A BABY ON
HER CHRISTMAS LIST

BY
LOUISA GEORGE

A FAMILY
THIS CHRISTMAS

BY
SUE MacKAY

A lifelong reader of most genres, **Louisa George** discovered romance novels later than most, but immediately fell in love with the intensity of emotion, the high drama and the family focus of Mills & Boon® Medical Romance™.

With a Bachelors Degree in Communication and a nursing qualification under her belt, writing medical romance seemed a natural progression and the perfect combination of her two interests. And making things up is a great way to spend the day!

An English ex-pat, Louisa now lives north of Auckland, New Zealand, with her husband, two teenage sons and two male cats. Writing romance is her opportunity to covertly inject a hefty dose of pink into her heavily testosterone-dominated household. When she's not writing or researching Louisa loves to spend time with her family and friends, enjoys travelling and adores great food. She's also hopelessly addicted to Zumba®.

With a background of working in medical laboratories and a love of the romance genre, it is no surprise that **Sue MacKay** writes Mills & Boon® Medical Romance™ stories. An avid reader all her life, she wrote her first story at age eight—about a prince, of course. She lives with her own hero in the beautiful Marlborough Sounds, at the top of New Zealand's South Island, where she indulges her passions for the outdoors, the sea and cycling.

A BABY ON
HER CHRISTMAS LIST

BY
LOUISA GEORGE

MILLS
BOON

Published in Great Britain 2014
by Mills & Boon, an imprint of Harlequin (UK) Limited,
Eton House, 18-24 Paradise Road, Richmond, Surrey, TW9 1SR

© 2014 Louisa George

ISBN: 978-0-263-90806-0

Printed and bound in Spain
by Blackprint CPI, Barcelona

Dedication

To Iona Jones, Sue MacKay, Barbara DeLeo,
Kate David and Nadine Taylor, my gorgeous Blenheim
girls—thank you for the great weekend at the cottage
and your amazing help to brainstorm this book.

You guys definitely know how to rock a writing retreat. xx

Praise for
Louisa George:

'HOW TO RESIST A HEARTBREAKER
keeps you hooked from beginning to end,
but make sure you have a tissue handy for this one
will break your heart only to heal it in the end.'
—*HarlequinJunkie*

'A moving, uplifting and feel-good romance, this
is packed with witty dialogue, intense emotion and
sizzling love scenes. Louisa George once again brings an
emotional and poignant story of past hurts, dealing with
grief and new beginnings which will keep a reader
turning pages with its captivating blend of
medical drama, family dynamics and romance.'
—*GoodReads* on
HOW TO RESIST A BEARTBREAKER

'Louisa George is a bright star at Mills & Boon®
and I can highly recommend this book
to those that believe romance rocks the world.'
—*GoodReads* reader review on
HOW TO RESIST A HEARTBREAKER

CHAPTER ONE

Nine months ago...

'I'VE FOUND A baby daddy!' Georgie's wide grin shone brighter than the Southern Cross, her dark brown eyes sparkling even in the bar's dim light.

Liam watched, dumbfounded, as excitement rolled off her, so intense it was almost tangible.

'Well, not a daddy as such. I should really stop saying that. But I have found someone who would be perfect to donate his sperm...which I know makes you shudder, so I'm sorry for saying The Word.' She gave Liam a wicked wink that was absolutely at odds with this whole one-sided conversation.

Whoa.

Too gobsmacked to speak, Liam indicated to her to sit. She tossed her silk wrap and bag on the back of a chair, put her drink down on the table and plonked in the seat opposite him at the only free table in Indigo's crowded lounge.

A baby?

He felt the frown forming and couldn't control it—even if he'd wanted to—and finally found his voice. 'Hey, back right up, missy. Am I dreaming here? I thought you just said something about a baby...'

It had been too long since he'd seen her looking so happy so he was wary about bursting her bubble—but, hell, he was going to burst it anyway. Because that's what real friends did—they talked sense. Just like she'd done the first time they'd met, in the sluice room of the ER; he a lowly med student, losing his cool at the sight of a lifeless newborn, she a student nurse with more calm and control and outright guts than anyone he'd ever met. She'd let him shake, allowed him five minutes to stress out, then had forced him back into the ER to help save the kid's life. And they'd been pretty much glued at the hip ever since.

So he needed to be honest. He raised his voice over the thump-thump-thump of the bar's background bass that usually fuelled their regular Friday night drinking session, but tonight the noise was irritating and obnoxious. 'I go away for three months and come back to sheer madness. What happened to the *Nothing's going to get in the way of those renovations this time*? *I'm on the real estate ladder now and going up.* What the hell, Geo? A baby? Since when was that on your to-do list?'

Stabbing the ice in her long glass with a straw, she looked up at him, eyes darker now, and he caught a yearning he'd seen glimpses of over the last ten years. She thought she hid it well, but sometimes, when she was distracted or excited, she let her tough guard slip. 'You, of all people, know I've always wanted a family, Liam. It may not have been at the top of my list because I always believed it would just happen at some point. But I can't keep putting it off and leaving it to chance, because chance isn't going my way. And I refuse to prioritise decorating over having a baby. That would be stupid.'

In his opinion, having a baby was right up at the top of stupid but he kept that to himself. And, for the record, it wasn't just decorating—her house needed knock-down-and-start-again renovations. 'But what's the hurry? You're only twenty-eight. It will happen, you've got plenty of time. You just need to find the right guy.' And why that made him shudder more than the *sperm* word, he didn't know.

She let the straw go, then pulled a hair tie from her wrist and curled her long wavy hair into a low pony-tail. Her hair was the same colour as caramel, with little streaks of honey and gold. He didn't need to get any closer to know that it smelt like apples or fruit or something vaguely edible. And clearly he'd been away too long if he was starting to notice stuff like that.

Luckily she was oblivious to him staring at her hair and thinking about its colour and smell. 'Oh, yes, and the candidates for husband are queuing up at the door, aren't they? You may have noticed that the pickings for Mr Perfect are slim and slimming further by the day in Auckland. There's a man drought. It's official apparently, New Zealand has a lot fewer men than women my age. Why do you think I've needed you to…*expedite* a few dates for me?' Her shoulders slumped. 'I know we've had fun setting each other up with potentials over the years, but I'm starting to think that—'

'That maybe you're too…picky?' He raised his glass to her. 'Hey, I don't know, but perhaps you could consider only having a one-page check-box list that potentials need to tick, instead of fifteen?'

Her eyes widened as she smiled. 'Get out of here. It is nowhere near fifteen.'

'Not on paper, no. But in your head it is. I've seen you in action, remember. *He's not funny enough. Too intense. Just a joker. Doesn't take me seriously. Just wanted a one-nighter.*' Truth was, Liam had been secretly pretty damned proud she'd spurned most of his mates' advances and that she'd ended most flings before they'd got serious. There was something special about Georgie and she deserved a special kind of bloke. He hadn't met one yet that would be worthy of her.

'So I have standards. I'd settle for Mr *Almost* Perfect if he existed—which he doesn't. I'm getting too short on time.' Her red, loose-fitting summer dress moved softly as she shrugged delicate shoulders. 'I don't know about you, but I get the feeling that asking a man to father your children on a first date might just scare him off.'

'Well, hell, if I asked a man to father my children on any date it'd either be in a nightmare or because I was hallucinating.'

She rolled her eyes. 'You know very well what I mean. And, yes, you are the straightest guy I've ever met.' Her eyes ran over his chest, lingering a little over his pecs, throat, mouth. Why he noticed he didn't know. And, even stranger, he felt a little hot. When her gaze met his she gave him her usual friendly smile. 'You're looking mighty fit these days, Dr MacAllister. How was Pakistan?'

'Hot, wet and desperate.' As with all his aid missions, he didn't want to relive what he had seen. Enough that he had those images in his own head, without sharing details with others.

'But at least you know you were doing good out there. What were the conditions like? Are you okay? How are you feeling? When do you leave again? Please be happy for me.'

This was always how it was with Georgie: random conversation detours and finishing each other's sentences. But things generally flowed and they knew each other so well that often they didn't have to speak to communicate. So with the sudden baby daddy bombshell he'd never felt so excluded from her life. 'I'm fine. Knackered, but fine, looking forward to a few weeks' locuming at the General's ER. At least there's running water and reliable electricity. And I have a decent bed to sleep in. The next planned rollout for me is in South Sudan in a couple of months.'

'But if they need you earlier…'

He nodded. 'Sure. It's the way it is.'

'I still don't know how you manage all that to-ing and fro-ing. Here a couple of months, then gone again. I like staying in one place.'

And he didn't. The longest he ever stayed anywhere was when he came back here because he needed a semi-permanent job to help fund his aid work. 'But I'm never going away again if it means I come back to crazyville baby talk.'

'It's not crazyville.' Again with the eye roll. He didn't even have to look. This time it was accompanied by an irritated shake of her head. 'I've made a decision to do this now. On my own. I know it'll be tough and it's not the perfect image I've always had in my head about a mum and dad and two point four kids, but that's too far out of reach right now. I've had to curtail my dreaming and get real. Being a solo mum is just fine.'

She stopped talking to take a long drink of what looked a lot like lemonade. On a Friday night? Could be that she was actually serious about this. 'I want to conceive and carry to term, and have a baby…*my* baby… and, if things work out, have another one too. But that's probably greedy and selfish.'

'You deserve to be, Geo, after what you've been through.' *But now? Why now?*

'So, I'm looking forward, and taking an opportunity.

Endo is a lot less active during pregnancy so if I could manage two pregnancies in quick succession…if the IUI works, that is… IVF would be a whole different ball game.'

Trying to keep up he lifted his palms towards her. 'IUI? IVF? Slow down a bit. So you're not thinking turkey baster? Or just plain old-fashioned sex? That is a relief.'

'Believe me, I'll do whatever's necessary.'

He didn't doubt it. And finally the reality was sinking in. She was going to do the one thing he'd sworn never to do—and because he was her friend she'd expect him to be supportive. 'So what tipped you over to the dark side?'

And, yes, his reaction would not be what she wanted, but: a) he couldn't help it and; b) he wasn't prepared to lie just to make her feel better. It was precisely because of their friendship that he knew he could be straight up with her.

'You are such a grump. For me there is no dark side. Being abandoned at two days old and having literally no one from then on in has made me want to feel part of something…a family. You know that. I just want what everyone else has, Liam—to feel loved, to be loved. To love. And I have no doubt that there will be some hard times, but I will never leave my baby on a doorstep for someone else to find, and condemn them to a life of foster-homes and social services, like my mum did to me. I will cherish any child I have. I've had my share of dark sides and being pregnant and a mother isn't one of them.'

Her nose wrinkled as she reached across and lightly punched him on the arm. 'So, I was worried things were getting worse endo-wise, so I asked Malcolm to run some more tests at work a few weeks ago.' Her hands palmed across her abdomen—subconsciously? Possibly. Protective? Definitely.

'You've been having more pain? Oh, God, I'm sorry, Georgie. That sucks. Really, I thought you were managing okay.' Liam hated that. Hated that even though he fixed people up every day he didn't have the answers to Georgie's problems and that they were running out of solutions as time ticked on. His heart thumped in sync with the music, hard and loud in his chest. 'What did he say?'

'That the endometriosis is indeed getting worse. That everything in there's getting blocked up and scarred and it won't be long before I'll need pretty major surgery. That it's only a matter of time before pregnancy is going to be nigh on impossible. At least, without a whole lot of effort and money and no promises at the end.'

Her eyes filled with tears. Which, for Georgie, was such a rarity Liam sat there like a useless lump and watched in horror, unable to move. She was the strongest woman he knew. She'd faced tough battles her whole life and she never tired of fighting. No matter how ridiculous her plan sounded, his heart twisted to see her hurting. 'You know how much I need this, Liam. I thought you'd understand. I thought you'd support me. You know, like good friends do? I've been there for you regardless and I kind of hoped you'd feel the same.' Her hand reached for her gut again. 'This idea? This is a good thing.'

It was the worst thing he'd ever heard. 'And so who is going to provide the...?' He couldn't bring himself to say the word. For an accomplished medic he had trouble imagining what went on behind closed doors at the IVF clinic.

'Sperm? I've decided I'm going to ask Malcolm.'

'What?' Liam almost choked on his beer. 'Your boss?'

'And that's wrong, why? He's smart. Not unattractive. Owns a successful IVF clinic and has helped thousands of women achieve their dreams, so he's compassionate too. Those are all the right kind of genes I'd look for in a father for my child.'

'He's still also your boss.'

She hip-planted both hands. 'And I'm pretty sure he'd want to help. He sees this kind of thing every day, so to him it's not an unusual request. I'll ask him to sign a contract to keep things simple. I have enough money put by to keep me going for a while and the clinic has agreed to reduce my hours after maternity leave.'

Maternity leave. Contracts. That sounded far from simple. And the money she had put by was supposed to be for renovations to help her become more financially independent. 'Seems like you have it all figured out.'

'He knows how much I want this. How much I need to know DNA and family history. It's been my life's dream. Just a little...*expedited*.' She gave him a smile at their shared joke.

Liam didn't feel much like laughing. Sure, she'd talked about this on and off over the years but now the reality hit him in the gut like a two-ton truck. She wanted a baby. A family. Kids. 'Surely asking your boss is downright unprofessional. Unethical.'

'A friend helping a friend? Since when did that cross any kind of line?'

'Where would you like me to start?' It crossed more lines than Liam cared to think of. It would be like...like if he offered to father her child. Ridiculous. Ludicrous.

Wouldn't it?

The thought flitted across a corner of his mind. He pushed it away. Ludicrous indeed.

'Malcolm saw how upset I was at the results.' As she

spoke she seemed to loosen up a little. Determined, but calm. 'I've asked to have a meeting with him next week. If he says no then I'll have a rethink.'

'It sounds messy to me. How about using one of the anonymous donors at the clinic? You get to know about their family history, too. You can choose anyone that ticks your fifteen pages of boxes.' He didn't know why someone anonymous fathering her child seemed like a better option. It just *felt* better. A long way from right, but better. 'And why didn't you ask me?'

What the hell?

He didn't even know where that question had come from. As she stared at him his chest tightened.

'Is that what this is all about? You're upset because I didn't ask you? Honestly? The man who comes out in hives when he even sees a baby?' As soon as the words left her mouth she closed her eyes and pressed her lips together. Too late. After a beat or two she slowly opened her eyes again and winced. 'Oh, my God, I'm sorry. Really. I'm sorry, Liam. I am. I didn't mean... I'm so sorry. But I just know how you feel about families.'

'Do you?'

She looked surprised at his question. Probably because he'd kept his past to himself and never spoke about what he wanted for the future. But families and babies were something he definitely had an aversion to. No, not an aversion, just a deep desire not to go there. Ever.

Her voice softened. 'Since you always refuse to talk about anything deeper than what you had for lunch, I have to surmise. You have a track record of emotional avoidance. So I've always assumed that big loving, meddling, messy, happy families aren't something on your wish list. In all honesty, you'd be the last person I'd ask. And, judging by your current reaction, I think I'm right.'

* * *

Liam's face was all shadows and hollows. His blue eyes had darkened to navy. Only once before had Georgie seen him look so utterly haunted, and that had been the day they'd met and she'd forced him to work on that newborn.

Later that night, when they'd gone for the first of many subsequent beers, the alcohol had made his tongue loose and he'd mentioned a family tragedy involving his sister, Lauren. But then had clammed up so tight Georgie had never been able to open him up to that particular hotspot conversation again. And since then he'd absorbed whatever it was that had thrown him off balance that day. Until now.

His voice was low when he eventually spoke. 'I just think you could have talked to me about it all first. Put more thought into it.'

'I don't think that's possible, it's all I've been thinking about for weeks, turning scenarios over and over in my head.' She watched as anger and hurt twitched through him until he wrestled it under control. Why couldn't he just smile and pat her hand and say what a brilliant idea it was? Her words had obviously been a low blow. She'd always respected that he had his reasons for not wanting a family, even if he'd never really fronted up and explained why.

Some support would have been nice, but hadn't she heard this kind of story so many times at work? Babies, IVF and the sometimes desperate journey towards parenthood made strong couples stronger and weak ones fall apart.

Then thank God she and Liam weren't a couple because, judging by this conversation, they'd fall at the first hurdle.

He was her friend, her closest friend in lots of ways;

she always took his advice, always went to him with problems. And now she was all kinds of confused, needing time to think and reaffirm.

She stood to leave. 'Look, this was clearly a mistake. I'm going to go home so we can both take some time out. I'm sorry if I've ruined our Friday night. But, you know, I don't know where we'd go from here. Trying to play your wingman and find a date for you with some poor unsuspecting woman just isn't my idea of fun right now.'

He tipped his glass towards her again, but he didn't get up. Didn't try to make her feel better. And he always tried to make her feel better.

Which was why his opposition was spooking her more than she'd anticipated. Still, she'd made this decision and she was sticking with it.

She had no choice. This was her life. Her chance.

And to hell with him if he wasn't going to be there right when she needed it most. She threw her wrap round her shoulders. 'I'll...I don't know...see you later?'

He watched her stand. He still didn't move but his voice was more controlled as he gave her a small smile. 'Heaven help us all when you start taking the hormone injections.'

'Oh? Why?'

'Aren't they supposed to make you all antsy and volatile?'

'What?' She couldn't bring herself to tell him she'd been taking them already. And, yes, she was being antsy. But it was his reaction that had made her like that, not the medications. 'Maybe, just maybe you have royally pissed me off. And to add insult to injury, you're now being condescending. Patronising.'

'Just honest. As always.' Yes, she supposed he was.

One of things she relied on him for was his frank honesty. 'So when is it all happening? The impregnating thing?'

'So very clinical, Liam.'

'Yes. Isn't it?'

'I was hoping it would be in the next couple of weeks if possible.'

The glass in his hand hit the table with a crash. 'What? So soon? You don't mess around, do you? You don't want to talk a bit more? At least listen to someone else's opinion?'

'And have you try to convince me against it? I don't think so. I don't need your negativity. It's a chance, Liam. I need to take it.'

For a few seconds he looked at her. Just stared at her. She couldn't read him. The man she'd thought she knew pretty much inside and out, and she couldn't even guess what he was thinking.

After a torturous silence that seemed to increase the tension tenfold, he spoke, 'Yes. Yes, you do. Take the chance, Geo.' Now he stood up and walked her to the door. Once outside he didn't wrap her in his usual goofy bear hug. Didn't graze her cheek with a kiss and a smile. Didn't give her a wink and make her laugh. 'Let me know how you get on.'

'Why? So you can make me doubt myself all over again?'

He took her by the shoulders and his gaze bored into her. 'Because I'm your friend, Georgie.'

And then she ached for him to give her one of his hugs more than anything else in the world. But he turned away. Back towards the bar and the white noise that seemed to be mingling with his words and filling her head with doubts.

What if he was right? What if this was the far side of

crazy? What the hell did she know about family anyway? About parenting? It wasn't as if she'd had any experience on either side of that particular fence. What if Malcolm didn't follow through? What if he did?

Worse, what if this rift meant that the friendship she had with Liam would be broken for ever? He was the closest thing she had to any notion of family, and the thought of not having him in her life made her suddenly feel empty and cold.

Torn and confused, she climbed into a waiting cab and watched him retreat to the bar, his dark T-shirt straining across well-defined broad shoulders, and a gait that screamed defiance.

And what the hell was going on with those pecs? The man had suddenly developed muscles of steel. Strange, too, that in the midst of all this turmoil she should even notice. That, and the shape of his lips, the way his mouth curved and softened as he smiled, which had been rare but welcome tonight. Those hormones were clearly playing havòc with her head.

But judging by the sudden strange slick of heat that hit her breasts and abdomen—which surely must be a reaction to the muggy Auckland evening—they were messing with her body too.

CHAPTER TWO

Mum's had a stroke. Had to go back to UK. Don't know for how long. Will keep you in the loop. Sorry. Can we have that meeting when I get back?

SHUTTING THE IVF clinic room door, so she could have a moment to take it all in, Georgie stared at the text, her gut clenching. Bile rose to the back of her throat. She felt dizzy.

And downright selfish.

Inhaling deeply, she pulled herself together. For goodness' sake, it wasn't the end of the world, just the end of an opportunity. That was all. There would be another chance, next month or the month after. Some time. With a different donor.

She should be feeling sorry for her boss, not herself.

No worries, Malcolm. Safe journey. Sending hugs for your mum x

And yet she felt as if her world was closing in on her, that she was fast running out of time and her dream was getting further out of reach. Scrolling through her texts, she found her conversation thread with Liam and started to type. Then stopped. She hadn't heard a thing from him for four days, and even though she knew he'd be busy, catching up on everything at work, she felt a little lost. Normally he'd text her with funny stories from his shift, jokes, stuff. Just stuff. But ever since Friday she'd been hit by silence. And it hurt a little that he knew what she was going through but didn't want to see how she was doing.

Okay, it hurt a lot.

So maybe that would be the norm from now on. She didn't want to think about that. But for the last few days it hadn't been just his absence that had been on her mind. It had been that crazy tingly feeling that had swept through her body the other night, just looking at him. And then an out-of-proportion feeling of loss that he wasn't being supportive. It was absurd. Seemed those meds made her overreact in lots of different ways.

The clinic room phone interrupted her thoughts and brought her back to reality. 'Georgie speaking.'

It was Helen, the receptionist, and Georgie's good friend. 'I have a patient here, Kate Holland. Says she doesn't feel too great. Can you see her straight away?'

'Kate? Sure, I remember her, she was in just the other day. I'll be right through.' Helen rarely showed any kind of emotion, so the anxiety in her voice made Georgie take notice. Putting her own worries aside, she made sure the clinic couch was ready, opened up Kate's notes on the laptop then collected her patient, who appeared noticeably short of breath, flushed and anxious.

'Kate. What's the problem? Are you okay?'

'No. I feel pretty rubbish, actually. My stomach hurts and I'm so thirsty.' For a toned and fit marathon runner Kate climbed onto the bed with a lot of effort.

Alarm bells began to ring. Georgie settled the young woman against the pillow, silently counting the laboured respiratory rate. 'You've been having the injections, right? Any other problems? Nausea? Vomiting?'

Kate nodded. 'Yes. Twice this morning and I feel really sick now. But so thirsty.'

Georgie took her patient's hand and measured her pulse. Fast and thready. Any number of scenarios raced through her mind. Fertility drugs had a tranche of usually mild and temporary side-effects, but when they were severe they could be life-threatening. 'Peeing okay? If you can do us a sample, that'd be great.'

'Not much at all. But I'll try.'

'Okay, when you next need to go, yell out.' Giving Kate a quick examination and piecing together her patient's history, Georgie reached a preliminary diagnosis. It wasn't what either she or her patient wanted to hear. 'How long have you felt like this?'

'The past couple of days or so. I started feeling really sick yesterday.' Kate gripped Georgie's hand, her flushed face tight and scared. 'But please don't tell me we have to stop the injections. Please say we can do this. It's our last chance.'

Georgie gently encouraged her to lie back down, not wanting to upset her even more but realising that time was of the essence. 'I know, Kate. I know. But don't get ahead of yourself. I'll quickly get the doctor to come check you over, he'll probably suggest you have a short stay in hospital, just a few days or so, to check everything's okay…'

After the doctor had confirmed Kate's diagnosis, Georgie arranged the next few steps. 'Because you're publicly funded, we'll transfer you to the General Hospital gynae ward, that's the closest to your home. They'll look after you. I promise.'

'What about the IVF? Will that happen now?'

Georgie took her hand again. 'Sweetheart, you re-member the doctor saying you had something called OHSS? That's our medical shorthand for ovarian hyper-stimulation syndrome. That means your body has reacted very strongly to the drugs. You have too much fluid in your abdomen, which is why you're out of breath. You're dehydrated, but we need to watch how much fluid you drink because we don't want you overloaded. You have a swollen red calf, which might mean you have a blood clot. We've arranged for some scans and a few more tests at the hospital. You need to rest and let your body heal before you do any more.'

'We can't afford any more. This is it, our last chance. Mark will be so disappointed. He's been really positive this time round, we both have. We talked about a Christ-mas baby, he got so excited. He wants to be a dad so much.' Fat tears rolled down Kate's red cheeks and Geor-gie's heart melted.

Some people, such as Kate, were lucky enough to be eligible for publicly funded treatment for a limited num-ber of cycles. Having already waited for months and had one failed attempt, this was indeed Kate's last chance. She and her husband Mark had a low income and there was no way could they afford the high costs and even more time off work for private IVF. Life was so unfair sometimes.

Georgie dealt with these scenarios in her job every day, and she'd always managed to keep a professional emotional distance, but today it felt deeply personal. She knew how desperate it was to have a ticking clock. And a chance that could be blown for any random reason. 'We'll do the best we can for you, Kate.' But she wouldn't make any promises. It wasn't her style to give her patients false hope, no matter how much her heart ached in sync with them. 'In the meantime, you have to get better.'

If anything, it made Georgie more determined to grab her chance as soon as she could. Deciding to go through with it was the first step on what she knew was going to be a long road. She had no illusions as to the prospect of being a single pregnant woman, then a solo mother. It would be immensely rewarding. It would be hard. And with no one else to help shoulder the burden she knew there would be times she'd find it difficult to cope. But she would. She'd been on her own her whole life. She didn't need anyone else. But needing and wanting were two different things.

On days like these she'd usually ring Liam and have a whinge. Often he'd suggest a drink or a movie or something to cheer her up. But as he'd gone AWOL and she didn't fancy another grim conversation, she'd do things differently tonight. He certainly wasn't the only friend she had in the world.

'Okay, that's me over and out. See you in the morning,' Liam called to his secretary, then grabbed his work bag and made his way through the crowded ER to the exit. It had been one hell of a day, dealing with staff shortages, bus-crash casualties and the usual walk-ins. What he needed now was a sundowner at the local and an early night.

The hospital doors swept open and he took his first breath of fresh air for eleven hours. It was tinged with a familiar fragrance that had him turning his head. She was standing way over to his left, half-hidden by a tall confident-looking man, and Liam would have missed her and walked by if he hadn't caught that sweet, flowery scent.

For some reason, as he saw her deep in conversation

with a stranger, his heart hammered. Mainly, he suspected, because he'd bawled her out the other day and hadn't had the chance to make things right. 'Georgie. Hi. What are you doing here?'

She whirled round, her cheeks reddening, her green nursing scrubs making her look younger somehow. Vulnerable, which she'd hate. There was a ripple of tension as her shoulders straightened, but she masked it. 'Oh. Hey. I'm dropping off a patient's bag. She had to be admitted unexpectedly and left it at the clinic by mistake. This is her husband, Mark.'

'Liam. Hi, I work here.' As he shook hands with the guy the heart-hammering slowed a little. Was it wrong to feel relief that his friend wasn't sick, but that another man's wife was? Damn right it was. But relief shuddered through him anyway. 'Is everything okay?'

'Mark's wife, Kate, has OHSS, so she's feeling a bit fragile. Mark's on his way up to see her on Ward Three.'

'Ah, yes. I remember seeing her name on the admissions board. She'll be okay, mate. She's in good hands.'

The man nodded grimly and headed through the main entrance. Leaving just Liam and Georgie and a weird sense of displacement. Georgie played with the handle of her handbag, looked at her feet. 'I should probably go.'

Not without some kind of resolution, he thought grimly. This was painful. They'd never had this kind of weird, tense scenario play out before. 'Wait. Are you okay?'

What he meant was, *Are we okay?*

'Yes. Thanks. You?' She raised her head and looked at him. She looked tired, drawn. The edges of her eyes were ringed with black. Which was a far cry from the last time he'd seen her when she'd been brimful of excitement, and he'd stomped all over her happy mood.

Was the dark look just for him or had something else happened to her?

Okay, stop guessing and cut the crap. 'Look, Geo, I didn't mean to pee all over your parade. I'm sorry about the other night. I was tired and just caught by surprise.'

'Clearly. And you've been too busy to send a text?' But the iron-clad barriers seemed to give just a little with his apology. 'Or did they get lost in cyberspace, along with your good manners?'

'As it happens, things have been manic here. I've done four long days with the last vestiges of jet-lag messing with my brain.' She didn't need to hear all that. 'I did think about texting you more than a few times. But I wasn't sure whether you'd slap me or eye-stab me with one of those killer looks you save for especially annoying people that drive you mad on purpose. And I wasn't up to taking the risk.'

That, at least, got a smile. 'Aw, Liam, I'd never eye-stab you. How could you say such a thing?'

'I know what you're capable of, my girl. Downright scary at times.' He walked with her towards the car park, feeling a little more relaxed. 'Er...done the deed yet?'

'By which you mean the assisted fertility?' Georgie slowed and gave him what he had come to recognise as one of her false smiles. Her mouth flipped up into the usual grin, but her eyes didn't shine. In fact, nothing about her was shining tonight. Even her *caramel* hair—it was just plain weird that he'd started to notice things that he'd always glossed over—seemed dulled. 'Malcolm's had to go away due to a family crisis, so I've put off asking him.'

'Oh. I see.' And with that news he really should have been cock-a-hoop but he wasn't. Strange emotions rippled through him, mainly disappointment for her. It was what she wanted. She'd been so excited and determined the other day, to the point that he'd been unable to talk any sense into her.

Now she looked like she needed bolstering. 'Okay. So you've got plenty of time. I'm sure you'll be fine waiting just a little while longer. Have you had any thoughts about asking anyone else? What about the donor lists?'

She frowned. 'Yes, well, it's far from ideal. And, like I said, time is something I don't have a lot of.'

'You sound like you're waiting for the guillotine or something. Just a touch dramatic, Geo?'

'You think so?' As they closed in on her car they stopped. She pointed up to the second floor of the hospital with a taut finger that was definitely capable of eye-stabbing if she so wished. 'That lady in there has been trying to get pregnant for five years. And nothing. Zilch. Nil. She's had one chance at IVF, which came up with disappointment, and now everything's on hold until she gets better from the side effects of trying to stimulate her ovaries. I expect that if she gets the go-ahead again she'll have to pay megabucks...and even then it might not work for her.

'I do not want to be that lady, possibly looking at years of pressure and stress. I've got to start the ball rolling and damn well soon. Otherwise when and if I'm finally in a committed relationship with someone who loves me, it might be too late. I have a window of opportunity in my cycle coming up very soon. And I'm disappointed that I can't take advantage of it. Dramatic? If you say so. But, then, you're not the one staring down the barrel of a ticking time bomb.'

'Wow. See? Scary.' He stepped back. 'I'll just make sure I'm out of eye-stabbing range.'

She stalked off to her car, then stopped abruptly and

turned on him, gravel scraping underfoot. Never before
had he seen such passion and anger and determination
and spirit in anyone. 'For once in your life, Liam, take
me seriously.'

'I do. All the time. I was just trying to make you feel
better.'

'Well, you didn't. You know what? I bet we could
spend the next few weeks going round in circles with
this and you'd never understand.'

Oh, he understood all right. He'd been thinking about
it for days, ever since she'd brought the subject up. In fact,
that ludicrous idea that had flitted through his head had
taken seed and would not let go.

But the ramifications were huge.

She glared at him, her eyes fierce, curls springing
loose and free around her face. Her mouth taut and determined. She looked magnificent and terrifying, like
the time she'd pushed him into Resus for that baby. And
many times since when she'd been hell-bent on partying
hard or just grasping life in her hands and making the
most of it. She'd been like that since he'd known her—
reaching, grasping, dreaming. Making her life full, taking what she wanted. Because she'd had so little for so
long she hadn't wanted to waste a moment, and she de-
fied anyone who stood in her way.

She was strong and staunch and loyal and in that second he knew that if *his* back was against the wall, she'd
do anything for him. Anything.

And so here they were at an impasse. All he had to do
was offer her what she wanted.

Great to help out a friend, but at the same time he was
held back by...abject *fear*. Fear, that was it. The increased
heart rate, sweaty palms, gut clench. He was scared as
hell at the prospect of it all, of letting everyone down. Of

not loving enough. Or, worse, loving too much. And he knew damned well how that panned out. He wouldn't be able to function around a child or be part of her cosy family. But if he didn't do it then she'd be forced to choose someone she didn't know or give up altogether—and he knew, too, that that was not part of her dream.

Despite all the late-night musings and the words going round and round in his head, he knew it was the most stupid idea he'd ever had.

But the words lingered. Lingered still as he saw her shrug her shoulders. As she turned her back to him and opened the car door. Lingered as he watched her swipe her hand across her face to stop a rogue tear. She wouldn't even allow herself to show her bitter disappointment. That almost broke him in two.

It would cost him little in time and effort. Not overtly anyway. He'd have to deal with the ramifications later. But right now his friend was hurting and there was something he could do to help. One singular thing. He could be that guy. The one he wanted to be, the one who took an emotional risk and helped a friend in need, whatever the personal cost.

Before he'd had a chance to second guess himself the words were tumbling out. 'Georgie, wait. I'll do it.'

Her voice was small and he could hear the pain, and yet deep down there was some hope as she turned to face him. 'Do what?'

'I'll be the donor.'

'You? *You?* Why?' Her laugh was bordering on sarcastic.

He took a step forward. 'Because I'm taking you seriously. This is what you want. What you deserve.'

She wagged her finger, fast. 'Oh, no. No. No. No. No. No. No. Not happening.'

'Unless you have a particular aversion to passing along my DNA? If I were to look objectively I'd say I was pretty okay. I'm a doctor, so not dumb. Oh, and my compassion knows no bounds. Apparently you like that in a father figure. I'm funny—always a winner.' He pointed to his abs, which he sucked in for effect. 'And pretty much the most devastatingly good-looking man in town.'

And bingo—his aid work meant he'd be out of the country for most of the rest of his life if he wanted. So he wouldn't be forced into any emotional attachment. This was a purely altruistic act. Which begged the question—what the hell did he want?

This wasn't about him, he reminded himself. It was about Georgie. 'How could you not want to use my *sperm*?' He whispered the last word as reality started to seep through his feel-good fuzzies.

The sarcasm melted away and the laugh was pure Georgie. 'Yeah, right. That's objective? Don't get above yourself. For one, you have a slightly crooked nose.'

He ran his down his ethmoid bone and he gave her his profile view. 'Rugby injury, not genetic. Besides, you can hardly see it.'

She cocked her hip to one side as she perused him. 'You have particularly broad shoulders.'

'Great for tackling and giving great hugs.' And he should know. He'd done it often enough. Usually as he was patting women on the back and wishing them well. *It wasn't them, it was him.*

She frowned. 'But not great for wearing halter-neck tops.'

'Ah shucks, and now you've spoilt my dress plans for tomorrow.' Funny, but it felt strange, being analysed in such a way by a friend.

'On the other hand, you do have…long legs.' Her voice cracked a little as her gaze scanned his trousers. Her pupils did a funny widening thing. A flash of something—and then it was gone. Two red spots appeared on her cheeks. 'Ahem, big feet.'

'And we all know what that means.' He winked. 'Any boy would be happy with the MacAllister brand of DNA. If you bottled it you'd get a fortune.'

'Oh, yeah? No girl wants big feet. Bad for shoe buying.' She gave him a final once-over glance. Then her voice softened. 'Really, it's a lovely offer and I'd be stupid not to take you up on it. But what about you? You don't want this. You really don't want this.'

'But you do, Georgie.' There was a long beat while he tried to put into words the weird feelings he was experiencing. He could give her the chance she wanted, on one condition. 'But we'll need a contract. I don't want any involvement.'

'Oh.' Giving the minutest shake of her head, she held her palm up. 'You'll be the baby daddy but don't want to be *the* daddy?'

'Yep.'

'Oh. Okay. Then I'm utterly shocked that you've offered. Why would you do that?'

Not wanting to dig up something he'd pushed to the darkest part of his soul, he gave her the scantest of explanations. 'Happy families isn't my style. But a happy Georgie is. I'll do it. Just agree before I change my mind.'

'Oh, this is fast and so out of left field.' She put a hand to his shoulder, ran her fingers down his arm. And in the cool late summer evening goosebumps followed the trail of her warm skin against his. 'Can I think about it? Get used to the idea?'

'Sure.' He needed time too, his chest felt blown wide open.

'It would mean a lot of changes. For us.'

'I know. I realise that.' And if it hadn't been Georgie's dream on the line, no way would he ever contemplate something like this.

She looked hesitant, shocked, but hopeful. 'So…well, we could have a contract similar to the clinic's standard donor document. We can use that as a blueprint. If that's what you really want?'

'That's what I want. No involvement, nothing.'

'I won't ask you for anything else. Ever. Trust me.'

He did. Absolutely. He just wasn't sure how much he could trust himself. 'Yes. Definitely. A contract will be best.'

'And it'll mean tests. Soon. Like this week.'

'Whatever it takes.' Although the altruistic vibe was fast morphing into panic.

'Oh, my God, is this really happening?' She reached round his waist and pulled him into one of her generous hugs. His nostrils filled with her perfume and he fought a sudden urge not to let go.

Her body felt good close to his. She was soft in his arms and her head against his chest made his heart hurt a little. He'd missed her these last few weeks. Especially these last few days. They never argued.

And this…was just a hug. Nothing strange there. She gave them all the time. And yet… He was aware of the softness of her body, the curve of her waist… He swallowed.

Nah. She felt just the same as always. Just the same old Georgie. She turned her head and looked up at him, her dark eyes dancing with excitement, the evening sun catching her profile. For a second she just looked into his eyes. One. Two. He lost count. She had amazing eyes. Flecked with warm gold and honey that matched her hair. His gaze drifted across the face he knew so well, and a shiver of something he didn't want to recognise tightened through him.

She pulled away quickly and the connection broke.

Thank God, because he was getting carried away in all her emotion. And that was definitely not something he was planning on doing. Emotional distance was the only thing that stopped him wreaking any more damage on those he loved. Hell, he was his father's son after all. Emotional distance was what MacAllister men did better than anyone else. But somehow he didn't think that that admission would go down well on Georgie's tick list.

'Thank you. Thank you so much. It means a lot to me.' She placed a gentle kiss on his cheek. Again with the goosebumps. This time they prickled all the way to his gut and lower. 'I'll mull it over and...um...let you know? Soon as possible?'

'Okay, and I'll get the turkey baster sorted for when you say yes.' Now he needed to ignore the strange feelings and off-load some of this ache in his chest. He saw a damned long run in his immediate future.

Her demeanour changed. She brushed a hand down over her scrub trousers, all business and organisation as she took a shaky little step away from him. 'Like I said, we'll do it the clinic way.'

'For sure. Any other way would be just too—'

Her head tilted a little to the side. 'Ick?'

He grinned. 'Is that a technical term?'

'Absolutely. For that weird feeling you get when you think about sleeping with your best friend? Like sex with your cousin? Right? Weird.' Shuddering, she looked to him for reassurance.

Which he gave unreservedly. 'Right. Yes. Ick's the word.'

The notion of them having sex had rarely arisen. Back in the early days he'd caught himself looking at her and wondering. She'd walked through his dreams many nights. He'd tried to imagine what kissing her would have been like. How she would taste. How she would feel underneath him. Around him. But he'd never put any of that into words for fear she'd run a mile. He'd never asked more from her than what they'd already had and, frankly, he'd believed that any kind of fling would inevitably ruin the great friendship they'd built up.

She was worth more to him than just sex. And seeing as that was the only thing he ever offered to women, he'd never wanted to risk doing something so pointlessly stupid and losing her.

Plus, while Georgie was funny and loyal, she'd never made a move or seemed interested in him in that way. They'd had an implicit agreement that anything of a sexual nature could never happen. So he'd sublimated those imaginings until he'd stopped having them. Had lost himself in other women.

Which made it all the more nonsensical that he'd started noticing things again…like her smell, the colour of her hair, her eyes. Surely it could only mean some sort of nostalgia for the younger Georgie in his past when the present was shifting out of his control?

CHAPTER THREE

Eight months ago...

Hey, stranger. Thought you'd want to know that your genius sperm has done what it was designed to do... I'm pregnant!

Great news. Congratulations.

FINALLY, AN ANSWER. Biggest news she'd ever had and not one exclamation mark. Not one. No cheers or fanfares. No questions. Was he not just a little curious? Pleased for her? Maybe it was the whole emotionless text thing stuffing up the sentiment of his message, but hadn't the man heard about emoticons?

Disappointed, Georgie texted him back.

I'm so excited! :) Catch up soon?

Sure. Things are a bit busy right now. Packing. South Sudan. In two days. I'll try come over to say bye.

Okay, your call.
He was heading off again and he'd try to come and

see her? *Try?* What the hell…? Packing didn't take two whole days. He was the world's lightest traveller.

And, actually, it was her call just as much as his. Worrying about contacting him had never been an issue before and it shouldn't be now just because she was carrying his baby. *No. Her* baby. He'd made that very clear. But surely they could still be friends? She wasn't going to allow this to change what they had. Why should pregnancy make a difference?

But it did, she realised. Not just to her relationship with Liam, but to her. She was going to be a mum. *A mother.* With a family. Something she'd never had before. She was going to be part of something…more.

She put a hand to her very flat, very *un*pregnant-looking stomach and her heart did another flip. It was still so early, too early to grow attached; any number of things could go wrong. But it was already too late. Her stomach tumbled as she closed her eyes, imagining.

Hey, there, little one. Nice to meet you.

And that was about all she dared say. She felt something tug deep inside her. These days she seemed to be so emotional about things. About the baby. About Liam…

Well, if he wasn't going to make an effort then she damn well would. She wanted to celebrate and send him off on his travels with no tension between them. Georgie stabbed his number into the phone and left a message: 'Hey, step away from your backpack. Let's do something. I won't take no for an answer. I get the feeling you're avoiding me. But if you are, please don't admit it. Just say you've been busy. Mission Bay? Six-thirty. I'm hiring bikes. No excuses.'

'Are you bonkers or just straight up certifiable?' Three hours later his voice, behind her, although irritated and loud, made her heart jig in her chest. He'd turned up at least, and for that she was grateful. 'Cycling? In your condition? Seriously?'

'Oh, for goodness' sake, I'm fine. How many times have we done this?' She turned and pretended to scowl, but her scowl dropped the moment she set eyes on him. He was wearing a scruffy old T-shirt that hugged his toned muscles and was the same vibrant blue as his eyes. Faded jeans graced his long legs, framing his bum…and, no, she'd never really studied it before, but it was deliciously gorgeous. No wonder he had a queue of women trying to encourage him to commit.

Heat hit her cheeks and shimmied down to her belly, where it transformed into *What would he be like in bed*?

And that was just one of too many thoughts about him recently that were way out of line.

To distract herself from staring too long at the man who had suddenly become a whole new fascination for her, she clipped on her helmet and prepared to use up some of this nervous energy. Pregnant, yes. Petrified, indeedy. Strangely excited just to see her long-lost best mate? Very definitely. And that made her legs twitch and her stomach roll.

'I needed some fresh air. It's such a beautiful evening and it's the weekend tomorrow. Freedom! We could get fish and chips and eat them on the beach later.'

He frowned and pointed to her helmet. 'Take it off, Georgie. It's too dangerous. We haven't been cycling for years, you could fall off. Why you suddenly want to do it now I don't know.'

'Because it used to be fun and I don't know why we got out of the habit of doing it. I want the fun back.' She shook her head in defiance. 'And stop being ridiculous. You're a doctor, you know very well that at this stage in pregnancy it's perfectly fine to exercise. Come on, I'll be fine, it's not as if I'm bungee jumping. Although, there is a free slot at the Skytower at eight. So if we hurry…' She handed him his helmet and stood, arms crossed over her chest, until he'd put it on over that grumpy face. 'Breathe, Liam. Breathe. It was a joke. And do try to keep up!'

The sea air was filled with salt and heat and the smell of a distant barbecue. Overhead, seagulls dived and squawked, making the most of a bright summer evening's scavenging. Mission Bay was, as always, filled with smiling people, cycling, blading or running along the seaside promenade. On the right, beyond small beach inlets and a turquoise sea dotted with anchored yachts, the mighty volcanic Rangitoto Island stood verdant and powerful. On the left they cycled past coastal suburbia, higgledy-piggledy candy-coloured houses clinging to the steep hillside.

Georgie pedalled hard, keeping him in her slipstream, ignoring his concerned cries. She could do this. She needed to do this to show him—and herself—that she was still the same old Georgie. And if she could also purge those weird fluttery feelings that seemed to happen whenever she saw him, that would be even better. Because this new Georgie who kept popping up with hot thoughts about Liam was unsettling in the extreme.

Usually he raced ahead, screaming over his shoulder for her to go faster, but today he seemed happy to pootle behind. She had the distinct feeling that, in his own way, he was keeping watch over her.

After a few kilometres, pedalling towards towering city skyscrapers, she turned and cycled back to the row of Victorian buildings flanking a children's playground and large fountain. Toddlers kicked and splashed in the spraying water, watched over by attentive parents.

Georgie braked, imagining being here some time in the future, showing her little one the exciting new world. Making everything a game, lining up her pram with the others, chatting to parents about nappy changing, bedtimes and the terrible twos. Her heart zinged. It seemed that, despite all her best efforts, she was starting to see everything through a different, pregnancy-coloured lens. With a heavy heart she glanced at the young dads splashing around and on the reserve, throwing balls to their sons, cheering, encouraging and, most of all, laughing.

Liam had been definite in his refusal to be a father. She understood that some people didn't have the need for kids in their lives, but that didn't mean she liked the idea. How could someone not want to know their own flesh and blood? It had been a question burning through her for her whole life. How could you just walk away and not want to be found, not want to make contact? What the hell ever happened to unconditional love?

It went against everything she knew about him. He was gregarious, funny, and cared deeply about the people he helped. But if he really meant he wasn't going to be involved she'd have to be Mum and Dad to her child. After all, in the children's home where she'd eventually settled, one parent was always better than none at all.

As Liam approached she flicked the bike into gear and cycled on to a small caravan advertising fish and chips and ice-cold drinks. 'Usual? Snapper?'

'Of course. And a large portion of chips. Tomato sauce...' He grinned, pointing to a can of cola. 'And all the trimmings.'

'I don't know where you put it all.' His belly was hard and taut. Body lean. Again with the full-on flush as she looked at him, this was becoming an uncomfortable habit. 'If I ate half of what you ate I'd be the side of a house.'

'You can't exactly worry about putting on weight now, can you?' He laughed and gave her a look she couldn't quite decipher.

Having returned their bikes to the hire shop, they walked in step down to the beach and found a spot on the sand in the warm, soothing last rays of the day. Liam sat beside her and they ate out of the paper in companionable silence, pausing every now and then to comment on the food. The fish was divine, as always, the chips hot and salty, the cola too cold and too fizzy. Everything seemed exactly the same as it always was, except that it wasn't. She didn't know how to begin to have any kind of conversation that referred to being pregnant without causing another rift between them.

In the end she decided that rather than going over and over things in her head she was just going to say what was bothering her. She waited until he met her eyes. 'I wanted to say thank you, thank you, thank you for what you did.'

'It's fine. Honestly. Congratulations. You must be pleased.' He didn't look fine, he looked troubled as he leaned in and kissed her cheek, long eyelashes grazing her skin. 'You're looking good. Feeling okay so far?'

'Feeling a little numb all round, to be honest. It's real and happening and I can't quite believe it. I'm so lucky for it to have worked first time round. But it does happen.' She ran her palm across her tender breasts. 'No morning sickness yet, but my boobs are pretty sore.'

'Yeah. It happens. Wait till the varicose veins and heartburn kick in then you'll really be rocking.' He gave her a small smile, smoothing the tiny lines around his eyes, and for a second she was ten years younger, meeting him for the first time. All über-confident medical student who had been knocked sideways by the tiniest of beings—so small she'd fitted almost into the palm of his hand. Never had Georgie seen anyone look so frightened by something so frail, the cheery self-assurance whipped from him as if he'd been sucker-punched.

He'd been honest and open and warm. And since then she'd stood with pride at his graduation, cheered him on the sidelines at rugby games, dragged him kicking and screaming to ballet performances and musical theatre, entirely happy with what he'd had to give her. Just a simple, uncomplicated friendship.

But now his eyes roved her face and then his gaze dipped to where her hand was over her breast. Suddenly she felt a little exposed and hot again under his scrutiny. She kept her eyes focused on the top of his head but eventually he looked back at her as if he was going to speak. A flash of something rippled through those ocean-blue eyes. Something that connected with her, something more than warm, which made her belly clutch and her cheeks burn. Heat prickled through her, intense and breath-sapping.

Her fingers ached to just reach out and touch his cheek. Just touch it. To see what his skin felt like. To feel his breath on her face. Her mouth watered just looking at his lips. Open a little. Just a little… Her breath hitched. He was so close. His familiar scent of male and fresh air wrapped around her like a blanket.

Close enough to—

He shook his head as if confused and disorientated. Then he shifted away and focused on the remainder of his food. Meanwhile, she breathed out slowly, trying to steady her ridiculously sputtering heartbeat. Had she imagined that flash of heat? Those feelings?

Yes.

It was all just her stupid clunky imagination.

She would rather die than ask him and be laughed at… or worse. That kind of conversational subject was explicitly off limits and would only cause tension. It was bad enough that she'd created this difficult atmosphere in the first place. But now, to… Oh, my God. The thought flitted into her brain and rooted itself there, so obvious, so immense, so downright out of this world… *No*. Surely not. She didn't. Couldn't.

She fancied him? Fancied the pants off Liam MacAllister? The guy she'd got drunk with, thrown up on, told her deepest dirty secrets to? She wanted to kiss him? Really? Truly? Her heart thudded with a sinking realisation. Things between them were complicated enough, not least because he was going halfway across the world in less than twenty-four hours and she had no idea when she would see him next.

She couldn't want him, and he certainly wouldn't want her, especially with a baby in tow. Not now. Not ever. End of.

Hell, no.

Georgie was wearing a soft white lacy bra.

That was all Liam could think of. Not how amazing it was that she was pregnant. Although that was pretty amazing. Foolish and foolhardy and well beyond his comprehension too. But she did have a kind of warm glow about her, a softness he'd never seen before. He was no longer even registering how far beyond stupid she'd been to race along the pavement on two thin wheels when anything could have happened to her.

No, the only thing that took up room in his thick head was that her small perfect breasts were covered in lace.

As she leaned forward to take another hot chip, her top gaped a little more and he caught a glimpse of dark nipples. Cream skin. He swallowed. Dragged his gaze away and looked out at the boats bobbing on the turquoise water. What the hell was wrong with him?

Why, when he needed to put distance between them, had that whole concept suddenly become too hard to contemplate? He'd gone from not thinking about her in that way to not being able to stop thinking about her in the matter of a few weeks. He'd kept away, making excuses not to see her, just to get his head around everything. And it had failed spectacularly because the moment she'd told him she was getting on a saddle he'd thundered down here with a distinct determination to convince her not to. He'd always teased her, had fun with her, joked around with her, but never until now had he had this need to protect her. Even if it was from herself.

And he was damned sure it wasn't just because she was pregnant. But he wished to hell it was. Because that was none of his business. Because that he could distance himself from.

Couldn't he?

Man, his life was changing in a direction that was beyond his control and it was taking a lot of getting used to. His life, yes. But another life, a new life, was growing inside her and he was struggling to get past that.

After finishing her dinner and crinkling up the paper into a tight ball, she spoke. 'You didn't have to sneak into the clinic during my lunch hour, you know. I would have given you some space.'

'It just didn't feel right.' He looked everywhere but at her. The finer details of how he'd provided the sperm were definitely not for this conversation. Even more, he'd really not wanted to alert her to the fact he'd been in her workplace, doing the deed in a side room. 'Man, they ask a lot of questions.'

'Tell me about it. They always ask a heap of stuff about

your parents too. Any genetic conditions, inherited diseases. Has either parent had cancer, heart problems, high blood pressure? It kills me just a little bit to not know. In some ways it's a whole clean slate and I don't know about any inherited illnesses that may be hanging over my head. But in other ways it's a jigsaw, trying to piece bits together.' She shrugged, trying for nonchalance, but Liam knew just how much she'd ached to know just something about her mum and dad. 'I don't even know who I got my eye colour from, for God's sake.'

He wanted to say it didn't matter. Because even if you did know who your parents were, it didn't mean a damned thing. It sure as hell didn't mean they loved you. Or maybe that was just his. But, then, how could he blame them? 'Well, at least you know little Nugget there will have big beautiful blue ones, to break the girls' hearts.'

'Or brown. She could have my brown ones.' She glanced over at him with a curious look and he immediately regretted mentioning any kind of pet name. He was not going to get involved. He would not feel anything for this baby. Which was currently only a collection of cells, not a baby at all. Not really.

His chest tightened. Who was he trying to fool? He could barely look at Georgie without imagining what was growing in her belly.

Who. Who was growing in her belly. *His baby.* He was going to be a father. And what had seemed such a simple warm-hearted gesture to help out a friend a few weeks ago had taken on a whole new meaning. This was real. This was happening. She was having his baby.

For a moment he allowed himself the luxury of the thrill of that prospect, let the overpowering innate need to protect overwhelm him.

Then he remembered a very long time ago, as a young

boy of eight, the excitement deep in his heart as he'd felt a baby's kick. His hand on a swollen bump. The soft, cooing voice. A new life.

Then it was gone.

Ice-cold dread stole across him like a shadow. It didn't matter how far you ran, your nightmares still caught up with you.

He quickly tried to focus on something else. 'So, plans for the weekend? After the bungee is it whitewater rafting? Paragliding? How about base jumping? All perfectly suitable under the circumstances.'

'First I thought I'd go running with the bulls, then perhaps a little heli-skiing.' She threw the rolled-up paper ball at him. Missed. Completely. 'Idiot!'

He threw it back at her. 'Bingo. On the head. Your aim is appalling.'

'Show-off!' She threw it towards him. Missed by a mile. Went to grab it. He reached it first and held it high above her head. Way out of her reach. She jumped to get it. Failed. Jumped again. Then she playfully poked him in the stomach so he flinched. 'Ouch!'

'Yes! Got it.'

He grabbed her arms and pulled her into a hug. Tickled her ribs until she yelped for mercy. Felt the soft heat of her breath on his skin. The way she moulded into him. Warm. 'Play fair.'

'Says the man with elastic arms. You have a natural advantage.'

'And you...'

Grinning and breathless, she pulled away, but not before he'd got a noseful of her flowery scent. She smelt like everything good. Everything fresh and vibrant and new. Something spiralled through him. A keening need. Rippling to his heart, where it wrapped itself into a ball of content, then lower to his groin, where content rapidly turned into a fiery need.

He let her go as his world shifted slightly. This could not be happening.

She sat back down, pink-cheeked but smiling. 'Actually, I thought I'd rip up the carpet in the spare room and see what's underneath. I'm hoping it's going to be one of those miracle moments—*Ooh, look, the last owner covered a perfectly intact parquet floor*—like on the DIY TV shows. But somehow I doubt it.'

'So do I. You'll be lucky if there's a decent layer of concrete there. Thinking about your dilapidated house makes me laugh. Either that or I'd cry. It needs serious work.' And thinking about something tangible and solid made a lot more sense than thinking about the searing lusty reaction he'd just had that had thrown him way off kilter. 'Don't get your hopes up. I've seen that old scabby carpet. The walls. The roof. My guess is that the previous owners only spent time covering up just how badly falling down the place was.'

'Aw, you know it was all I could afford. And it's a nice neighbourhood, good school zone, so will be worth a lot more by the time I've finished. Worst house on the best street and all that. And the roof is sound, it just needs some TLC.' She pouted a little and his gaze zeroed in on her mouth. Plump lips. Slightly parted. The tiniest glisten of moisture. He leaned over and dabbed a drop of ketchup away from her bottom lip. His thumb brushed against warmth. And his body overreacted again in some kind of total body heat swamp, accompanied by a strange tachycardia that knocked hard against his rib cage. The beach seemed to go fuzzy out of his peripheral vision as she blinked up at him, surprised by the sudden contact.

Her lips parted a fraction more and if he leaned in he could have placed his over them.

And now he was seriously losing his mind.

Clearly he needed to get laid and quickly. With someone else.

Georgie moved away, frowning. She might have said his name. He didn't know. He willed his breathing back to normal.

Where were they? Oh, yes. The house. For God's sake, he needed to get up and go. This was crazy. This irrational pointless need thrumming through his veins. Crazy and sudden and he didn't know what the hell he was doing any more. Or where this had come from. But he wished it would go as suddenly as it arrived. 'It'll be great when you're done. Lots of potential.'

'So you said when I bought it. But now I've got to capitalise on that. I've chosen some paint. I thought a soft cream would be nice and I'll add colour with blinds and cushions, nursery furniture. I saw a great changing table in a second-hand shop down the road from work—all it needs is a lick of paint, I'm not going to be one of those mums who—'

'A bit early for nesting, surely?' He gathered all the wrappers up then stood, offering his hand to pull her up.

She threw him a look filled with hurt, brushed her clothes down and reached for her bag. 'Well, I've got to start somewhere. Nine months flies by, believe me. I see it all the time at work—people often don't even come up with a name in that time.'

Ignoring his hand, she stood without help and looked out at the ocean. Her shoulders taut, back rigid. Her jaw tightened.

He'd meant that she shouldn't be too sure that this early pregnancy would last the course, that she needed to wait before she spent money on things. Invested. But saying that would be crass. Distasteful. Working at the fertility clinic, she was well aware of all the pitfalls and rewards of pregnancy. And judging by the way her eyes glittered with any baby talk, she was very invested already.

When she turned back to him her eyes were blazing. 'You remember that first night in my house, Liam? When we sat on packing crates and talked all night about the plans I had for renovations?'

'Of course I do.'

'I'm still the same person. I still have that dream. It's going to be a fabulous place. Then I will sell it and climb that property ladder, baby in tow. We'll be zillionaires by the time I've finished. It just needs a bit of imagination, more time and a few willing hands.'

There was a long pause in which he felt sure she was waiting for him to offer to help with the decorating.

He'd returned from Pakistan planning on doing just that. But if he got involved in doing up her house that would mean more time spent with her and that was diametrically opposed to his plan. Which had been to ease himself out of her and her baby's lives. Gently. Without her really noticing. Just longer absences that she could fill with her antenatal classes, nursery shopping, other pregnant friends—because she must have them. Everywhere he looked these days there were blossoming bellies and tiny squawking babies.

But now, seeing her pregnant and the immediate emotions that instilled in him, his plan seemed like a crock full of madness.

So all the more reason for him to get out quickly. He couldn't be ruled by emotions, he never let that happen

in his professional or his personal life. It was too dangerous to do otherwise.

'Anyhoo…' Her eyes were clouded now as she blinked
away. She rooted in her bag and pulled out a folder of papers, clearly trying to keep her voice steady. Goddamn,
everything he did hurt her. She cleared her throat. 'Here's
your signed copy of the contract from the clinic. Helen
was supposed to mail it to you, but I offered to bring it
along here instead. As you saw, it's pretty standard stuff.
You get no claims, no guardianship or visitation rights,
you're not a legal parent, you have no parental rights….
yada-yada. Just what you wanted.'

'Oh. Okay. Great. Thanks.' In black and white it
seemed so cold-hearted. And yet it absolved him of everything. No responsibilities. He took it and shoved it
in to his backpack. He didn't need to reread it. He was
signing every right to this child away.

Truth was, his thoughts about this baby were so
blurred now. He'd thought it would be easy to walk away.
But…well, it wasn't easy at all. He felt like he was giving
his child the same fate he'd had—a life with little contact
with his father. A life wanting something…guidance,
truth, recognition. He couldn't give his child that. He just
couldn't. But what could he give? What did he have left?

Georgie peered up at him and everything he knew
about her was in that guarded look in her eyes. She understood his pain, but was equally angry. She was putting her needs first. And she needed to, he didn't blame
her a jot for that. 'That's what you really want, isn't it,
Liam? You don't want to help me get a nursery ready—
that is clear. Or choose decor. Or talk about baby things.
You don't want me to be pregnant. You don't want any
of this…'

'Look, Geo, that's not it. I'm thrilled for you. I am. It's

what you want and you look so happy, how could I not be pleased for you? I thought this was what you wanted.'

'Me too. But I don't know how you can do it. The more I think about it, the more I don't understand you. I've known all along that you cut yourself off from any kind of decent meaningful human connection...' She twisted in the sand and stepped towards him. 'So just explain to me one thing: what are you so afraid of?'

'I'm not afraid of anything.' And that was the biggest lie he'd ever told. He was afraid of the responsibility of another baby's life, of not being able to protect it from harm. Of loving too much. Of dealing with the utter heartbreak if something went wrong, because he didn't think he could live through that again. His heart raced as blood drained from his head, from his face. 'Nothing.'

'I watched you, Liam...that day in Resus, when your whole world crumbled at the sight of a sick baby. I know you are carrying some terrible burden and, through knowing you for ten years, I think it has something to do with your family. Your sister Lauren?'

He railed around, wishing he didn't know her so well, wishing she couldn't see through the barriers he'd erected. 'It has got nothing to do with anyone.'

'If you choose to let whatever happened colour everything you do for the rest of your life then I can't help you. And I want to, I really do. But I can't bear that every time I mention my baby—*our* baby—you flinch. So I'm going to do this my own way. I'm sorry if that doesn't work for you. Just go off to the South Sudan and do your precious job.'

'What?' His heart thumped harder, fast and furious. 'Is this about my job now as well? You don't like it that I'm going to be leaving all the time, is that it?'

'It's about everything, Liam. About your attitude,

about your refusal to admit what's bothering you, the damned contract that means you will willingly let our friendship irrevocably change and allow a baby to be fatherless, and, yes, it's about your job. It's dangerous, and scary for those of us left behind.'

He shoved his hands in his pockets. He could barely look at her. By donating his…by delivering the goods, he'd done what he'd thought was the right thing—he *had* done the right thing—but the fallout kept coming. 'That job keeps me sane.'

'And drives me mad with worry. But I don't know why we're even bothering talking about this. You've got your contract, you can go off unhindered by any kind of sense of responsibility.'

Responsibility? That was the one single thing that drove him to do what he did. Every damned day.

She whirled around and stalked away, but paused, momentarily to turn back. Scraping her hair back from her face, she glared at him, her body language so at odds with her words. 'Stay safe.'

CHAPTER FOUR

Four months ago...

'ONCE THE PAIN relief kicks in you can take him to X-Ray. Let's see exactly how far up the little tyke stuffed the ball bearing, shall we? Depending on where it is, he might need a sedative for us to get it out. But we need to know more before we do anything else.' Through the fog of his sleep-deprived brain Liam offered the concerned mum a smile. Just a little shut-eye between his plane hitting the tarmac and coming into work would have been nice. Still, boys would be boys, and stuffing things up nostrils was par for the course for a four-year-old.

Hopeful images of a little boy who looked a lot like him flashed through his head. He batted them away. He'd call Georgie and talk to her *later*, explain his plan, what he wanted...once he'd worked out exactly what it was he was going to say. Theoretically it made sense to have some contact with his baby. He'd be responsible for finances and guidance, provide things. No emotional involvement. No day-to-day stuff—he didn't want to tread on Georgie's toes. But enough that his child would be able to identify him as his father. He was responsible, for God's sake.

All very good in theory, but in practice he had no idea.

Maybe this was just another of his ludicrous plans that would be fraught with endless fallout. But somehow he did not like the idea of being a dad and not having at least some contact with the child.

The little boy's mum laughed, but Liam could see by her lined forehead and forced smile that she was still anxious. It didn't matter what befell a kid, their parent always worried.

'I don't know why he decided it needed to go all the way up his nose. I just wish he hadn't found it at all. I'll kill his dad when we get home. Leaving little things on the floor is so dangerous.'

'I guess having kids means big changes. It takes a bit of getting used to.'

That thought had been running over and over in his head since he'd left. Would he be like that with his child? Worried sick if it stuffed something up its nose? Would he refuse to let them play outside in case they injured themselves? He'd seen extremes in this job. Neglect that almost tore his heart in two, and the worried well who caused a fuss over nothing. Where children were concerned, it was difficult to get the balance right. But generally it didn't matter where he was—flooded Pakistan, drought-ridden Africa—parents were the same the world over. They loved. They gave their children what they could. They worried.

He tried to find the wee lad a smile.

The boy grinned back. With sticky-out ears beneath sand-coloured hair he was pretty cute. And now, with the analgesic kicking in, clearly unbothered by the metal ball in his left nostril. 'I liked it. It was silver. I wanted to smell it.'

'Oh.' Kids said the strangest things. Stupefied by his inadequacy where children were concerned, Liam wondered whether you should talk to them like adults or use special kiddy words. He stuck to plain and simple. 'Metal ball bearings don't have a smell, buddy. Now, don't put anything else up your nose. Not even your finger. Off you go.' He turned to the mum and relaxed a little. It was far easier to talk to a grown-up. 'See you when you get back from X-Ray.'

The kid laughed at Liam's grumbling stomach, clearly unfazed by whichever way Liam spoke to him. 'What's that funny noise?'

'It's…er…' Not often he was lost for words. 'I'm hungry. My tummy's asking for lunch.'

'Metal balls don't smell and tummies don't talk.'

'No. Well, I don't suppose they do. But they growl, like mine, so go on and get your picture taken so we can see inside you. Skedaddle.'

And lunch was supposed to have been six hours ago. But since then he'd had a steady stream of minor emergencies on top of a few pretty major ones. Now, shift almost over, he could finally go home. Looking forward to getting something into his stomach that wasn't yet another Sudanese stew or tasteless plane mush, he strode across the ER floor, past the whiteboard. And stopped. Turned. Refocused on the names. *What the…?*

White noise filled his ears, his appetite replaced by an empty hole deep in his gut as he hot-footed it back to Minors and threw the cubicle curtain open. Sure enough, she was there, head in her hands, making soft snuffling noises.

'Georgie? What the hell—?' Four months he'd lain sweltering in a too-hot tent and she'd been tattooed onto the back of his eyelids as he'd gone to sleep, their last conversation going over and over in his head. Making things right hadn't seemed possible from the dodgy dirty-walled internet cafés he'd visited sporadically, so his emails had been short and perfunctory.

He'd spent weeks wondering what he'd say when he saw her in person, how he'd feel when he saw her carrying his baby. How he'd feel when he saw her, period. He hated it that she had put a line under their friendship, ending everything so abruptly. But none of that mattered now, none of it.

He tugged her into his arms, hauled her head against his chest and stroked her back. 'Hey, don't cry. It's okay. It's okay. Whatever's happened we'll fix it. It's okay.'

Firm hands pressed on his chest and gripped his shirt. Her voice was low but not upset. In fact...was she laughing? 'Oh, my God! Liam. You're back! When?'

He'd finally stopped shaking enough to concentrate. Goddamned ER doctor and he'd crumbled the second he'd seen her name. *Georgie. The baby.* He didn't know which thought had come first—one had been so quickly followed by the other. And if that wasn't the most bizarre sequence of mind mess he didn't know what was.

And now she was here, damaged somehow—because this was where damaged people came. And that was just the staff. Worst-case scenarios flitted through his doctor's brain, fuelled by his own awful experiences. 'Early this morning. I was going to call you once I'd had a sleep, but they needed me here urgently. I didn't even get the chance to go home. But what the hell—?'

'Don't get carried away. And, no, I'm not crying.'

'What happened? The baby?' He took a step back and surveyed her belly with quick observations. She had a rounded-out bump now, small and perfect, but the rest of her was thin. Too thin. Grimy, dusty. None of this added up. 'Is the baby okay?'

'Yes, everything's fine. Except…' She finally let him go and moved her hand away from her face. 'I hurt my eye.'

Her right eye was weeping, closed and puffy. Her cheek was swollen. 'Whoa. Great job. What did you do?'

'I smashed a wall through and got dust or shards of chipboard or plaster or something in it. It hurts like hell.' She grimaced, swabbing at her damp face with a dusty fist.

Thank God she was okay. Thank God the baby was okay. Unfamiliar feelings sliced through him, accompanied by a strange lumpy sensation in his throat that made words hard to find. 'You were knocking a wall through? On your own? Are you mad?' He hauled in air. 'Don't answer that. I know the answer. Which one?'

'The kitchen-lounge one. I thought it'd be nice to have one big sunny room all finished in time for Christmas. Imagine what fun it'll be to have dinner in there.'

'The legendary Georgie Taylor Christmas, with enough liquor to sink a ship. And enough food to feed an army. But couldn't it have waited until you got help? Christmas is months away.'

'I've got to be prepared, Liam. This renovating lark takes time and I want Christmas to be perfect this year. I have grand plans.' With her one good eye she glared at him. 'If all you're going to do is tell me off, I'll ask for someone else to deal with my injury.'

'Go right ahead, missy. I think you'll find I'm the most experienced doctor here but, please, feel free to find someone better. I'll take you on a tour if you like. See if any one takes your fancy.' He thumbed the teary trail across her cheek. As he touched her an immediate heat suffused his body. He took his hand away, shaken by such an intense response. 'Oh, sorry, I forgot, you can't see.'

'Excuse my bluntness, Dr Mac, but your bedside manner is slipping. You're supposed to be nice to people when they come and see you with an injury. Basic ER doctoring.' She stuck her tongue out and if she'd felt any electric surge at his touch she didn't show it. He'd thought he'd purged her from his heart, that if he'd worked harder, faster, later then he wouldn't care so much. *Feel* so much. Too bad it hadn't worked. He didn't want to feel anything at all.

'Looks like I suck at interpersonal skills.' He picked up her chart and feigned calmness. 'That was meant to be an apology, by the way.'

'Must try harder. See me after class.' Her lips pressed together tightly. She took a breath and let it out slowly. She definitely looked thinner than the last time he'd seen her, cheeks a little more hollow. Her hair, T-shirt and jeans were covered in bits of wood chip and plaster, but her eyes…well, her good eye had darkened shadows round it. She gave him a reluctant smile that had him craving more. 'Oh, Liam, I've missed you. Missed this.'

Me too. 'Okay. So sit still and let me have a good look.' He tipped her chin towards him. And, yes, it would break every damned oath he'd ever made but, hell, if those lips weren't made for kissing. Which would be a pretty dumb move all round, because things would never be the same again. 'Trust me, I'm a doctor.'

She laughed. 'The old ones are the best. I bet you use that on all incapacitated women?'

'Only the bloody foolish ones who are hell-bent on being so independent they do themselves a mischief. You tried to knock down a wall on your own?' He focused on her eye, not her lips. Damaged or downright sexy. Either way his heart hurt.

'And who else could help me? I'm hardly going to pay someone.'

'You could have waited for me.'

'We both know that that wasn't an ideal option. I didn't know when you were coming back or if we were still friends. Are we?'

The heart hurt intensified. 'Come on, we'll always be friends, whatever happens. Now, let me look.'

'Okay. Give it your best shot.' She managed to open her eyelid a tad but blinked so rapidly he knew it was painful. It slammed closed again, tears rolling down her cheek.

He grabbed a tissue and wiped them away, unwilling to risk a skin-on-skin encounter again. 'Hey, it's okay. I forgive you.'

One eye widened in disbelief. 'What? You? Forgive me? But you were the one—'

'Seriously, no need to cry over me.'

Her lips pursed. Pouted. 'I'm not crying over you, matey. I just can't stop it watering.'

He looked away and began writing on her charts, mainly because it was far easier to do that than look at her. At least he didn't want to kiss the charts better. 'Well, whatever you've done, you've made an almighty mess in there. We're going to need to give you an eye bath to get the gunk out and then get an ophthalmic opinion.'

Her shrugging shoulders confirmed her agreement. 'So you'd better get it organised, then. You must be busy with more needy people than me. I don't mind seeing someone else. That would be if I could see at all.'

'Actually, I'm finishing my shift very shortly. I've got one patient to review then I'll sort out your referral while you have an eye bath. As soon as I'm done I'll wait with you.'

She shook her head. 'No need, honestly. If you don't want to.'

'Of course I want to.' He wasn't letting her go that easily. 'I know I made you angry and for that I'm sorry. I know I can be blunt and unthinking at times, but I realise there are two of us in this friendship...'

'Three now,' she hissed at him, rubbing her belly. His heart gave a little jerk. *His baby.* At once he felt proud and anxious. Excited and terrified.

Protective. Should he say something now?

No. She was damaged and he needed to deal with that, get things on a firmer footing. And work out exactly what it was he wanted to say. What kind of involvement he wanted. He rubbed his hand across his forehead. 'Come out with me for dinner, like old times. We could do fish and chips with extra grease, your favourite. Or curry. Thai, Chinese?'

'Urgh. Please. Don't mention—' She held up her hand then covered her mouth. 'I should have... Oh. No.' She grabbed the back of her chair and stood. Swayed a little.

'Should have what?'

She murmured through her fingers, 'Eaten something. I'm sorry, I have to—'

Then she was ripping back the curtain and staggering across the corridor to the toilet, leaving grubby handprints along the wall. He was beside her in a millisecond. Maybe she'd hit her head too and forgotten to mention it? Concussion? 'What's wrong?'

'Morning sickness? *Morning?* Yeah, right. Liars. All-day sickness, more like. Switches on at the thought of food. Goes away when I eat. In all this excitement I forgot to eat.' She pushed him back away from the bathroom door. 'Wait. Please, wait here. Before I chuck on your shoes.'

And he got a distinct impression that she probably didn't care if she did. 'No, Georgie, you can't see a thing. I will not wait. I will stay here and make sure you're okay.'

'Go do your patient review. You're not the boss of me.'

'How old are you?' He'd spent ten years getting to know that no one could ever be the boss of Georgie. He could hardly leave her and go back to ball-bearing-in-nostril kid when she was like this. 'You infuriating woman—'

But he stopped arguing as she slammed the door open and crouched down while he held her hair back in a thick makeshift ponytail. Her body shook. He held her steady.

This was his fault. He'd allowed this to happen. He'd facilitated this. He ran his hands across her back, felt the knobbly bones of her spine through her loose-fitting T-shirt. Jeans hanging off her hips. She was definitely thinner. This pregnancy was taking a toll on her and she was so damned proud she would never think of mentioning it. She needed a good meal. To be looked after. Someone to take care of her while she grew her baby, instead of believing she could do it all on her own. 'Does this happen a lot?'

'Enough.' She rocked back on her heels and wiped her mouth with toilet tissue.

Putting his hands under her arms, he hauled her up, made sure she was steady on her feet, watched her wash her hands and splash her face, wincing as cold water hit her eye. 'You're losing weight.'

She looked at him in the bathroom mirror, dried her hands and threw the paper towel in the bin. Peered at her eye in the glass. The swelling had worsened. Her one good eye pierced him. 'So are you.'

'South Sudan can do that to a guy.'

'Don't tell me you gave half your food away again?'

'I can survive. They don't have enough. I had plenty even with half-rations.'

'So how was it?'

'Messy. Murky. Complicated.' Like the rest of his life. 'But I'm back here and I want to know about you. How long have you been vomiting and how many times?'

'Simmer down. A few times a day. Counting wasn't helping. Let's just say, too much. It's perfectly normal. It's supposed to go once I hit the second trimester, so it'll be gone any day now. I'm fine.'

Fine? She was a mess. 'And in between the vomiting you're working full time and then taking out your frustration on your house walls? When do you rest?'

She threw him a smile that stopped way short of her dark eyes. 'Well, you know what they say about giving a job to a busy person. That's me! I like being busy.'

'No, you don't, Georgie. You like getting drunk in grungy bars playing loud eighties rock anthems, you like blobbing on the couch and watching reruns of your favourite soaps until you can say the dialogue better than the actors, you like strawberry ice cream, but not berry swirl. You like doing nothing at all if you can help it. You do not like to be busy.'

Uh-oh. Hip-planting was occurring. Both hands fisted. Bad sign. 'Well, you can add doing renovations when pregnant to that list. Go figure, you learn something new about people every day.'

'You know what they say about people like you?'

'No.' She turned to him and swayed a little, her cheeks drained of colour. Her eyes fluttered closed as she steadied herself, leaning against the sink, hands flopped to her sides. She looked exhausted. He wanted to swoop her into his arms, wrap her up in bed and look after her. As if she'd ever let him. 'Tell me, Liam, what do they say?'

'That only the pig-headed, wilful, independent and stubborn will not listen to anyone else. To the detriment of their health. You can't get sick, this baby needs you to be well. You need to stop and rest.' And he was not going to stand by and let anything bad happen. Period.

But contrary to everything he expected from her, she didn't rally. Her shoulders sagged as she gripped the sink, her voice so small he had to strain to hear her. 'Okay, okay, I get it. I'm done arguing. Whatever you say, you're the doc.'

Things must be bad. Never in all the years he'd known her had she so much as uttered a single word that would make her appear less than über-confident and capable.

He took her by the shoulders and steered her out into the waiting room. Found her a chair. Sat her in it. Put a finger over her mouth to hush any complaints.

She needed him and he wasn't going to let her get sick on his watch. It wasn't as if she could call a relative to come look after her—she didn't have any. No one to look out for her, to give her a break when she needed it. To take the baby for a few hours when she needed sleep. To babysit. Did she really have a clue how hard this parenting was going to be? 'You're going to start taking it easy. Doctor's orders.'

CHAPTER FIVE

'LET ME HELP YOU. Be careful, you have a nasty corneal abrasion.'

'So you keep saying. Urgh. So I'll play pirates and keep wearing the eye patch, me hearty.' Georgie had to confess that even though the thick white cotton wool patch didn't help much with healing, and made her look a lot like a numpty, it protected her eye from the glare of her house lights and made her think seriously about wearing safety goggles in the future.

But one thing she'd be reluctant to confess out loud was that the moment Liam had said she needed to take things easy it had felt as if a huge weight had been lifted from her shoulders. Because it was all very well trying to be big and brave and bold but sometimes, just sometimes, she tired of having to rely solely on herself for everything.

A deep breath escaped her lungs as Liam pushed the front door open. She was home. She could relax. At least in theory. It was a little harder in practice, having him in her space, being big and bold for her. Why had he suddenly come over all macho? Why did that make him even more desirable?

For that matter, why hadn't her desire dampened down over the last few months? And why was a man in combat kit and biker boots infinitely more attractive than anything else? She turned on the doorstep. Pregnant and now injured, this was not a good time to be finding her friend attractive. 'Thanks for getting me home. I'll be fine from here. Maybe we could catch up tomorrow when we're both feeling better.'

'Hey, what's the hurry? Are you scared about what I'll do?' He shook his head, eyes glittering with tease as he surveyed her body. If she wasn't mistaken, tension of a very sexual kind rippled between them.

Air whooshed into her lungs as she gave a sharp intake of breath. She wasn't afraid of Liam at all, she was more scared about what *she* might do, suddenly alone with him and very, very hot. 'No…er…I—'

'Don't panic. If it's a total mess I won't get mad. I'm here to help.'

He was talking about the state of her house. Not…*of course not*…anything else. 'I'll be okay. Honestly. Go home, you look beat, Liam. You must be jet-lagged and knackered.'

'Listen to yourself, Geo. You're not letting me help. You don't have to do everything on your own.'

'Of course I do. And I like it. That way I don't have to compromise on anyone else's plans, don't have to work to their timetable, I can just please myself.' She placed her hand against the wall and kept him on the doorstep.

He shook his head. 'Has anyone ever told you that you're the most stubborn person in the world?'

'You? Many times. But you're saying it as if I might care. And I don't.'

'Well, today you're my responsibility and I promised the discharging medical officer I'd take care of you.'

'But you were the discharging medical officer.'

'Go figure. So I'll fix you some dinner, have a look at the damage you've inflicted on your poor house. Make sure you're OK. Then, once I'm satisfied, I'll leave.' He went to squeeze past her, but she blocked his way.

'Promise?'

He frowned. 'If that's what you want.'

She wanted him to be happy about the baby—the single most important thing, and which he'd hardly mentioned. That was all. Well, and to hold her again. Possibly kiss her. Make out, maybe… But that would be a wish too far. 'What do you want, Liam?'

'To make sure you're safe, crazy lady. That's all.'

As he peered through the dust and grime he scratched his head, fluffing his short dark hair into little tufts. 'Bloody hell, Georgie. It's worse than I imagined.' He stepped in, walked across the floor, leaving large thick footprints in the grey film that coated everything. 'What the hell have you done?'

She hid a smile as she followed him into the house where she'd half knocked through the wall, making her downstairs pretty much open-plan. She had grand plans for this room, plans she'd been aching to share with someone. Him, mainly.

And even though she'd been beyond angry with him for the last couple of months, it was good to be able to see him—through her one useful eye—and talk to him. Because she'd been honest when she'd said she'd missed him.

She hadn't expected to have those strange feelings rattling through her again, though. She'd put it down to a cluster of hormones, but when he'd held her, cradling her head like she was something very precious, her heart had done a little leap. More, her body had started to hum with something dangerous. It was a bad idea, having him in her space. 'Personally, I think it's looking great. That old partition wall made everything dark and dingy. Just needs a little bit of cosmetic work and it'll be fine.'

'Plus finishing off. Cornices, a new floor.' He tapped along what remained of the plasterboard wall. 'You go and sit down in the lounge, if you can find the sofa under all this mess. I'll finish this off, clear up, then sort out something to eat.'

'You're hardly dressed for it.'

He looked down at his ex-army fatigues. 'They're old. I don't care. You just sit tight. That is, Miss Independent, if you know how to let someone else do the work.' He picked up the hammer and his forearms tightened. Capable hands, plus mussed-up hair already, and he hadn't even lifted a finger. How was she going to cope?

For a few minutes she lay back on her couch, closed her eyes and let relaxation take hold. It was lovely to lie there, listening to the crash of the hammer. The crumble of plaster, his deep male grunts as he swung and hit. He worked for a while then there was silence.

It stretched.

Suddenly interested in what was happening—or not—Georgie opened her eye and peered across the settling dust.

Oh, good Lord. Her stomach contracted as she inhaled a mouth full of dust. He'd taken off his shirt and was now measuring across the space with an industrial tape measure. Defined muscles stretched and contracted as he moved. Tight abs ridged down to his trouser waistband, a sexy smattering of dark hair pointed to a promised land. The man had no business looking like that, all sunburnt and muscular and just too damned hot. She swallowed, her mouth suddenly dry. Her throat was tight. Her breathing came quick and fast.

Staring was rude.

She reclosed her eye.

No good.

She wanted to look again. It was like watching bad reality TV: she knew she shouldn't watch, but she couldn't help herself. The man was gorgeous. And, heck, she'd always known what his body was like. Days spent with him at the beach had had little effect on her in the past. But now... Wow. He'd developed strength and solidity and muscles. Filled out into those broad shoulders. Her body hummed with need.

He turned to face her. 'You okay? You need anything?'

Not the kind of thing he'd want to give her. 'I'm just fine, thanks. But I wanted to let you know I'm sorry that you left and we'd fallen out. I was worried about you, you know, the whole time.'

He winked at her. 'Forgiven. Just about. I hate this arguing. It's not like us. We don't argue.'

So many firsts for them. 'You do realise that not once have you asked me for any details about the baby? About when it's due. Or if I've had any scans. Which I have.'

'I didn't know where to start.' Dropping the hammer to the floor, he looked lost. Shame faced. Terrified. 'This is all so new. It's pretty intense to get my head round.'

He was a long way behind her in this. For the last few months she'd been wondering whether her child having a father around mattered. Whether, in the long term, it would matter to him.

God, there were so many things she hadn't thought of when she'd gone hurtling into this process. Things she should have talked to him about. Things that could make or break their friendship for ever. It was already spinning out of control.

She pulled a scrap of paper from her purse, taking another risk at rejection. If he baulked at this then she'd reconsider. She got up and walked over to him. 'Here, have a look. An early scan. More of a blob really, but there she is.'

'She?' He took the paper in a shaking hand but didn't look at it. His face paled, he swallowed. And again. 'Too early to talk about gender, isn't it?'

She shrugged. 'I just think of her as a girl. Don't know why.' She pushed the paper closer to him. 'Take a look.'

His fingers closed over the top corner of the paper. He took a deep breath and looked down. No sound. No emotion. Nothing flickered across his face. Nothing to register that this was his child. That she was carrying his baby. Then he raised his head and gave her the scan picture back. 'My God.'

His voice was hollow and raw and she wondered what he was thinking. Maybe he was happy that she was happy but didn't know how to show it.

Her throat filled. 'I don't know what to say or do to make this easier...or less complicated. I know this is going to sound very selfish, but I want everything, Liam. I want this baby, but I don't want to lose your friendship.'

'And I...'

She thought he was going to say more but he didn't. His hands dropped to his sides as he shook his head and turned away.

Despite his doubts, he'd given her this gift. How could she have been so angry with him? He looked so empty and confused that she stepped forward and wrapped her arms round him, pulled him to her, and he responded by holding her close.

Her hands ran over muscles, dips and grooves of naked hot skin, slick with a light sheen of sweat. Her heart began to pound as awareness surged through her. His smell of surgical soap, aftershave and pure male heat filled the air. She inhaled it. And again.

His face was inches from hers. His breath feathered her skin. But she daren't move. Something stirred inside her deep and low. Her breasts tingled for his touch. Was he feeling this too? She hoped…but then what? This whole crazy messed-up situation didn't need complicating further. If he knew what was running through her brain right this second he'd probably walk away and never come back. For all she knew, he was probably planning that anyway.

Keeping her eyes tightly closed, she held her breath, felt him relax against her, felt his grip on her lessen. She didn't want him to let go. She wanted…

'Thanks for that, you old bat,' he whispered, lips pressed against her cheek, his scent intensified along with the tingling through her body, pooling in her groin. She couldn't think of anything but him, being in his arms, how good this felt.

Heat swamped her. There was no point pretending that what she felt for him wasn't real, that this was just a hormonal response. For goodness' sake, she'd been struggling with these weird emotions for months now. And, yes, she wanted to kiss him. She had to know what he tasted like. How he would feel.

With every risk of him leaving—and with no thought for the consequences—she turned her head, met his mouth. Felt his surprise resonate against her lips. Then a groan. A growl. A need.

Liam registered the first touch of Georgie's lips as his heart slammed loud and thunderous in his chest. For one split second a dark corner somewhere in his brain considered that this was the far side of madness—but then that thought was gone and he was left with nothing but heat and need raging through his veins.

Cupping her face in his hands, he opened his mouth to her. Felt her shaking body, heard the guttural moan from her throat, felt her tight fists grip his trouser waistband as he dragged her closer. And each of her responses fed his need. She tasted wet and hot and soft. Of salty tears and fresh pure joy. He closed his eyes at the sweet sensations she instilled in him.

Her hands made a slow trail to his backside as she clamped her body to his and she moaned again as she felt him harden at the press of her hips. He liked the way she felt against him. Liked the feel of her fingers on his body. The thrill of her touch.

As his hands slid down her back he brushed against her bra strap and the memory of those perfect nipples covered in lace made him ache to touch them. Slipping his hand under her T-shirt, he worked his fingers to her breast, felt the hardening nipples beneath silk. He wanted to feel them against his skin. Naked. Wanted to suck those dark buds into his mouth. To taste her everywhere. Wanted to feel her around him.

'Oh, God, Liam.'

'Georgie…' He opened his eyes, and immediately registered the harsh reality. *Damn.* This was Georgie. She was injured and pregnant and he was supposed to be looking after her.

Not taking advantage of her. This was Georgie. His best friend. The hands-off friend.

Who was pregnant.

With his child.

And, yes—ever since he'd held that picture in his hand and felt the deep singular ache in his heart he'd known that he'd fight heaven and earth for his baby. This was something that was a part of him and he couldn't turn his back on that.

He'd been about to tell her his plan. About the financial help he'd decided he wanted to give. About giving his son or daughter the best. Because they deserved it, Georgie did too. But…when it had come to it, after holding the scan in his hands, he'd panicked. He needed to be sure.

And then…this…had blown his heart wide open.

My God. Kissing Georgie.

In the cold stark light of day that dark corner of doubt started to flourish. Another person he would let down. His life was littered them. He sure as hell didn't want to include Georgie and the baby in that line-up.

The shock of what they were doing made him break away. He did it with little finesse and immediately saw the embarrassment or disappointment or just plain confusion flash across her gaze.

What the hell just happened? He coughed, cleared his throat, tried to sound a lot less shaken up than he felt. 'Well, that was unexpected. And not at all like kissing my cousin. But, then, Mike never was much good at tongues, apparently. You, however…'

'Always the joker.' She twisted away and stalked back into the lounge area, wringing her hands in front of her, clearly trying to work out how they'd gone from friends to…this. And what the heck they were supposed to do now they'd crossed an unspoken line. 'I'm sorry. I shouldn't have done that.'

'No.' He followed her but couldn't find it in him to sit down. His first and only instinct was to get the hell out. But running out on a woman who was sick and confused would make him a jerk and a coward. Although he couldn't help feeling that he'd already started to put distance there. He wasn't sitting down and talking reasonably, he was edging subconsciously closer to the door. He made himself stand still and focused on her. '*We* shouldn't have done that.'

'No, Liam. *I* kissed you. Embarrassment totally one hundred per cent complete.'

And he'd kissed her back—without any encouragement. What happened to reining in his libido, like any other decent man would? But something a lot like a mind meld had happened, pushing him to continue, and he'd been unable to stop.

Her lips were a little swollen, her good eye misty, hair messy, as if she'd just scrambled out of bed. She looked sexier than anyone he'd ever seen. Sexy and very off limits.

Actually, sexy, off limits and torn. 'Really, Liam, I think you should go.'

'Yes. I'll come back and finish this off another time.' He went to get his T-shirt, shook off some of the debris stuck to it before pulling it over his head. 'I should order you a pizza or something. You need to eat. Regularly and properly.'

'I can manage a phone quite well.' Waving her hand in front of her, she gave him a brief smile that was laced with hurt. 'Please, just go. You're officially off the hook. Go, and let me die a thousand embarrassed deaths in peace.'

He didn't know what was running through her mind, but he'd take a big guess that it wasn't him actually agreeing with her and leaving. The last thing she needed right now was uncertainty. But everything was messed up and muddied; there he was tangling her pregnancy with his feelings. He was having a hard time separating the baby issue from his attraction to Georgie. If they didn't get everything out in the open, this would be hanging over them for ever. 'But shouldn't we talk about what just happened?'

'No. That's not going to get us anywhere but deeper in trouble. It's pretty clear from your face that you're shocked. Please. Please. Just go.'

'I'll be back tomorrow to help you.'

'Off the hook, I said. I can manage. Please...' She was biting her bottom lip and looking so regretful that he did her bidding. She didn't want him around. And the truth was he didn't much feel like staying when his head and his body were so much at odds and he was at risk of making things worse. Or, even more catastrophic in the long run, helping to make her feel better in the only way he wanted to right now, which would be a one-way ticket to the far side of stupid.

CHAPTER SIX

MORTIFIED. JUST DOWNRIGHT mortified. Georgie was surprised her cheeks hadn't burnt a hole right through her pillow. Twelve hours later and she was still…utterly mortified. Half peering, half feeling her way around her house, she went downstairs to the kitchen, finished wet dusting all the surfaces, popped the kettle on and contemplated pushing two pieces of wholegrain bread into the toaster. Then gave up on the idea. Ruining friendships had sent her appetite running and hiding along with her pride.

And, okay, so he'd kissed her back, and appeared to have been enjoying it, but the moment he'd cut loose and let her go she'd seen doubt and fear and confusion run across those eyes. Eyes that had turned, once again, a darker shade of navy.

But, man, he'd tasted so good. *Felt* so good. Until the moment he'd jerked away and she'd wished she could have been swallowed up in the house's perennial dust cloud and whirled back to five minutes previously. Before the kiss that had probably, finally, broken their friendship.

And it was all her fault. She'd pushed him in one direction to give her his sperm, acknowledged he didn't want to go there at all but had done it anyway, and then had pulled him to her in a selfish moment of unwarranted and uninhibited need. Putting her head in her hands, she leaned against the grey kitchen bench, dusty again already, and groaned. Stupid. *Stupid.*

God knew where they'd go from here.

The doorbell rang quick and sharp and then Liam was calling out, and then standing in her lounge, muscled arms filled with brushes and buckets and tools, which he put on the floor in the corner of the room.

'Morning.' He stopped short and frowned, and her stomach contracted. 'Holy cow, you look awful.'

'Thanks a bunch. So do you. Why don't you come right in and make yourself at home?' She tried to make her voice sound nonchalant instead of shaky, but it all just came out weird and high-pitched. She was a little bit relieved to see that he looked like he'd just finished night duty—tired, paler and shadowed with a perfectly stubbled jaw. Which inevitably made her stomach contract again, but this time for a totally different reason.

She peered up at him, trying to measure his mood while at the same time trying to quell the nausea in the pit of her stomach. And she knew it was nothing to do with her morning sickness and everything to do with kissing her oldest mate—and even now, despite the mortification, wanting to do it again. The hot spots on her cheeks reappeared. 'I thought I said you didn't have to come and help. I know you have little time off as it is without bothering about me. I can manage fine.'

'And leave you here knowing what disaster was lurking behind this door? No way. No doubt if I left you in here with a hammer for any length of time you'd be completely blind and crippled within the hour. So basically I'm doing my colleagues at A and E a favour by keeping you out of their hair.' He made no effort to hide his smile. 'I thought we should go out for a while first, take a walk to the French market. Get out of this dust bowl and clear your lungs.' AKA not wanting to be in a confined space with her. She understood, loud and clear. 'You don't need an asthma attack added to your medical history.'

'My lungs are perfectly clear, thank you.' *Unlike my head*, she thought, which was filled with grimy confusion. 'The dust settles downwards all over the surfaces rather than floating upwards to my bedroom.' And at the mere mention of where she slept, usually near-naked, she had an unwelcome image of him also naked, in her sheets. Okay, so not unwelcome…in fact, very welcome indeed. Just unrealistic. And never going to happen. 'So…er… how are you? Good sleep?'

And maybe it was the mention of her bed that did funny things to him too, because all of a sudden his bravado slipped, he shoved his hands deep in his pockets and his gaze was not at her, but beyond, or around, or anywhere else but meeting her eyes. *Eye*.

An awkward unspoken tension hovered between them as he shifted from one foot to the other. 'I'm fine. How are you feeling? How's the eye? Using the drops as prescribed?'

'Yes, Dr MacAllister.' She patted the new patch gently, knowing that, added to the sleepless eye bags and the uncombed hair, it gave her a pathetically ill look. Still, having managed perfectly well for twenty-eight years pretty much on her own, she was far from fragile, but it did feel nice to have someone ask how she was feeling, even if it was just to avoid talking about the kiss or what the heck they should do now. 'The prickly headache's gone. I feel okay, a little sore, but raring to get going in here.'

'Well, first brioche and espresso are calling. Then you can go and do whatever you want to do for the day and leave me in peace to get this place sorted. I've got more stuff in the car—plaster, rollers, cornices, skirting, protective goggles and face masks. It'll keep me busy for a few…' His fingers speared his hair as he looked at the room, the magnitude of the utter mess they'd made clearly dawning. *And not just the house*. She'd made a mess of everything. 'Weeks.'

And he was also playing the *let's not talk about it* game. She could do that too. And perhaps, by the time they'd got to the market normality would be restored and her appetite would come out of hiding. 'Okay. Well, I'll just drag a brush through my hair and grab a jumper. Give me a minute or two.'

The sky was a brilliant cloudless cobalt blue as they strode down the hill, past rows of perfectly maintained colonial-style houses, just like hers was going to be…possibly next millennium. Luckily the market wasn't far so they didn't have too many moments of difficult silence to fill before they got there.

They walked through the car park to the stalls dotted around the forecourt of a large open-fronted building selling everything French. Colourful Provençale earthenware sat next to tins of *foie gras* and jars of bright thick jams; soft linens and dainty sprigs of lavender graced traditional wooden dressers; blue and white chequered tablecloths covered a hotchpotch of mismatched tables. People sat around, chatting and eating and laughing.

A stack of antique furniture sat in one corner of the building, rickety tables and chairs, kitchen and bedroom heirloom pieces. Georgie spied a quaint rocking bassinet in need of a little care and attention, adorned with the softest cream-coloured blankets and the cutest coverlets, and her heart did a little jig. It was perfect. But, as with most things here, it was also too far out of her price bracket.

She sighed, dragging herself away from such beautiful things. Buying would have to happen when she could afford it, not when it took her fancy. Liam noticed her gaze drift back to the bassinet but, then, he would. Annoyingly, he knew her through and through. Her heart jig went into a serious funeral dirge. It seemed everything was an issue between them these days. He nodded at the bassinet. 'Planning ahead?'

'Window shopping. At least that's free. I have to get my priorities straight. Firstly, I have to provide a decent place to sleep. Then I have to provide something to sleep in.'

'Babies cost a lot, eh? So much to think about, it's mind-blowing.' His forehead crinkled as he frowned. He looked as if he was about to say something, then changed his mind and tugged her to the juice bar instead. 'Okay, now you're going to have a fresh juice. Then we'll get a decent coffee and something to eat.'

'But—'

He placed a gentle palm against the small of her back and manoeuvred her towards the juice stall. 'No buts. And we're going to be the same as we always are when we come here. We're going to *ooh* at the cheese and hold our noses at the smell. And buy way too much and not eat it all. And then we'll have to fumigate your kitchen-diner-lounge room thing, whatever you want to call it.'

'I call it my living area, and it's going to be fabulous. But unfortunately I'm not going to eat any unprocessed soft cheese there or anywhere else. Along with alcohol, pâté and most kinds of processed meat that I love, stinky cheese is out for a while. Remember?' She patted her stomach. Damn the man, she was going to mention her pregnancy. It was part of her. Soon it would be most of her, plumping her out like a huge fat cushion. And then there'd be no denying it. Whether he liked it or not.

To her surprise, he grinned.

'Okay, so you're going to look at the cheese section and be downright miserable. Walk straight past the pâté, giving it a cold hard stare. Cast eye-daggers on that devilish salami and *jambon*. And then order a double helping of *pain au chocolat* and a *chocolat chaud* with lashings of cream, and still wallow in what you can't have instead of what you've got. Which, in my book, is three helpings of chocolate and it's not even ten o'clock.'

He stopped at the juice stall and ordered a freshly squeezed OJ for himself and a 'Brain Booster' for her, like always.

'Which is why you need this vitamin blast to counteract the sugar rush. And now we're going to talk about what happened last night, and when we've stopped cringing we're going to laugh about it. We will laugh. Eventually.'

At her shocked face he smiled again, but this time it was softer and more tender. And she liked it that he was trying to make things normal, that he was making sure she had the right things to eat, and that she was as content as she could be under the circumstances. This was the Liam she'd grown to love. Whoa. *Love?*

Platonically, yes. She loved him as any friend would love a friend. And fancied him, just a little bit. Which was understandable, because a lot of women did. He was just the type that appealed—dashing doctor with a great sense of humour and nice hands. Looking lower, she admired other parts of him too.

Okay, if he kept on staring at her and smiling like that she could definitely fancy him a lot.

'Na-ah.' Georgie shook her head as her cheeks heated

again. 'I'm not going to talk about it, I'm just pretending it didn't happen.'

'Well, I'm not. That's not going to work. It's going to be the big elephant in the…market, stomping around with us for ever. So we'll acknowledge that it happened. We'll agree it was—'

'A mistake,' she butted in, before he could say anything else. Because that's what it had been. A huge silly mistake.

'Here you go, you two. Your usual. Beautiful day…' The juice lady passed over large plastic cups of vividly coloured juice with perfect timing. Georgie took hers and handed Liam his. Then she wandered through the stalls, perusing the locally grown fruit and vegetables, the huge bowls of oily olives and myriad savoury dips, and feigned interest in everything apart from this conversation.

He was by her side in a moment. On any other day she wouldn't have paid much attention but today all her body seemed interested in was getting closer to that smell, in being near him, in having his lips on her skin again. His mouth was dangerously close to her ear. 'I was going to say it was nice. More than nice. In fact, it was a bloody revelation. I didn't think you'd be so…unleashed. But if you want to say it was a mistake, go ahead.'

She twisted to see him, his eyes glinting with tease. And heat. 'It was a mistake. And I'm so-o-o embarrassed.'

His arm snaked across her shoulder and he wrapped her in a sort of guy-style headlock hug thing. Which shouldn't have been remotely sexy but was the biggest turn on since her lips had touched his last night. 'It's okay, Geo. We can move on. It is possible.'

'You think?' Wiggling from his grip, she faced him. 'I kissed you! In fact, I almost attacked you!' The clatter of teacups reverberated around the space, and then ended in an abrupt silence. People stared and then turned away and pretended not to stare, which made everything ten times worse. She lowered her voice and her words came out a lot like a hiss. 'But, then, you kiss so many women you probably didn't even think much about it.'

Hadn't he? Had it been really not special? Had she not turned him on while she'd been burning up? By saying they could move on, was he trying to say that he didn't want her? Which was what she wanted, wasn't it? An end to these weird feelings? So why did she feel as if she'd been stabbed through the gut?

'To be honest, it's all I've been thinking about for the last twelve hours.' He steered her to a table and sat her down, grinning. He was enjoying this. Well, of course he was, this was Liam, the great non-committer. 'But what I need to know, Geo, is why?'

'Well…' If she knew that, she'd be up for a Nobel prize or something. The secrets of the universe. The chemistry of attraction. The laws of inconvenience and mortification. All started and ended with the *but why?* of that kiss. 'Haven't you ever wondered about…you know…us? What it would be like? What we would be like?'

He shrugged his gorgeous shoulders, but a tiny muscle moved in his jaw. 'I seem to remember you used the descriptor *ick* the last time we talked about this. So, honestly, it wasn't something I imagined could happen. Then, suddenly…*wham*.'

'I attacked you. I did—*do*—think it's an ick idea. But, then, for some reason last night I felt really connected to you. I'm sorry.'

'Stop apologising. Never apologise for kissing like that.' The waitress brought their order and he took a bite from his *croque monsieur,* which oozed melted cheese over the plate and looked almost as delicious as the man sinking his teeth into it. He swallowed and took a sip of espresso. 'Do you think it's because of the baby? Is this all because I'm the father? Because, frankly, you never gave me any reason to think you liked me…in that way. And, yes, we're going to keep talking about it like we talk about everything, so take your hands away from your face.'

'No. Yes. No. I don't know. It's all become too complicated. I felt weird when I saw you that day in the bar after you came back from Pakistan. Something was different. You seemed different, I felt different. Maybe it was the fertility drugs.' But that was a lame excuse. Lots of women took them and didn't go around kissing inappropriately. She finally had the courage to look up at him. Yes, something was still very definitely different. The feeling hadn't gone, it had got worse. 'Anyhoo, I got it out of my system last night, and we both know that nothing can happen, don't we…?'

'Absolutely. Understood.'

What she wanted him to say she didn't know. Except, possibly, that he wanted to do it again and again. That he fancied her in just the same way. Okay, she wanted the whole dang fairytale—but Liam had never been much of a Prince Charming, and she definitely didn't suit the Cinderella role, apart from the having no money bit. In that part she was absolutely typecast.

Placing his cup slowly into the white bone china saucer, Liam looked like he was carefully choosing the right words. 'We are in no state to start anything. Imagine if we did the sex thing and then fell out. Imagine if we took anything any further. Me the playboy and you pregnant and vulnerable. You need to think of the baby.'

'So I don't get to have a sex life? Women can have sex

when they're pregnant. Numpty.' Her eyes almost ping-
ing out of her head, she picked up her fork and pointed it
at him. 'And I am not vulnerable. Dare to say that again
and I'll fork you to death.'

'No, never. Please. Anything but that.' His voice rose
a teasing octave. Then got serious. 'You are one of the
strongest people I've met. It was the wrong choice of
words. Your situation makes you vulnerable. But you
need someone who'll stick around. Someone who—'

'Wants me?' She closed her eyes wishing to hell she
hadn't said that. It sounded so needy, and she wasn't.
Just uncertain. And frustrated. Because she wanted to
kiss him, she wanted to take him to her bed and tangle
in the sheets, like she'd imagined. She wanted him…in
a way she hadn't known could be possible. But he didn't
want her. And he was trying so hard to put it gently and
nicely and in a friendly way. It was humiliating that he
even thought she needed the gentle treatment.

A sharp twist of pain radiated through her solar plexus.
Even her own mother hadn't wanted her and had left her
in a box on steps outside a church hall with nothing except a small cream woollen blanket and the clothes she'd
been wearing. No one had ever claimed her. And bureau-
cracy and mixed-up paperwork had meant she hadn't
been put up for adoption until she'd been too old, so she'd
never belonged. Period. No one had ever wanted her.

And to a certain extent Liam was right. He didn't stick
around anywhere for long, his job took him to some of the
most dangerous parts of the world, and for the most part
she thought it was exciting, glamorous even. But in reality it was dangerous. He ran a serious risk of being killed,
caught or tortured. Did she want that kind of anxiety to
infiltrate her life and that of her child's from here on?

His warm hand covered hers. 'You know I wouldn't do

anything to hurt you, right? But we can't put our whole friendship under threat because of curiosity. Things would inevitably change. They couldn't not change. Everything would come under the spotlight—past partners, broken promises, how we fill the dishwasher, whose turn it is to empty the bins. And everything we've ever done with other people will come under scrutiny too, what we've said, what we've done. There'll be expectations, and I'm not good with that. You know that. I don't want things to get complicated.'

Too late, mate. 'Like me having your baby?'

'Yeah. That. It's complicated already, without getting things involved sexually too. Not that I don't want to… wouldn't…you know…mind. That kiss wasn't ick. It was good. Very good.' He shook his head. 'God, this is awful. I think I preferred your way of pretending it didn't happen. Let's go back an hour, shall we?'

Or twelve?

He held her gaze for a few seconds and smiled apologetically. Then his smile melted. As if distracted by something over his shoulder, he turned away. When he looked back he didn't give her eye contact at all. Just stared down at his cup. 'And…'

'And?'

His head jerked up, and he looked spooked and shocked. 'Nothing. Forget it. Just that. I can't give you what you need.'

'I don't need anything. It was only a kiss.' But the caution in his eyes told her he had been about to say something else. Had broken off before he'd dared say it. What the hell? Her heart began to rattle against her rib cage. 'Wait a minute. What are you hiding?'

'Nothing. I don't know what you mean.'

'You look edgy and worried and I've seen that look on

your face many times. Right before you give your poor sap of a girlfriend the old heave-ho.'

He looked down at his hands and dragged in a breath. 'Georgie, there's something else. Something I've been meaning to say since I got back, but haven't...quite found the right words.'

The chocolate croissant felt like a hard lump in her churning stomach. Things had become really messed up. 'I won't jump you again, if that's what you're worried about.'

'Of course I'm not worried.' No? Well, he just looked it, then. 'I'm going to help you renovate your house, I promised I'd do that. And I will.'

She knew a man was stalling when she saw it. 'And then, when you've done your dutiful bit and fulfilled the promises, you're going to adhere to the baby daddy contract and do a runner.'

'Far from it. In fact, just the opposite.' He stood up, took her by the arm and began to walk back through the market. 'Not at all. Georgie, I know it's taken me a long time to outright say it, but I wanted to make sure. I was trying not to mess you around.'

'What? What is it?' *You've met someone. Someone important.* Words clogged in her throat, thick and fast. 'Spit it out, man. I'm on tenterhooks here.'

He gave her a sideways smile. 'Thing is, I do want to be the father of this child. I want to provide, I want to take responsibility for my baby.'

'What? *Your* baby? Your baby? Whoa. That's a surprise.'

'Yes. My baby. It's got my DNA. Just like we agreed. Like you wanted.'

'But you said...' All her ideas tumbled around in her head with a sharp mix of frustration.

All she'd known about him for ten years suggested he didn't want a child. He didn't want a family. He'd signed a damned contract, made that the only condition. So instead of being the far side of elated, her gut felt churned up. Would he change his mind again?

And again?

And then there was the small matter of the kiss, which coloured everything.

His involvement was what she'd wanted ever since he'd offered to be the donor, but this was not how she'd imagined it would make her feel.

Irritated, she shook her arm free from his. Shoppers jostled against them as they headed back towards the house. The busy street was so not the place to be having this conversation. 'I know it's what I wanted, but I thought you didn't…weren't…aren't…' She pulled herself together and chose bluntness and honesty. 'Why now? Why this all of a sudden? How can I trust that you'll take this seriously? You're so confusing.'

Unlike her, he seemed far from irritated, his voice steady and determined. 'It's not confusing at all. This is the most serious and the most single-minded I've ever been about anything.'

'And you decide to tell me now? Here, on Parnell Road?'

'Okay, I have to admit my timing's lousy.'

'You can say that again.' She whirled round to face him, her head woozy at the sudden and fundamental change in her life. She didn't know how she felt about this. He hadn't exactly declared his overwhelming love for the baby, and she didn't know how she *felt* about him—except that he'd just completely blindsided her and everything was getting more complicated by the second.

And more, she had to be sure this wasn't some passing

phase he'd move out of next week, next month, next year. 'Is this some kind of misdirected duty thing? Because you don't get to do that. You don't get to mess around with other people's lives just because it makes you feel better. Here one minute, changing your mind the next.'

'I won't change my mind.'

She tried to stay calm. 'A contract has been signed, Liam. You're legally bound, remember? Clause number six? *"You will have no paternal rights whatsoever over the child, and will have no authority of any kind with respect to the child, or any decisions regarding the child."*'

'Whoa. Really? Off by heart?' He stared at her open-mouthed.

'What? I counsel about this exact dilemma every damned day, Liam. So I know the wording. Okay?'

'So you'll remember clause ten, then? You can agree to me having social contact—at your discretion.'

He'd certainly read it. He'd taken the time and effort to read and research. He was serious. 'Yes, I can, if I think contact will be good for the child. But what do you know about bringing up a child? About being a father? What's changed for you?'

Love, she thought. She hoped.

Because love for her child, even though it was still so small and so precious, had changed her fundamentally.

But Liam's expression turned thunderous. 'This is ridiculous. I don't want to mess anyone around, I want to be involved—the two things are completely different. I knew you were going to react like this. You just don't want anyone butting in on your little family of two.'

'How dare you? I would love my baby to have a father, you know that. You know I want that more than anything.' She shook her head. Amazing that he could think that. 'Is that what you think of me? That I'm selfish? That I want to keep this child purely for myself, like some kind of…toy?'

'Of course not. But surely, as the father, I have a say in things?' He really meant it. He wanted to be part of this. But could she trust him to be wholly there for them?

'No. Actually, you don't. You signed your rights away. All I know is that not many months ago you demanded a contract and now you don't want that. Maybe next month you'll want the contract again.'

He stopped short, breathing hard, dragged a wad of paper out of his jacket pocket. 'Here. Here's the contract.' He held the papers up and tore them in half. Then half again. Then again. Pieces of ripped paper fluttered to her feet like large bits of confetti. Only this was the severing of something, not celebrating the uniting of something. 'I want to be a father. The father of the child you are carrying. My child.'

And the word 'love' is still not there.

She'd listened hard and it was still missing. No matter how much she wanted it to be there, no matter how much she strained to hear it in the cadence of his words, in the silence between them.

He wanted to be a father, but he didn't want to be a daddy. That was the fundamental difference. He wanted the label but not the emotional involvement. That was Liam through and through.

But, on the other hand, if he was truly serious and did want to be involved, she couldn't deny him that, couldn't deny her child the right to know its father.

Why did this have to be so complicated? Why couldn't he have kept to his side of the deal? Why did she have to have developed more than friendly feelings for him? Those emotions were tainting things, making her think in a way she'd never done before. This whole morning wasn't about the kiss at all. It had never been about the kiss.

His hand was on her arm now. 'Georgie, I don't want to have this conversation here on the street and I don't want to argue. This was the furthest thing from my mind. You look upset and that really wasn't my intention. I honestly thought you'd be pleased.'

Pleased? If his intentions were genuine then she'd be delighted. How could she not want him to be a father? He was smart, funny and, if she was honest, would make a great daddy—if he stuck around long enough. And there it was again, her immediate concern: he just wasn't the staying sort of guy. For whatever reason—and she only knew half of his story—he didn't commit.

She picked the pieces of paper up and shoved them at him. Then hesitated on her doorstep. 'Can we talk later? This is pretty big for me, I need some time to think things through.'

'Yes, by all means, think it through.' He followed her up the steps and when it was clear he wasn't giving up, she took her key out of her bag. As he watched her he shook his head. 'But I need to say this now, Geo, and I need you to listen. It's tough work, bringing up a child. I don't want you to go through it on your own and I don't want our child to miss out on having a father. I know how that feels and I couldn't condemn my own flesh and blood to that kind of life. Don't you want me to be involved?'

'This is my flesh and blood too. My only flesh and blood. So I've got to be careful, make the right decisions.' At least he had a family. He might not want to have them, but he was tied to them. And now she would be tied to him for ever. Oh, why the hell hadn't she thought this through more thoroughly at the beginning? 'What exactly do you mean by "involved"? Cash? Because that's not enough. Is that why you're here? To pay us off or something?'

'It's been in my head for the last few weeks, I just didn't know how to say it. When to say it. What to say, even. But the more I see you, the more I think about it, the more it makes sense.'

'It's not about making sense, it's about how you feel. In here.' She touched her chest. It felt a little cracked open and raw. 'In your heart and your soul. You can't do something because it makes sense, otherwise we'd never do any of the rash, amazing stuff we do. Like this pregnancy thing from the start. None of it made sense, not to you or anyone else. But it did to me.'

'And it does to me now.'

His words hovered in the air as she thrust the key in the lock and threw the door open. She took several long deep breaths and tried to clear her thoughts.

Then tried to explain them to him. 'If I was going to co-parent I would expect a fully one hundred per cent committed father who was around, who wouldn't flinch during the darker times. Because there will be some, I'm sure.' And although she adored Liam, he wasn't reliable. He was away a lot of the time, never knowing when he'd be home. And she couldn't get past the fact that he'd told her that this baby plan was the worst thing he'd ever heard.

'It's got to be for ever, you can't change your mind again. I don't want to open our child up to a whole world of hurt. I saw plenty of kids at the home whose families made promises and broke them, and in the end broke their kids' hearts and crushed their spirits.'

'I know you had a hard time, Georgie. And that's why

I'm here now. So our child doesn't have to go through what you went through.'

'You have no idea. You don't know what it means to be alone. To make up a pretend family because you don't have any. To watch others being chosen. To wish that someone, anyone, would choose you. And to try to be, oh, so brave when they didn't, when inside every part of you is crumbling.' She would never crumble again. This child inside her gave her twice the strength and three times the resolve. 'This is your last chance to decide, Liam. I'll hold you to whatever decision you make now. This is it. No going back. No coming to me in three years, six, twelve and saying you made a mistake and you've changed your mind again. You have to be in or out—for ever.'

This was something Liam could answer. Because this was the one thing he knew. He would not let his child down. He'd known that with every damned fibre of his being since the moment he'd seen her carrying his child. Since he'd seen that scan of a real living being. His child. Their child.

Every single mention of a baby, every thought of who was growing inside her, brought back the crushing pain again. And with that hurt still beating against his rib cage he knew he'd make every effort to make his child safe. Because that was his job. A father did that.

But he was also going to keep any emotions out of it. Because, hell, he needed to keep his heart safe, too. He would provide from a distance. He would have visits but he wouldn't—couldn't—put any of them at risk by allowing himself to care for them. He would treat his child with the same compassion and consideration he treated his patients, no more and certainly no less.

'I know what I said. I didn't think it through. But this

is my child and my responsibility and I will never shirk from that. I don't want your experiences for our child, or mine either. This child will know he's always wanted.' This was not how Liam had imagined this scenario play-ing out, but he had to go with it. He'd already stumbled too far along without saying what he felt. Although he'd been shocked by the ferocity of Georgie's reaction. He'd seriously misjudged her. She was growing braver and stronger and more independent every moment she car-ried that baby. 'I am in it for ever.'

'How can I be sure?' Her hands were on her hips while her dark eyes blazed.

'So tearing up the contract isn't enough for you?'

'No. Actions speak, Liam. I want actions—and not dramatic hollow ones like those shreds of paper.'

Now this was well and truly out in the open he knew there could never be any more kisses. He needed to keep a good long distance from her, too. Anything else would make things far too complicated. They could both be good parents if they were a team, a *platonic* team. Mess-ing with that, opening a whole potential for destruction, would be a recipe for disaster.

He knew how much pain a child suffered when their parents couldn't bear to look at each other. Knew how destructive it was, watching arguments unfold, always calculating when the bomb was going to drop. Always being on guard. Always feeling, believing, *knowing* that every single ounce of friction was his fault. He couldn't put his own child through that, so if there was no inti-macy there would be no chance of that damaging scenario happening. 'You'll know, Georgie, because I'll damned well prove it to you.'

CHAPTER SEVEN

Three months ago...

'IT'LL KEEP ME busy for weeks.'

Ha. He wished.

By Liam's reckoning it should have been finished months ago, but whenever he turned around this tinpot wreck of a house threw another job at him. Georgie had been wrong about the roof. With the winter came high winds that blew off and cracked more than enough tiles for the whole thing to need replacing.

Then there was the floor in the kitchen. Weathered and abused over seventy years, it took four consecutive weekends to sand it down enough that it was even and usable. Then three coats of varnish. A perfect parquet floor it was not, but it was now an acceptably usable one. All done on a tight budget, and fitted in between exhausting twelve-hour shifts at work. It had taken a lot of coercing Georgie to even allow him to do that.

Climbing down the stepladder from where he'd been fixing the new light fitting in the flash living area, he huffed out a long breath. He had to admit she'd had a point about knocking the wall down, the open-plan space was amazing. With the renovated floor and antique white walls it was impressively large and light, with a good flow from one area to the next. She'd managed to find, on the cheap from a trading website, a set of elegant French doors that opened the kitchen out onto the small deck. Beyond that was a riotous garden, overgrown and dingy. But he had no doubt she had plans for there too. The woman clearly had a gift for renovation.

A loud bang and a very unladylike curse came from above him. Liam was up the stairs and in the bathroom in two seconds flat. 'You okay? What the hell was that?'

'Just a little contretemps with a tin of paint. And… damn, I was so nearly finished.' From her crouched position on the floor she grimaced up at him as a pool of off-white gloop seeped across stained dustsheets. A paintbrush stuck out of her denim dungarees pockets, her face was splattered with paint and she wore a plastic carrier bag tied round her hair. She dabbed at the ever-increasing seepage with a rag, huffing and puffing a little. 'I'm going to have to nip out to the hardware store and get some more paint now. Do we need anything else?'

His eyes flickered from her to the stepladder, back to her. *Unbelievable.* 'You were painting the ceiling?'

'Um…yes?'

'After I specifically told you it was next on my list of jobs?'

'Um…yes.' This time there was no hint of apology. 'It needed doing and it was next on *my* list. I was free to do it, so I made a start.'

'Why can't you accept more than the slightest bit of help without a row? You are slowly driving me crazy. No—make that rapidly driving me crazy.' There was only so much independence a guy could take before it became downright stubbornness, and then it made him really mad. 'You were supposed to be taking a break.'

'Breaks are boring. There's nothing more satisfying

than seeing the instant difference a coat of paint can make to a room. Look, isn't it great?' She gestured at the white over the dirty green and, yes, it looked good. That was not the point.

'And risk a broken collarbone…or worse?' He didn't allow his brain to follow that train of thought. Already she was showing signs of discomfort with her growing bump—all it had needed was one wrong step. 'These ladders are unsteady, and those trainers have a slippery grip. You said so yourself.'

'I was fine.'

'Oh, clearly. So fine that you dropped the paint can?'

'No one likes a smartass.' With an irritated groan she whipped the plastic bag from her head and stuffed it into her pocket, then gripped the side of the bath to assist her to transition from sitting to standing—flatly refusing his outstretched hand. Once up she rubbed her back, which pushed out her stomach, fat and round and very obviously pregnant. Her face had filled out a little too, her long hair, which she'd piled on the top of her head in some sort of fancy clip, was glossy. Man, was it shiny, and it took him all his strength not to pull her close and inhale. Somehow the more annoying she became, the more he wanted her. Seemed he was hard-wired to protect her too.

But he'd never contemplated giving her this job and hadn't thought she'd be so hell-bent on doing what she wanted. How much did he need to do to show her he was invested too? She'd taken him at his word and had never referred to the contract again, but he knew she watched him and wondered. Every day. And every day he tried to prove to her he was up to the father job.

He just hadn't contemplated how hard it would be to keep his emotions out of the agenda.

'How about you sort out the cupboards in the kitchen

instead, like we talked about earlier? I'll do this when I've finished the lights downstairs.'

And, yes, it was like this every week. She had a problem or, more usually, the house had a problem and he had an insatiable, irrational need to fix it. Except the biggest problem was that he shouldn't be here at all. The baby wasn't due for months, so in theory he could let her get on with it. But, well, he couldn't.

Her voice had a sudden edge to it. 'You can't bear to be in the same room as me for five minutes, can you?'

'Sorry? What on earth are you on about?'

'It's just that every time I go into a room you leave it. It's been going on for weeks, it's like there's a revolving door. Me. You. Me. You. I'm getting dizzy.'

'Ridiculous.' Truth was, he couldn't bear to *not* be in the same room. Being with her was killing him. A long, drawn-out agonising death of lust. He was doing this for the sake of his child, making sure they had everything they needed. At least, that was what he told himself, and not because he didn't want to wake up every morning and not have the prospect of seeing Georgie's smiling face or inhaling her scent that pervaded everything in the house.

'Is it me? Is it seeing me like this that you don't like?' She paraded in front of him, laughing, sticking her tummy out—there was a bubble where her belly button protruded. 'Because I happen to love it.'

He laughed. 'Or maybe it's a coincidence, ever thought of that? Perhaps I just always happen to be about to leave when you come dashing in. Bad timing, maybe, and you're looking for it so you have confirmation bias?'

'Yeah, right. Never try arguing with a know-it-all doctor. I notice it because it happens, matey. And don't deny it.'

Avoiding the wet paint, he took her hands and faced

her, putting a serious tone in his voice, ignoring the immediate sharp jolt of electricity that ran through him as he touched her. 'Okay, yes, Geo, you're right. I'm sorry to have to break it to you, but you do look terrible, hideous, unsightly. In fact, I was going to ask you to cover up with that dust sheet. But now you've spilled on it I'll just have to put up with you as you are.' He laughed at her tongue sticking out of her mouth. 'Yeah, really, I can't bear being with you, and that's why I spend every spare hour here, doing your bidding.'

If only she knew how partly true those words were. It was seeing her, full stop. Seeing Georgie carrying his child, seeing her turn this dilapidated wreck into a home for her family. His family.

Every time he turned around there was something else: the piles of gifted baby clothes; the stockpile of nappies for newborns. The baby scans on the fridge—the most recent one at twenty weeks, where he could see every finger and toe. Where the ribs encased his baby's fast-beating heart. Its chubby belly. The MacAllister nose.

Liam's heart swelled, then tightened. The memories threatened to swamp him again. He rubbed his chest, but the pain wasn't physical, it was psychological. And every time he saw Georgie it got worse.

And still he kept on coming back. Because he couldn't not. Because he couldn't contemplate an hour of his life when he didn't see her.

She dropped her hand from his grip and began wiping a paintbrush on the rim of the can. 'I am grateful, really. You don't have to give up all your spare time...' Her hand went to her belly and she made a sharp noise. 'Oh!'

He knew that look. He knew most of them now, thank God, because she never complained about any of the changes she was experiencing and he knew a few of them must have taken some getting used to. A rise of eyebrows and a gentle smile meant baby movement. A frown but determined-not-to-show-it stubbornly stiff jaw meant she had backache. A fist against her chest meant heartburn. He'd never been so aware of anyone in his whole life. 'Kicking again?'

'Yes. It doesn't hurt, it just makes me jump. It's weird. though, I don't know if I'll ever get used to it—it's like a whole crowd of butterflies stretching their wings. He's a little wriggler, this fella. I think he might be a martial arts expert when he grows up.'

He nodded towards her belly, his heart suddenly aching. 'She might be a dancer? Cheerleading? Gymnast? Scottish country dancing? That has kicks, doesn't it?'

Her eyebrows rose. 'The ones I learnt at school had a lot of skipping in circles and peeling off. I don't remember kicking. Apart from hot sharp prods to my nine-year-old partner's ankles. He had no clue what he was doing and was far happier pulling faces at his friends than swinging me in a do-si-do.'

Then clearly the boy had been a prize idiot.

Clearing the paint pot and mess out of the way, Liam stood her in front of him. Goddamn, she was beautiful, all flushed and smiling. He had to admit that being pregnant suited her. She'd never seemed so content. Apart from the odd moment when he'd catch her staring out of the window into the distance, or looking at him with a strange expression on her face. 'Show me?'

'What? Scottish dancing, in a tiny bathroom? Are you nuts? Silly me, of course you are.'

'Probably.' He took her hands in his and twirled her round. 'Like this?'

'Not even remotely.' Her head tipped back as she laughed, and for the first time in for ever things were back to normal between them. There was no baby, no contract, no tension, just two old friends messing about, like they'd done hundreds of times before. He twirled her again, faster, and caught her in his arms and she squealed, 'Stop! I'm covered in paint, my hands—'

'Are fine. Now, show me what to do. Like this?' He made a woeful attempt at a highland jig that had him stumbling over the stepladder. 'Clearly this needs practice.'

'And a lot more space.' She sucked in air, and again, doubling over with laughter. 'You are a lot worse than David Sterling.'

'David?'

'My nine-year-old partner. Broke my poor innocent heart when he kissed Amy Jenkins at the Year Four social, but at least he had rhythm.'

'I have rhythm.' And Georgie's heart was too damned precious to be broken again. Although Liam had a feeling that when all this was done, he'd be no better than David-bloody-Sterling.

'Oh, yeah?' She prodded him in the stomach, and he wondered whether that was a step up or down from being kicked in the ankle. 'I've seen your rhythm, mate, at Indigo, late at night, when you're filled with booze.'

'Bad, huh?'

'Actually, no, not at all. You're a good dancer, probably better than I am if I'm honest. But I'm not exactly going to want to admit that, am I?'

'You, my lady, are such a tease.' Feeling suddenly way out of his depth, he gave her a smile and it was pure stubborn willpower that stopped him from kissing her again.

'Really? You think so? I haven't even started.' She smiled back and the air between them stilled. Her hand slipped into his and squeezed, and she peered up at him through thick dark eyelashes. And he was sure she was just being Georgie, but that kiss hovered between them again, in her words, in the frisson of electricity that shivered through him. In the touch of skin on skin. Her voice was raspy. 'Is it just me or is it very hot in here?'

'Hmm. You want to try peeling off? That might help. I could give you a hand. That is one thing I am very good at.' He rested his palm on her shoulder, toying with her T-shirt sleeve. Her pupils widened at his touch, heat misted her gaze and he knew then that she was struggling too. That just maybe she wanted the physical contact that he craved.

But, goddamn, he knew that was the most stupid thing to say, especially when they'd agreed to go back to situation normal between them—but it was out there now. He was tired of fighting this…and absolutely sure he shouldn't have said those words.

Time seemed to stretch and he didn't know what to do. Apologise? 'Georgie—'

'Oh. There it is again. It always takes me by surprise.' Shaking her hand free from his, she pressed her hand to her belly again watching his reaction, eyes wary now. She gave her head a little shake as she stepped away. 'And don't look so worried. I won't ask.'

'No.' She wasn't talking about his faux pas. Once she'd asked him if she wanted to feel the baby kick and he'd refused. Point blank. And she'd never asked him again, but sometimes made a point of telling him when it was happening. And, by God, he wanted to, but he knew he couldn't, that with one touch of her, and of their baby, he'd be compelled to want more. And that didn't fit in with the emotionless parenting idea. Or the platonic parenting either.

The atmosphere in this minuscule room was reaching suffocation point, he needed to cut loose. 'Okay, so break time. You go put your feet up and I'll pop out to the hardware store. We need more sandpaper anyway. I'll get more paint, and I've got to get the right bulb for the light fitting—you got screw-in instead of bayonet.'

'Oops. Sorry. And when you come back, do you think we could spend more than two minutes in the same place? You won't run out on me?'

The ten-million-dollar question. 'This house is throwing us so many problems we have to divide and rule if we're going to win. Now, get that kettle on and I'll bring back biscuits for afternoon tea.'

'Are you sure?'

'Buying biscuits isn't exactly a difficult task. Of course I'm sure.' And, yes, he knew that wasn't what she'd meant. Dodging bullets seemed the aim of today. 'Chocolate? I know, white chocolate with raspberry. Two packets.'

She threw him a huge grin. 'Oh, Liam, I do like it when you talk dirty.'

He could have been out for another few months and it wouldn't have been enough to stop the need surging through his veins. In less than an hour he was back, trying to locate her, with his peace offering of her favourite biscuits. She wasn't in the kitchen, and the contents of the cupboards were still in boxes in the same place on the floor.

Wondering if she was actually doing as he'd suggested and taking a nap, or on that damned stepladder again, he mounted the stairs two by two, in total silence, glad that he'd fixed the creaking floorboards. The bathroom was empty.

Intrigued, he walked along to her bedroom, heard the

radio, a song he didn't recognise, and she was singing along. It sounded ditsy and bright and he knew he should call out, make her aware of his presence, but something compelled him to be quiet as he approached her room. He told himself that he didn't want to make her jump.

She was standing in front of her closet, holding a black lace dress up against her body and looking in the mirror, turning from side to side, stretching the fabric across her belly. The work dungarees had gone, and now she was wearing flannel shorts and a baggy blue T-shirt. After a few seconds she frowned and threw the dress on the chair then shook her hair free from the hair slide. It cascaded down her back, a river of lush honey curls. Her breasts strained against the T-shirt. She was dusty and paint-streaked and fertile and ripe. She looked sexier than any skinny model on the front of the magazines, sexier than any woman he'd ever laid his eyes on. His heart stuttered. He took a step forward, paused.

She still hadn't heard him. Her humming continued. Taking a brush from the closet, she gathered a fistful of hair and started to brush rhythmically. And even though he knew he shouldn't be standing here, watching her do this, knew he was breaking a zillion unspoken promises they'd made in the aftermath of the single kiss, he still couldn't bring himself to speak. His throat was scratchy and raw, and his body was on fire. Each swipe through her hair was considered and resolute, her slender arm moving up and down, almost trancelike, what he could see of her face was calm and relaxed.

She was lost in thought, and still singing the upbeat, happy song. The reverence with which she took each brushstroke made his heart contract. The glossy sheen of her hair, the ridges of her back as she moved and shifted from foot to foot. Her body swayed a little, her backside bopping to and fro; and maybe it was the heat from before, the soft light in the room, the smell of her, the intimate nature of watching her, but he struggled with a powerful urge to carry her to her bed and make love to her.

He realised he was hard, that his hands were clenched against his body's strain towards her. That he had to consciously control his feet and make them still.

How could someone doing something as mundane as brushing their hair bring him to the edge of reason?

After a few moments she started to coil her hair back up onto the top of her head again—and that was it—his control was lost. In a second he was behind her, hands on hers, whispering close to her ear. 'Don't. Leave it down.'

In response to his sudden arrival she turned, shaking. Confusion racing across her face. And heat too. 'Oh, my God, Liam. You made me jump.'

'Sorry. I just…' He curled a lock of her hair around his fingers, pressed it to his mouth.

She placed her hands on his chest, that intimate gesture firing more need through him. 'What?'

'I can't do this any more.'

'Can't do what?'

'I can't keep away from you. Ever since that kiss I've been hiding out.'

She let out a long breath and her face creased into a soft smile. 'I knew it. I knew you were up to something. See. I told you. You are avoiding me. I was right. I'm always right.'

'Intuitive, perhaps. Give a guy a break. I was doing the right thing.' He touched her lips with the pad of his thumb, tracing the soft path, the delicate curve. They were pink and moist and kissable. He remembered how good she had tasted and suddenly he couldn't wait any longer. Finesse lost, he dragged her to him. 'Come here.'

She inhaled a stuttered breath, her lips opening a little, her body trembling. And made a concentrated effort to calm it. She briefly closed her eyes, opened them again. 'But I thought—'

'Shh… Thinking is overrated.' He reached his arms round her thickened waist, pulled her closer, spiked his hands through her hair and nuzzled right into it. Cupping the back of her head, he held her face close against his throat. Just held her against him until the shaking stopped. Until he could look at her again. He wanted to kiss her, but he wouldn't, wouldn't make things difficult. But he could hold her. Could feel her soft curves and taut belly pressing against him.

Breathe.

He prayed for the awareness and attraction to go, to be left here with just his old friend Georgie and nothing else, nothing complicated, because he knew that by taking those steps across the room he'd made things muddier than ever. But it was so compelling to hold her, to feel part of something so good. To be, for once in his life, actively looking forward, instead of just running from the past. To be accepted for the man he'd grown into.

Only now he knew how it felt, he didn't want to go back. Couldn't go back.

And then…the strangest of sensations. A tiny shiver against his hip, something almost ethereal…then it was gone.

His baby kicking.

Breathe.

But there was no oxygen. His chest hurt as he tried sucking in air, there was no space for anything more, emotion had filled his chest. A hard core of deep affection, a protective need, a desperate ache. And pride. His baby was moving, stirring in her belly. The shaking started again, but this time it was his body that was on the edge of control. 'Was that…?'

'The Scottish country dancer?' She pulled away a little and pressed a palm against his cheek. 'Yes, Liam. It was. There it is again.' She reached for his hand and pressed it against her bump. It was a flutter, not a whack. At least, not against his palm. The whack to his heart was mighty, though. And, God, no, he didn't want to feel this. Not this ache. Not this wanting. He didn't want to feel anything.

'Wow.' It was all he could manage. His throat was thick, his heart rampaging as all the pain came hurtling back. Pain, and yet something else, something profound that made his soul soar.

He didn't know what to think or what to say as he stepped back. He'd been trying to avoid any kind of physical contact with Georgie but he'd been unable to stay away, had been compelled to hold her. Now his reasoning had been proved right. All his emotions were getting tangled up and he didn't want that. Didn't want any emotions to get in the way of clear thinking.

Obviously sensing him detaching already, she tugged at his hand and pulled him to sit on the bed, her other hand stroking his shoulder. And it was tempting to sit with her and let her stroke the tensions away, but he couldn't sit, so instead he walked to the window and looked out at the encroaching night. Dark shadows filled the garden, like the dark shadows in his heart. He needed to find some place where he could breathe normally again.

Georgie's voice reached to him. 'I know this is hard for you. I just don't know why. I'm trying to understand, I really am, and I'm trying not to push, but I want to know. I might be able to help. Tell me about your sister, about…Lauren.'

'I can't… I don't want to.' Didn't want to spoil this moment, where *this* child was vivid and vibrant and had so much potential.

There was a long silence where the night breathed darkness into the room, and he thought she might have fallen asleep.

When she eventually spoke she sounded disappointed, and that was so not his intention. 'Some time, then. Tell me some time.'

But it was too much to ask of him. He didn't even know what words to use. Lauren…had been there, and then she hadn't been. And a huge hole had blown open in his eight-year-old heart that had never been filled with anything other than anger. At himself, mainly. At his parents.

And now… 'It'll only spoil everything.' He forced air out and inhaled again, trying to make some space in his chest, but still he felt constricted and tight. 'Let's get the hell out of here. I need to breathe.'

CHAPTER EIGHT

'THE PUDDING PLACE?'

'The right choice?'

'Oh, yes. Most definitely. These desserts are to die for. I couldn't think of anywhere more perfect.' Georgie's gaze slid over the rows and rows of chocolate éclairs, mini-Pavlovas and baked cheesecakes in the little dessert-only café, and then landed on Liam. She regarded him with caution. Whatever had been haunting him had passed. The shadows on his face had cleared a little, leaving him pale and reserved and yet trying so hard to act normal. She hadn't realised how emotionally distant he could make himself, even when he was in the same room.

For so many years his background had never mattered to her and she'd respected his need for privacy and put his quirky way with relationships down to immaturity at first, then pickiness, but now she believed it was meshed in fear. Of what, she wasn't sure. But now…now it meant everything. It meant the difference between them surviving this strange set-up they'd created or failing it.

If she could understand why he held back so much, perhaps she could help him surmount it. Because although he'd shown commitment with his time, she still didn't wholly trust that he would be there when it mattered. That he wouldn't change his mind and run. And she wasn't prepared to take that risk with her heart or her child's.

A waitress arrived and asked for their order. Georgie couldn't decide. 'I think I'll have one of each. To start with.'

'You sure that's enough?' Liam laughed, a little more carefree. 'Or are you just keeping it light until your appetite really gets going?'

'This eating-for-two business is pretty damned good. I'm going to miss it after the baby comes.'

He gave his order then turned the menu over and over in his hands as he spoke. 'In South Sudan it's not uncommon for women to have large families, sometimes up to twelve kids. Imagine the fun you'd have then: eating for two for ever.'

'I'd be the size of an elephant if I did that and be on a perpetual diet for the rest of my life.' The chocolate éclair was divine. Great choice. Thick and rich and moist. It slid very easily down her throat. 'But, listen, you never tell me properly about your trips. It's always *murky* or *dry* or *messy*. But it must be way more than that.'

Leaning back in his chair, he crossed his arms and watched her eat. His gaze wandered over her, causing a riot of goosebumps over her skin, and she stared right back. Splatters of cream paint stuck to his old grey T-shirt. Funny, she remembered buying that for him years ago at a gig she'd been to when he'd been covering the night shift. It had been a little baggy on him back then but now it barely contained his solid biceps and stretched across a chest of muscle. His hair was sticking up in odd places, and he was dusty.

His knuckles were scratched and his skin torn. He looked rugged and edgy and it was such a turn on to watch him move she could barely think straight. This was dangerous territory. Every second spent with him was pushing her closer to an edge she knew was going to be at once delicious and yet potentially soul-damagingly painful.

He took a sip of hot black coffee. He'd ordered just that, no food. With wall-to-wall dessert on offer the man was clearly mad. 'So what exactly do you want to know?'

'What kinds of things do you get up to out in the field? The people you meet. I know you usually work at the tent cities, but what are the real cities like?'

His shoulders lifted in a sort of nonchalant shrug. 'The agency gang are pretty solid— people who want to do good, but all fed with a huge dose of reality. We know our limitations, there's never enough of anything—resources, people, help—but there's no point beating yourself up about what you can't achieve, you just get on and do what you can. While we're there the team always develops a huge bond, but such intensity can also drive you completely nuts. We do what we can in desolate and desperate parts of the world. There are, sadly, too many of them. But we do make a difference.'

'Well, there's no shortage of work, judging by the stories in the papers about floods, earthquakes and war zones. There's endless need for you everywhere.' He went to them all without any hesitation and she'd never once heard him utter one word of complaint about the harsh conditions he must have to endure, and the terrible things he must have seen. He kept everything tight inside him, but she didn't doubt he made a difference. He must have saved hundreds of lives and given thousands more help and much-needed hope. 'And the people you help? What are they like?'

'Desperate. Stoic. Honest. Victims. They have nothing apart from the clothes they stand up in. No homes, nowhere to call their own. There's always a threat—if it's not soldiers and fighting, or landmines and rogue devices, it's weather. Too much rain, or not enough. They need so much more than we can give them. But we fight to save their kids' lives. It's important to have a generation of hope that can break through the cycle of poverty and suffering.'

Pride rippled through her chest, her already tender heart bruising just a little more. Between him and her baby her emotions were being bumped around all over the place. 'But isn't it desperately heartbreaking? I know when I worked on the paeds oncology ward it damn near broke my heart.'

Again with the shrug. 'Of course, but it's uplifting too. You try to keep the emotion out of it, or you'd never survive. You can't carry all that and more around with you all the time, you just get on and do the job. I've learnt to detach.'

Hallelujah. 'Oh, yes. I've seen you detach, my friend. I have personal experience. You're pretty expert at it.'

'Yeah, well. I don't like getting in too deep.' He tried for a smile, which at once made him look boyish and yet very, very sexy. 'It brings me out in hives.'

'That much is obvious. You have form. Lots and lots of form. I'm thinking Sally the medical student, Jenny from Hamilton and Hannah the interior decorator. Poor Hannah, she was nice. You really broke her heart.'

'She was talking babies, mortgages, retirement homes...' He visibly shuddered. 'She had our whole future mapped out on the first date. And she even had a cutesie name for me. Seriously, one evening spent together and suddenly I was Macadoodle-doo. No one does that.'

Georgie couldn't help but smile. 'Oh, yes, they do. It's

part of the relationship ritual. It's about creating a whole new world of two, developing a language you wouldn't speak to anyone else. I think it's endearing.'

'It isn't.'

She laughed. 'You know your trouble? You just need to let people in a little.'

'Really? My trouble?' His laugh was brief. 'My relationships have given you lots of entertainment over the years, missy, and vice versa. But I've never thought you had trouble that needed fixing. I just took you the way you are. I still do.'

'Even pregnant? Because that took a bit of getting used to, didn't it?'

His eyebrows rose and he let out a big breath. 'Yes, even pregnant. Look, things have been very weird since this whole pregnancy thing started, but I'm doing my best to deal with it.'

'I know you've been working really hard on the house. And it's been brilliant.' But he still had a damned long way to go—like talking about the baby unhindered, like being in the same room with her, like being able to look at the baby scans with joy instead of concern and fear, as if he expected pain.

Although the last day had proved he could spend some time with her. But with what consequences? She'd almost dragged him to the bed the minute his breath had touched her neck. Holding back was the single most difficult thing she'd ever had to do.

Up until now she'd been the only woman he'd never detached from and it broke her heart to think she could well end up being just another one to add to his list. One kiss and they'd been on shaky ground ever since. Every movement he made, every space he filled, she was aware of him. Too much. Way too much. And that stunt in the bedroom had her flustered all over again. She was fighting the attraction but she didn't know how long she could hold out.

'I'm sorry. You're right. It's just…I can't help noticing that when you're struggling or getting close to someone you always cut loose right at the point when things start getting interesting. Like…' She wasn't sure of the wisdom of bringing this up, but if she didn't then he probably would anyway, if the conversation at the French market was anything to go by. 'Like earlier. Weird, but I really thought for a minute that you were going to kiss me.'

'Oh. That.' His mouth had been close to hers, his raw masculinity emanating from every pore. She'd wanted him with a fierce and frightening urgency, had wanted him every day while he'd been up that ladder, flexing his arms to the ceiling, carrying timber around the house, hammering nails. Every. Damned. Nail. Each hit with the hammer had made her hot and bothered—and she was sure it wasn't good for her, or the baby, to have such a need that was being unfulfilled.

At what point, she wondered, did desire ever go away? Because for her it seemed to be getting worse by the minute, and just when she thought it was waning, he'd do something as simple as open a damned can of paint and just watching his hands move so confidently made her all hot and bothered again. Worse, the way he looked at her with such heat in his eyes made her believe he felt the same but that he was fighting it every step of the way.

But why?

Friendship. They had a decade of past and a long future hanging on the choices they made now.

There was a beat before he answered, as if he was debating what to say and how to say it, and she wished this situation hadn't made him so guarded. 'Georgie, make no mistake, I do want to kiss you, but I have just about enough self-control to hold myself back. It may not be a good idea to talk about this.'

'You did at the market.'

'That was before it had become a…habit.' He looked at his hands. They were still damned confident, even wrapped around a coffee cup, and she remembered what it had been like to feel so wanted as he'd hugged her.

'One kiss is hardly a habit.'

'Not the kiss. The wanting.'

'Ah.' Words were lost somehow between her throat and her mouth. The café sounds around her dimmed and her senses hyped up to acute overdrive. It was hard to breathe. Hard not to stare at those lips, those eyes, that face. Hard not to imagine what he could do to her and what she could do right back. Hell, he'd just admitted he wanted to do it again, so should she just kiss him anyway?

She felt like she was on a seesaw, her heart pulling one way, her head tugging the other. Up. Down. Up. Down. It was exhausting and exhilarating. With one look she could be flying, one word and she'd be hurtling back down to earth.

She struggled with her composure, but as always was falling deeper and deeper under his spell. And she could have struggled just a little bit harder, walked away, called a halt, but she didn't. Pure and simple. 'And why would you want to be so self-controlled?'

'Because it's too much to ask of us.' His eyes were burning with a sudden heat that felt as if it reached out and stroked her insides.

'We've already been through ten years. We already ask a lot of each other.'

'But now you're asking questions I don't know the

answers to. You never did that before. You're trying to fix me and I don't need fixing. I don't want to be fixed. If we continue like this, things will change. Things have changed, and I'm not sure I like it, or want it, or know how to handle it, without letting you down.'

Part of her believed that to be right. He was being chivalrous and living up to his values, being honest about where things could or couldn't go for them. There was surely no future, especially with his emotional barriers. They were utterly and completely incompatible.

The other part of her wished he'd give up on his good intentions and kiss her anyway. Because she could see neither outcome sat comfortably with him. Perhaps she should just make it easier for him. It wasn't as if she didn't know exactly what she was getting into. And if something didn't happen soon she would finally know what it was like to die from desire. *Fan the flames and let them burn out.*

'I've a feeling it's already a little late to worry about things changing between us. Don't you think? I'm not the only one here wondering what it would be like if we kissed again.' Pricking some vanilla cheesecake onto her fork, she offered it to him across the table. 'Don't you get just a little tired of being so saintly?'

'Yes. Every single moment I'm with you.' He leaned forward again and she was transfixed as he closed his mouth over the morsel of food. Heat shimmied through her as he very slowly chewed then swallowed, the movement of his Adam's apple dipping up and down strangely and compellingly sexy. Her eyes slid from his throat to his mouth, a guarded smile on a face filled with dips and curves she knew so well but had never really explored. How she wanted to trace her finger along those lips, to run her hand across his cheek and feel the rasp of his stubble against her skin. To scale the furrows of his cheekbones.

His voice was an octave dirtier when he spoke. 'My mind is working overtime, thinking of the things we could do together. But I'm sure it's just a passing phase. All interest in the new curves and stuff. I just want to touch you. It's a man thing—feral and protective and in-stinctive. We can't help it. Nature's a bitch sometimes. If we act on these instincts and then it doesn't work out, that's a lot of friendship down the drain. We need to co-parent on a platonic and sensible basis, not give in to rash lust and then have regret to deal with too.'

'Oh, so you mean the bigger boobs are distracting you? Interesting...' She very slightly arched her back as he lowered his gaze to her breasts. A powerful need zinged through her. She wanted him and was resorting to seduc-tion of the clumsiest kind. But she couldn't get him out of her head. She needed to know what it would be like to be with him. If only one time. Just to hold each other as lovers, unlike the way they touched each other now, as friends. She wanted to stroke him, kiss every part of him. And if she didn't do it soon she'd go completely mad.

One day they'd look back on this and laugh. If they were still speaking to each other. 'So it's nature that's making you look at me like that?'

'Like what?'

'Sex.'

His pupils flared at the word. 'It'll wear off.'

'I sincerely hope not.' She finished the last bit of des-sert in one big, almost but not quite satisfying mouthful. She had a feeling there was only one thing that could sat-isfy her right now, and it wasn't cheesecake. 'We should give in to our natural urges sometimes, it's bad for us to repress them all the time, apparently.'

'It's even worse to break something that's pretty solid.'

Their friendship. But that was true and lasting and proven. 'Why would it break? It doesn't have to break, not if we don't want it to. We can do whatever we want. It's our choice.' She couldn't resist stretching her fingers across the table towards his. For a few seconds just their fingertips touched. Then, without looking at her, he slid his fingers across hers, intertwined them, stroked his hand across hers. His skin was rough but his touch was soft. His heat spread through her, up her arms, to her back, down to her belly.

After a moment of such an excruciatingly sexy caress he turned her palm over and lifted it to his mouth. His kiss was hot. He licked a wet trail to her forefinger. She snatched her hand away before a moan erupted from her throat. Even so, her voice was filled with need. 'We should be getting home.'

'We? Is that an invitation?' His face cautious, and turned on at the same time, he scraped his chair back to go.

Finding him her sexiest smile, she whispered back, 'Honestly, Macadoodle-doo, since when have you ever needed an invitation to my house?'

'I think maybe this time I do.'

She hadn't answered him in words, but she'd taken his hand and led him out of the café like a woman on a mission. Thank God she lived only a short drive away because he couldn't have waited many moments longer. Liam didn't know when he'd ever been so burnt up about a woman.

They bypassed the living area and made it to her bedroom without words, without kissing. He went in first, held open the door and she walked straight in and turned to face him, a question on her face. A dare. A promise. There was space between them. It would only need one step.

Just one.

He faltered. For a few moments neither moved as they stared at each other. This was happening. Really happening. The step from friends to…to whatever this was. *Lovers* might have been doubtful, but the trajectory from restaurant to street to bed was unstoppable. The air in the room seemed to still. One second. Two. With every lingering moment heat spread through his body like a raging fire, threatening to engulf him. If he touched her now there would be no going back.

This could have been a time to leave. He almost took a sideways step, his hand lingering on the doorhandle, but faltered again.

As she watched him a slow sexy smile appeared on Georgie's lips, and if he'd had any flicker of doubt that she didn't want this it fled right then. And that was when, he supposed, he should have drawn that line, the one they shouldn't have stepped over. Or where they should have agreed what this meant. But he was too consumed by her, by this need to utter a word.

In the end he didn't know who made the first move but suddenly she was in front of him, or he was in front of her and his mouth was hard against hers. This time there was no hesitation, no coy shaking. This was pure need and desire. She tasted of chocolate and vanilla and every flavour in between. Her mouth was wet and hungry and it fired a deeper, hotter want within him. Jaws clashed, tongues danced, teeth grazed. There was nothing sophisticated about the kiss, no gentle sucking or tender caress. It was messy. Dirty. Hungry.

His lips were on her throat as he dragged her T-shirt

up around her neck, ripping it as it snagged on its journey
to the floor. Finding what they wanted his hands cupped
her beautiful breasts over her bra, then under her bra to
the accompaniment of a deep guttural moan. She pressed
against him, writhing against his thigh. 'Liam, oh, my
God, I want you now.'

'I want you.' For a brief moment he acknowledged that
this could be the singularly most stupid thing he'd ever
done. Then that thought was gone, erased with more of
her kisses and the press of her fingertips against the top
of his jeans. He sucked in air as she played with his zip.
And, no, he did not want to hesitate for a second—but
his hand covered hers. 'You first.'

Her bra hit the floor and then her shorts, and he was
walking her to her bed and laying her down on the flowery duvet he'd seen a hundred times before but never in
this light, never at a moment like this. Everything was
familiar and yet unfamiliar, like her. His mouth found
her dark hard nipple and sucked it in. She was divine, so
sexy, her nipples so responsive. *She* was so responsive
as she writhed against him, nails digging into his back
until he groaned.

As his mouth started its journey south, kissing carefully over the undulation of her belly, her hand stopped
his and her voice was, for the first time, wary. 'Is this
really stupid?'

'Without a doubt.'

'Yeah, I thought so. Dumb and then some.' Her mouth
was swollen and red. He knew it had been a long time
since Georgie had been kissed, and kissed like that—because he had been the last one to do it. God only knew
when she'd last had sex but unless he was mistaken he
could count the time in years, not months. So this was
important. She'd chosen him.

He relieved her of her panties, hands skimming a belly that was plump and soft. He followed a trail of dark hair down her midline, watching her squirm as he parted her thighs and found her centre. He slipped a finger in, two, and felt her contract. She moaned, 'Oh, yes.'

'Crazy?'

'Madness.' She arched against him. 'But that feels so good.'

He kissed a slick trail to a nipple and smiled against it as she bucked in pleasure against his hand. Then he found her mouth again, her tongue tangling with his as she unzipped his jeans and took him in her hand. His gut contracted. He was so hard, so hot for her, and, damn, if he didn't have her soon he was going to explode.

She rubbed his erection against her sweet spot and he could feel the wet heat of her. Then she pushed him against the mattress and straddled him. 'I want you inside me, Liam. Now. Please don't do the whole slow build-up thing. That's been happening for days, months if we're honest. I just need to feel you inside me. Otherwise I'm going to just about die.'

'Don't do that. No. We can't have that.' And without any further encouragement he slid deep into her. She was so ready for him, he could feel her orgasm building already, her walls contracting around him as she pulsed with him. She met his rhythm, found his mouth again and he was lost in sensation after sensation of her mouth, her centre, her weight on his thighs. Her scent around him, her heat around him. Deeper. Harder.

He wanted to slow down time, to hold onto this moment but the luscious heat of her, her sexy, knowing smile made him sink deep into her. 'Oh, my God, Georgie, you're going to make me lose it.'

He fisted her hair and dragged her face to him, kissing

her long and hard until he was fighting for breath, until the pace increased, faster and faster. Her eyes closed as he felt her contract around him, her body shaking with the strength of her orgasm. *'Liam. Liam.'*

Never had his name sounded so sweet, so wanted, so precious. He was lost in her, in her voice, in her heat, grinding against her, hard and fast and deep, until he felt his own climax rising and then crashing on a wave of chaos and kisses.

For a few seconds she was quiet against him, Liam could feel her heart beating a frantic pulse against his chest. Her hair was over his face. She was covered in a fine sheen of sweat, fists still clinging to his shoulders, pinning him against the sheets. He was already hard again, thinking about a few moments' repose, then maybe a shower— preferably with her in it. It was startling, surprising and felt surreal to be here, with her, doing this.

So he wasn't prepared for her words as she bolted up-right and her hand went to her belly. 'Oh, God, Liam. Oh, my God.'

The baby. For those fleeting moments he'd forgotten, blown away by the sultriness of her ripe body, of being inside her, of losing himself completely in the best sex of his life. He'd wanted Georgie the woman. Not Georgie the mother. Although she came as a package deal, he knew that.

No, he hadn't forgotten but blocked out that thought.

And then things got very murky in his head. 'What is it? Are you okay? What's wrong?'

'No, I'm not okay.' Twisting away from him, she climbed off his thighs, wrapped the top sheet across her front and curled onto the bed in a protective foetal position, her hands in front of her face. 'Oh, God, best-friend sex. Kill me now.'

'Why the hell would I want to do that?' The laugh erupting from his throat was part relief, part concern because she was right; in fact, they'd both been right. This was the most half-cocked stupid thing they'd ever done.

'I can't believe we've just done that when I look like this.' Her cheeks were red and hot. 'I've never cared how I looked to you before. You've seen me in all states of soberness and drunken debauchery, when I was sick, when I was glammed up to the nines. You've seen me lose my bikini completely in an ill-timed dive into the pool, even caught sight of me in my scaggy weekday bra and pants, and none of it mattered. Ever. But now? Now I'm so embarrassed.'

He stroked fingers down her spine, tenderness for her goofy display of embarrassment meshing with something else in his heart. This was not meant to happen. He was supposed to be creating a safe place for his child, proving he could be a good father. Making sound choices. It was okay to give in to a little sexual play with someone who had no strings attached—but they had a ten-year history and an uncertain and very shaky-looking future that involved another life. They shouldn't be playing at all. He was getting in too deep, getting himself into a situation he didn't know how to get out of. 'And maybe you're just a little bit crazy? Why do you think I care how you look?'

'Because it's suddenly important. Everything is. I didn't think it would be, but it matters.'

'I don't believe this.' Pulling her hands away from her face, he made sure she was looking right at him. Because, yes, this mattered. She mattered. Whatever else happened now—and already a thousand doubts were stampeding into his head—she had to hear what he was saying. Because she still needed to hear the truth, regardless of what he thought or felt about it. 'Is it enough for me to say that you're beautiful?'

'No. Not really. I'm six months pregnant, for goodness' sake. I'm fat. I'm getting stretch marks. My boobs are huge.'

'Really? I hadn't noticed.' He pretended to take a sneaky peek. And then wished that he hadn't. He could make light of this, but the honest fact was she was beautiful. So beautiful it made his heart ache and he wanted to kiss her again, to make her scream with pleasure. To make her realise just how much she was wanted.

'Well, you've been staring at them for long enough.'

'That's because you are amazing. Beautiful. Fertile. Vibrant.' He took her hand, gently kissed her knuckles and brought her fist to his cheek. 'And I don't care how you look, Georgie. Because, honestly, the wrapping's not what I was making love to.'

Honestly? *Honestly?* His heart banged fiercely as if protesting. What the hell were they doing? She was his friend and by doing this he'd let her down. Period. He was supposed to be the strong one, dammit.

'You know, we should really have stopped before we started.' Dragging her hand from his grip, she sat up. 'If that makes sense.'

'Things stopped making sense a while ago.'

'Yes, you can say that again.' She let out a long sigh but snuggled against him, her hair tickling his nose, baby-soft skin touching his, then closed her eyes. 'That was good, though. Damned good, Macadoodle-doo.'

He glanced towards the bedside table and saw a baby name book, a pregnancy book. In the corner of the room there was a bottle steriliser still in its wrapper next to a bundle of baby clothes. On the floor to his left was a magazine open at a page about safety in online dating. She'd gone through the questionnaire and circled a few As, some Cs, a smattering of Bs. Was she thinking about dating again? Before all this she'd have filled in the questionnaire with him and they'd have been in fits of laughter at the results. But this one she'd done on her own. In private.

Despite the post-coital warm fuzzies he realised with a jolt that he might not be a real and integral part of her new life. She was thinking about a future without him in it. That was what he'd wanted, right? That was why he'd signed the contract in the first place. So she could have her dream life—a partner would be the icing on the cake for her. A husband, two kids and a dog. The family she'd missed out on, growing up in that children's home she'd hated. Traceable DNA.

A husband who didn't keep running away. She deserved that. She deserved the very best.

And even though he knew all the reasons he shouldn't be here, he still kept batting them away, trying to find good enough reasons to stay. But he didn't have many, apart from selfish ones that meant he got the best sex with an amazing woman and then broke both their hearts.

He edged his arm out from under her neck, lay for a few minutes and watched her. She looked so relaxed, so peaceful, so hot that he couldn't bear to think of her with another man. But did that mean he had to commit? What if it fell apart? That would be all kinds of messy. A family didn't need that. He didn't need that, and she certainly didn't. From his own bitter experience he knew damned well what damage a broken family could do to a child.

Better to stay friends for ever than fall apart as lovers.

Snaking away from her, he sat on the edge of the bed

and looked around for his jeans. 'I guess I'd better get off home.'

'Oh, no. Don't you dare move, matey.' Her hands were on his shoulders, gripping them with more force than when he'd taken her over the edge, forcing him to sit back down. She picked up one of the books he'd seen and flicked through it, shoving it under his nose. 'So, I was thinking Desdemona for a girl. Albert for a boy? What do you think?'

'What? You're joking.' Not what he'd choose in a million years. What he would choose he didn't know. He hadn't allowed his mind to wander down that route as yet.

'And in the morning we need to go shopping for a breast pump. There's a new babyware shop opened up on High Street. And I know it's early but I want to get some Christmas decorations from that pop-up shop in Regents mall.'

'Christmas? Already? It's September.'

'My first Christmas in my first home. A baby on the way. I want it to be special.' Her voice was wistful. 'No harm in starting early, and they'll sell out of all the good stuff pretty quickly, you'll see.'

'What was Christmas like at the home?' He knew she tried to make a huge effort to celebrate it every year and asked everyone she'd ever met to eat around her large wooden table—waifs and strays, everyone's uncle's cat… she just didn't want to be on her own.

There was a pause as if she didn't want to go back there. He couldn't blame her. The bits she'd mentioned about growing up had been a far cry from his early experiences. Until his perfect world had imploded.

She put on her *I'm okay* voice. 'Oh, the social workers and carers tried to make it feel special, but we all knew they just wanted to get our celebrations out of the way so they could finish up and get home to their real families. It was depressing, in truth. This year I'm going to go big. I'm going to get the biggest tree and the most decorations anyone has ever had and cover the place—the tree, the walls, the outside. You know, like on Franklin Road, where every house has decorations and lights? It'll be like that, a Christmas to remember. And then next year I'm going to give Desdemona—or Albert—every damned thing they want. Because I couldn't have what I wanted. Ever.'

He imagined her, stuck in the home, wishing her little heart out and always being disappointed. Life sucked sometimes. For Georgie life had sucked a lot. 'What did you want, Geo? What did you wish for?'

'Ah, you know, the usual stuff.'

He propped himself up on his elbow and ran his fingers across her curves, down her shoulder, to the side of her breast, and stopped for a moment as she shivered under his touch. Then continued stroking her hip. 'No. Really, what did you want?'

She laughed, shyly. 'I wanted to start a collection of Beanie Babies—these little stuffed-toy things. Man, they were expensive and all the girls at school had them for birthdays or Christmas. I saved up my allowance every week and eventually bought a second-hand whale. He was my favourite.'

So he wasn't the only one here who was expert at dodging a question. 'No. Really. You're always telling me to stop hedging—but you're champion of it too. What did you deep down want?'

'Oh, God. However I say it, it's going to sound twee and crass but…well, I really wanted to be part of something. And now I am. So I got it in the end.' She laughed. 'It only took twenty-eight years.'

Did she mean him? Did she mean they were now part of something? Or did she mean the baby? *Family?* His heart started to pound. What had he done? Given her hope that she belonged to him?

Didn't she? No. No one did. No one could.

What the hell had he done? 'Oh. I see.'

'Anyway, before we go shopping I thought perhaps a big brunch in town first. That's what we'll need, right? A good sleep and then some decent food. Or maybe some food now? Are you hungry? Sex makes me hungry.'

'These days everything makes you hungry.' Okay. He got it that it would be rude and insensitive to split right now. He slumped against the pillow, trying to reconcile his head with his heart, but it seemed they were cursed to be at odds with each other for ever. 'Whatever you want.'

'Really?' Her foot dug him in the thigh. 'What I want is for you to stay. Talk to me.'

'God knows how you have the energy to talk after mind-blowing sex.' He ignored her assertion that he stay. For how long? Tonight? Tomorrow? A year? For ever? Reality was blurring dangerously with the ache in his heart.

One eye opened. 'It's not because we've just had sex, it's because *we* talk, Liam, that's what you and I do. We talk endlessly and have done for a decade. About everything. *Mostly.* We've never not known what to talk about before. How about we talk about stuff…about your work, my pregnancy, this child, your family, why you don't contact them ever? What the heck it is that spooks you so much about creating something that everyone else in the world craves. I want to know about you growing up, and I want to know about Lauren.'

The walls were closing in. It was time for evasive action, because he did not want to go there. At all. 'You know, suddenly I'm really fascinated about how breast pumps work. Talk me through—'

'No way, José. You don't get out of stuff that easily.'

'Oh, but I do. By fair means or foul…' The sheet covered most of her body, but her right foot was sticking out. He took it, leaned forward and slowly sucked her big toe into his mouth. He felt her soften against the mattress and her moan stoked more heat in him. That shower scenario was looking more and more attractive.

'Yeow. Definitely not fair.' Four vermilion-varnished toes wriggled against his chin. 'Use that mouth for talking, Macadoodle-doo.'

'Why, when it's so much better at doing other things?' His mouth hit her ankle, the back of her knee, her inner thigh, and he licked a wet trail northwards. As she squirmed he gave a wry smile. Any more wriggling was halted by his hands on her thighs. 'See?'

'But I want to— Oh, yes, that feels good. Just a little to the… Oh, yes.' Her hands fisted into his hair. 'Don't stop now, Liam…'

'I have no intention of stopping.'

'We…can…talk…later…'

Like never. 'Hush. Relax. Enjoy.'

And with that her mouth clamped shut and as he grasped her hand, she did exactly what he'd suggested.

CHAPTER NINE

WHEN GEORGIE WOKE the next morning the left side of the bed was cold. He was gone. As she'd thought he would be. It had all been too good to be true. He'd had second thoughts and hot-footed it to Afghanistan or somewhere equally unreachable. Typical Liam. Typical men. She lay back on the pillow and growled.

And then growled again, because since when had her mood been determined by a man?

Since Liam MacAllister had become…whatever he'd become. More than a friend…and with added and rather nice benefits. He certainly was very, very good at the bedroom side of things, even if he was quiet—*mute*—on the history side. But, hey, a forward-thinking man was always better than one looking back, right?

Although his past had shaped who he was, and that intrigued her. It had also created those barriers he was so keen at throwing up between himself and anyone who wanted to get close. The sex had been a really crazy idea. Lovely but crazy, and now she was even more confused than before. Ask him for clarification? Not likely. She imagined how that conversation might go and decided she didn't need to have him actually voice the rejection out loud.

After a few minutes of lying there, debating what

to do, there was a gentle tapping at the door and in he walked, topless, with jeans slouching off his hips, a tray in hand, a pot of coffee and a plate of something that smelled nice but looked a little…suspect. He gave her a smile as he placed the tray on the bed. 'Morning. Here's a sad-looking croissant I found at the back of the freezer, along with a couple of rogue frozen peas and a lot of ice. There was literally nothing else to eat. Nothing. You really do need to go food shopping.'

'The trouble is I eat it as fast as I buy it. I can't keep up.' Without his shirt *he* looked good enough to eat—did she need anything else? And he hadn't run off, he was here, making sure she ate properly. Was this a dream?

She rubbed her eyes, which she really shouldn't have done because the corneal abrasion was still healing, but it was too late and… Yes, he was still here, not an apparition. With food. And coffee. The man was a god.

The god sat on the edge of the bed. 'Well, seeing as we're having a day off renovating today, I'll make sure we fill up the fridge before we're done.' He buttered a piece of croissant, offered it to her, then waited until she'd opened her mouth and popped it in. 'Come on, get your strength up, we're going to need that soon enough.'

'Thanks. Eugh. Not such a great croissant. I can't even remember when I bought— Wait…we're having a day off? Who says?'

'You said you wanted to go shopping. And I'm tired of sanding and painting and you look like you need a decent break. I want to forget about this dust and dirt and do something else. So I've made some calls. I have a plan: your breast pump will have to wait, along with the Christmas decorations. Eat up and then we'll get going.' He got up as if to leave.

'Not so fast.' She caught his hand and he took it,

wrapped his fingers around hers and squeezed. In all the years of knowing him she'd never been aware of this tender side to him. She liked it. Goddamn, she liked it, just when she was trying to think of more reasons not to like him. Not to lose her heart or herself to someone who wouldn't want it. 'To where?'

'It's a surprise. But there'll be proper fresh air. The sea. Decent food. No dust.'

'Is this just another tactic to avoid the issue? You know…talking?'

He gave her a guilty grin. 'I feel restless. I just need to get going. Out. Somewhere.'

This was the guy who spent most of his life travelling and the last few months cooped up in her house. He never stayed anywhere for long, so she could see why he'd need to cut loose sometimes. Plus, a break would be fun. 'Then what are we waiting for?'

'Well…' He pulled the sheet down a little and exposed her breasts. Then he kissed her neck, her throat, her nipples, and she was putting her arms around his neck and drawing him to her. He whispered against her skin, 'I really need a shower before I set foot outside. You?'

'What? Me and you? In that tiny bathroom? You think we'll fit?'

'If it's big enough for a highland jig, it's big enough for a shared shower. We'll squeeze in somehow.' His fingers stroked down her back and she could see the bulge in his jeans. He was hot and hard for her.

Which made her hot in return. She couldn't resist reaching her hand to his chest. Felt his heart beating underneath her fingers. Solid. Steady. *Liam.* This was Liam. This was all kinds of surreal. She remembered his little dance in her tiny bathroom, the way he'd looked at her, the way she'd wanted to touch him then. How touching him now made her feel excited and jittery and turned on. Not solid or steady at all. 'But it wasn't big enough for a highland jig, remember?'

'We'll fit. Trust me?'

'I don't know.' That was half the problem. And, yes, he'd stuck to his words and been there for her throughout this pregnancy. Not once had he mentioned the contract again. He seemed committed to the baby, even though there were times when she caught his worried face and just knew the spooks were there, haunting him a little. But he'd surprised her with his resolve. And kept on surprising her, but could a man really change? She just didn't know. For a few minutes last night she'd thought he'd been having doubts, had felt his restless legs keen to leave, had known that if she'd let him he'd have gone. Would she always have to keep anchoring him here? Would she never be enough for his first instinct to be to want to stay?

For now, though, he was here and was asking for nothing more than to spend time with her. Time she didn't want to waste analysing things to death. 'Oh, okay. Where's there a will, there's always a way.'

'Always…' His laugh was deep and sexy and there was no way she was going to put up any kind of fight against those fingers, that mouth, those eyes. Had she been thinking about fighting? She couldn't remember. Her whole world narrowed to this single moment when she could forget everything else. 'So what are we waiting for?'

His hands closed around her fingers. 'Absolutely nothing.'

An hour and a half later, which truly could have been only thirty minutes had it not been for a lovely long shower and a very deliciously sexy start to her day, Georgie let out a yelp of excitement as Liam steered his expensive and very un-child-friendly two-seater coupé into a car ferry terminal. 'Waiheke Island? A day trip?'

'If that's okay?' He looked genuinely concerned that she was happy with his choice. 'I thought it'd be nice to do something different.'

'Yes, it's fabulous. It's a lovely idea. I haven't been there since a school trip years ago.'

He stared across at the ferry. 'My grandparents lived there, we used to go over and stay at their house every holiday when I was little. I can't remember the last time I visited.'

And there was something else she hadn't known about him. Maybe that concern on his face was really apprehension? 'Oh, I had no idea. Will it bring back bad memories for you?'

'I'm hoping to cement some new ones. It's a big enough island for me not to even go there.' A stream of vehicles appeared and queued up behind them as a crew member gestured for the cars to embark. Cranking the car into gear, Liam drove up the metal ramp and parked the car on the ferry platform. Once out, and breathing a lungful of fresh sea air, he slipped his hand into hers and whisked her towards the bar area. 'Come on, let's get a coffee and watch the world go by.'

The short journey across the Hauraki Gulf was smooth and pleasant, enhanced greatly by a pod of dolphins that came alongside to play. Diving and chasing and showing off, they added extra magic to this unexpected trip. Standing on deck, watching him walk towards her with two cups of coffee in his hands, grinning and gesticulating to the wildlife, Georgie's stomach gave a little hearty jump at the thought of a stolen day with Liam. Things were definitely changing, moving along in a direction she hadn't ever imagined. She didn't know if the changes were for the good, but she did know she would never be the same after all this.

Waiheke, famed for its vineyards and olive oil, was showing the tentative beginnings of the new spring season. After a long wet winter the hills were green, the acres of vines stretching on and on to the horizon were budding and leafy, while ewes watched over lambs in the fields adjacent to the roads. Once away from the main township they headed east along a winding road that eventually opened to vistas of clean empty beaches and blue water sparkling in the pale sunshine. Such a difference from her city house, which she adored—but stepping onto green fields would be nice for a change. Liam had been right, time out would do them both some good.

After half an hour or so he pulled left into a white gravel driveway that led towards the sea. On their right was a large whitewashed colonial house with a sign advertising wine sales and tastings. Georgie was surprised he'd pick a place like this. 'Oh? You booked us lunch at a vineyard? I assume you want to sample the wares?'

'I may have a small glass. But it's not so much the vineyard I was planning to see.' He threw the car into park and got out.

She stepped out of the door and sighed at the wisteria just starting to flower and framing the large wooden door. The soft pink against the white was startling and soothing, and like something from a film set. 'Oh? So what is it? What's the big secret?'

'It's not so big really, more a thought than a secret. Wait and see. And apparently they do a very nice lunch platter. It's huge. Which seems to be the only consideration you make these days when choosing meals.' There was a flurry of activity as their hosts found them a table out in the garden, bottled water and much-needed shade.

The garden was private and secluded, but felt somehow open rather than cloistered. Cushioned candy-striped hammocks hung between trees flanking a small neat square of grass. Palms and large ferns gave much-needed shade. There were fairy lights entwined around the vegetation that she imagined would give a pretty effect in the evenings, along with tealights in coloured glass jars on the ornate ironwork tables. It was tranquil, cool and very calming, and as they sat she felt some of the tensions of the last few months float away.

The menu was limited but sounded delicious. Suddenly she felt famished and so ordered a large mixed platter that promised fish, freshly cooked meats, a selection of local hard cheeses and lots and lots of bread. Most of which, she knew, she could eat and not worry about them having any effect on her baby. The rest she'd leave for Liam.

As they waited for the food he started to chat. 'Chris, the owner of this place, is an old school friend of mine. He inherited the vineyard from his dad and has turned it into a very successful business.'

As she listened to the sound of…nothing, except the fuzzy hum of bees and faint birdcalls, and took in the impossibly breathtaking surroundings, she felt the most peaceful she'd felt in weeks. Either that, or the sex-induced endorphins had made her limbs turn half to rubber. 'It's amazing.'

'Isn't it?'

'So what made you decide to come here of all places?'

'He sent me a link to his new website the other day. I took a look, saw the photos of the deck and the garden.'

They were momentarily interrupted as their drinks

arrived, then were left alone again. Liam took a sip of pinot gris, then put his glass down on the table. 'Then, when I was standing on your deck this morning, looking out at the garden, I thought that we really need to sort it out. The wood's rotting in places and there are nails popping up all over. It's a wreck, Georgie, and could be dangerous if we don't do something about it. The inside of your house is almost complete now so I thought we should finish things off properly. The baby's coming in the summer, and with the usual Auckland humidity you're going to want to sit outside. I thought the hammock idea would be great. And the palms give great shade. A lawn in the middle would be a pretty cool place for a baby to learn to crawl—no risk of injury.'

'Well, wow. That's really thoughtful. And, yes, it's absolutely gorgeous. I can see it working perfectly in the space I have. That's very kind of you, and especially to bring us all the way out here to actually see it.' She felt a little as if the ground was shifting. Half hope, half... what?

He shrugged, looking a little embarrassed at her enthusiasm. 'It's just a day trip, Georgie.'

But it was one of the kindest things anyone had ever done for her. Why did he have to keep getting better and better? Why couldn't he slink off and make her feel unhappy and not pine for more? In cold, harsh reality she was scared that she'd get too attached to a man who would break her heart. Because even if he did want to be involved in her family, how could she be sure he'd be in it for the long term? With her? How could she be sure he'd love *her*?

'But it's—'

'Oh, here's lunch. And here's Chris. Clearly a busy man, he owns the place, makes the wine and so, it seems,

serves the food.' He stood and shook the hand of a thick-
set man who looked older than Liam's thirty-two years.
'Good to see you, mate.'

'You too.' Liam's friend's eyes grazed over Georgie,
down to her belly, and he beamed. 'And you must be
Georgie. I'd know you anywhere, that social media's a
beast, isn't it? You feel like you know people without
ever meeting them.'

'Yes. Isn't it? Hello.' She may have been Liam's friend
on any number of social network sites, but Georgie wondered how much Chris really knew and what Liam had
said, if anything, about their unusual situation. After
all, not many couples got pregnant first and then had
sex. Everything was happening the wrong way round.
Besides, the word 'couple' hadn't been breathed out of
either of their lips.

They hadn't discussed yet what to say, if anything, to
anyone who enquired about their situation. But as that
seemed to be changing by the day, it was probably better that they hadn't come up with any definite descrip-
tion. Just Liam and Georgie, same as it ever had been.

Still, the winemaker seemed gentleman enough not to
pry and diverted his gaze from her bump back to Liam.
'Look, I've got a bit of a rush on, can't stay and chat.
Give my regards to your father, Mac. I hear he's retir-
ing up north.'

Liam's eyebrows lifted. 'Oh? Really?'

It was his friend's turn to raise eyebrows. 'You didn't
know?'

'I haven't caught up with him for a while.'

'No. He said as much last time he was over. He seemed
a bit miffed. But, then, he always did. Are you going to
pop over to The Pines?'

Liam shook his head. 'No. He sold it years ago. No point going backwards, is there?'

'I don't suppose so. Look, thanks for coming. Lunch is on the house. Good to see you.' Chris turned to leave then paused. 'Oh, make sure you try the syrah too. Delicious.'

Lunch was lovely, and as filling as Liam had promised, and Georgie ate as much as she could, managing almost the whole meal without mentioning the last conversation. But in the end it got the better of her. Her heart began to race as she brought up the difficult subject, so she tried to keep her voice level. 'So, when did you last talk to your dad?

Liam shrugged. 'I don't know. Two years ago?'

'Two?' It seemed nonsensical to have no communication with family members. If she—

'Look…' Pushing aside his empty plate, he let out a long breath. 'Please don't give me a lecture on how lucky I am to have a father and that I need to make the most of him. I know that's how you feel about families. But it isn't how I do.'

'But—'

'It's a lovely day. I really don't want to spoil things.'

'That may be a little late.' Although she knew she shouldn't have pushed it, he'd brought her out of a desire to help her, and to give her a rest. She was the one spoiling things.

For a moment she thought he was going to stamp or growl, but he fought with his emotions and put them back in that place that he never let anyone see. The man must have some ghosts, she thought, if he was so unwilling to talk. But he was tight-lipped about his work too—he kept everything tied in. Some people needed counselling, but he just wore it all in his skin, would never consider any kind of help, not even to get things straight in his head.

He saw that as a strength. 'Let's not do this today, Geo. Let's enjoy ourselves, plan the garden, take a walk, anything but this. Talking about my family tends to put a huge downer on everything.'

'Okay.' But something niggled at her. Ate away at her gut. She was genuinely trying to help. 'Or we could say everything really quickly and get it out in the open.'

He shook his head with irritation, but he smiled. 'Or say nothing at all.'

'Or I could ask Chris.'

'He doesn't know everything.'

Now she knew she could leave it and walk away and pretend this conversation hadn't happened. Or she could take it a step further…hell, he knew everything about her. Everything. 'And I know nothing. When did you last see your mother? What is The Pines?'

'Okay, so we *are* doing this.'

She took a sharp breath and threw him her most winning smile. 'I see it as my duty as a friend to annoy you until you actually get to the nitty-gritty.'

'You don't have to take that role so much to heart, Georgie. Maybe the nitty-gritty isn't what you think it is.' He placed his napkin on the table and stood, offering her his hand, but he looked impatient rather than annoyed. 'The Pines was my grandad's house and I am resolutely not going there so don't even ask. Just don't. It's a no. There is no point going over stuff, it doesn't help. You can't change the past and some of it is best not remembered. And I last saw my mother on Mother's Day. I took her out for tea. And it was awkward as always.'

'No. You were in Pakistan, or South Sudan—somewhere. Either way, you weren't here. Make it the year before.' They walked out into the vineyard. Rows and rows of vines stretched before them on and on into the distance. They wandered aimlessly down a row, inhaling the smell of freshly mown grass. 'You know, Liam, your parents will be the only grandparents our child has. Seriously, they are the only other people in the whole world with a connection to him…or her. They are flesh and blood. I really wish you could try to make things work between you all. If not for anyone else's sake, for Nugget's.'

He shook his head. 'Sometimes I wish I didn't know you as well as I do, because then I wouldn't have to put up with this. Trouble is, I do know you and I know you won't give up. At all. Digging and digging.'

'It's what makes me such a good nurse, and why you love me.'

'Love?' He stopped short and stared at her. For too long. For so long she wondered what the heck was going on in his head. She closed her heart to his shocked question…*love?* She didn't want to know his answer. Or maybe it had always been there and she'd been afraid to look. But in the end he just shook his head. 'My parents divorced when I was ten, and neither of them have shown any interest in me since well before then. The feeling's mutual.'

'Why?'

'You really do want to do this, don't you?' He ran his fingers through his hair, opened his mouth, closed it. Opened it again. 'Because Lauren died. And rightly or wrongly we all blame me.'

'Why? What on earth happened? What could you have done that was so bad?' Over the years Georgie had pondered this. She knew his sister had died, knew his parents were separated. But piecing the bits together had been like trying to do a jigsaw with no picture as reference.

They walked in silence to the very end of the row and onwards towards the ocean, found a crop of rocks in the little bay and sat on them. A breeze had whipped up, but the sun still cast a warm glow over them. Even so, Georgie shivered at the look haunting Liam's face. The dark shadows were back. His shoulders hunched a little. He'd already let go of her hand and even though they were sitting side by side it seemed almost as if he'd retreated within himself.

His voice was low when he finally spoke. 'She was a premmie, born at thirty weeks, and had a struggle, but she finally got discharged home. She was doing well. She was amazing. Really amazing. The light of our lives.'

Georgie sensed something terrible was coming. She laid a hand on his shoulder and waited, holding her breath. The sound of waves crashing onto the shore was the only thing that broke another prolonged silence. That, and her heartbeat pounding in her ears.

'I caught a winter bug. Nothing serious, just a stupid cough, fever and a snotty nose that laid me low for a few days, one of those that most kids get. Mum banned me from being near her. Very sensible, in hindsight. I just thought she was being mean.'

He looked like he wanted to continue but couldn't find words. When he composed himself enough to speak his voice was cracked and barely more than a whisper, 'But Lauren was so fascinating, such a little puzzle of noises and sounds with an achingly beautiful smile, that, as an eight-year-old big brother with a strong sense of responsibility and a lot of curiosity, I didn't want to keep away. So one morning when she was crying I sneaked into her room and picked her up, soothed her back to sleep. I held her for ages, I don't know how long, but long enough for her to go to sleep and for me to care enough not to wake her, so I held her some more.

'A few days later she came down with the same bad

bug, but she couldn't fight it off. She tried, though. Tried damned hard. But she just wasn't strong enough.'

He hauled in air and stood, hands in pockets, looking out to sea. So alone and lost that it almost broke Georgie in two. She imagined what it must have been like for a young boy to go through something like that, and her heart twisted in pain. He'd been doing what he'd thought was the right thing. Not knowing how wrong it could be. But the baby could have caught a bug anywhere—in a shop, at the doctor's surgery, in a playgroup. It had been bad luck she'd caught it from her brother. Bad luck that had kept him in some kind of emotional prison for the rest of his life.

At least, Georgie thought, she hadn't had something and then lost it. She just hadn't had anything at all, and in some ways that seemed almost preferable to suffering the way Liam had. Again she couldn't think of anything helpful to say, and couldn't have managed many words even if she'd known some formulaic platitudes that might have helped. Her throat was raw and filled with an almost tangible sorrow for him. 'I'm so sorry, Liam.'

'To cut to the chase, my parents were never the same after that. Eventually the grief was too much for their marriage. I got lost in the slipstream of guilt and blame. We've all rarely spoken since, doing only the perfunctory family necessities, if that. I suppose you could say it's pretty damned loveless.'

No. *He* was loveless. Losing his sister and then being neglected by grieving parents must have been almost unbearable, especially countered by a flimsy excuse that it had all somehow been his fault. He'd been a child too, for goodness' sake. How could you lay blame on someone who only wanted to give a baby more love?

Georgie knew Liam well enough to know there was

little point in trying to convince him that he was anything other than culpable. If he didn't believe it himself, and if his parents, the people who mattered, had never tried to reassure him, then what would her words mean to him?

But she stepped forward and wrapped her arms around his waist, hoping that somehow the physical sensation of her touch might convey her empathy for him in a way that words never could. 'And that's why you fight so hard year after year to save all those babies in those disaster-stricken countries.'

'They just need a chance. I can't right any wrongs and I can't wave a magic wand but I can give them real help.'

'And that's also why you don't want a family of your own.'

'Yeah, I didn't do so well with mine. Lauren dying was hard going, but you get through it. Somehow. Eventually. But what I needed most was help, support, love. And I got nothing. Families can hurt you so badly. I wouldn't want to do that to any child of mine. Worse, judging by my experiences, I'd probably do more harm than good.' He shook his head, shook himself free of her grip, and walked back towards the vines.

'No. You're going to be a great dad.'

He pulled up to a halt. 'Really? You think? After what I just told you? I don't want to go through anything like that again. I don't think I'd survive it. I don't want to…' He started to walk again. Head down. Shoulders hunched.

She kept a few feet behind him, giving him the space he clearly craved. 'To what?'

'To lose something like that again.'

'You wouldn't.'

He railed round at her. 'How can you be sure? How can you stand there and make promises no one can keep?'

It was all so clear now. His idea of family was broken.

His image of love was filled with so many negative connotations he couldn't dare risk himself again with that
emotion. That was why she'd found him so distraught that
first day she'd met him—caring for a sick baby had di-
minished him, reminded him of what he'd lost. But he'd
taken that loss and turned it into his vocation. Not many
could do that. Not many would face their fears every day.

Although he never let it get personal. He never let anything get to him. Ever. That was what the death of his
sister had taught him, to keep everything and everyone
at a safe distance. So he wouldn't feel responsible, so he
wouldn't have to face the prospect of more pain if things
got sticky. Hell, she'd been watching him do it for years,
and had never felt how much it mattered. But now, *God*,
now it mattered.

And still she was left only with questions. If that was
how he felt, why had he torn up the contract? Was this
all just some duty kick he was getting?

What would become of them all?

Sometimes she wished she had a crystal ball and could
look into her future and see how it all worked out. But
this time she was afraid. Afraid that what she'd see wasn't
what she wanted.

She left him to meander through the vineyard, stopping to look at the tight fists of bright red buds at the end
of each row, gathering strength to grow into flourishing
roses, and to watch tiny white butterflies skitter past. And
as they walked she noticed his shoulders begin to relax
again. The sunshine and quietness chased the shadows
away and eventually he came back to her, took her hand
in his and walked towards a cluster of old stone buildings.

But before they left the vines Georgie paused and
looked at the tiny fruit gripping tightly onto ancient

gnarled wood. 'Do you think Chris would mind if we tried one of the grapes?'

He laughed. 'I think he probably would, but they're not remotely ripe anyway. They'll make our stomachs hurt.'

'But they're award winning, it said so on a big certificate on the wall back at the restaurant. Should we try? I've never had anything award winning straight off the vine before. How about you? You should try one.'

'No.' He pulled her hand away from the plant and hauled her against him. His eyes were hungry, his breathing quickened as he looked into her face, at her eyes, at her mouth. He was a complex man filled with conflicting emotions—but that didn't make her want him less. He was real and, yes, he was complicated. He was layered and that was what made him all the more intriguing.

He cupped her face and stared into it, his expression a mix of heat and fun and affection. Then he pressed his mouth to hers and kissed her hard. It was a kiss filled with need, with deep and genuine desire. This was new, this…trust, this depth, sharing his worse times and dark past. It was intense and it was raw but Georgie felt a shift of understanding to a new level. A new need. His grip on her back was strong as he held her and for a few moments she thought he would never let her go. And, holding him tight against her, she wished that very same thing with every ounce of her soul.

'Can I drive the car? Please?' Georgie grabbed the keys from Liam's hand and he let her take them. Let her run to his pride and joy and take the driver's seat, which he would never ever normally do. But, well hell, just telling her about his old life had set something free from his chest. He felt strangely lighter, freed up a little.

But then, as he climbed in beside her, his gaze flicked

to her belly and there was that hitch again, the one that reminded him that happiness was always fleeting. That love could hurt just as much as it could give joy. He'd thought he'd be able to distance himself emotionally from her, and from the baby, but in reality the feelings just kept hurtling at his rib cage, ripping his breaths away, one after the other. Hard and fast until he didn't think he'd ever be able to breathe properly again. He didn't know whether to run away from her or keep a tight grip. But staying close opened them all up to him wreaking havoc again.

'Where are you going to drive to? Palm Beach is nice. There are some good shops in Oneroa. Or we could go for a walk along Rocky Bay.'

She ran her fingers over the leather steering wheel. 'No. I remember from my school history classes that there are tunnels somewhere left over from the Second World War. Do you know anything about them?'

'Stony Batter tunnels? Sure. My grandfather helped build them actually. He was born here, camped in the fields just up past Man O'War Bay through the last years of the war.' Sheesh, he'd opened his mouth and now he couldn't stop his past pouring out. 'He used to take me up there when I was a kid.'

She flicked the ignition and drove back towards the main road. 'Do you want to take a look?'

Did he? That would mean a drive past The Pines and a whole lot more memories. The weeks they'd spent here as a real family. Complete. God, why had he decided to come here to relive everything again? Why? Because, for some reason, Georgie made him feel as if anything was possible. Even overcoming a dark and murky past. Who knew, maybe he could squeeze his eyes shut as they drove past The Pines and he wouldn't feel the dread already stealing up his spine. 'Okay. If you insist.'

'I do.'

But that was a mistake. Memories joined the swirl of pain in his chest as they closed the kilometres between the vineyard and his old holiday home. Part of him wanted to grab the steering wheel and head straight back to the ferry terminal. But it was too late.

The Pines stood tall and dark and ominous as they drove past, the short driveway leading to the front door, still painted dark blue, ancient pohutakawa trees flanking the lawn, laundry flapping on the line, all gave his gut a strange kick. Memories of happier times filtered into his head—his father swinging him round and round, his mother laughing at their antics and calling them for dinner. The long leisurely Christmas lunches filled with fun and excitement—midnight mass, waiting for Santa, opening presents on Christmas Day morning.

They had been happy, once upon a time. But once that dream had been shattered, it had never been possible to reach that state again.

He let his gaze wander, turning his head slightly as the large rambling house went out of view. Glancing at him, Georgie jerked the car to a halt. 'That was it, wasn't it? The house?'

There was no point lying. 'Yes. It looks as if someone is renovating it.'

'Do you want to go and take a look?' Her eyes were kind as they settled on him and he knew she was trying to do the right thing by making him confront his demons. But he didn't need to do that here, he confronted them most days as it was. 'I'll come with you, you won't be on your own.'

'Let's keep driving.'

'Actually, no.' She drew up at the side of the road and

before he could stop her she'd done a U-turn and they were back at the house.

'Georgie, I know what you're trying to do. It's okay. I'm fine. Things are fine.'

'Sure. If you say that enough times you might just believe it. I, however, take a little more convincing. Come on.' She stepped out, leaned against the car and wrapped her arms around her chest as she stared at the house. 'I can imagine you playing there in the garden. Causing mayhem. It's a real family home. Three generations all together. Nice.'

'It was once.' He wrenched himself out of the car and looked over at the house, fighting the tightness in his throat. 'The last time I was here was for my grandad's funeral.'

She turned to him, hair blowing wildly in the sudden breeze. 'I'm so sorry.'

'He lived here all his life, he loved the place, said he didn't need to go anywhere else.'

'It's nice that you have family history. It must be reassuring to hear about the past, thinking that your grandad walked along these same paths as you. It gives a connection, doesn't it?' Slipping her hand into his, she left it at that. But her words kept coming back to him as they walked across the road past the house and looked out over the bay towards the tiny islands dotted around the horizon.

Liam remembered his grandad telling him about the antics he and his mates had got up to here on the island— fishing, drinking, farming. How he'd courted Liam's grandmother for two years but had always known he'd marry her. How they'd devoted years of their lives to the community here. Liam had always known his ties to this place but it had been too easy to take them for granted.

Then he'd tried to put as much space between him and them as he could.

He looked at Georgie now in profile, those gorgeous lush curls whipping in the wind; she would never know if they came from her mother's side or her father's. Those soft brown eyes—a hint of Maori blood? Italian? Again, she'd never know. That staunch tilt of the jaw—well, that was pure Georgie, from years of forging her independence and stamping her place in this world. How she'd turned her life into such a success from her rocky beginnings, he would always wonder at. She had no memories of any kind of family time, good or bad, no special Christmases, no history to talk of, no stories to tell her baby.

Nugget.

Fear washed through him. Fear and hope mingling into a mish-mash of chaos in his gut. He was going to be a father.

He was going to have to create memories for his child too. A history. And a future.

See, this was why he'd been against families for so long. Because the unbearable weight of responsibility meant you had to stop hiding yourself and be someone good. Deep down good. Unselfishly open and honest. You had to let go of the past and be that person, the one everyone relied on. The one everyone looked up to. The one who knew there was danger and risk in opening his heart, but did it anyway.

Trouble was, he just didn't know if he could be that man.

CHAPTER TEN

One month ago...

TIME WAS MOVING FAST. Too fast.

The next few weeks were a blur of sensual lovemaking and laughter. It seemed, to Georgie at least, that sex could be a good mix with friendship after all. Liam was still funny and helpful, he still hammered nails and painted walls. He made her laugh and sigh with delight. They chatted and joked about pretty much everything, as ever—and it seemed almost as if something inside him had been set free.

Except...there was that nagging worry that things were rattling towards an abrupt end. And there was still a part of himself that he held back, that she couldn't break through.

Georgie's head was in a state of flux. She didn't know what he wanted, and she wasn't sure what she wanted out of this either. There'd been no discussion of expectations and she was too scared to ask him about...*what next*. All she knew was that having him in her bed and by her side made her feel the very best she'd ever felt. Although she'd never again mentioned his past, she also didn't want to discuss a future.

Because for the immediate future—which in her terms

amounted to the next eighteen years—she wanted what she had never had: a stable, loving environment for her child. She wanted her baby to feel loved and nurtured, as if it were the centre of the universe and not, like her, alone and unwanted. She wanted her child to not have to fight every day to be noticed. She wanted her child to feel completely and utterly confident and…loved. Just loved.

So, in reality, she needed to forget about any kind of intimacy with Liam, shouldn't waste precious time wondering how it was going to work out—because she should be concentrating on getting through the pregnancy and planning to bring up a child as a co-parent with a friend.

Which didn't work so well for her when she was lying next to him in bed, or trying to do the nine-to-five at her day job when her head was full of naked images of him earlier that morning.

'Georgie, did you manage to get the blood-test results for Kate Holland? She's coming in this afternoon and I want to make sure she's all set.' Malcolm had returned from settling his mum into a nursing home in Dorset and had hit the clinic with renewed vigour.

Georgie watched as he bustled around the office, ordered and officious. He was a nice guy, but had some traits that she found just a little irritating. In retrospect it was good that she hadn't asked him to be the donor for her child. What on earth had she been thinking? But, then, on the other hand, Malcolm was nice. Just nice. Not anything else. Not complicated, not sexy as all hell, not a brilliant kisser—okay, so she didn't know that, but he didn't have sexy lips.

'Georgie?'

Malcolm. He was sitting at the desk opposite her now, face masked by a computer screen. 'Oh, sorry. Yes?'

'Blood results for Kate Holland?'

'Yes, I phoned the lab to chase them again an hour ago and they said they'd email them through. They should be here...' She tapped on her keyboard and brought the work up on screen. 'There you go. I've directed them to her file. All looking good. She'll be pleased.'

'Thanks.' Her boss's head popped up over the monitor. 'Georgie, are you okay?'

'Absolutely fine, thanks.' And so far she hadn't let her thoughts interfere with her job, but they were definitely trying to filter in. Which was annoying in the extreme, because she loved this job, needed the pay, loved helping people reach their dreams, so *focus* was the watchword of the day.

'If you need to talk anything through I'd be more than happy...' Malcolm's face disappeared back behind the computer screen, but after a few moments it reappeared again. 'No pressure, though.'

'Seriously, I'm fine. Tired, but that's to be expected.' And in truth the lack of sleep wasn't all pregnancy related.

Malcolm looked hugely relieved at the prospect of not having a stressing-out employee on his hands. She hadn't mentioned to anyone at work who the father was and wanted to keep things quiet. It was far too complicated to try talking about this kind of thing here. Everyone thought they knew everything, everyone thought they understood and they were all so lovely and well meaning, but how could they understand when she didn't even understand half of it herself?

Malcolm went back to tapping on the keyboard. 'Ah, I see we have Jo Kinney arriving in ten minutes for follicular monitoring.'

'I know, I made the booking, but don't worry—I'll make myself scarce. I understand how frustrating it is to see pregnant tummies in a fertility clinic when you're struggling to get even a fraction of the way.'

Her boss's voice was concerned. 'I'm hoping the counselling sessions are helping her.'

'I think so. The last time she was in she confessed to feelings of uncontrollable jealousy if any of her friends told her they were pregnant. And she's not talking to her sister at the moment because she's carrying twins. It's all so very difficult for her.' Since she'd become pregnant Georgie had been at pains to make sure she'd been extra-compassionate with her patients. She had what many of them only dreamt about and that was something she would never take for granted. 'I do have a feeling that she'll get there in the end, though.'

'We can only hope so. Don't look so worried, I'll give her the best shot we have.' Malcolm stood to leave. 'So do me a favour and take a lunch break for a change. The sun's shining and the yachts are racing out on the gulf. Get some fresh air. And while you're out, buy some tinsel, we need to Christmas this place up a bit, and last year's decorations are looking a bit sad.'

'Now you've definitely asked the right person for that job. I don't need to be asked twice to go Christmas shopping.' Smiling, Georgie stood and took off her name badge. She had plans to meet Liam for lunch, but had kept that information under wraps. Meeting him in secret for snatched lunches added to the excitement. 'Actually, I'm also going to go and take a sneak peek at that new baby shop. They import things from Europe apparently, it sounds wonderful.'

'Don't go buying the whole place up.'

'I won't. I'm just going for ideas. After the renovations I don't have much left over for the frills.' She grabbed her bag and made a quick mental list of things she needed.

A pram, a cot, cloth nappies, a stroller. Basically, the essentials. It was only window shopping, but it was lovely to dream.

The light warm breeze was welcome after the cloistered atmosphere in the clinic. Summer was edging in and starting to make its presence felt; the shoppers and office workers on High Street had shed their thick woollen coats and knee-length boots. The shop displays had Christmassy reds, greens and silvers instead of wintry blacks and browns, Georgie noted, and that made her feel bright. Despite not knowing which way was up with Liam, there was so much she should be thankful for. She had a great house, a great job with understanding and supportive colleagues. She had a future right here in her belly. There were many not so fortunate.

She almost broke into song, with the buskers churning out the old Christmas favourites…and, strangely, hearing 'Away In A Manger' brought a lump to her throat. A happy lump.

Choosing a colour theme for her tree this year was hard, but in the end she went with traditional red and gold. A few new baubles. And a named one for her and one for Liam. And for Nugget too… Desdemona didn't fit.

The baby shop was exclusive and expensive, she could see that just from the window displays with beautiful hand-carved cots and no price tags. When she entered the well-dressed shop assistants greeted her with expectant smiles.

'Just looking, thanks,' she answered their questioning faces, and wondered whether she'd have been better walking past and on to the more affordable chain stores further down the road. But, oh, it was such an adorable place, decorated with luxury Christmas items—'Baby's

First Christmas' bibs, blankets, towels. Miniature stockings hung from a makeshift mantelpiece. She eyed a kit for a hand-sewn advent calendar and made a mental note to add it to her ever-growing list. That would all have to wait until next year. Nugget's real first Christmas, and she'd make sure everything would be just perfect.

No, this Christmas would be special too. She had the feeling that waddling around trying to feed an army would be too much for her this year, so it would be just her and Liam, if she could lure him away from that ER... for the first time in her adult life she'd have a quiet one. At the thought of just the two of them spending such a special day together she grew a little hot. She imagined waking up to a special Liam Christmas surprise...and her cheeks flushed.

But where was he?

Clearly, he'd been held up by some emergency or other, but soon she'd need to get back to work, so she headed for the exit.

'Georgie? Hey, is that you, Georgie? Wow! Look at you. I had no idea...' It was Kate and Mark Holland, hand in hand staring into the same shop window.

'Kate?' The woman looked a darned sight healthier than she'd looked before, when she'd been bloated and on bed rest and pretty damned miserable. 'Lovely to see you. How are you doing?'

Kate's eyes twinkled. 'Not as well as you, clearly. My goodness, this is a surprise. When are you due?'

Georgie resisted running her hand over her now huge bump. 'Eight more weeks, end of January. A summer baby. Believe me, I am not looking forward to waddling around in that humidity.'

'Do you know the gender? What about names?'

More things on her list. She'd been putting off talking to Liam about names again, and when she'd jokingly mentioned it he'd ended up…well…it had been very nice indeed. 'No, I don't know the sex, I want it to be a surprise. And names are so hard to choose, don't you think? Picking one's hard enough, but a middle name too? That's all kinds of heavy-duty responsibility. Imagine picking a name and them hating it for the rest of their lives.'

'So you have some planning to do. I like the traditional ones myself. Make a list.' Kate seemed genuinely pleased for her and wrapped her in a gentle hug. 'Lucky you. I really am pleased.'

Georgie told herself to get a grip as her throat filled with emotion for Kate. Her hormones were all over the place today. 'I saw you'd booked into the clinic this afternoon—what's the plan?'

Her patient gripped her husband's hand as they both smiled. 'My mum's given us some money for one more round, an early and very unexpected Christmas present. I can't tell you how amazing that is. I just can't give up. I just can't.'

'That's great news. Really brilliant. I'll keep everything crossed for you and we'll do everything we can at the clinic.' Georgie knew exactly how Kate felt and wondered just how hard she'd have fought to feel the way she felt right now. Hell, she'd have kept on fighting until she'd had no fight left. And then she'd have fought harder still. Nothing was as precious as this child, getting this child. Having this child. It was the first time that Georgie had ever sensed what it would be like to be part of a family. To belong. To love and be loved, unconditionally. And Liam fitted into that picture too. No matter how much she tried not to, she couldn't help but do some serious Christmas wishing on that account.

'Thanks.' Kate bit her lip and her eyes briefly fluttered

closed. 'I'm a bit worried, to be honest. I don't want to have another major disaster like last time.'

'Okay, so the first thing you have to do is stop worrying. That's not going to help at all. We'll start you on a lower dose of stimulation drugs this time and monitor you very closely. There's nothing to say that you'll have the same experience again. Really, try to relax, that's the best thing you can do. I'll see you later and we can talk more then.'

'Okay. See you soon.'

Georgie was about to leave when she felt a prickling along her neckline. Turning, she saw Liam approaching and felt the immediate rush of bright light whenever she saw him. 'Hey. Did you forget the time?'

'I'm so sorry. Just one thing after another today.' He shook his head and pecked a kiss on her cheek. 'Did I miss the shopping? Come on, let's go. I'm starving.'

'Me too.'

He grinned. 'No surprises there. What's in the bags?'

She hid the bag of named baubles behind her back and grinned right back—he'd probably think she was just a sentimental old sook. 'Not telling.'

'Aw…come on.' As he spoke his mobile phone went off. He shook his head in irritation, dragged his phone out of his pocket and looked at the display. 'Look, I've got to get this.'

'Who is it?'

'Just MAI.'

'The agency? Why? What do they want?' She felt the colour drain from her face. He'd been home so long this time. Long nights she'd kept him to herself like a delicious secret, always knowing that this day might come but pretending that it wouldn't. Convincing herself that it wouldn't matter anyway, that she was on top of her feelings about him. She'd managed to leave herself enough space and hadn't fallen for him so completely that his leaving would damage her.

Besides, he didn't have to go. The baby was due soon. He would turn them down. He would stay. 'What do they want?'

'No idea.' He shrugged. 'Sorry again. I won't be long.'

He turned a little away from her and she stared into the shop window, half looking at the too-expensive wares, half-listening to his side of the conversation. It would be fine. She would be fine. He wouldn't run, she trusted that he wouldn't go now, not when she needed him.

'Hey. No worries. Where…? How long…? Why…? What do you need?' Suddenly his voice went quiet and the bright light inside her went out.

He stayed quiet for a few moments as he listened to the caller. Then he looked over and caught her eye. There was something about his tense expression that made her heart stumble. Guilt? Panic? He tried for a smile, but it was more regretful than reassuring. Then he closed his eyes, turned his back to her, shoulders hitched.

Something was wrong.

She strained to listen, but whether he was hiding the information from her or protecting her she didn't know.

She heard her name.

She heard 'pregnant'.

She heard, 'Yes, I'll do it.'

Then he stood stock-still.

Something was wrong. Numbness crept through her. The only things she could feel were the fast, unsteady beat of her heart and the clench of her fists around the shopping bag handles.

Something was wrong but, unlike her house, or the

garden or the zillion things that had broken over the last few years, Liam wasn't going to fix this.

Liam snapped the phone into his pocket and turned to face her, already understanding that she'd heard a little and assumed a lot. Things were careering out of control in every direction he turned. 'I'm sorry. Again.' It was inadequate, he knew, but it was heartfelt.

'So you keep saying. What for? Being late for lunch or agreeing to whatever it was you just agreed to?' Her eyes were dark, her cheeks hollowed. She knew him too well, Liam realised. He couldn't hide things from her. 'What did they want? No...more to the point, when are you leaving? Where are you going?'

'Sudan. Tonight.'

'They need you, right? There's no one else? Absolutely no one else? Tell me they were desperate. You had no choice?'

The pause he gave was too long. Long enough for her to read between the lines. They'd sort of asked and he'd sort of offered. And, yes, there were others who could have gone. He'd just fast-tracked himself to the top of the list.

Things between them had got so complicated so quickly, he was thrashing around trying to make sense of it. But he couldn't.

Yes, he loved waking up with her. Yes, he loved spending time with her. Too much. It was all too much and he was starting to want things, to feel things he shouldn't about the baby and about her. He was supposed to have kept his emotions out of all this and yet here they were washing through him. Guilt. Panic. Adoration. Need. *Fear*.

And taking that risk was a step too far. He needed to

get his head straight. To have time to think. Sudan was the perfect place. It wouldn't be for ever, but it might just be enough to get things in order again, so he could be rational and stop these gut-wrenching emotions messing with his head. 'Well…'

He could hardly look at her, but he had to face her anger.

Which was swift and fierce and almost tangible. He could see her starting to close down.

She shook her head and strode past him. 'Okay. So you've made your decision. I have to go to work. I'm going to be late.'

Liam followed her down Queen Street towards her clinic, trying to keep up. The way she'd looked at him he could have sworn she'd wanted him to say something more. Something profound. But he wouldn't lie to her, let her think one thing, believe something—*want* something—that he wasn't sure he could give. Hell, she was hearts and flowers all the way and he was, in comparison, a lost cause. He shouldn't have let things get to this point. 'For a woman who's seven months pregnant you can sure keep a good pace.'

'That's because I'm in a hurry. My clinic's due to start and you're making me late for *my* job. You're not the only one with a strong work ethic.' She was in front of him now, grumping over her shoulder. And watching her stalk ahead, all proud and indignant, made him want her more. Which gave him every reason why he should get that damn flight.

'Georgie, we need to talk about this.'

'Really? You think?' She stopped outside the clinic. 'When you've already made your decision? You jumped at the chance. No hesitation. I didn't see much talking going on between us.'

He followed her up the stairs and into a meeting room. He closed the door and went to sit opposite her across a table. The table was too big, the room too sterile.

Her words echoed off the walls. 'And you don't know for how long. You never do. It could be months.'

'Look, it'll be okay. Everything will be fine. The deck's almost finished, the garden just needs some final touches. Don't do anything until I get back.'

Those lifeless eyes regained a spark that flamed. 'So this is your idea of being in it for ever? A lifetime commitment, and this is what you're promising? You won't be here geographically—and I can probably handle that. A lot of mothers have to deal with that. But…oh, this is unfair. I'm being unfair.' She stood up. 'I knew this all along, but—'

'What? Say it… Say what you're thinking.' He reached across for her hand, but she pulled it away. She was closing down. 'Talk to me, Georgie.'

'What's the point?'

'It's what we do. Talking.'

'Not, it appears, about the important things. Not when it matters. You should have discussed it with me first. *We* should have decided.' She took a deep breath and huffed it out. 'You say you're committed, that you want to work as a team, as a co-parent, but the moment they call, you jump. *You* choose. You can say no. You can stay here. There is a get-out clause. I do know.'

It was important that he remain calm and let her anger bounce off him. 'It's my job, Georgie. I've been home for a long time.' *Home.* That thought made Liam's stomach clench— it was the first time he'd thought of anywhere as home. Georgie's home. His heart swelled in pride at what they'd achieved at her house, but simultaneously he felt as if it was being slashed into pieces. 'This will be the last time. I'll make sure I resign completely after this.'

'I'm sure that's what they all say, and I'm sure they mean it too. Besides, I know why you do it, month after month, serving your penance to Lauren. I get that. I wouldn't ask you to give it up. But now? Right now? When you have a choice and you chose them. You chose them. Unbelievable.' She began to pace the room, glancing every few seconds at the clock. Which ticked away the minutes sonorously, ominously, like a sentinel counting down.

She stopped walking. Her hands gripped the back of a chair. There was a small hole in the dark grey fabric, the edges frayed. She seemed to stare at it as she spoke. 'So you told them? About the baby?'

'Yes.'

'And you might not be here for the birth?'

'They said they'd try to make it happen.' The ache that had started in his throat seeped into his chest, getting more raw and more real.

Distance. That's what they needed, then they'd be able to think and talk and act rationally, without the sideshow of pumping hearts and that long aching need. He needed to feel about her and the baby the way he felt about everyone else, not infused with some sort of mind-melding, heart-softening drug. That way he would be able to make good decisions, act responsibly.

He walked to the window and looked out at the street below. It had started to rain. Heavy clouds spewed thick drops over the passers-by below.

Finally, she came to him and made eye contact. But it wasn't what he wanted to see. All affection had gone, all excitement and hopefulness.

Somewhere along the way all his emotions had got

locked up with her. Every day started and ended with thoughts of Georgie. As he turned to the window he caught sight of a stack of magazines and remembered the online dating article. She was hoping for something more.

She wanted a declaration, he supposed. Something that told her how he felt about her, about this. But he didn't know what to say. Couldn't express the chaos, couldn't see through those clouds, only that his heart felt raw at the prospect of not being here. Of letting her down. But it wasn't fair to make her believe a lie.

Her voice was cold. 'And they're going to try? Is that what we've got to look forward to? You trying?'

'Surely that's better than me not trying? I'll call when I get there. I'll call as often as I can. I'm sorry it's not going to work out exactly to plan.'

'We didn't have a plan, Liam. That's just the problem. We just pretended everything would be fine, and it's not. It won't be.' She shook her head, her ponytail bobbing from side to side. She looked so young. And so cross. So magnificently annoyed. 'I won't hold my breath about the calls. I know what those satellite phones are like. You've never managed it before.'

It had never mattered so much before.

She was distancing herself from him, he could see. She was systematically putting space from her emotions, he recognised it because he'd done it himself so many times—but she never had.

When she looked back at him her resolve seemed clear. The emotions were settled, she was cold and distant. Things had irrevocably changed—including the emotions whirling in his chest like some sort of dark storm cloud, whipping away the oxygen and leaving nothing in its place. An empty chasm that hurt so hard.

He was going to help those who didn't have the wherewithal to help themselves. But, bone deep, he knew he was going because he couldn't not. Because facing other people's truths was always easier than facing up to his own. 'They need me there.'

'And we need you here.'

He looked over at the shopping bags she'd dropped on the floor. 'You bought decorations?'

'Suddenly I'm not feeling very festive. You're not going to be here.'

'I doubt it.' And that was all his fault. She'd been looking forward to spending Christmas together and he'd ruined it.

He turned to face her as hurt and pain whipped across his heart.

Her arms hugged across her chest. Her eyebrows rose as she infused her voice with a brightness she clearly didn't feel. 'So go. Save some lives. Come back safe and then be a good father to your child.'

'It'll only be for a few weeks. I'll get back for the birth. I'll make it happen.' His child. It was so close now, a few more weeks and he'd be able to hold his child.

Was that why he'd taken this job? Because he was too afraid? Was he too afraid to love his child?

To love Georgie?

That idea shunted him off balance. He didn't want to look too deeply inside himself, at his motivations, so he was going by gut feeling here, because that was all he had to go on. His head wasn't making any sense. 'And what about us?'

'Oh, Liam, we want different things, I understand that now. I feel that now. I want a big messy family with two parents who love each other, with doting grandparents who want to share the joy, and you don't want any of that.' She touched her heart and a little piece of him shattered because he knew what she was saying. That this was the end. 'We just don't have the same dream.'

No. Now his heart was being ripped away. He didn't want to hear those words, to feel this hurt. But he knew that it was the only way they would ever be able to get by, to see each other and survive. Maybe one day they'd find a place where they could be friends again. 'And when I come back?'

'We'll have rewound in time to before the baby. To before you came back from Pakistan. Back to when we were just friends. When things weren't complicated. You can have your life and I'll have mine and we'll meet somehow in the middle, for this little fella. Co-parents, like we agreed.'

'But—'

'No.' Her hand flicked up to stop him speaking. 'It's what I want, Liam. What I need to get through all this. Things are going to be hard enough as they are without wondering what you want from me too, worrying if you're going to change your mind or choose something else, something more appealing. Because you do that... don't you? So it'll be better if we have no promises. No pretence. No ties between *us*. No *us*. Just this baby.'

'But—' He wanted to fight her, to fight for them, but she was right. It was easier, cleaner if they broke everything off now and got back to being friends again. If that could ever happen. Time apart would help. It had to.

'I'm used to being on my own, Liam. That way there aren't any expectations. I can't spend my life wanting people to love me if they don't. If I'm not enough, that's fine. I'll be enough for this little one.'

You're more than enough for me. For anyone. But love? That was another level he hadn't dared strive for since Lauren. Something he'd closed himself to. Love?

Nah, he couldn't trust himself to go there. 'I'll be back as soon as I can. I'm sorry, about everything.'

'No. This is all my fault, Liam. I should have listened to you in the first place. It was a beyond crazy idea. And now our friendship is ruined, we can't talk without shouting. You're leaving and we're arguing. We never did this before, we used to go to the pub and give you a good send off, and off you'd trot, with a damned fine hangover, to save the world. And we cheered from the sidelines, proud and happy that you were doing something most excellent and good.

'But look at me, I'm not cheering now. I resent you for going and that's not how it should be. You'd resent me if I asked you stay. We're caught between our own needs and wants and it's too hard to live like that. Everything's changed between us. You said it would and it has. It's me who should be sorry. I made you do this. I kissed you first. I took you to my bed. I'm sorry for all of it.'

'Never. We've created something. A child. *Our* child. We can't ever be sorry for that.' He tried to pull her into his arms, to kiss her once more. To taste those honeyed lips, to feel her, soft and gorgeously round, in his arms. To feel that sense of belonging that she gave him, that reason to stay. To make him stop running from the past and look ahead to something different, something better, something not haunted by what happened before. Something more than good. But she stepped away, out of reach.

So far out of reach he didn't know if he'd ever find a way back to her.

'I need you to leave now.' She wanted him to stay. Wanted him to want to stay with her and the baby, and make a family of three. Oh, God, she wanted him. Wanted more. Wanted so much more. Wanted a different way to describe what the two of them had shared. It didn't necessarily need paperwork—she didn't expect marriage, but she did want commitment. Not just to the baby but to her. She wanted to be part of something long term. With him. She wanted her dream.

But he was running away, and he'd given her no choice in the matter.

And, yes, he'd shown commitment to the pregnancy despite her initial doubts. Not once had he wavered when even she'd had the odd wobble about impending parenthood. Hadn't he helped her create a beautiful space for her and their child? Hadn't he designed a garden? Hadn't he made sure she was safe, that she ate the right things, that his child was cocooned in the right environment to grow?

But he had still never said the word 'love' to her. Not about her or his child. Or about anyone or anything, for that matter, ever. He was all locked up in the tragedy of his baby sister and it was desperately sad but she wanted him to love someone.

She wanted him to love her.

And he couldn't. Because if he did he wouldn't be heading off on some mission that he didn't need to go on. He'd be here, holding her hand and planning a happy Christmas, supporting her in her last couple of months of pregnancy.

Was it too much to ask? Was she expecting too much?

No. It was what every couple strove for. She wanted him to feel the same way about it all as she did. She wanted him to share that excitement she felt whenever she lay in his arms. The way her heart soared when he was inside her. The sensation of utter completeness when he looked at her, when he made her laugh. She wanted him to love her and the baby the way she loved him. Wholly. Totally. Without reservation.

And there it was. The naked, ugly truth. She'd fallen in love with him.

When she should have been putting all her attention into this baby, she'd gone and fallen for its father—the wrong kind of man to love.

No.

She tried not to show her alarm and fixed her face as best as she could into an emotion-free mask as she walked away from him, while he stared at her uncomprehendingly, his hand on the doorhandle.

No. Don't go. She wanted to shout it at him. To hurl herself at him and be a barrier between him and the door. But what would be the point? Letting him go was the right thing to do. What was the point in making someone stay, hoping they would learn to love you? Hoping…

She loved him. Completely. Devastatingly. Instead of protecting herself against more heartache, she'd allowed her life to be bowled over by a man who couldn't and wouldn't ever love her. It was a simple and as difficult as that. How stupid.

And now, even worse, she was tied to him for ever. She'd insisted on that. And he'd agreed. He'd torn up the contract in a dramatic gesture of commitment and determination that had both impressed and scared her. And despite everything she knew about him, she'd believed him and somewhere deep inside a little light had fired into life and it had grown and she'd hoped…

And now the light had blown right out.

Because, after all, she'd been the silly one in all this, she'd allowed herself to dream, had allowed herself to slip under his spell, had willingly given her heart to him. He'd always been upfront. And you couldn't be more upfront than jumping on the first plane out of Dodge.

Liam had been right all along. Love could be damned cruel. She could never let him know. 'I need you to leave. Now. I need you to go, Liam.'

'Georgie—'

'Go. I have to work.' She watched the door close behind him, and almost cried out, almost declared herself, to see if that would make a difference to him going or staying. But she wasn't about to play games, give him tests, make him say something he'd regret. Or that they'd both regret.

But, still, nothing took away from the fact that she loved him. She had probably always loved him—as a friend, as someone who she could confide in and share a joke with. He was, deep down, a good man who was conflicted, who was trying to hide from hurt, and after his experiences who could blame him? His flaws made him even more likable. Falling romantically in love with him had been the icing on the cake and she would be proud for her child to have him as a father. One day she would tell him that. When she could look him in the face again. When her heart had stopped shattering into tiny pieces.

With shaking hands she picked up her shopping bags, took out the tinsel and gaudy baubles and threw them on the table. That would be for later, for a time when she felt like celebrating. Right now Christmas loomed ahead a sad and sorry affair. A Christmas without Liam. She'd wrapped him up in her festive excitement, made him the best present a girl could have, and he'd gone. Left her, just like her mother had.

One day she'd find someone who wanted her enough to stay around.

She took a few deep breaths, swiped a hand across

her face and caught a tear. And another one. Then gave up the fight and let them flow.

My God, she thought as she looked in the staff-room mirror, she needed to pull herself together; this clinic could be hard enough without the nurses falling apart too.

'Come on, girl.' Plumped up her cheeks and dried her eyes. 'There are plenty who are much worse off.' Like the people Liam was going out to save. Like the ones she had booked in now, who looked to her for support and advice. Who didn't have a healthy baby in their bellies. Who needed her dedication and attention to get them through. She allowed herself two more tears. Exactly that. One for her, one for her baby, then she took another deep breath, put on her game face and went back out into the world.

CHAPTER ELEVEN

Two weeks ago...

LIAM LURCHED AGAINST the cold hard passenger seat as the Jeep bumped over potholes along the pitted dirt track. 'Man, these roads don't get any better. I'm going to be covered in bruises before we get to the camp.'

'Aren't you pleased to be back?' Pierre Leclerc shouted above the din of the engine, his words tinted with his French-Canadian accent and vestiges of the countless places he'd visited in his long aid career. He cracked a booming laugh and hit Liam on the thigh. 'We missed you.'

'Ah, shucks, mate, I missed you too.' Like hell he'd missed them. He'd struggled every kilometre, every minute of the interminable flight, the uncomfortable transit, the stench. The seven-day layover in Juba, getting supplies, waiting for the right documents, stuck in bureaucratic hell. The long drive out here. Every second wishing he'd had the courage to stay in Auckland with Georgie.

He just couldn't get rid of the memory of her. All grumpy and stroppy, stomping down the crowded street, the swing of her backside, the tense holding of her shoulders, the swish of her ponytail. The closed-off posture.

The truth of her words. *Our friendship is ruined*. But it was all too late.

Pierre leaned across. 'I hope you bought us something decent for our Christmas stockings?'

'I have something to help us forget, if that's what you mean.' Patting his duty-free purchases of rum and whisky, he joined in the laughter, trying to be friendly, wishing like mad he was back in New Zealand, far away from this nightmare of dry earth and flies.

I made a mistake, he thought. *I made a million of them*.

They pulled into the camp compound, the dull corrugated roof of the medical building half-hidden by a layer of brown sand whipped up by the morning wind. A thin pale grey sky stretched above them, promising little relief from the scorching sun.

Liam looked around at the thousands of tents and crudely made straw structures lining the gravel and mud path. Sun-bleached rags, tied between sticks and corrugated metal, provided the best shelter they could from relentless heat. A group of women huddled around a water tap. 'It hasn't changed at all.'

'Nothing much changes around here. It's like *Groundhog Day*.' Pierre pulled out a handkerchief and swiped it across his forehead. 'People still arrive every day seeking help, and we still struggle to house them, to feed them, to provide adequate clean water. There aren't enough toilets, the kids are all getting sick. Nothing changes at all.'

Except last time Liam couldn't wait to get here. And this time he couldn't wait to leave. 'So, what's planned for today?'

'Immunisation programme. Training the new assistants so they can go on and run it solo.'

'Okay. Let's do it.' Liam jumped down into the fog of red dust created by the Jeep wheels.

Within seconds, dozens of semi-naked children appeared screaming, laughing and singing, surrounding Liam and Pierre and clinging to their legs. Such joy in everything, even in the direst circumstances. But that was kids for you: they didn't overthink, they didn't worry or analyse, they just got on with life, running forward to the next great adventure. There was a lesson there.

Pierre steered him into the medical centre. As they squeezed past the long queue of sick people waiting to be treated Liam found himself wondering where to begin, but as always Pierre had the routine down like clockwork. And Liam easily slipped back into it.

'Okay, your turn.' He beckoned to a mother holding a small child in her arms. 'How old?'

The woman looked at him, not understanding. She offered him the child, a boy of about twelve months, scrawny and lethargic with the telltale potbelly signs of malnutrition.

'He's about one year and a half.' The base nurse translated the woman's local dialect, 'His name is Garmai. Just out of the supplementary feeding programme two weeks ago.'

Liam checked him over and measured the child's arm circumference to determine the extent of malnutrition. Garmai would probably spend the best part of his life growing up in a refugee camp, his home town too dangerous to go back to as rebels terrorised the streets and drought stole their crops. So different from the life his own child would lead in New Zealand, where water came through invisible pipes below the ground, machines worked with the swipe of a finger and food was plentiful.

And a father half a world away.

What the hell had he been thinking?

'Eighteen months old? Really?' He spoke to the nurse.

'It looks like he still has signs of mild malnutrition. He needs to go back to the feeding centre, not stay here where he's probably only going to get sick again.'

'There isn't room. They discharged him because there's too many more coming every day.'

'They'll have to make room. This child needs help and I don't want a half-hearted effort.' He turned and smiled at the mother, trying to dredge some hope when there was little. 'I'm going to have a child. To be a father.'

He'd never given any personal information to anyone here before, not even to the staff—but the words just tumbled out. Pride laced his voice as his thoughts returned again to Georgie for the umpteenth time that day, along with the familiar sting of regret and yet startling uplift of his heart. Every thought of her brought a tumbling mishmash of emotions and a fog of chaos. 'Soon. Very soon.'

The mother gave him a toothy grin and gabbled something to him, but a high-pitched scream grabbed their attention. A heavily pregnant woman half walked, half crawled into the room, clutching her stomach. She was immediately ushered back out and into the emergency area by two nurses.

Georgie? *Georgie.* Of course it wasn't Georgie. He'd left her to face her biggest challenge alone back at home. How would she cope with the pain of childbirth? Did she have a plan? Why the hell hadn't he made sure she had a plan? He'd phone her again, at least try to, tonight, and make sure she was okay. That was, of course, if she ever deigned to speak to him again. Her silence had been deafening.

Unlike the squawk of chattering voices and laughter and screams that filled the room as a huddle of women walked towards the emergency area. He looked up at the nurse for an explanation. 'The pregnant woman's sisters, here to help.'

'Great. She'll need some support.' He looked back at the boy, then jerked his head up again at another straggle of women walking through the room.

'The birthing attendants. The mother's mother. Her aunts.'

'Are they going to have a party or something? There's a lot of them.'

The nurse beamed. 'Of course. Family is very important here.'

As it was to Georgie. And she was going to be alone.

And that was his fault.

Watching those people come together to help their sister, to celebrate family in all its messy glory, made his heart clutch tight and he realised that Georgie had been wrong about one thing: he did want the same dream. He'd spent the last nine months trying to fight it with his head, but his hands had worked on her house, her garden, building a home for them all, a home that he loved. His arms had held the woman he adored, cradled her belly holding the baby he so desperately wanted.

For the first time in years he saw his own needs with startling clarity. He wanted to look forward instead of back. He wanted to be a father his child would be proud of. He wanted a family.

Hell, Georgie had even got him thinking about his own mother and father. And how much, deep down, he wanted to make some kind of contact with them again. He'd make a start tonight. He'd phone them and tell them they were going to be grandparents.

He wanted to be part of something good. He wanted somewhere to call home, a community of friends. Someone to love. And to be loved. The same simple dreams as every single person in this camp. He just hadn't realised it until now.

Most of all he wanted Georgie, with such a passion it stripped the air from his lungs. But he knew her heart came with a proviso. He had to love her. She wouldn't accept any less than that.

He had to love her. *Had to?* Could he do that? He sat for a moment and that thought shook through him like a physical force. He let her image fill his brain, suffuse his body with so many wild emotions. His throat filled with a raw and unfettered need.

Man, how he wanted her. He missed everything about her. He wanted her. Dreamt about her, saw her soft beautiful eyes in everyone's here, her kindness in the gentle touch of strangers, her compassion, her independence that frustrated and endeared her to him. He missed her so intensely it hurt. He needed to touch her, to lie with her, to fight with her. And, of course, to make love to her over and over and over. And such a need and such a want could only amount to one thing.

He did love her.

He'd been fighting so hard to protect himself he hadn't seen the single most important thing that had been happening.

God. He loved her and he'd walked away. No, he'd *run* away, afraid of how much she made him feel things. He'd messed up everything and now was it too late to start again? Would she even let him in the house? Would she let him love her?

Did she love him back?

He needed to know. He needed to make things right. He needed to go home.

A scream and a healthy wail echoed through the flimsy walls. New life. New beginnings. Not just for that family in there. But for him. Being here reminded him how fragile life was, and he needed to spend the rest of it with the woman he loved.

It was time to act. He needed to get back to her. Before Christmas, before the baby came. Before he lost any more time being here instead of there. He stood up and realised that a queue of people had formed, all staring at him in this tin-roofed lean-to in a place, it seemed, even God had forgotten.

Damn. He'd made too many mistakes and being here was one of them.

But how the hell to get out of this godforsaken dust-bowl and bridge the fifteen thousand kilometre gap to be home in time?

Christmas Eve...

'Kate? Is that you? Hey, it's Georgie. From the clinic.' Georgie gripped the phone to her ear and tried to keep her feelings in check. This part was always the most emotional bit of her job but she wished, just this once, that she could see Kate's face when she told her the news. Knowing exactly how her patient would be feeling at this moment, she wanted to wrap her in a hug. In fact, wrapping anyone in a hug would be lovely—it felt so long since she'd done that. One month, two days and about twelve hours, to be exact. Not that she was counting.

And the loneliness was dissipating a bit now, especially when she distracted herself. Which she felt like she had to do most minutes of most hours, because he was always on her mind. Just there. The look on his face as she'd called the whole thing off, haunting her. But it had been the right thing to do. A very right thing.

'Yes?' Kate's voice wavered. The line was crackly. 'Yes?'

'I've got the results from the blood test you came in for earlier today.'

A sharp intake of breath. 'Yes?'

'So…' Georgie read out all the numbers, knowing that this gobbledegook would mean the difference between heartache and ecstasy for this couple. 'So, all that means we have good news. Great news. You have a positive pregnancy test. Looks like you're going to have a very happy Christmas. Huge congratulations. I know how much this means to you.'

There was a slight pause then a scream. 'Oh. My God. Really? Really? Are you sure?'

Georgie couldn't help her smile. Her heart felt the fullest it had in a month. Since, exactly, the moment she'd watched Liam disappear from the clinic. 'Yes. It's very early days, obviously, and we still have to take one day at a time. But, yes, you are pregnant.'

'Oh, thank you. Thank you so much. Mark will be so thrilled. I know how much he wanted this. We both do. We can't thank you enough.'

Georgie ignored the twist in her heart at the thought of how gloriously happy this couple would be, together. Expecting a baby, making a family. Of how much Mark would be involved, and how much his love and concern for his wife always shone through his face.

It did not matter, she kept telling herself, that she was facing all this on her own. She would be fine and one day, maybe, she'd find a man who wanted her too. 'Okay, so we need to make another appointment for you for a few days' time to check the HCG levels are rising as well as we want them to, which means you'll have to come in before the New Year,' Georgie explained. 'I also need to book you an ultrasound scan…'

'Not long to go for you now?' Kate asked, after they'd finished the business end of the call. 'How are you feeling? Excited?'

'Very. There's just over a month to go and I don't feel remotely ready. I still have heaps of shopping to do, and I haven't even thought about preparing my delivery bag.'

'Get your man to spoil you rotten over the holidays, then. Make him do the fetching and carrying while you put your feet up.'

Familiar hurt rolled through her. Emails had been sporadic. Phone calls virtually non-existent. The only news she got was on the TV or radio. But even then she wished she hadn't heard anything. Too many people being killed. It was too unsafe. And all this stress just couldn't be good for the baby, so in the end she'd switched the damned TV off and played Christmas music to calm her down. 'He's overseas at the moment. I'm not sure when he'll be back.'

'That's a shame. What are your plans for Christmas?'

'Oh, just a quiet one at home.' She thought about her Christmas tree with the lavish decorations that she'd eventually found the motivation to finish last night. The small rolled turkey she'd bought and the DVDs of old Christmas movie favourites stacked up waiting for her to watch in the evenings. It was going to be an old-style Christmas, just her and Nugget. Not what she'd hoped for. And that was fine. It really was.

'Well, have a good one. *Kia kaha.*' *Stay strong.*

'Yes, thanks. Bye.' Georgie smiled as she put the phone in the cradle. Broken heart or not, she fully intended to.

Six hours later she was standing on the deck, adding the final touches to the outside decorations to the jolly and earnest accompaniment of carol singers blasting through her speakers. The deck may not have been quite finished, but the garden looked beautiful, with the candles flickering in the darkness. Liam had been right, the winery garden idea had worked well—just a shame that the edges still needed to be finished off.

But tomorrow's forecast was for sunshine and she had no intention of sitting inside when she had such a fairytale place to spend the day. The hammock had her name on it, along with a glass of cranberry and raspberry juice, a large helping of Christmas pudding and a damned good romance novel.

There was just one more string of lights to hitch onto a branch to make everything perfect. Standing on tiptoe, she reached up and tried to throw the lights around the branch.

Missed. *Damn.*

She tried again. Missed again. Stretching forward, she flung the lights towards the branches, the weight of her baby tummy dragging her forward and off balance.

Stepped out into...air.

She felt the scream before she heard it, rattling up through her lungs, into her throat that was filled with panic. The one single word that came to her, the only thing she wanted right now. 'Liam!'

Then she flailed around like a windmill as there was nothing and no one to stop her fall into darkness.

Now...

Pain seared up her leg with even the slightest movement. She was sure she'd broken her ankle—it was twisted at such a strange angle caught in the gap between splintered

wood and the garden wall. A bad sprain anyway, too sore
for her to put her weight on, and she was too wedged in
to be able to lever her big fat belly upwards.

So she was stuck. *Damn.*

And hurting. *Double damn.*

And how long she'd lain here calling for help, she
didn't know, but the moon was high in the sky now. Typical that she'd left her phone in the house. Typical that the
neighbours had gone to their holiday home by the sea.
Typical that it was Christmas and she was on her own.
And the music she'd been playing seemed to be on repeat
and if someone didn't turn it off soon she'd go down in
history for being the first woman to have been turned
clinically insane by Rudolph and his damned red nose.

And it hurt. Everything hurt. Including her heart, because she felt stupid and sad, here on Christmas Eve,
alone and stuck. And for some reason her usually capable
mind set had got all mushy and she felt a tear threaten.
And more than anything she missed Liam.

That was it. She loved him and she missed him with
every ounce of her being. And he wasn't here and he
never would be. Not in the way she wanted.

She tried again to wriggle free but her ankle gave way
and she didn't want to put more pressure on it. Thank
God it was summer and the night was warm. At least she
could be grateful for that small mercy.

No. She wasn't grateful, she was angry. With herself,
with Liam, with everyone and everything. Was she going
to be stuck here all damned holiday? 'Hey! Anyone? Lady
with a baby here. Stuck. Help?'

Rudolph with your nose so bright...

'Shut up! Please. Someone. Help.'

Once she'd calmed down a little she tried pulling herself up again. This time she managed an inch. Two...

but then nothing more. She was about to call out again when a sudden searing pain fisted across her body. And her feet got wet.

Her heart hammered just a little bit more. No. Surely not?

The baby? Now? She pressed a hand to her belly and spoke in the softest voice she could muster. 'No, Nugget! Don't you dare make your appearance here. You've got five more weeks to cook. You stay exactly where you are.'

She waited, biting back the pain from her foot. Trying not to cry. Maybe it had been a Braxton-Hicks contraction? Maybe it was all just practice?

No such luck. More pain rippled across her abdomen, sapping her breath and making her grip tight onto the side of the deck. That one had hurt. A lot. 'You are just like your father, you hear me? You have lousy timing.'

How could she have a baby here, when she couldn't even lift her leg up half an inch? Never mind that it was five weeks early. What was she going to do? Her lips began to tremble.

No. She wasn't going to cry. She was going to be fine.

More contractions rippled through her. Faster and more regular and every time they hurt just a little bit more. Time ticked on and she wanted so much to move, to free herself. To walk, to bend, to stretch.

And then more contractions came and the night got darker.

To cope with the pain she tried to conjure up an image of Liam, pretending he was here with her. Pretending he was helping her. Pretending he loved her. Because only that would be enough.

Think. Think. What could she do?

She didn't want to think. She wanted someone to do that for her, for a change. She wanted to be tucked up in bed, her head on Liam's shoulder, wrapped safe in his arms. She wanted— 'Owwwww. This is all your fault, Liam MacAllister. I hate you. I hate…*youooooww.*'

'I'm sorry. Is this not a good time?'

And now she was hallucinating, because through all this thick soupy darkness and Rudolph on repeat and searing pain she could have sworn she'd heard his voice.

She decided she was going to go with it. Maybe she was already clinically insane after all. 'Yes. You bet your damned Christmas socks it isn't a good time. I'm caught between a deck and a hard place. My foot's broken and I'm having your baby.'

'Right now?'

'Yes, right now.' She spoke to the Liam-shaped smudge that appeared so real it was uncanny. And to her endless irritation her heart did a little skipping thing. She didn't want it to skip. She wanted it to stay angry because that was the only way she was going to get through this. 'What the hell are you doing here anyway? Aren't you supposed to be healing the sick? Giving alms to the poor?'

Then he was there, really right there, with his scent and his capable hands, and he wasn't panicking like she was, he was talking to her in a soothing, very understanding voice. 'Let's get you… Oh.' His hands shoved under her armpits and he tugged. 'You're stuck.'

'Give the man a medal. Yes, I'm stuck. I've broken my ankle and Desdemona's about to make her— *Owwwwww.*' Pain ripped through her again. The contractions were coming faster now. More regular and more intense.

But he was here. Like some goddamned guardian angel, he was here. For her. He'd come back. For her?

Or was it just for the baby? She couldn't think about any of that right now. He was here.

His voice soothed over her again. 'You're going to be fine, really, but I think we need the fire brigade or someone else to help lift you out. I don't want to hurt you…'

You already have. 'No way. No way are you getting those good people out of bed on this special night just to come with their special lifting equipment and heft me out of— *Oowwwwww.*'

'Contractions are that regular, eh? We've got to get you out. How about if I…?' He put his foot against the wall and heaved her upwards, and if he hadn't been tugging at her she might have melted into his embrace just for a moment. Just held on tight, just for one solitary moment, to absorb some of his strength and his heat. Just held right on. 'Twist left a bit…wait…slowly…'

'Whoa. Watch it…' Then she was somehow shrugged up and sitting on the deck and her foot was throbbing and her stomach contracting and she gripped onto his old T-shirt while sudden enormous pain rattled through her. 'It hurts, Liam. It all hurts.'

He grimaced a little, she thought. She could just about make him out. The candles had blown out hours ago and she hadn't managed to even plug the fairy-lights in. Some other time she might have thought this was romantic. It wasn't. It hurt.

But then he pushed her hair back from her face and rubbed his thumb over her cheek and she bit her lip to stop herself from crying because he was here and she wanted him so much. But he didn't want her.

He looked right into her eyes. 'I know, darling. I know it hurts. It'll be fine. Honestly. It'll be okay.'

'No, it won't. This baby can't come yet, it doesn't have anywhere to sleep…and I haven't had my baby shower,

I want my party. I want to play games—I don't want to do this.'

And I don't want you here to torment me and be the macho hero and loving father when you'll go and break my heart a million times over every time I see your face.

'This. Is. Not. My. Birth. Plan. I want gas and air. Pethidine. *Drugs.*'

'Roll with it, Geo. Looks like you're going to have a special guest of honour at that party. Because this baby is coming, whether you want it to or not. I get the feeling it has your genes when it comes to independence.'

'Oh. Oh. *Owww.*'

'Let's get you inside. It's too dark. I don't know how to help if I can't see.' Half carrying her, half walking her, he managed to get her inside and onto the lounge floor. 'The bedroom's too far. Okay. I'm calling back-up. This baby's in a hurry.'

After stabbing numbers into a phone, he rattled off information and only then did she hear the anxiety in his voice. When he turned back to her she saw him in full light. My God, he was breathtaking. But he looked concerned. No, more than that. He looked haunted. *Lauren.* 'It won't happen again, Liam. It will be fine.'

'I know, I know. Everything's okay.'

'And I think I want to push—'

Everything was not okay.

Liam consciously regulated his breathing, but there was nothing he could do about his pounding heart rate and his overwhelming sense of dread. There was every chance that this could go wrong. This was a prem scenario. The one nightmare he wanted to avoid. It was happening all over again.

He tried to shake away the image of tubes and an incubator and a tiny pink thing that grew into his crying wailing sister, but had looked so quiet and so sick that it had almost broken his heart. And of the tiny coffin that had barely filled the space in the dirt.

So, no, everything was not okay.

He inhaled sharply and took Georgie's hand and waited until she'd stopped screaming and screwing up her face. 'That's it. It's all good. You're doing well.'

How many babies had he delivered? He'd lost count. Out in the field where there was little help and lots of disease, when mum and baby had less than a good chance of surviving. And he'd never panicked. Not once. But right now he'd never wanted so much for medical equipment. For back-up. For the pain in his heart to dislodge so he could think straight. For the woman and the child he loved to be okay. 'You're doing good. Now breathe… breathe…'

At what point had he so hopelessly and completely fallen in love with her? Maybe right then that second as she stared up at him with such fear and love and relief in her eyes that it made his heart jolt. Or maybe when she'd told him to leave and he'd seen the same love shimmering in her face, even though she had been trying so hard to hide it from him. Maybe when he'd found her in the ER with a damaged eye. Or when she'd told him she was pregnant.

Or even that very first day in the sluice room ten years ago when she'd taken no nonsense and told him to harden up.

But in the last few days that thought had taken hold of him and he just couldn't shake it off. Damn fine time to realise you loved someone, right when you had a chance of losing them. But whatever happened he had to love her now, from this minute on, and protect her and care for her. And help her. And be brave for her. 'I can see the head, Geo. Breathe for me. Just a second. Breathe.'

'I don't hate you.'

A smile flowered in his heart—enough to take him past the fear and into a place of calm. They'd get through this together. 'I know. I know you don't hate me, Geo. Concentrate on the breathing.'

'Really, I'm sorry. I don't hate you— *Owwwwww.*' Then with an ear-splitting scream a slick baby slithered into his arms. The doorbell rang. Footsteps pounded into the room. Georgie cried. The baby cried. The cord was cut, a murmur of voices. A hearty chorus of congratulations!

And, able to finally breathe again, he was left staring at this miracle. His son. All ten fingers and ten toes and a hefty set of lungs. Who was managing just fine on his own. And suddenly Liam's heart was blown wide open with a different kind of emotion. A searing riotous joy and a feeling that life was just about to get gloriously messy.

Then he looked at his son's mother, who was the most red-faced, tear-stained disaster he'd ever seen. And his heart swelled some more, shifting and finding more space for love for her. And he knew in that moment that nothing would ever be the same because he'd allowed these people into his heart and that was where they were going to stay. For ever. 'You are amazing, Georgie Taylor. He is amazing.'

'It's a boy? Yes?'

'Yes. He's doing fine. Just fine.' He passed the baby to her to hold, watched as the tiny bundle nuzzled towards her nipple. 'A boy, with great instincts and a particularly well-defined MacAllister package, if I do say so myself.'

'One minute old and you're assessing his genitals?'

'It's a guy thing.' Unable to resist kissing her any longer, he lifted his head and pressed his mouth to hers. 'I love you. I love you, but I need to explain—'

'Whoa? Really? Now?' She nodded towards the team of busy paramedics. 'I've just had a baby and we have an audience, and you want to do this now?'

'Yes. Now, and always. My timing is legendary, didn't you know? I don't care who hears it, I love you, Georgie.'

Her eyes widened but she put a hand between them to create space. 'It's the hormones. You'll grow out of it in a day or two. Then you'll be hot-footing it back to South Sudan at the first opportunity.'

'No. It's taken me a decade to come to my senses, but I love you. I want to be with you. Nowhere else in the world has you, so I want to be here, to make you happy.' His throat caught a little. 'And now we have this one.'

Those wide dark eyes brimmed with tears. 'No. It's because of him that you're here. Not me. You don't love me. You want to. Oh, how you want to. But you don't.'

'Are you for real? I've called in every favour I've ever had and flown halfway across the world. Dashed straight to you. Which part of *I love you* don't you believe?'

She bit her lip and as always her stark honesty was there in her face, in her words. 'I'm scared, Liam. I want to believe it all. Wow, that would be such an awesome dream to have come true, really. I couldn't think of a better thing I could have. But you don't have to get carried away. I get that you don't like connection.'

She was rejecting him? He hadn't factored that into his plan. 'I have spent every available waking hour for the last eight months here. I have pimped your house, transformed your garden, been at your beck and call. I've been your friend through thick and thin. I am still your friend, Geo. That is the best part about all of this. We are friends first. Doesn't that prove that I love you?'

'I want your heart. Not your duty or your responsibility, or some friendship loyalty thing. I want your true love.' It was there in her face and mirrored in his heart, unfettered, truthful, raw. He needed to make her believe him. She clearly took some persuading. 'I want your true love. For me. I won't take anything less.'

'Wait. Wait right there.' He dashed out to the car, grabbed his things and dashed back. 'The paramedics are waiting outside, they want to take little Nugget—we need a name. Really, we need a name. Just to be checked out at the hospital. And to get your foot sorted. But I want to give you this first.'

He dragged the cot into the lounge and placed it next to the biggest, brightest Christmas tree loaded down with the most garish baubles he'd ever seen. 'Here. I got this.'

Her hand went to her mouth. 'You bought the cot from the French market? And you've painted it? That's very sweet, very kind of you. He'll love it. I love it.'

'And I love you. I bought this for you back then, the day after you fell in love with it. Because you wanted it so much. Because it makes you happy. I just want to do things that make you smile. I love you. Please believe me.'

'Oh, Liam.' Georgie shuffled across the sofa, trying to avoid the pain in her nether regions, her foot, and just about everywhere on her body. But it all faded just a little bit. He loved her? Did he? She'd listened out for it for so long, but he'd never used the words. She'd wanted to hear it, had waited so patiently for someone somewhere to say those three words to her. She had believed that a declaration of love could only be spoken. The deeds, though—they'd been plentiful. He'd shown her his love instead of declaring it. Every day for ten years.

For some reason she couldn't breathe, her lungs were filled with nothing, her throat choked with a lump of emotion. 'I don't know what to say.'

'Well, don't, then. Don't say a thing. Just listen. I didn't want to fall in love because love can be damned painful. I pushed everyone away to protect myself. I didn't want a family, I didn't want those things you craved. But you've shown me how to make it work, how to take a risk. That fighting for the people you love is the most important thing of all. I love you. Because you are you. You're funny and weird and you laugh at my jokes and your smile warms my heart every time I see it. But best of all we can get through anything—hell, we've stood by each other ten years already. I'm ready for another thirty, forty, eighty… You?'

'Yes. Yes, of course.' She wrapped him into her arms, with a slight protest from the little fella. 'Thank you. Thank you so much. I love you too. Really. Truly.'

'And if you want me to give up the aid work, I will. I'll find something else.'

She shook her head. 'Enough with the crazyville talk. I know how much you need to do that work. Just maybe shorter stints? And we'll definitely discuss it, right? You won't just decide.'

'Of course not. We're in this together.' And the way he was looking at her convinced Georgie that he really did mean it. He planted a kiss on her cheeks, then laughed. 'Hey, it's Christmas Day, you realise? We'll have to think of something festive to call him. I'm sorry, but Nugget doesn't cut it.'

She looked over at the twinkling lights on the tree, at the three baubles centre stage with their names on. At the stack of DVDs and the romance novel. This was not how she'd intended spending Christmas Day, but she couldn't think of a better way. Two guys to look after. Two guys to love her. A family. A proper family—now that had always been at the top of her Christmas wish list. 'There's always Noel or Gabriel…Joseph, maybe? We could call him Joe?'

'Or…Rudolph? Rudi?'

That damned music was still playing in the background. 'Not on your life. Come here and kiss me again.'

His nose nuzzled into her hair. 'I can't think of anything else when I kiss you, my mind goes to mush.'

'That's the plan, I don't want any more suggestions like that. Besides, we've got plenty of time to think of a name, but way too many kisses to catch up on…'

He did as requested. When he pulled away it wasn't as far as he usually went. She liked that. Liked the way he was intent on staying. Liked the way he loved her.

'Happy Christmas, darling.'

'Happy Christmas, Macadoodle-doo.' She gave her man another kiss. Then snuggled into the baby snuffling in her arms. 'Happy first Christmas, Nugget.'

And many, many more to come.

* * * * *

A FAMILY
THIS CHRISTMAS

BY
SUE MacKAY

Published in Great Britain 2014
by Mills & Boon, an imprint of Harlequin (UK) Limited,
Eton House, 18-24 Paradise Road, Richmond, Surrey, TW9 1SR

© 2014 Sue MacKay

ISBN: 978-0-263-90806-0

Harlequin (UK) Limited's policy is to use papers that are natural,
renewable and recyclable products and made from wood grown in
sustainable forests. The logging and manufacturing processes conform
to the legal environmental regulations of the country of origin.

Printed and bound in Spain
by Blackprint CPI, Barcelona

Dear Reader

Havelock is at the head of the Pelorus Sound in New Zealand's Marlborough Sounds, just twenty minutes down the road from where I live. It's known as the Green Mussel Capital of the World, for its locally grown mussels, and every year there is a mussel festival with bands, arts and crafts, and of course lots of mussels to eat. It is a vibrant small town and very focused on the sea.

When I was planning A FAMILY THIS CHRISTMAS Havelock seemed just the right place for Jenny and Cam to get together and work through their issues. Both of them have city backgrounds, and yet both find the lifestyle in this small place fits with what they want to give and receive in life. It's a perfect place to bring up two small boys struggling with the departure of their mum.

I hope you enjoy reading Jenny and Cam's story, and also enjoy learning about a little treasure at the top of the South Island.

I'd love to hear from you on sue.mackay56@yahoo.com

You can also drop by www.suemackay.co.nz to catch up on my latest releases and get a copy of the recipe of the month.

Cheers!

Sue

CHAPTER ONE

'WATCH OUT!' THE SHOUT was followed by something like a muffled scream ricocheting through the air, lifting the hairs on the back of Cameron Roberts's neck.

Then the clattering sound of what Cam swore was one of the twins' skateboards hitting the pavement the wrong way up. His gut tightened, and his heart squeezed. What now? Was there no end to the trouble his boys could get into? They were only eight yet could kick up more messy problems than a team of rugby players out on the town after a hard game.

Already moving towards the front of his house, he dropped the hedge trimmer on the barbecue table on the way past. 'Marcus? Andrew? You guys okay?'

'Dad, hurry. She needs a doctor. I didn't mean it. I promise. I'm sorry.' Marcus appeared at the end of their drive, tears streaming down his worried little face.

Cam's gut became a knot. What had Marcus done this time? And where was Andrew? Had something happened to him? That would explain the fear in Marcus's cry. Except he'd said *she* needed a doctor. 'What's happened?' He ruffled Marcus's hair on the way past, begging the parenting gods to give him a break for once.

As usual those particular gods were on holiday if the sight before him was anything to go by. 'One day, just one whole, disaster-free day, is all I ask for,' he muttered under his breath as he reached the redhead lying in an awkward bundle on the pavement.

Her face was contorted in agony and the eyes she raised to him were darkened with that pain. Judging by the rapid rise and fall of her chest, her resp rate was raised. Blood smeared across her left elbow and down her arm, probably from scraping along the concrete.

Andrew stood, hopping from one foot to the other, his skateboard dangling from his hand as he stared down at the woman as though he couldn't understand how she'd got there. A second skateboard lay upside down beside her. Marcus's.

'What happened?' Cam repeated, as he dropped to his knees beside the woman. Swearing was forbidden in their house, and that went for out on the pavement too, but Cam came very close to breaking that rule right at this moment.

'Dad, the lady's hurt, but—'

'We didn't mean it. True.' The wobble in Andrew's voice as he finished Marcus's sentence told Cam heaps.

The woman moved, groaned. 'My ankle's broken.'

Glancing down her leg, he noted one foot and ankle already swelling. Fracture or sprain? 'We don't know that for sure yet.'

'I do.' She sounded very certain. Not to mention angry.

Guess he couldn't blame her for that. 'I'm a doctor. Is it all right if I take a look and access the damage?'

Her eyes locked with his. Forest-green eyes, reminding him of long-ago summers spent walking in the hills. 'The front edge of that boy's board slammed directly into my talus. The pain was instant and excruciating. It's broken.'

Talus, eh? Not ankle bone. Then she knew a medical thing or two. With a sinking stomach he studied the extended foot. She was also probably right about the fracture. Unless she'd twisted her ankle as she'd fallen. 'I apologise for this. My sons tend to be over-exuberant about everything they do.' Understatement of the year, but he wasn't about to spill his guts and tell this woman that most days he struggled to cope with their antics. That was none of her business even if they were to blame for her current predicament.

Wow, she's beautiful.

Where the hell had that come from? He glanced around, saw nothing out of the ordinary, no one speaking over his shoulder. He returned to looking at the woman, sucking in a groan of raw need. Despite the pain distorting her face, she was drop-dead stunning. *Do the job and get her packed up and on the way to hospital. Do not think about anything else. This might be one stunning female but the point is she is a female and therefore nothing but trouble.*

'They were in a hurry,' said the woman, easily distracting him. Then she shifted on her butt and gasped. Her knuckles whitened as she clenched her hands and waited for the pain to subside. Despite the situation her voice held a gentle lilt, in the way a Southlander spoke.

'Scottish ancestry?' Now, why had he asked that? None of his business, and nothing to do with this foot that needed to be eased out of a worn slip-on shoe.

'Not a drop. Growing up at the bottom end of the country tends to mean we don't speak like the rest of you kiwis.'

The roll of her 'r's tickled him, warmed him. He'd always been a sucker for women with accents. Yeah, and look where that had got him.

He instantly refocused on the rapidly swelling ankle. He shouldn't need any reminders about beautiful women with sexy accents and how shallow they could turn out to be. 'I'll call the ambulance crew. They'll have nitrous oxide on board for you to suck on while they remove your shoe.' The knowing glint in her eyes told him she knew what nitrous oxide was. 'Andrew, get my phone. Now.'

'Yes, Dad.'

'Marcus, bring the cushions from the couch out here for the lady.'

'Yes, Dad. But we—'

'Do as I say.' His calm tone belied his anxiety for this woman and the annoyance that just for once his boys could've held back on arguing with him.

'Very obedient,' muttered the woman, as the boys disappeared inside the house.

You think? 'Only because they know they're in deep trouble right at this moment.' Cam gently straightened her leg, making sure he didn't jar that ankle. 'I'm Cameron Roberts, by the way. A GP at the local medical centre. Make that the only GP at the centre.'

'Jenny Bostock.' Her full lips pressed flat, and the green of her eyes dimmed as she stared over his shoulder as though trying to focus on something other than her ankle. Her hair might've originally been tied back in that band now hanging down her back, but it must've sprung free when she'd gone tumbling down in a heap. Thick, red waves cascaded over her shoulders, down her back, even over one side of her face.

Resisting the urge to lift the hair back from her cheek wasn't as easy as it should've been. But following up on that impulse could get him struck off the medical practitioners' register, if not a slap across her face. 'Are you visiting Havelock for the day or stopping on the way through?' *I am not being nosy, merely trying to distract you while I tend to this painful ankle.*

Blinking, she refocused on him. 'I crossed over on the ferry this morning and decided to take Queen Charlotte Drive instead of going direct to Blenheim. Then at Havelock I decided to take a walk along the main street before having lunch at that café beside the marina.'

'My sons have put paid to that idea. I'm very sorry. They get a bit carried away at times.' The only place she was going now was hospital.

'Double trouble, eh?' Those lips lifted into the semblance of a smile, surprising and warming him. The anger had abated. Hardly surprising given what she was coping with. She'd be focusing on dealing with the pain.

'Forget that saying. Whoever made it up hadn't had twins of their own. Try tenfold trouble.' He grimaced, then dug deep for a smile of his own, the movement of his mouth a little strained. 'But on the plus side I get ten times the love.'

'They came skating out of nowhere. Don't be too hard on them. For all I know, this could've been my fault. I was watching a boat heading out of the marina and not looking where I was going.'

'You're being kind. I've told them more times than I can count to be very careful of pedestrians. Not that we get many this end of town.'

'They're boys—of course they're not going to listen to you.'

'Don't I know it.' Time to lock those skateboards away till they learned to control their actions. 'Any numbness?' Cam asked, as he lightly tapped her foot. When she nodded he continued with, 'Want to try and move your foot?'

'Not really.' But her lips flattened and her eyes took on a determined look.

He knew the moment she tried by the spike of pain in her eyes. 'Stop. I'm sure you're right about this not being a sprain.'

'Here's the phone.' Andrew appeared on the other side of Jenny.

'I got the cushions.' His other boy scuttled along to join them, his arms laden with every cushion to be found in the house. Not many.

'Place them behind the lady one at a time. Careful. Don't bump her. You'll hurt her some more.' He wanted to growl at the boys, shout at them for being careless, but it seemed he did too much of that these days. His goal at the moment was to refrain from being a grump all the time. Maybe they'd learn from this accident without him reading them the riot act or banning the boards. They got so much fun out of skateboarding he hated to take that from them.

Jenny directed the placing of the cushions, talking softly to the boys like this happened to her every day. They lapped it up, tossing him a look that suggested he should be taking heed and learning something from this.

Standing up, Cam direct-dialled the volunteer ambulance chief. 'Hey, Braden, you're needed outside my gate. Lady with a suspected broken ankle needs pain relief and transport to Wairau.'

'Wairau?' Thick eyebrows rose as those forest eyes focused on him from down on the pavement.

His knees clicked as he hunched down again. 'Hospital in Blenheim. You need an X-ray and an orthopaedic surgeon's take on what that shows up.'

'There goes my catwalk career.' Was that a twinkle through the pain in her eyes?

Catwalk? Yep, come to think of it, those long, slim legs filling his view were made for modelling. *Thinking's not always wise,* said his brain, while his eyes cruised the length of her. The rest of her body was A1 too, topped off with that glorious hair and a face that could tempt a eunuch. *Which you pretty much are these days, boyo.* Given the chance, Jenny Bostock could certainly change his mind on avoiding the female half of the population. *So don't give her a chance.* He straightened up again, putting space between them. Hell, he was up and down like a yoyo.

Time to get practical. 'I presume you've got a car parked up somewhere around here. It can go in my garage until you're ready to drive again.' It was the least he could do, considering who'd had put her out of action.

Her fingers slid into the hip pocket of snug-fitting, mid-thigh-length shorts and tugged a key ring free. 'Red sports car, registration HGH 345, parked outside the woodcarver's.'

He nearly missed the keys as his gaze remained fixed on that hip. Catching them at the last moment, her words finally registered. Sports car, yeah, right. 'You're very trusting.' Which probably meant the vehicle was an old bomb in need of lots of repairs.

'Dr Cameron Roberts, Havelock GP. Shouldn't be too hard to track down. Anyway, I'm lying outside his front gate: 5C Rose Street.'

Far too observant. Just then he heard a siren. 'They're turning it on for you.'

'All ambos like to play with their bells and whistles, don't they? But I admit I'll be glad of that nitrous oxide. This is doing my head in.' A grimace tightened her mouth. She'd run out of smiles. Those bewitching eyes looked plain old tired now. Her attention to him and the boys had all been for show, something to take her mind off what was really happening.

'Should've asked you this sooner. Is there someone I can call for you? Get them to meet you at the hospital?'

Those eyes went blank as she withdrew completely. 'No, thanks.'

'You'll need to be picked up after the medical team has put you back together.'

'I'll sort it.' She looked away, but not before he saw desolation glittering out at the world. Then, 'Hi, guys. You come to get me? I hope you've brought lots of pain-killers.'

Braden and his sidekick, Lyn, jogged over with a stretcher, a cardboard splint, their medical kit and the tank of gas Jenny was longing for.

Cam said, 'Hi, guys. Meet Jenny Bostock.' Guilt assailed him again, this time brought on by that desolation she was busy trying to hide, and knowing if it hadn't been for his sons she wouldn't be in whatever predicament she now found herself.

'Dad, can we go to the shops?'

'We saw Mum get out of a car at the end of the road.'

His heart crashed. They'd seen their mother? There was more likelihood of pigs flying by. Would this ever stop? As if it wasn't enough that they'd broken this woman's ankle, they thought they'd seen their selfish mother. When would the boys accept that that particular woman had no intention of ever returning? Even if she deigned to drop by because she'd had a rush of oxygen to the brain, she certainly would not want two eight-year-olds interfering with her career plans.

'There isn't time. You're meant to be at the softball

juniors' Christmas party in an hour and you still have to clean your faces and put on decent clothes.'

The disappointment blinking out at him from two almost identical faces hurt as much as that broken ankle was hurting Jenny. Better he give it to them straight than have them walking up and down the short main street peering into every shop and café, looking for someone who was hundreds of k's away in the North Island. He hated having to be the big bad ogre breaking their hearts by telling them that when it was their mother who'd caused their anguish.

He looked away, his gaze encountering Jenny's as she drew in deep breaths of gas. This time he couldn't read the expression in those green eyes at all. He didn't try to guess because he wouldn't be seeing her again. Whatever she was thinking didn't matter.

Braden said, 'We'll be off as soon as we've got a splint on this here leg and loaded Jenny in the ambulance. You going to happy hour at the pub tonight?'

The fundraiser for the school swimming pool maintenance. 'That depends on what time the boys' Christmas do finishes and we get back here.' He and the kids had become experts at socialising, being invited to just about every celebration happening in Havelock. Anything from a cat's birthday to the theatre group's finishing night was an excuse to have fun around here. Which was fine, except when someone took it into their head to arrange a function in Blenheim, a thirty-minute drive away. Not far except when appointments were stacking up or, like at this time of year, there were too many social engagements to attend.

'Might see you later.' Braden and Lyn shifted their

patient onto the stretcher and rolled her across to the ambulance.

Cam followed, unable to walk away. 'I hope all goes well for you at Wairau, Jenny. And once again, I'm sorry for my boys' actions.'

Removing the gas inhaler from her mouth, she gave a semblance of a smile. 'Accidents happen all the time. I should've been looking where I was going.'

This woman was very quick to forgive. Not many people would've said that. A genuine, good-hearted lady? Or was the laughing gas mellowing that despair that had been glittering out from those suck-him-in eyes?

Watching the ambulance pull away and head towards the intersection, he felt a tug of longing he hadn't felt in years. Longing for what? Something about Jenny's bravery had caused it, made him feel he should be following in his car, going to the ED with her. Holding her hand? Yeah, right. Holding a beautiful woman's hand was so not on his agenda. He shrugged. Couldn't deny feeling responsible for her.

If there'd been someone with her, or even meeting her at the other end, he wouldn't be thinking like this. But it sounded like she was alone. So when she came out of hospital, where would she go? How would she get there? She hadn't been carrying a bag, wasn't wearing a jacket with pockets to hold money or credit cards. Or a phone. Just the keys she'd handed him to the car he had to retrieve and park at home. He swore, once, softly. He was going to have to deliver her bag to her.

He spied the boys carrying the cushions up the drive, flicking him worried looks from under their too-long hair, having obviously heard his bad language but not willing to tell him off as they normally did. At least

they'd got the seriousness of the situation. He sighed.
Time to get moving if they weren't to be late for the party.

Oh, and note to self: arrange for two haircuts at the
hair salon on Monday afternoon after school.

CHAPTER TWO

JENNY STARED AROUND the ED and shivered. 'I want out of here. Like now.'

Not going to happen. The ED specialist had told her what she'd already suspected—that he was waiting for an orthopaedic surgeon to come in and look at her X-rays, and who knew when that would be. Apparently the surgeon had been out fishing on Queen Charlotte Sound when the ED staff had eventually got hold of him.

Waiting patiently wasn't her forte any more. And waiting in an ED was cruel. There'd been a time she'd loved nothing more than turning up for her shift in the emergency department. She'd thrived on the heightened anticipation brought on when waiting for the unknown to come through the doors, and by helping put people back together after some disaster had befallen them. 'Yeah, well, you turned out to be useless at that, didn't you?'

The ED was full to overflowing. The adjacent cubicle wasn't completely curtained off, leaving her open to scrutiny from a blue-eyed toddler with curls to die for. A young man lay on the bed in obvious pain, after apparently coming off his farm bike and being pinned underneath for an hour until his wife had found him. The injuries couldn't be life-threatening or he'd be in Theatre already.

'Up.' A very imperious tone for someone so young.

'No, Emma, leave the lady alone.' The child's mother snatched her out of reach to plonk her on a chair by the man's bed. 'I'm sorry about that,' said the harried woman.

'No problem.' Jenny dredged up a smile and watched as the little girl clambered off the chair the moment her mother's attention left her.

'You all right there?' asked a chirpy trainee nurse from the other side of Jenny's bed. Too happy for her own good. 'Anything I can get you?'

Didn't they teach nursing students not to tease their patients? 'I'd kill for a strong coffee right about now.'

'Nil by mouth, I'm sorry. At least until after Mr Mc-Namara has seen you, and then only if you're not having surgery.'

'I totally get it. It's called wishful thinking.' Talk about getting more than her share of apologies today. Cameron Roberts had looked and sounded more than apologetic, with tiredness and stress blinking out at her from those coffee-brown eyes peeking from under a mass of wayward blond curls. Bet those gorgeous twins were more than a handful. Trouble and twins were synonymous. She had first-hand experience of that.

The nurse smoothed the already smooth bedcover. 'If you want anything, call me. There are some magazines lying around somewhere but they're years out of date.'

'I'm fine.' She could pretend, couldn't she?

'Great.' The student flashed another smile and went to charm another patient, leaving her in relative peace to contemplate her situation. Which was looking rather dire.

Stuck. That's what she was. Stopped in her tracks, all because of a boy on an out-of-control skateboard. He'd wrecked everything. Like she'd slammed into a brick wall and there was no way round. She'd wanted to yell at those boys, tell them they should've been looking where they were going, not shouting and taunting each other to go faster. She did remember turning to see what the noise was about seconds before the boy—Marcus?—had crashed into her. But in all reality she'd been miles away, unaware of much except that boat heading out and the sun on her face.

The boys had looked so repentant. They'd also appeared as if they'd had enough of being told off and wanted to be given a break. She totally knew what that was like. How many times had she and Alison driven Mum insane with their mischief? Cameron Roberts hadn't known she knew what she was talking about. 'Bet I could teach those boys a thing or two about being naughty.'

Then an image of Cam's tired and frustrated expression slipped into her mind and she retracted that thought. The man didn't need any more problems.

'Emma? What's the matter, baby?' In the next cubicle the mother's panic was immediately apparent. 'Why's she gone so red? Emma. She's not breathing.'

Jenny swung her legs over the side of the bed, ground her teeth on the flare of pain. 'I'm a doctor. Pass her here.' One look at the child's terrified face, which only minutes ago had been grinning at her, had Jenny reaching back to slam her hand against the emergency button on the wall behind her bed. 'What was she playing with?'

'I'm not sure. Cotton balls, I think.'

Grabbing the child from the distraught mother's arms, Jenny ran a finger around the inside of her mouth, scooped out sodden cotton balls. Had the child swallowed any? 'Does Emma have any allergies that you know of?' she demanded.

'No.'

Emma definitely wasn't breathing. Instantly laying the child over her knees with her head hanging down, Jenny began striking the child firmly between the shoulder blades with the flat of her hand. Strike one. Two. Come on, baby. Breathe for me. Three. Please. Four. Please, please, please. Five. Where are the doctors? Check the resp rate. The tiny chest wasn't moving at all.

Jenny knew the mother was screaming at her but she ignored her, focused on saving this little girl. Quickly standing on her good foot, ignoring the pain slicing up her leg, she held Emma around her waist and located her belly button with her finger.

'What's going on?' A doctor raced into the cubicle, followed by two nurses.

At last. But handing over now meant wasting precious seconds. Jenny fisted one hand. 'This child appears to have choked. No resp rate. I've done five back strikes.' Oh. Tell him. 'I am an ED doctor.' I *was* an ED doctor. Her fist thrust upward into Emma's abdomen. One. Two. Emma coughed hard and a small round object shot across the floor.

'A lid off a pill bottle by the look of it.' One of the nurses retrieved it from under the next bed.

The doctor took the now crying and bewildered child from Jenny's arms and laid her on the bed. 'Shh, sweetheart. You're going to be all right.' He looked over his shoulder at the crying woman and the frantic father trying to get off his bed. 'Mum? Come and hold your little girl while I examine her. What's her name?'

'Emma.' The mother scooped up her baby and held her tight.

'Easy. I need to give her a complete exam. Nurse, bring me a child's blanket. Jason, get back on that bed. You shouldn't be moving. You'll start that wound bleeding again.' The doctor turned back to his little patient and gave her a quick but thorough going over. 'She's going to be fine, thanks to this doctor.'

The mother had lost all colour in her cheeks. 'Thank you so much, all of you. If you hadn't done what you did…' She swallowed.

Jenny eased her butt back onto her bed. The pain in her ankle had intensified now that she wasn't being distracted. 'Don't go there,' she advised with a smile she hoped wasn't a grimace as pain stabbed repeatedly. 'Instead be glad you were here and not at home when it happened.'

Within minutes the department had returned to normal. Except for the hiccups in the next cubicle as the mother slowly calmed down, only muted voices could be heard once more.

With a sigh Jenny lay back. Talk about having the day from hell. But a broken ankle was low on the scale of urgency and really she was incredibly lucky. Euphoria nudged her despair aside. That child would've been saved by any of the doctors or nurses on duty but she'd done it. Her old instincts had kicked in instantly. She hadn't had to spend precious moments trying to recall the procedure. It had been there, lying in some unused corner of her brain waiting to be summoned.

It was good to know she still had it, even though she wasn't about to do anything stupid like go back to being a doctor. Yet the words 'I'm a doctor' had spilled off her tongue without thought. If she had stopped to consider that, she'd probably have handed Emma to another medic and lost precious seconds.

Wriggling further back against the pillows, she wondered what she'd do once she was discharged. Originally she'd planned on staying in Blenheim for a couple of nights and visiting the vineyards she'd gone to with Alison two years ago and having a glass of her sister's favourite bubbly.

Did she still stop here until she was capable of getting around again? Doing what? Reading, eating, sleeping. Boring. What about going to Havelock? Her chuckle was humourless. Less than five hundred people lived there. So not her, a place like that. All too soon the locals would start saying hello, and then asking how her day was going. She shuddered. Face it. Stopping for more than three nights anywhere was so not her at the moment. But as of now she was no longer on the move.

Almost six months on the road hadn't solved anything, hadn't given her the forgiveness she ached for, hadn't brought her any closer to accepting what had happened.

This road trip had just about run its course anyway. There were only two more stops to go. Yeah, well, like climbing mountainsides in the Kahurangi National Park was going to happen now. Saying goodbye to Alison might have to wait another year.

Tears welled up, spilled down her face. 'So sorry, sis. I intended being at the place where you left me on the first anniversary.' Now that final goodbye had been taken from her in a single hit. A little like Alison's death. One fall off a mountainside and she'd gone. For ever.

'You look like you could do with some company.'

Now, that wasn't a memory. That voice was from three hours ago. Ducking her head further down to hide her face, she croaked around her clogged throat, 'Dr Cameron Roberts.' Who didn't sound overly pleased to be here. Surprise, surprise.

'You remembered, then. Most people call me Cam.'

She'd always had a phenomenal memory. Right down to the very last word Alison had ever said to her. She drew a deep breath, and put Alison to one side—for now at least. 'You can't find the location of the boys' Christmas party?'

He sat on the edge of her bed without asking. At least he was careful not to disturb her broken foot. 'Safely delivered and for once I'm not putting on the red suit and handing out parcels to over-excited kids.'

'Sounds like fun all round.' She looked up, momentarily forgetting about her tears.

'Hey, you're crying.' He looked nonplussed, like crying women threw him.

Sure am. 'Guess it's just a reaction to finding myself in here, instead of enjoying that lunch down on the marina.' Telling a virtual stranger the truth would sound like she was looking for sympathy and that was the very last thing she intended. She didn't deserve it, for starters. 'Don't mind me. I'm fine, really.'

He looked relieved. Because the tears hadn't become a torrent? 'I hear you're waiting for Angus McNamara to show up.'

'Is he any good?' Like, hello? What choice did she have?

'You don't except me to say otherwise, do you?' Cam was still watching her closely, but now a small smile slowly appeared, like he wasn't used to smiling.

'Not really.' He should try the smile thing more often as it turned an already good-looking face into something beyond handsome. Her stomach sucked in and her heart knocked gently against her ribs, as if to say, Hey, sit up and take note. He's one cool dude. *Except, dear heart, the man has a wife. Those boys mentioned seeing their mother.* She shifted a little and groaned, grinding out, 'You'd tell me if I'd be better off seeing a chainsaw specialist, wouldn't you?'

Cam grimaced with her then told her, 'Angus is very good.' He swung her car keys between them. 'The car's parked in my garage, out of the way. I brought in your case. Thought you'd want a change of clothes some time.' Thoughtful as well as a hunk. 'It's in the ED office until they know whether you're having surgery or just getting a proper splint and crutches.'

'Would you mind putting the keys in my case? Losing them would only give me another headache to deal with.'

'Sure.' Cam stared thoughtfully at a spot somewhere around his feet. 'If you're discharged, where will you go?'

She had no idea. 'Yesterday I looked up motels in Blenheim and found heaps of vacancies so I didn't bother making a booking. I'll phone around when I know what's going on here.'

'You sure that's what you want to do? You could catch a flight home as soon as they kick you out of here.' The question in his eyes asked where home was.

She wasn't answering it. 'I'll be fine. Lots of options, really.' She played mental ping-pong. A motel where she'd have to get take-out delivered because of her inability to move around? Or a flight out to where? Which town would she settle in and pretend it felt like home until she was okay to move on again? According to some, home was where the heart was, and her heart was lost right now.

At the moment all her worldly possessions were locked up in a container in a storage yard in Auckland, no doubt going mouldy. She suspected that after her road trip she'd like somewhere new to start again.

'I'll leave you my numbers so you can call me if you want anything else out of your car.'

'Thanks.' The carton of medical journals could wait a month or so. The hiking boots, running shoes and camping gear were absolutely useless at the moment. Blink,

blink. *Stop feeling sorry for yourself. It's a broken ankle, not a catastrophe, even if you are stuck here for a while.* Her gaze drifted to Cam, over his expansive chest and on down to the long legs stretched half across the cubicle. 'How did you manage to get behind the steering wheel of my car? Your knees must've been up around your ears.'

'That's something I'm used to. Though driving a sports car was a novelty, even if only for half a kilometre. The boys couldn't believe what they were seeing when I pulled up at home.'

'I can picture their faces.' She continued checking him out. *Why?* She had no idea.

This guy spent time in the sun. His skin had a mouth-watering tan. Those calf muscles were well honed. Her stomach squeezed. *Settle.* The last thing she needed right now was to get interested in a man. She had nothing to offer anyone. She ran on empty all the time. Anyway, this particular man was taken. *Remember?* Remember. 'You look fit. You run?' Why was she even asking? He'd disappear any minute and that would be the end of that.

Surprise widened his eyes. 'It's the one thing that keeps me sane some days.'

She'd focus on his running, nothing else. 'That can't be easy with only a handful of short streets or the main highway to pound out on.' An hour in Havelock had been ample time to get the idea of how small the place was.

'I use Queen Charlotte Drive. The hill's a bit of a grunter but the traffic moves at a far slower pace than out on the main road. Sometimes the boys cycle with me. I'd never take them on the main road. Too many large trucks rolling through all the time.'

'Your boys are cute.' Where was their mother? Had she gone to the party with them?

'Don't you dare tell them that. They absolutely hate

anyone using the "cute" word.' Another smile, more expansive this time, lifted his mouth into a delicious curve and lightened the brown of his eyes.

'They're strong-willed?'

Cam nodded his head slowly. 'Unfortunately, yes.'

'You'd want your kids to be pushovers?' she asked, wondering exactly why he'd dropped by. She wasn't his patient or his friend.

His sigh filled with sadness as the smile switched off and his gaze dulled. 'They're a funny mix of strong and soft. Kind of nice, I guess, but there are things I wish they were stronger about.'

If only she knew how to wipe away that look, bring back the warm smile. But it wasn't her place. They were strangers who were going to remain so. 'I'm sure all parents think that.' How enlightening. Not.

'You got kids?' His question was nothing startling, fitted into their conversation, and yet it arrowed in for her heart.

'No.' She'd always hoped she'd get married and have a family. That had been part of her life plan, along with the medical career, the extended travel to Europe and watching Alison achieve her goal to become an international airline pilot. Except Alison had died because *she* had failed as a doctor. Her new life plan was waiting to be rewritten, but one thing she knew for certain was that having a family would be a part of it. Losing her sister had heightened that need.

'Hello, Cam. Didn't expect to find you here. You know my patient?' A middle-aged man strode around the curtain and stopped at the end of her bed.

'Not really. My boys are responsible for this. A skateboarding accident of no mean proportions.'

'Ouch.' The casually presented man turned to her. 'I'm Angus, your surgeon.'

She held out her hand. 'Jenny Bostock. Should I be asking if you caught any fish? Or will that make you go a little harder on me?' Plastering on a smile she didn't feel much like making, she watched closely to see how he reacted to her.

'Your timing was perfect. Dinner's ready and waiting in the fridge at home. Blue cod. The best fish in our waters, as far as I'm concerned.' His friendly smile faded. 'I've seen your X-rays. The lower tibia has a fine fracture, but it's the talus that needs attending to, I'm afraid. You require plates to be attached.'

'That's what I expected.' And didn't want. But there was nothing she could do about it, except rewind the clock four hours and stay in her car, instead of walking around Havelock.

'Do you want me to outline the whole procedure, *Dr* Bostock?' The surgeon emphasised her title.

Beside him, Cam lifted his eyebrows. 'So you are a doctor. I wondered if you were.'

'Angus has been reading my admission slip.' She should've put dog walker or cleaning lady but some habits didn't disappear, even after six months. 'Anyway, it was irrelevant to the situation. I'm presuming you'd have treated me the same, no matter what my job was.'

Cam shrugged. 'Of course.'

She didn't go around telling anyone she was a doctor. People might ask her to treat them or give them advice, and they really didn't need that from her. But when it came to filling in paperwork she tended to honest. Just in case she ever got her life back on track.

'Jenny—I can call you that?' The surgeon's eyebrow rose in query.

'Sure.'

'Jenny's being coy. I'm surprised you haven't heard how she saved a child who was choking not more than thirty minutes ago. Everyone's talking about her.'

Cam's eyes widened. 'Truly? That's awesome. I have to say you seem to have a habit of finding yourself in the middle of trouble. Is that usual? Or is today the exception?'

Define trouble. Crossing her fingers, she muttered, 'It's been one of those days when I shouldn't have got out of bed.'

'Well, you're back in one now.' Cam's smile was cheeky, warming her where she didn't want to be warmed. Right around her heart.

'Right.' Angus became brisk. 'Let's get this under way. The anaesthetist should be here any minute. I'll head over to Theatre and wait for you there.' He flicked the curtain wide to stride out.

Cam took his cue. 'I'd better go and check on those boys of mine, see what other mischief they've managed to get themselves into.'

She called after him, 'Thanks for dropping by. I'll sort out what to do about my car when I'm a bit more mobile. I'll give you a buzz some time tomorrow. Is that okay?'

'It can stay where it is for weeks, if necessary. Call me if you want anything else.' He was only being helpful to a stranger for whom his boys had caused trouble. It was there in his eyes, in the now flat smile he gave.

'Thanks.' Suddenly she didn't want him to go. Her fingers picked at the sheet covering her. The idea of being anaesthetised made her feel tetchy. All the what-if scenarios popped into her mind. Surgery was not without its risks. *So talk to Cam, ask him questions about anything at all to keep him here for a bit.*

'I can hang around until Sheree gets here.' So he read minds.

'Sheree?'

'The anaesthetist on duty this weekend.' His butt sank back onto the edge of the bed. 'In what field of medicine do you practise?'

The down side of having him stay was fielding the unwanted questions. 'Emergency.'

'You feel weird, being an ED patient?' Those eyebrows rose again.

Kind of cute when they did that. Did *he* like the 'cute' word? Why was she even asking herself that? The man had a family, wasn't available. But it had been a long time since she'd been interested in a man that way. 'Not weird, just scary being on the receiving end of all the attention.'

'I had keyhole surgery for appendicitis ten months ago. If it hadn't been for the pain and knowing how fast the whole thing could've turned bad, I'd have bailed out of having the operation. Call me a wimp, but I knew everything that was going to happen, and that made it worse.'

'You mean you understood what could go wrong.' Like she did.

A big, warm hand covered hers. 'You'll be fine. Sheree and Angus know what they're doing. The worst of this will come afterwards, when you can't get around easily. I could send my boys in to be your slaves for as long as it takes to get back on your feet.' His brow crinkled. 'They're not very good at cooking, or cleaning, or making decent coffee. Great at fetching and carrying, though.'

Surprised he could joke with her, the nervousness took a step back. 'You make them sound like puppies. Fetch, Booboo.' The warmth seeping into her from that small contact made her relax even more. Then she tensed.

Tugged her hand free. *He has a wife.* 'Thanks for your concern, but I'm fine. Really.'

Cam's gaze cruised over her face, studying her intently. Looking for what? Then with a brief nod he stood up. 'I can hear Sheree talking out there. I'll head away. Take care.'

She stared at the curtain long after he'd gone. What would it be like to have Cameron Roberts to come home to at the end of a busy day in the department? *Excuse me, you don't work in an ED any more. You don't work at all. As for coming home to that particular man, you must be high on laughing gas. He's taken, remember?*

A girl was allowed to dream, wasn't she?

CHAPTER THREE

JENNY WOKE TO a nurse pumping a blood-pressure cuff wrapped around her arm. 'Did I miss the party?'

The nurse frowned. 'Party?'

'The dry mouth and fuzzy head.'

An easy smile. 'The revolting after-effects of anaesthetic. Your blood pressure's normal. I need to take your temperature.' A thermometer was slipped into her mouth as the nurse continued to talk. 'Breakfast will be along shortly. You've got visitors, too.'

'Visitors?' Jenny spluttered around the glass stick between her lips. 'I don't know—' Anyone except Cam and his boys. 'Oh.'

'Those boys are so gorgeous.' Then the girl winked. 'Just like their dad.'

'True.' It had to be post-op trauma that made her agree. 'Does Mr McNamara do rounds on Sundays?'

'He phoned earlier to say he'd drop by to see you this morning.'

'Hey, sunshine, you're looking more comfortable,' Cam called from the doorway. 'Up to visitors? As in three of us?'

'You bet.' Shuffling up the bed, she pulled the sheet up to her throat and settled back on the pillows the nurse rearranged at her back. Sunshine, eh? More like a disaster zone, with hair that hadn't been brushed and probably yesterday's mascara making dark smudges under her eyes. But it felt inordinately good to see him.

Cam stepped into the tiny room, followed by his sons carefully carrying coffee and something smelling suspiciously like a hot croissant.

'Hello, guys. Is that for me?'

They nodded in unison. 'Yes.'

'You're crackerjacks, you know that? I've been hanging out for a proper coffee since I arrived in this place.' To think she could've blown this by venting her anger at them yesterday.

'There's a bacon and egg thing, too.' One of them held out the bag to her.

'Bacon and egg croissant,' the other explained.

'Okay, tell me, is there a trick to knowing who's Marcus and who's Andrew?' They were darned near identical, though now that she was looking for differences she could see one of the boys had a tiny scar on his chin. Tapping it gently, she asked, 'What happened there?'

'Marcus pushed me off the swing when we were little.'

'Gotcha. You're Andrew.' Now all she had to do was remember to look for that pale scar every time she bumped into these two scallywags. Like how often would that happen?

Andrew smiled a bigger, more impish version of that smile his father had given her yesterday when he'd visited the ED. 'Marcus has got a scar on his bottom.'

'Have not.' The other twin stuck his chin out and glared at his brother.

'Have too.' Andrew scowled and made to haul his brother's shorts down.

Cam stepped in. 'That's enough, boys. We came to visit, not turn the ward into a war zone.'

Jenny felt something oddly like laughter beginning to bubble up. When was the last time she'd laughed? 'Better than the boring place it is at the moment. So how was your party? Did Santa Claus bring presents?'

'Santa Claus isn't real. He's—'

'Just an old man dressed up funny.'

Her breath hitched. A lump blocked her throat. She and Alison used to finish each other's sentences. Oh, boy, this just got hard. Harder. *Think of something to say. They're all staring at you.* 'Bet you accepted the presents he gave you.'

'Of course. They are cool. I got a remote-control plane.'

'I got a helicopter.'

'Pilots, eh? Have you been flying in real planes?' She wanted to tell them how cute they were but knew not to if she wanted to remain friends with them, and, strangely, despite that little glitch over the way they shared sentences, she found she did. Though the chances of seeing them again once they walked out of here were very remote.

Cam was shaking his head at the three of them. 'Don't any of you come up for air?'

All three of them shook their heads and smiled at Cam, who said, 'Great, so I'm the only sensible, sane one around here. Jenny, do you want milk for your coffee? Sugar? I can scrounge some off the nurses.'

'Milk and sugar would be good.'

'Dad, can we bring our presents to show her?' Marcus—or was it Andrew?—asked. They weren't directly facing her so there were no identifying marks in sight.

'The lady has a name. Miss…' His brow wrinkled as he glanced at her hands. 'Miss Bostock, or Dr Bostock.'

Jenny locked gazes with him, and felt a nudge in the

pit of her stomach. He really was gorgeous. She hadn't been imagining it through the haze of nitrous oxide. 'I'm happy with Jenny, unless you object.' Definitely not Dr. She didn't deserve that title any more.

He shrugged. 'No problem. Okay, lads, give Jenny the food and coffee. No, don't climb on the bed. She has a very sore foot.'

Instantly Marcus's smile disappeared and his head dropped forward. 'I'm sorry.'

So was she, but it had happened and grumping about it wouldn't make him feel good. Wouldn't do her any favours either. Leaning forward, she raised the boy's head with her hand under his chin so he had to look at her. 'Listen to me. It was an accident. You didn't mean it, did you?' His head slid from side to side. 'You didn't see me and I didn't see you. I was watching the fishing boat out on the water. So let's not worry about this again. Okay?'

Marcus nodded and looked at his dad. 'She's nice, Dad. I like her.'

Heat seeped into her cheeks, probably making her usually pale face resemble a stop light. That was the nicest thing anyone had said to her in a long while. She could even feel tears collecting in the back of her eyes. Great. Crying twice in less than twenty-four hours. Cam would think she should be in the mental health ward and rush his boys away.

'Breakfast time,' called an older woman, as she pushed in a cart that rattled with plates and cups.

Saved by the cart. 'Can I have some milk and sugar, please?'

'Certainly. Your family brought in some decent coffee for you. That's lovely. Here, lads, hand Mum the milk, will you?'

Marcus stared at the woman with his mouth open and

something like anguish in his brown eyes, while Andrew took the plastic bottle and passed it to Jenny, looking bemused but not upset.

'She's not our mother,' he informed the woman. 'She hurt herself on our skateboard so we're visiting.'

'That's nice of you. Is that breakfast in that bag? It will probably be tastier than the cereal I've got here for Dr Bostock.' With the number of patients she saw every day the woman would be used to making similar mistakes.

Cam finally got a word in. 'Jenny, do you want the hospital breakfast? We won't be insulted if you do.'

She shook her head. 'Just the milk and sugar, thanks, Sadie.' A quick read of the name badge pinned to the woman's ample chest earned her another smile.

'Here you go, then.'

Then another voice spoke from the doorway. 'Good morning, Jenny.' Angus strolled into the room, dressed in light slacks and a T-shirt. 'Morning, Cam, boys. How's everyone today?'

It was getting to be like a bus station in here. She looked around, found everyone watching her, waiting for her to answer. 'I'm good. Not that I've got out of bed yet so I've no idea how I'll go on crutches.'

'Crutches?' The twins' eyes lit up.

She grinned at them. Their innocent sense of fun made her feel good about a lot of things. 'It's going to be exciting driving my car, don't you think?'

'Time we left Jenny alone.' Cam headed for the door. 'She's got to talk to Mr McNamara.'

Disappointment tugged. With all the chatter between her and the twins Cam hadn't said a lot, and now she wished for a rerun of the minutes they'd all been here. This time she'd talk to Cam, find out more about living in Havelock, just because it would be a safe subject and she could listen to his deep, husky voice. But they were already on the way through the door, the boys pushing each other.

'Cam,' she called. 'Thanks for dropping by. I appreciate it.'

He turned a steady gaze her way, that anguish under control. 'I could leave the boys with you for the day if you want company.'

I'd like that. I really would. They're gorgeous fun. One day, Jenny, one day in the distant future. 'Guess the ward staff might have something say about that.'

'So would you after the first hour. We'd better not keep Angus waiting. He's dressed for golf, I'd say.'

'You're not wrong, Cam. I won't be long with Jenny if you want to wait.'

Cam shook his head. 'We've got things to do in town. I want to be done and home before the temperature really cranks up. It's hot out there already.' Cam turned to her again. 'See you later.'

Really? He'd drop by again? She nodded, afraid if she spoke the sudden lump in her throat might dissolve into tears. She was so used to being on her own it was like being knocked in the back of the knees to have had the Roberts trio turn up here to see her. Watching Cam walk away, she drank in the sight of his broad shoulders and a very tidy butt clad in khaki chinos.

Angus cleared his throat and she turned her attention back to him. 'What happens next? Am I out of here this morning?'

'Have you got anywhere to go?'

'Yes.' They had taxis in Blenheim, didn't they?

The surgeon was shaking his head. 'You'll have to do better than that. Your admittance form gave a post box number—in Dunedin.'

Caught. 'I'm staying in a motel.'

'Which one?'

Hell. What was the name of one she'd checked out on line two days ago? The Grape Castle? The Vineyard Retreat? Her shoulders slumped. 'I'll make a booking before I leave here.'

'That will be tomorrow at the earliest. If you had someone to take care of you I'd discharge you today, but I don't want you tottering around on your own until you've got the hang of using crutches. Anyway, you shouldn't be walking anywhere, even across a room, until the swelling's gone down, and I suspect checking into a motel would involve more movement than I would be happy with.'

'Give me all the gory details and then go and enjoy that round of golf. I'll stay put. For now.'

The look he gave her suggested he didn't trust her to behave. Neither did she, but she'd keep that to herself. By the time Angus had filled her in on the operation and written a prescription for painkillers she no longer had the energy to get out of bed. Round one to the surgeon.

The moment they got home Cam headed for the third, and rarely used, bedroom. He'd made his mind up. It was probably the dumbest thing he'd contemplated in a long line of dumb things but, hey, he'd do it anyway. 'Guys, come and give me a hand.'

Marcus and Andrew appeared in the doorway in a flash. 'What are you doing, Dad?'

'I want you to take all these books and toys and store them in your bedroom. In the back of the wardrobe if necessary.'

'Why?' came the usual question.

Because he'd seen despair in Jenny Bostock's eyes at

the mention of sorting out what to do with her car tomorrow when she'd no doubt be feeling like hell on crutches. Plus because she seemed filled with sadness and loneliness, something he could understand. What he should be taking notice of was that restless expression that trawled through her gaze at times.

That expression he'd seen all too often in Margaret's eyes in the months before she'd packed her bags and left them, except Margaret had been more of a caged lioness waiting to attack the world, whereas Jenny looked lost. A few days bunked down in Havelock wouldn't hurt her. His heart sighed. As long as that didn't hurt him.

There was something indefinable about Jenny that teased him. Beyond her physical attributes, that was. Despite that frailty he sensed a selflessness and a need to put things right. Would a woman like that walk out on her man after vowing to love him for ever?

'Dad, why are we cleaning this room?'

'Because I'm going to ask Jenny if she'd like to stay with us for a while.'

'Yay, that's cool.' The boys leapt into the air and high-fived each other. 'We like her.'

'She didn't tell us off or get mad or anything like that.'

That was the final reason he'd invite her. A thank-you and an apology. 'You're very lucky she's such an understanding lady.' He was curious why she hadn't immediately revealed to him that she was a doctor. Had something gone wrong with a case that had led to that sadness leaking out of her eyes and dulling her face when she'd thought no one was watching her? It would have to be bad for her to stop practising, if that's what she'd done. It was a rocky road at times, being a doctor.

Cam picked up a pile of books and handed them to Marcus. 'Put those away.'

Andrew lifted an even bigger pile and staggered after his twin. Warmth stole through Cam. They really were great kids. If only he didn't get so tired and busy, and forget that sometimes.

Within minutes they were back scooping up armloads of toys and traipsing out again. Getting ahead of him and what he had to do to make this room habitable for Jenny. Even as he pulled off the bedcovers and began spreading freshly laundered sheets the doubts nudged at the corner of his mind. What if he was making an idiot of himself? Jenny might think he was making a move on her and that would lead to all sorts of difficulties. But, seriously, the most likely scenario would be her laughing and telling him she could manage on her own.

She probably could, but her vulnerability had nudged him, made him sit up and take notice, had got him trying to read what was going on behind those beautiful big eyes she'd often turned on him. Eyes that turned him on. Talk about another reason not to invite her here.

'Do I need this when I've already got more to cope with than I can manage?' But guilt was a heavy taskmaster. He owed her. 'You sure that's what's behind this mad idea?'

'What did you say, Dad?'

'Talking to myself. Sorry, mate.' He might be overloaded with work and kids, but he couldn't walk away from Jenny. He'd invite her to come to Havelock, and then it was up to her.

Lighten up, Cameron. You are entitled to some fun, too. Really? *Really.*

Note to self: ask Mrs Warner to do the grocery shopping earlier this week in case there's an extra mouth to feed.

* * *

'Where do you think you're going?' Cam shoved his hands in his pockets and rested a shoulder against the doorframe of Jenny's hospital room, watching as she leaned against the bed. So slim, yet physically as strong as a whippet. The frailty was in her eyes, not her body.

Her head shot up so fast he heard vertebrae click, saw her wince. 'Don't sneak up on me like that.' Guilt darkened those green eyes glittering at him fiercely, reminding him of the sea when the kahawai were churning it up as they chased smaller fish.

'You were so engrossed in being stealthy you didn't hear me coming along the ward.' He couldn't hold back his smile any longer. It had been growing from the moment he'd seen her juggling her crutches and trying to pick up her bag from the chair. Which really should be a warning to hightail it out of there, instead of getting involved with her. He should be thinking apology here, not getting up close and interested in Jenny Bostock, pretty woman and sometime doctor.

'I was not.' Her turn to smile, though hers appeared very strained.

Shaking his head at her, he crossed to pick up her case himself. 'Give up arguing with me. I live with two experts, remember?'

'Where are you taking my case?' All pretence of smiling disappeared. 'Seriously, Cam, what do you think you're doing?'

'Taking you home.' So much for finesse. That must've gone down the plughole with the dishwater that morning. Had he thought he could railroad her into coming along quietly? If he had then he needed a brain scan. 'We have a spare bedroom available. You can hole up there for as long as you like. Once you're mobile again, as in using those crutches with more aptitude, we have cafés and a bakery, jewellery and fudge shops, all for you get lost in for hours on end.'

'I don't do shops. Not lately, at any rate. Though the café could be a plus.' Bewilderment etched her face. Maybe a bit of hope was in there, too. 'Is there a motel in Havelock?'

Had he really expected her to be thrilled about this? 'Backpackers' accommodation only.'

'Oh.' Her gaze dropped from him to her case and then to her crutches. She seemed to be weighing up her options.

He helped her along with making up her mind. 'The boys have got your room ready. They're really excited about having a visitor, even a practically useless one who won't be playing cricket on the front lawn any time soon.'

'You play dirty.' Her forefinger tapped the handle of one of the crutches.

Not normally, but he couldn't walk out of here leaving Jenny to her own devices. She was ill prepared to go it alone for the next few days. 'Trying to make it easier for you to accept. You can leave any time you like, straight after dinner if you want to.'

'I see.' Tap, tap, tap went her finger on the crutch. 'What about your wife? Or did you bully her into this as well?'

Now who was playing dirty? 'I'm divorced.' Was he a slow learner, or what? Jenny was gorgeous, but she might not be any more trustworthy than his ex had been. So what? This was going to be a brief stay, not a lifelong one.

She sucked in air. 'I'm sorry, but I needed to know. Not about your divorce but that I wasn't treading on anyone's toes.'

'You're not treading on anything at the moment,' Cam quipped, in an effort to dispel his unease, but then thoughtlessly asked, 'You heard the boys saying they'd seen their mother yesterday?'

'Yes.'

'They hadn't. She lives in Auckland, last I heard.' That's all she needed to know. Probably out-of-date news anyway.

'That must be hard for all of you. Do they make a habit of seeing their mum in places she's not?'

'Unfortunately, yes. Margaret—my ex—left rather abruptly two years ago.' That's definitely all he was saying. Jenny had cleverly sidetracked him from his mission. 'Jenny, you are in a bind, partly due to my sons' antics. I don't know why you don't want to go home, wherever that is, but I'm more than happy to help you out until you're up and running again. That's all I'm offering. Though be warned, life in our house is hectic and noisy, but during the day you'll have peace and quiet while the boys are at school. Take it or leave it.'

He studied her small case. She travelled light, if this and what was in her car was anything to go by. His sisters would think Jenny needed lessons on what to take away on a trip, but then she'd need a truck, not a sports car.

She swung the crutches, took two wonky steps. Her eyes locked with his as she tipped her head to one side. Sizing him up?

He went for broke, lifted the case and headed for the door. 'Coming?'

The silence was deafening. He kept walking, slowly so that if she decided to join him she wouldn't feel compelled to hurry. Why so little luggage? Those medical journals in her boot were hardly scintillating reading for a trip.

Clump, thump. She was moving, hopping on those sticks. Clump, thump.

Cam relaxed and kept walking, slowing even more.

Clump, thump.

Warmth spread through him. Jenny was coming home with him. He hadn't realised how much he wanted this until faced with the real possibility she'd turn him down. Being pushy had worked.

'I guess Havelock is as good a place to be as Blenheim.'

'Better, as far as I'm concerned. More community spirited.' Something he'd come to appreciate. It had taken time for him to get used to living in such a small place after spending ten years in Wellington. Nowadays he doubted he'd cope with the stress of city living with two young boys to keep a firm hand on.

'Only until I've got the hang of these damned things.' Bang, bang, the crutches slammed down on the floor. 'A couple of days at the most.'

'Sure.' The warmth spread. He'd asked out of guilt and yet now he was feeling good about the whole situation. *Steady, boy, steady. You might've leapt into the deepest part of the pond and have no way of surviving.*

'There she is.'

'Hello, Jenny. Are you coming to our house?' The twins mobbed her, threatening her precarious balance.

But before Cam got a word out Jenny was laughing with them and saying, 'How can I refuse that welcome?'

He hadn't got a laugh, or even a thank you. Did he need to take lessons from his sons on how to get onside with a pretty woman?

'Boys, wait here with Jenny while I bring the car to the door. Mind those crutches, will you?'

As he stepped out into the sunshine he heard Marcus asking, 'Can we have a go on the crutches later? They're cool.'

Unfortunately the doors slid shut before he heard Jenny's reply, but something told him she'd have agreed. She got on with the boys so easily. As long as she didn't get too close and they got hurt when she left. He'd knew too well the devastation their mother had caused them when she'd walked away. But what were the odds Jenny would stay more than a night, two at the most? How attached could Marcus and Andrew get in that short time?

How attached would he get? He so wasn't ready to trust his heart again. Doubted he ever would be.

No getting away from the fact this had definitely been the dumbest idea he'd ever come up with. Not once had he factored the boys' hearts into the equation, let alone his own. *Blast you, Margaret, for doing this to us.* How long did it take for youngsters to truly understand what being abandoned by their mother meant? Or did they already get it and this searching for her was just part of the acceptance process?

Note to self: go see a shrink and get my head space tidied up so I understand my boys and don't make stupid mistakes about a woman with beautiful eyes that I could drown in.

CHAPTER FOUR

'I'VE NEVER BEEN treated like royalty before.' Jenny smiled at the twins as a glass of chilled water slid onto the top of the small table beside the chair she'd been banished to. At least the lounge, dining area and kitchen all ran together so she didn't feel isolated from what everyone was up to. 'I could get used to this.'

'Dad said we had to make you—'

'Comfortable and get anything you need.'

Cam spoke from behind the kitchen counter. 'That also means not bothering Jenny all the time.'

Jenny spoke up before an argument ensued. 'Guys, maybe we could play a game on the computer or something later?'

The boys high-fived each other and shouted 'Yes' at the tops of their voices.

Cam nodded at them. 'That means you can go outside to play now.'

She watched them scrambling over each other in their haste to go out into the yard, then asked Cam, 'Do they ever slow down?'

'Exhausting to watch, aren't they?' That half smile appeared as his gaze followed his sons. 'You look sleepy. Do you want to go to bed for a while?'

That had to be the most uninviting invitation to bed

she'd ever had. How would that deep, gravelly voice sound if he was really asking her to take a romp in bed? And why did she even want to know? Shaking her head abruptly, she looked up into the steadiest brown gaze she'd seen in a long time. A hint of amusement shone out at her. Had he picked up on her reaction to his question? Probably. Ouch.

'Jenny? You're space tripping.' His gaze was still locked with hers. Odd, really. Usually people who knew her and what had happened tended to look away. But, then, Cam hadn't a clue about her life up until yesterday.

'If it's all the same to you I'll stay right where I am. If I do nod off, don't insist on the boys being quiet. That'd make me feel bad.' She'd caused enough trouble for this family already.

'We're having a barbecue. Steak all right with you?'

'Perfect. Can I make the salad?' Though right at this moment telling the difference between a tomato and a cucumber might be difficult.

Her question got her a small smile. 'I don't think so.'

'Had to offer.' Actually, she felt glad he'd turned her down. Those crutches were turning out to be a little trickier to master than she'd have believed. His kitchen was safer without her clunking around in there.

'Is there anything you don't like to eat?' Cam asked.

'Tripe, Brussels sprouts and broad beans.'

'You're more than safe here.'

As Cam dug around in the pantry she studied his back view and found it still very delectable now her brain was clear of drugs and post-op fog. But, of course, finding herself here with a man she barely knew, she was bound to be overreacting to all sorts of things. Then Cam turned to place bottles of sauces on the counter and caught her staring.

'Yes?' His eyebrows rose, and that smile hovered on his mouth.

Definitely ouch. Heat crept up her throat and spread across her cheeks. Caught, like a teenager ogling the teacher as he wrote on the board. 'Nothing.' Glancing around, she hurried to find something neutral to talk about. 'You've got a lovely home. Spacious and light, warm and cosy.' *Home and Garden* reporter she was not. 'Been here long?'

'Two and a half years. I was looking for a less hectic work schedule. On a holiday at the family farm out in the sounds, someone mentioned Havelock needed a GP. So here we are.'

'Is there enough work for a full-time doctor?' The town was less than small.

'I do mornings here four days a week and the rest of my time in Blenheim at the practice this one's linked to.'

'How do you manage? A GP's life is never quiet. Then there are your kids.'

'Solo parenting is a balancing act but I wouldn't swap it for anything.' He sprinkled oil onto the steaks and reached for the pepper grinder.

As she watched those strong hands twisting the utensil, her stomach did a wee shake. Long, strong fingers. It didn't take any effort to imagine them tripping over her skin. Her cheeks burned like a furnace. In fact, her whole body had come alive.

'Did I knock my head when I fell yesterday?'

Instantly Cam was wiping his hands and coming towards her. 'Have you got a headache?' There was nothing but concern on his face, bringing her up short as he stared into her eyes. Looking for signs of concussion?

Abruptly shaking her head to break that searching look—who knew what he'd see in there?—she curled in on herself and muttered, 'Sorry. Not a headache.' Though one was beginning to tap behind her eyes. 'I didn't mean to say that out loud.'

That concern didn't lift. 'I think you're a dab hand at downplaying situations. So, do you have a headache or not?'

'No. Promise.' Just a dose of reawakened hormones. No problem. They'd soon get tired of not being let out to play and go back to their cave. But Cam wasn't moving away so some explanation was apparently expected. Like what? Where were the twins when she needed their boisterous exuberance? 'Promise,' she reiterated, and tried for nonchalance as she lifted the glass of water. For the life of her she couldn't think of anything to say that wouldn't have him packing her back into that four-wheel drive of his and delivering her to that backpackers' lodge up the road.

Finally he moved away, returned to his bench and dinner preparations. 'You didn't mention hitting your head yesterday, neither did you show any signs of a bang on the skull when I checked you out.'

'As I thought.' Sipping the refreshing water, she stared into the bottom of the glass. When was the last time she'd held a man, or been held in strong male arms? When was the last time she'd shared a kiss? Months ago, weeks before she and Colby had split.

Colby. A man driven by his background of poverty, he didn't know when to stop and enjoy what he'd achieved. He'd always wanted more, and had expected her to be into all that too. When she'd mentioned that one day she hoped to have a family, he'd regarded her as if he didn't know her at all. Maybe he hadn't known who she'd become. Face it, she struggled to recognise herself sometimes. The one definite to come from losing Alison was that she wanted children. But first she had to find a man with the same beliefs and objectives. An image of a firm butt in fitting trousers flicked into her mind.

There hadn't been a man, any man, since Colby. Hadn't been the need. During her grand tour of places she and Alison had been it had left little energy or inclination for sex and romance. Anyway, sex with strangers so wasn't her thing, and she hadn't stopped anywhere long enough to get to know anyone. Until now. Again an image of Cam floated across her mind, this time a smiling, helpful Cam.

She jerked upright in the chair. Something cold and wet trickled over her stomach. The glass in her hand was empty. 'Did I nod off?'

'You did.' A large hand removed the glass. 'Want a replacement?' Cam asked, a hint of amusement in his voice.

Who could blame him? The guy already had two kids to mind, he didn't need a delinquent adult as well. 'No, thanks.'

'Dad, we're hungry.'

'Now, there's surprise. Go and wash your hands, then set the table on the deck.'

'Is Jenny coming outside with us?'

Cam raised one eyebrow. 'I can bring your dinner in here if you like.'

'I don't think so.' She made to push up from the armchair and there was a steadying hand on her elbow. 'I'll join you out there.'

'Easy.' Cam handed her the blasted crutches.

'I could've hopped,' she growled, as she tucked the poles under her armpits and tried to balance without tipping over into a heap.

'You could have, and it would've hurt.' That was such a doctor tone.

She tried glaring at him. 'You have all the answers, don't you?' Then a smile broke over her mouth. It was impossible to be mad at him when he was being so kind and downright appealing.

'You'd better believe it.' Finally, those lips lifted into a return smile.

This time, thankfully, those hormones stayed in their cave. But warmth trickled through her. When Cam smiled it was like a light in a blackout. Even though he didn't do full-blown, face-crinkling smiles, what he did give was rare and special, making her feel special. Which, of course, she wasn't. Not to Cam anyway.

She headed for the deck, carefully manoeuvring around furniture. No way was she tipping onto her face and giving him more to deal with.

'Goodnight, you two. No talking once the light's out.' As if they'd take the slightest bit of notice. Cam tried to pull on a serious face but how could he when Marcus and Andrew looked so darned cute—make that cool—lying in their beds pretending to be ready for sleep. He knew the moment he closed the bedroom door they'd roll over to face each other and yack their heads off for as long as he pretended not to know.

'Goodnight, Dad.' They both giggled.

How could Margaret have left them? He still couldn't get his head around that. Leave him? Yes, fine, if that was what she wanted. That particular pain had finally begun ebbing away. Shame the distrust couldn't do the same. But these guys deserved so much better from their mother. Bile rose in his throat.

It had been as if the bond that mothers presumably had from the moment they knew they were carrying a child had been missing in Margaret. Sure, the pregnancy had been unplanned. He should've seen the warning signs then. While he'd been ecstatic, she'd been upset. Unfortunately his belief that she'd get past that and fall in love with her babies when she held them for the first time hadn't eventuated. Instead, she'd focused more and more on her career until finally that had attracted her more than her children or her husband.

'Goodnight, Dad,' Marcus repeated. 'We want to go to sleep,' the little imp added, with eyes wide and the sheet already half off his skinny body.

'Dad?' Andrew sounded worried.

Three strides and he stood between the beds. Bending down, he scooped first Marcus then Andrew into his arms for a family hug. The scent of small boys filtered up his nose, warming him deep inside. 'I love you guys so much,' he whispered around the lump suddenly clogging his throat. How long since he'd last told them? These days he did more telling off than offering endearments. Something he really needed to work on.

Wriggle, wriggle. The boys slipped down and climbed back into bed. 'We love you, too.'

'Do you think Jenny's got anyone to love her?' asked Andrew.

Not if that desolation that tripped into her eyes at unexpected moments was anything to go by. 'I'm sure she has,' he lied. 'But it's not something you can ask her.'

'Why not?' The inevitable question hung between them all.

How to shut this down without upsetting the boys? 'When you don't know someone very well you can't ask a question like that. It's personal.' *That goes for you, too, Cam.* As Andrew's mouth opened Cam held up his hand. 'Wait. You don't want to make Jenny unhappy, and asking who loves her might make her very sad if there isn't anyone special.'

'We make her happy. She laughs with us.'

'You're right. She does that a lot when she's with you.' But not as much with him. Which might be a good thing. Too much laughter between them might lead to complications neither of them needed. He had his life mapped out: get these two through to adulthood as unscathed as possible. That meant focusing entirely on their needs and not his own.

Huh? What needs do I have anyway? I have food, warmth, shelter. I've a job that provides all those and helps towards keeping me sane. I'm the father of the greatest, coolest, funniest two kids ever born. It would be greedy to want more.

But when he stepped into the lounge and spied Jenny in the big old rocking chair Grandma had left him, the question repeated in his head. *Do I have other needs?* Loneliness surfaced, knocking the breath from his lungs. Strange because he was usually surrounded by people. But when was the last time he'd told anyone his dreams? Or made plans to go on a holiday with another adult to share everything with?

At the moment there was no one around to discuss decisions with about what to buy the boys for Christmas, or whether to apply for a partnership in the medical centre. Cam grimaced. Some people would tell him he was lucky not having to take on board another person's ideas.

Glancing at Jenny, he wondered what it was about her that stirred up these pointless emotions and questions. Her chin rested on her gently rising and falling sternum, her eyes were firmly shut, those long, slim hands lying in her lap: the picture of abandonment. She'd finally succumbed to the exhaustion plaguing her all evening, which she'd been fighting with the tenacity of a bull terrier.

The sound of a small snore reached him. He grinned. She even sounded like a bull terrier. Kind of cute.

Smack. His palm banged his forehead. Cute? His boys were cute. Not this woman, who'd be gone within a day or two.

He might know next to nothing about Jenny Bostosk, but only a blind man wouldn't see that she moved on all the time. It was there in her eyes as they roved the horizon, in her short, sharp movements as if her body couldn't handle staying in one place for very long.

Which was just as well. Despite inviting Jenny into his home, he was not getting involved. It had taken a long time to get over Margaret dumping him. Even now he could feel the disbelief that had slammed through him when she'd announced she was leaving him and the boys. So, no, cute as Jenny was, he wasn't getting involved.

As his eyes scoped over her it dawned on him that at this very moment she was completely, and unusually, still. Her mind had obviously closed up shop for the night. Bet that didn't happen often.

Jenny needed to be in bed, not scrunched up in a chair. He headed for the bedroom he'd made hers for now and folded back the covers on the bed, closed the curtains and turned on the bedside light. Returning to the living area, he drew a deep, steadying breath and bent down to slide his arms under her. Straightening his back, he lifted her warm body and headed for the bedroom as fast as possible without disturbing her. Having an antsy woman wake up in this situation would probably get his head beaten in.

But she didn't wake up. No, instead she snuggled in closer, causing his lungs to stall and his muscles to tighten. All of them. Yeah, even that one. Now, there was a surprise. It did still work. Even when it shouldn't.

Why did the spare bedroom have to be furthest from the lounge? His strides lengthened. Another of those cute little snores and warm air touched his chest through his shirt. Oh, hell. How was a man supposed to remain sane and responsible? How was his libido supposed to behave? There was a question he'd be wise not to dwell on. What was it about Jenny that had him waking up when he hadn't been the slightest bit interested in sex since before Margaret had left?

Almost dropping Jenny onto the bed, he dragged the covers over her, not bothering to remove any outer clothes—he didn't do stepping into lions' dens—and backed out of the room so fast he nearly tripped. Closing the door, he sagged against the wall and berated himself for a full five minutes. Thankfully swearing silently didn't count in the house rules. Not when the boys weren't in the same room as him anyway. If they had been he'd be coughing up buckets of cash in fines, not banking every spare dollar for their university fees in ten years' time.

Note to self: check how those investment funds he'd started for the boys were doing. And tell his hormones to take a hike. Jenny was off limits.

The next morning Cam watched the boys place a plate of toast and a cup of tea on the bedside table with all the finesse of a calf wallowing in mud. 'Okay, say goodbye and go get your school bags, you two.'

Jenny gave each boy the benefit of her big smile. 'Breakfast in bed. How decadent. Thank you so much, Andrew. Thank you so much, Marcus.'

She never roped both boys into the one thanks or compliment. No, she singled each of them out. The boys' biggest gripe about being twins was that everyone spoke to them as though they were one unit. Everyone except Jenny. 'Are you a twin?'

Instantly the light in her eyes snapped off. Her hands clenched into fists before she slid them under the covers. Her bottom lip trembled.

Every swear word he could think of slammed into his brain. Now what had he started? It had seemed an innocuous question.

Marcus's eyes lit up. 'Are you like us? Where's your sister? Or brother? Doesn't she want to be with you?'

Ice entered the room. Cam could feel his skin chilling and goosebumps rising. If he thought he'd seen desolation in her eyes yesterday, he didn't have a word to describe the shock, agony and the bewilderment darkening that summer green of her eyes to winter's darkest day.

'Out. Go get your bags and wait on the deck.' With a hand on their backs he nudged the boys towards the door, holding back the urge to rush them away before they added to his monumental blunder—whatever that was. 'Go. Now,' he growled, knowing this was his fault, not theirs, but needing them to do as he said quickly and quietly.

Maybe the frozen atmosphere of the bedroom had touched them too because they tiptoed away, glancing back over their shoulders with worried expressions on their faces. He gave a wave, hopefully reassuring, and turned back to the woman he'd obviously just knocked for a six.

'I apologise for putting my size elevens in my mouth, but you're so good with the boys the way you treat them as individuals and not as a double package that I figured you might know what it's like to be a twin. I never meant to upset you, but it seems I've done so in a big

way.' Stop burbling on and on. But he needed to see that
tension ease, to raise the tiniest of smiles on those now
white lips. 'You are really, really good with my boys. It
comes naturally to you.'

Her chest rose and fell sharply, quickly, continuously.

And finally he shut up except to say, 'Take a deep
breath.'

It took a few attempts but eventually Jenny had her
lungs under control. But not her eyes. They hadn't lightened, or met his gaze, or even blinked.

Leaning down, he tugged one of her hands free of
the cover and wrapped it in both of his. It was cold. And
shaking. Cam sat on the edge of the bed and held tight,
his thumb rubbing gentle circles over the back of her
hand. Slowly, slowly the quivering slowed, but didn't
stop entirely.

Then Jenny pulled free and sat back against the pillows. 'Alison.'

Did he acknowledge her? Or would that start another
episode of what he'd just witnessed? If he remained si-
lent she might think he was deliberately ignoring her. He
spoke as softly as he could manage. 'Your twin?'

Her head dipped. 'She died.'

He'd been getting to that. Her reaction had to have
meant more than a sisterly fallout. 'I'm sorry. I can't
begin to imagine how that must feel.'

'Stop apologising.'

'What?'

'You've been saying sorry ever since we met on the
footpath. You don't need to.'

That had nothing to do with her sister. Probably her
coping mechanism kicking into force. Jenny could relax
about that. He wasn't about to jump in and ask the big
questions about how, why, where. Hell, he wasn't going

ask what she wanted sent from the bakery for her lunch. He'd bring something of his choice. 'Deal. No more apologies. Now drink your tea before it's totally cold.'

'Anyone ever tell you you're bossy?'

'The tw—' Swallow. 'Marcus and Andrew. All the time.' He handed her the cup and tried not to notice how much it shook in her two-handed grasp.

'Go. They'll be wondering why you're taking so long.' Colour was returning to her face at last.

Note to self: do not mention her twin sister at all ever again.

CHAPTER FIVE

JENNY WANTED TO throw up. No one in all the months she'd spent on the road had asked if she had a family, let alone if she was a twin.

She sipped the lukewarm tea and bit into the heavily buttered toast the boys had made her. Hopefully that would settle her stomach faster than holding her breath or plain old wishing the nausea away could.

If her foot hadn't been aching and throbbing and difficult to manoeuvre she'd have been tempted to catch a bus out of town, away from intrusive questions and prying eyes. Cam missed nothing. He'd seen each and every one of her emotions when he'd asked that question. He'd known instantly he'd made a big mistake, probably even had an inkling as to why. At least he hadn't gone all effusive on her. That would've caused her stomach to do what she was so far managing to prevent.

'Yes, I am a twin, who failed her other half. Yes, I totally get what it's like to have people put me and my twin into the same pigeonhole. We were born identical, shared a birth date and parents, had the same passion for hiking in the bush, but that's where the similarities ended.'

Just like Marcus and Andrew. Already she could see differences. They both liked playing cricket in the yard, but Marcus preferred bowling, concentrating with everything he had to bowl the perfect ball, while Andrew just wanted to slog the ball as far as possible with no thought to where it might land in relation to the lone fieldsman, being their dad, or to the house windows.

Their dad. Cam, or Cameron Roberts, as he'd introduced himself. An enigma. He loved his kids massively yet often seemed to be cross with them for very little reason. The guy needed to loosen up.

Ha! Like she could talk. Loose did not describe her at all. In any connotation. A wound-up rubber band was getting close. Wind it too tight and it might snap.

Not only had her life come to a crashing halt in Havelock, having time on her hands was already forcing her to face things she'd had no intention of facing. There'd been some fun moments on this journey—like the beach at Whangamata where she and Alison had once given surfing a go. Neither of them had had the aptitude required to stay on a board long enough to ride a wave. This time she'd taken a surfing lesson, but had still bombed out. No doubt Alison had been laughing down at her.

Throwing the covers aside, she gingerly lowered her feet to the floor and stood up. Sucked in a breath and held onto it until the sharp jolt of pain faded.

After trying to juggle the cup and plate and use the crutches, she gave up, headed for the bathroom instead. She'd think of a way to take the cup and plate out to the kitchen later. Right now a shower was on the menu.

With Cam's usual thoughtfulness a large plastic bin liner and a roll of tape were on the sink top, and a stool had been placed strategically by the shower, with a towel folded neatly on top. He'd also placed her bathroom bag with her shampoo and conditioner beside the shower door.

She could get used to this. Cam was so caring. She wondered what had gone wrong with his marriage.

With her leg in the tightly taped bag, she hobbled under the jets of hot water and luxuriated in the heat pummelling her. Her body ached from top to toe from the thumping it had received when she'd hit the ground like a sack of spuds. Tipping her head back, she let the water saturate her hair then lathered in shampoo, at last returning the tangled mess to its silky texture. Now she felt half-human again. If only everything else needed to fix her problems came in a plastic bottle with a squeeze top.

Who knew that having a shower, getting dressed and making the bed could take so long? It was nearly lunchtime and Jenny stood at the kitchen bench with a cup of tea and pulled a face at the enticing sun-drenched deck. She wanted to be out there, drinking this, not standing here unable to move without her crutches.

Instead she turned to focus on the cork board next to the fridge. Covered in photos, school messages, party invitations and sports timetables, it gave her an insight into the Roberts family's day-to-day life. In a word— busy. And happy. In every photo one or all three of the males who lived in this house beamed out at the world.

'Big tick for you, Cam. You're obviously doing lots of things right with those two.'

Her heart squeezed. He was a great dad. His doctoring skills weren't shabby either. He'd been gentle and careful with her ankle, had asked the right questions. As for anything else, his long, lean body was pretty good, too, in great shape, if she dared to think about it.

Then there was that astute mind that picked up on vibes far too quickly. He didn't miss a trick. All in all, he added up to a very intriguing package. She hugged herself.

Don't go there, insisted a very familiar little voice in her head.

Finishing her tea, she carefully made her way out to the deck and dropped onto a wooden chair, breathed in the warmth and quiet.

Now what? She should've checked out that bookshelf to see if there was anything she could read. Even a mechanic's manual would be better than having nothing to distract her. Except she couldn't see Cam with his head under a bonnet. Though why not, she had no idea. Understanding men hadn't been one of her strong points.

'Hey, you're up and about.' Cam stepped onto the deck and stopped, his throat working overtime.

When the moment had stretched out too long and he obviously hadn't found his voice she asked, 'Has a bird left its calling card on my head?' Couldn't be food on her face. She hadn't eaten since her shower.

He swallowed hard. 'Yep, must've been a turkey from the size of the mess.'

Instinctively she ran her hand over her head and felt stupid for doing it, knowing he'd been teasing, or hiding something.

Cam held up two bulging paper bags. 'Lunch courtesy of the bakery.'

'Yum. I looked in their window on Saturday and everything looked very enticing.'

'Your hair is beautiful.' Then he disappeared inside to the kitchen.

Aha. That's what the throat movements had been about. He'd been stumped by her shocking red hair. No doubt the sun was highlighting all the tones and her head would be looking the colour of a cooked lobster. She called after him, 'I'm easily found in a crowd, that's for sure.'

'You don't like it?' Surprise registered on his face as

he popped his head out of the kitchen window. 'Or is it that you don't like standing out in said crowd?'

As she'd said, too damned astute for his own good. 'I tried blonde once. Had lots more fun.'

A quick flick of those lips into a brief smile. 'Redheads don't have fun?' he asked.

Did he want to know if she was into fun? 'Definitely not. We're very serious people.' There was no stopping the grin splitting her mouth wide. Cam had some magic power that made her smile more than she had in for ever.

'But they drive fast sports cars.' He approached with plates, glasses of juice and the bags from the bakery. 'Bread rolls with smoked chicken and cranberry salad okay with you?'

'Just what I was about to ring out for.'

'So, how's that foot?'

She watched as he bit into his roll, noticing for the first time what perfect, white teeth he had. *So what? They're teeth. Everyone has them.* But not everyone's teeth had her wondering how it would feel to be nibbled on her breasts or down her stomach.

'Jenny? A guy could be insulted with the number of times you go space tripping around him.'

Oh, I'm not insulting you, believe me. 'The foot's doing as well as expected. In other words, it's not ready to play football or do a tango. It does complain quite sharply at any sudden movement but, hey, we're still getting along.'

He shook his head at her. 'You are something, you know that?'

There really wasn't an answer to that. She bit into her lunch. 'How's your day going? Lots of patients?'

'The usual run of blood-pressure tabs, antihistamine scripts and general health checks. We're rarely rushed off our feet at this centre.' Was that longing in his eyes? 'But then there are the days when an emergency throws everything up in the air, and around here those tend to be messy.'

'You ever miss the busier practice in Wellington?'

'Do I?' He chewed thoughtfully. 'You know, I've been too busy making sure the boys get established in their new life and are happy to stop and think about it. Two friends from med school and I started that practice. We were doing very well. Then one day Greg went for a run after work and had a massive coronary on the side of the road.'

'He didn't make it?' It was a reminder that other people had bad stuff happen to them and didn't run away.

'Yes, he did. But it was a huge wake-up call. Sometimes we seemed to be working more hours than we had in the ED as interns. We brought in more partners, but it was never the same. So the long answer is, no, I don't miss that particular practice. Though I now work so far at the other end of the stress scale I'm almost horizontal.'

'Yeah, right. That explains the shadows under your eyes.'

'I knew I'd forgotten something. Didn't put any make-up on this morning.'

Had his wife disliked the slow pace of Havelock? She wasn't asking. Instead she tried, 'Where do the boys go after school?' Maybe she could look after them until Cam got home.

'Amanda, the mother of one of their friends, takes them. She also takes their swimming lessons.'

Disappointment tugged at her. Of course he'd have everything organised. He hadn't been waiting for her to fall into his life to help out. 'Does she look after the boys in the school holidays, too?'

'No. They go to my parents on the farm. They love it out there so much it's always a battle to bring them home at the start of term.'

Parents. *Parents.* She missed her mum and dad. They understood what she was doing and why. Didn't they?

Cam stood up. 'Time I headed to Blenheim. Anything you want before I go?'

'No, I'm fine, thanks.' *Oh, for pity's sake, it won't hurt to ask a favour of him.* Swallow. 'Um, you couldn't get my tablet for me, could you?'

'Of course.' He looked puzzled that she had to ask. 'Where is it?'

'At the bottom of my bag.' Which meant he'd have to dig through all her clothes, including her underwear. If he even found her slightly attractive he'd only have to remember the boring, plain white knickers and bras he'd find there and he'd sober up fast.

Within minutes Cam had placed a bottle of iced water, some fruit and her tablet on the table beside her. He added a notepad with his email address at the top. 'In case you need anything.'

A hug wouldn't go astray. Gulp. What? A hug? Why?

Because she felt a wee bit lonely right now. Being forced to stay put so wasn't helping her cause. Instead she was doing stupid things, like considering emailing Mum and Dad and telling them where she was and how she'd managed to end up here when usually she only said enough for them to know she was still alive and kicking.

A deep breath and her shoulders went back. 'Hopefully, I won't be annoying you. Have a good afternoon, and I'll see you later.'

A finger lifted her chin and knowing brown eyes locked with hers. 'Believe me, an hour after we get home you'll be wishing for the peace and quiet again.

School doesn't tire my boys. Instead, it winds them up even more.'

'They're like those battery bunnies from the TV ads.'

'Sometimes I wish I could just take out their batteries.' Cam's thumb slid across her chin before he dropped his hand to his side.

If she hadn't known better she'd have said it had been a caress. But she did know better. Cam had enough on his plate to deal with, without having the time or the need to be caressing her. 'Cam?' When she had his complete attention again she said, 'I really appreciate all you've done for me. Don't say you have to either, because you don't.'

'My lips are sealed.'

Her lips tipped up into a smile. 'Why did you bring me into your home?'

'My lips are sealed.'

Lips. Cam's lips. What would they feel like on hers? She watched as he stepped off the deck and headed for the front of the house without a backward glance. This whole scenario was alien to her, and yet it was tugging her in, wrapping around her, making her feel comfortable for brief moments of time. She tapped the tablet into life.

Hi Mum and Dad. That's great news about your trip to Sydney in the New Year.

This was where she'd normally sign off. But her fingers kept tapping the keys.

I am currently in Havelock. It's a quaint little town on the Pelorus Sound, famous for the green-lipped mussels grown in the sounds and packaged here at a small factory.

She stared out across the lawn to the hills beyond the Sound. According to her hiking book there were some walking tracks over there. Not that she'd been planning on doing any of those as she hadn't intended stopping here for longer than it took to eat lunch. But now she'd love the opportunity.

Mum, Dad, don't panic but I've broken my ankle. A silly little accident that has rendered me next to useless for a few days. The local doctor has kindly put me up until I'm ready to move on.

She chuckled. That made Cam sound old and avuncular.

He has two boys he's bringing up on his own. They're just adorable. Sigh. That's about it this time. Love you both heaps, Jenny.

She didn't hesitate, touched Send, and the longest email she'd written in a year headed off into cyberspace.

'Jenny, where are you?'

'We're home. Are you better?'

No way could she tell the twins apart by their voices. 'Hi, guys. I'm on the couch with a cat. Who does it belong to?' The black and white moggy had made itself very comfortable on her thighs an hour ago and she hadn't had the heart to send it packing.

'That's Socks. She lives at Mrs Warner's house, but Dad says we feed her more times.'

One boy appeared by the couch. Andrew? Fingers crossed she'd got it right, she said, 'Socks is quite heavy, isn't she? Andrew, can you lift her off so I can shift my legs?'

'Okay.'

Got the name right. Great. 'Thanks.'

'That cat's far too fat,' came an acerbic comment from the kitchen.

'Should I have put her outside, Cam?' Like that would be easy in her current situation.

'Good luck with that.' Cam strolled into view. 'How was your afternoon?'

'Excellent.' Joined the local theatre group and did a turn in the mussel-opening shed. 'It's unbelievably quiet here. I haven't done anything to help with dinner, I'm sorry.'

'You weren't expected to,' Cam glanced at her.

'We're having a barbecue.' Marcus bounced around the room until he found the TV remote.

'We always have barbecues,' Andrew explained in a bored tone.

Every time one boy spoke the other added his say. So like her and Alison it made her heart crunch. She'd stopped talking very much in those first months after Alison had left her because she'd found herself pausing and waiting for Alison to speak. Every time she hadn't, it had hurt all over again.

'Barbecuing is the easiest way to cook,' Cam muttered. 'Especially in summer.' Did he feel pressured about the meals he provided for his boys? They weren't exactly looking malnourished.

Licking her lips exaggeratedly, Jenny said, 'Barbecues are my favourite. Yummy food and no slaving over a hot stove.' Like she ever slaved over any kind of stove.

'Turn that TV off, Marcus. You haven't done your jobs yet. The washing needs bringing in.' Cam reached for the remote, tugged it from Marcus's hand. He raised his voice. 'Andrew, empty the dishwasher. Now. Bring your lunchboxes out to the kitchen first.'

Jenny grimaced. 'Can I do anything? Make a salad or peel some potatoes?' Sitting here while everyone else did the chores made her uncomfortable. She hadn't even noticed the washing on the line.

Cam was already returning to the kitchen. 'Stay where you are. We have a routine.' He turned and gave her a reluctant smile. 'For want of a better word.'

'I'd be in the way.' She got it. But tomorrow surely she'd be able to get around a bit better, and then she'd make herself useful.

'You would,' Cam agreed too easily.

The man looked so tired she wanted to insist on helping in one way or another, but she could see any interruption to his routine might be more of a hindrance than a help so she stroked the cat, which had returned to sprawl across her thighs, instead.

Marcus staggered in with an overladen washing basket and dropped it on the floor in the middle of the lounge.

'Push that over here and I can fold everything.' She nudged the cat aside and got a hiss for her effort.

'There's a novelty,' quipped the man himself, as he strode past to the glass doors opening on to the deck and that barbecue he was so fond of.

'Dad tips the clothes onto the table in the laundry and we take what we need when we want it.'

She had noticed the rumpled look worn by all three males in this house. Tomorrow she'd balance on her cast and iron some shirts.

'Give away all my secrets, why don't you?' Cam returned, ruffling his son's hair on the way past.

'I don't know anyone who likes ironing.' Except

Alison had, driving her crazy with her fussiness when it had come to clothes. The memory tugged, sent a small wave of warmth through her. She held her breath, waited for the explosion of pain that followed such memories. It didn't happen. Now, there was a first. The day was going from weird to weirder. First she'd sent an email to Mum and Dad that had involved more than *hello, how are you*. Now she'd recalled something about Alison that hadn't sent her heart plummeting to her toes.

Marcus said, 'Dad says it's a waste of time.'

'Your dad's a busy man.' She didn't dare look around to see if Cam had heard. She'd bet her crutches he had. The man had ears everywhere. Putting a folded towel on the couch beside her, she reached into the basket for another one. 'I bet he does the most important things first, and then there's probably no time left for other jobs like ironing.' Sticking up for Cam now, eh? What was that about? Plain old empathy for a man who at times appeared overwhelmed with everything, that's what.

Despite her determination not to look for him, her gaze drifted sideways, searching, finding him standing in the middle of the kitchen, a plate of chops in one hand, a bottle of cooking oil in the other, and a bemused expression on his face.

She winked.

His bemusement intensified.

Astonishment made her mouth gape. Since when did she do winks? Never, ever. So she'd just proved what a moron she was, winking at the man who'd opened up his home to her. Winks and lechery were synonymous.

'You're dribbling.' Cam winked back.

A deep-bellied laugh rolled up her throat and spilled between them. A muscle-relaxing, heart-warming, pants-wetting-if-she-wasn't-careful laugh. Smudging her moist eyes with the back of her hand, she struggled to contain the merriment before she embarrassed herself.

Cam probably already thought she was nuts.

But when she finally looked at him he wore that smile, only this time it was wider, softer, more heart-melting than she'd seen before.

He said, 'You're nuts.'

See? 'I know.' And I haven't laughed like that for a year.

Caution, Jenny. Two days after meeting Cam you're lightening up on the stress levels, the gloom is lifting and you're starting to see the world in colour rather than a grey monotone. Be very careful. You could be in for a fall.

'You've got a message,' Marcus called from out on the deck. 'Want your tablet?'

'Yes, please.' She hadn't meant to leave it outside but when she'd realised what she'd done she'd been comfortably ensconced on the couch. Not that she ever got much in the way of emails these days. She had to stay in touch with people for that.

Mum had replied. No surprise there. She'd be worried about her accident, had probably booked a flight up to see her and make sure she was looking after herself. *I shouldn't have told them.*

Darling Jenny, sorry to read about your broken ankle. That can be debilitating. The doctor sounds nice, taking you in like that when he's probably already very busy. I expect that you're doing all you can to help him. Big hugs and lots of love, Mum.

Huh? Where were the questions? The demands to be careful? The details of the flight she was arriving on?

Was this Mum's way of telling her it was time to stop moving and settle somewhere?

'Who emailed you?' Marcus asked.

'My mother.' I think.

'You're lucky.' That sweet little face turned sad.

'Yes, I am. But you've got your dad and Andrew.' Neither replaced his mother. She got that. She had her parents but they didn't fill the gap left by Alison. 'They love you heaps.' She wouldn't say they'd always be there for Andrew because no one could predict that with absolute certainty. Look what had happened to her for believing she'd have Alison in her life for ever.

'I love my mum heaps.' Marcus stared at the floor, his hair falling across his eyes.

Reaching out, she pulled him near and sat him on the couch beside her, away from the washing. 'Of course you do. Mums are special.'

Still staring at the floor, he nodded slowly. 'Ours is.'

'So are dads and brothers.'

The nodding continued. 'Mine are the best.'

'See? You're very lucky. I bet they think you're the best, too.'

Finally Marcus raised his head and looked at her. 'Are you really a twin?'

CHAPTER SIX

Cam held his breath and waited for Jenny's withdrawal from Marcus. He should interrupt, tell Marcus to stop asking questions and get his homework, but something in the way Jenny didn't sink in on herself the way she had that morning made him pause. Besides, if he was being honest, he wanted to hear this too. Letting Marcus do his dirty work?

'Yes, I am. I...' She stopped, swallowed hard, then kept going. 'My parents had two girls. I'm the oldest. Alison was the bossy one, always telling me what to do.'

'I'm the bossy one *and* the oldest.'

True.

'Who's the brainiest?' she asked. Deflecting the twin subject?

Marcus's chest puffed out. 'I am.'

Not quite so true.

'No, he's not,' Andrew yelled across the kitchen, where he was still slowly putting the clean dishes away, one piece of cutlery at a time. Why didn't he understand that if he just got on with the job it would be finished and he'd have more time for fun things? 'I got ninety-five for maths, you got eighty-one.'

Here came the war. Cam intervened, 'You're both intelligent in different subjects. Now, Marcus, set the table for dinner. Andrew, put four plates on the bench and get that dishwasher unpacked, will you? Before Christmas, if possible.'

Jenny stood up. 'I'll start hobbling towards the deck and hopefully I'll make it by dinnertime.' The smile she sent him was full of understanding and gratitude and warmth. She'd diverted the boys from asking more questions and he'd kept them diverted.

That's how it should be between parents, each backing the other subtly. Yet Jenny wasn't the boys' parent, didn't have kids of her own, and she'd managed to do that. Margaret had never done it, always looking for ways to come between him and the boys, finding an excuse for an argument. Was his main problem with Margaret that he'd chosen the wrong woman for himself? He'd loved her, deeply. Had he expected too much from that love? Something to think about when next he started getting serious about a woman. Huh. He'd better start thinking about that now then.

The knife fell from his hand to clatter into the sink. What the hell?

'You okay?' asked the woman responsible for his crazed brain.

'Sure.' Picking up the knife, he began slicing cucumber with a healthy regard for his fingers. Then he smiled.

Smiling used to come naturally. In fact, at one time he'd worn an almost permanent one. But that had been before everything had gone pear-shaped.

'Smells like burnt meat out here,' Jenny called, as she levered herself across to the barbecue. 'Nothing like a bit of crispy chop.' She started deftly flipping the chops over so the other sides could cook.

Great. Jenny's fault for distracting him so easily.

Note to self: keep focused around Jenny Bostock or more than the chops are going to get burned.

Another note to self: make those appointments for the boys' haircuts.

'Did you tell your parents about your fracture?' Cam asked, after he'd seen the boys to bed.

'Yes,' Jenny replied. 'They don't seem overly concerned, which is a relief, I guess.'

Jenny clicked shut the web page for the local bus company. There were plenty of choices for getting from Havelock to Blenheim if she chose to leave and find a motel. Maybe not tomorrow but the day after when she was bit more nimble.

'You making school lunches?' The guy hadn't stopped doing chores all evening.

Cam spread margarine on slices of bread. 'Yes. Every day except Friday when I let the kids buy their lunch from the bakery as a treat.'

'What other things need doing before you take a break?' He should be sitting down, watching TV or reading a book, talking to her over coffee, not moving from one job to the next. No wonder he looked exhausted all the time. Tomorrow she'd make sure to do some tidying up for him.

He glanced around the kitchen and shrugged. 'Think I'm nearly done. Did I mention you've got an appointment with Angus tomorrow? He called me, said I was the only contact he had for you. Hope that's all right. I kind of intimated I'm your GP for now.'

'What happened to calling my cell?' But he had been looking out for her yet again.

'I'd say Angus just phoned me without even considering checking your file. I made your appointment for the afternoon so that you can hitch a ride into Blenheim with me and I'll bring you home at the end of the day. You'll have to entertain yourself for a few hours after your appointment, that's all.'

'I can manage that.' Presumably there were cafés in Blenheim. Or she could find that motel she should be moving into. 'Thanks,' she added, as an afterthought. Cam had gone out of his way to help her and she'd neglected to be appreciative. 'Again, you've been more than helpful. I do appreciate it.'

'Even having me as your GP?' He gave her a glance that from anyone else would've been cheeky. With Cam she couldn't tell.

'Beggars can't be choosers.' She smiled. Amazing how easy it was to smile with him. Why wouldn't it be? He was a ten on the sexy scale. Any female with half a brain would be smiling at him.

'Where is your GP? Which town?' Cam spoke tentatively, as though afraid she'd tell him to mind his own business.

Which she normally would do. But what the heck? It wasn't as though she'd be giving anything major away if she answered. 'Dunedin. That's where I grew up and went to med school.'

'Your folks still live there?'

'Yes. They'll never leave, say there's no place like it. They're not wrong about that, but whether it's the best place in the country, I'm not so sure. The weather's the pits, for starters.' Too many freezing cold days with snow and ice interfering with plans.

'Where would you choose?' He snapped off a length of plastic wrap for the lunches.

'I have no idea. My last job was in Auckland but I can't say I liked that city much. Too big and sprawling for me.'

'Got a favourite place?'

'I used to have a fixation with mountains. Not as a place to live, though. The sea is appealing, though I've never lived on the waterfront.'

'What changed your mind about the mountains?'

So much for keeping this light. She should've kept her mouth firmly shut. 'I've done a lot of hiking, seen more of the back country than most people, and think it's time to find another interest.' A safer one. Mum and Dad didn't need to lose their other daughter.

It was apparent in his steady, sympathetic gaze and the way his smile slowly slid off those tempting lips that Cam knew she'd winged that answer. Thankfully he let it go. 'Feel like a coffee?'

'Can I have tea instead? Coffee will keep me awake half the night.'

'Sure, though I doubt anything's going to stop you from sleeping when you finally make it to bed. You've got serious bags under your eyes.'

'Charming.' Any time he mentioned her going to bed her tummy did a little skip. This time, as an added extra, her mouth dried. Bed and Cam in the same sentence were obviously too much to get her head around. He was hot. Scorching hot. But not a reason to get in a dither about. Oh, so her libido was meant to disappear for ever, was it? Was she not allowed to wake up and start looking at men again? It's not as though she was planning a long-term relationship with Cam. If anything—and that was a big if—she'd only want a fling. A very short one at that because she wouldn't be staying past Wednesday. A fling implied enjoying herself, something she wasn't ready for.

Cam said, 'I trained at Otago Med School, too. But I'd have been four, five, years ahead of you.'

She'd have remembered him. 'I'm thirty-one, started at university when I was eighteen.'

'Definitely long gone before you started.'

'So you're a geriatric?' He'd be about six years older than her, she reckoned.

'Definitely. Milk in your tea?'

Nodding, she asked, 'So why Wellington for your practice?'

Handing her the mug of tea, he sank into an armchair with his coffee. 'I went to boarding school there.'

'Why boarding school?'

'My parents have been farming in the sounds for forty-odd years. Mum home-schooled us until we were ready for high school.'

'How'd that go for you?'

'Loved it. I came home every opportunity, but being in the city was exciting, too.'

'It must've been poles apart from the life you grew up with.'

'Absolutely.' He blew on his coffee. Looked around the room, brought his gaze back to her. 'On Saturday you said you were travelling to Blenheim. Any particular reason?'

Time to drink up the tea and head to that bed he'd mentioned. This time her libido remained quiet. 'No, not really.'

He didn't look away or say a word. Just waited for an explanation. It would be hard to hide anything from him. But she didn't owe him an explanation.

The silence grew, not awkward but none too comfortable either. Gingerly sipping her tea, she thought about being here, doing something as ordinary as drinking tea and idly talking about life. How strange to have someone asking about what she did and where she did it. These past months the few people she'd crossed paths with hadn't even known she was a doctor. 'I haven't worked for a while. Taking a road trip instead.' And that's all I'm saying.

'A long road trip?'

'I'm nearly done.' The end was in sight. Except now she had no idea what she was going to do about getting to Kahurangi. Her foot wouldn't be in any fit state for driving, and there was no other way to get there. Buses went past but being dumped in the middle of nowhere without means of shelter and food wasn't viable. As for climbing to the accident site—forget it. Impossible.

'Jenny?' Cam called softly. 'If there's anything else I can do you'll tell me, won't you?'

His eyes looked as startled as hers felt, indicating that had come out of the blue as much for him as it had for her. Her eyes widened and a smile stretched her mouth. 'You've already done heaps. I'll be heading away, out of your hair, as soon as possible.' Then disappointment rocked her. She didn't want to move on. Not yet, not until she'd learned more about Cam. But staying would be unfair. He had more than enough to contend with, without adding her woes to his list.

'Will you eventually go back to working in an ED? Or do you want to change specialties?' At least he hadn't out and out asked why she'd given up medicine.

'Emergency medicine's always been my passion, and it's hard to imagine learning another specialty.' Even she could hear her voice dwindling away, getting quieter and quieter. Not wanting to face any more questions about any of this, she hauled herself upright and scooped up the crutches. 'Think I'll hit the sack.'

Cam's eyes widened, but thankfully he kept whatever had crossed his mind to himself. Instead, after a drawn-out moment he shocked her with, 'They're always looking for emergency specialists at Wairau.'

Bang. She was on her butt again and sucking in a pain-filled breath as her ankle protested at the sudden movement. 'I don't think so,' she finally spluttered.

He shrugged as if it was no big deal. Which it wasn't to him. 'Fine. Just letting you know. In case you were contemplating staying around.'

Thanks, but, no, thanks. It was one thing to feel disappointment at the thought of leaving, quite another to have Cam make it sound possible to stay. 'I'll keep it in mind.'

'Here, let me help you up.' Cam stood in front of her, hand extended. 'That was some thump you took just then.'

'Not sure what happened.' Yeah, right.

'I upset you again.' Contrition blinked out at her from those disturbing eyes.

Shaking her head from side to side, she said, 'Not your fault. Anyone would make the same suggestion given the situation.' Because they had no idea what she was up against. Placing her hand in his, the instant heat that warmed her had her making to tug away, except Cam closed his fingers around hers and held tight, pulling her to her feet.

Raising her gaze to meet his, she sucked in a breath at the need and loneliness and understanding she saw. Just as suddenly she wanted something from him too. Wanted friendship, closeness—wanted that fling she'd thought about earlier. It was there for the taking. She could see Cam's need in his eyes, feel it in his raised pulse as he held her hand, smell it in the thick air hanging between them.

Like a chrysalis slowly opening so that what lay inside could spread its wings and try to soar, it was as though

her life was starting over. That she was being given a
second chance. Her body swayed closer to his.

She didn't deserve a second chance. She pulled back.

Cam continued to watch her as he leaned close again.
She only had to lift ever so slightly on her toes and her
lips would be on his. And then she'd know what it was
like to kiss Cam, to taste him.

Tugging her gaze away from that beautiful face looking down at her, she glanced around the room. Looking
for? Approval? Condemnation? Toy trucks and a helicopter and a plane were stacked messily in one corner. *Toys,
Jenny, toys.* Children lived here, with this man. They had
first dibs on Cam, not her. She didn't have any dibs. What
had she been thinking? Maybe she *had* hit her head when
she'd fallen. She'd sure been acting strange ever since.

Jerking her hand free, Jenny hobbled sideways around
Cam. 'Sorry,' she muttered. 'I need to get some sleep.'
Then she might be able to put these out-of-left-field
thoughts about Cam to rest.

Silently he handed her the crutches, watched as she
tucked them under her arms. His face gave nothing away.
That need she'd seen moments earlier had been banished.
Thank goodness. It was hard enough controlling her own
wayward reaction, without seeing the same staring back
at her from the man who'd sent her libido into a tango
in the first place.

'Goodnight, Jenny.'

A sharp nod, a curt 'Goodnight' and she clomped
down the hall to the bedroom she used.

Now she really did have to find somewhere else to stay
until she could get around more easily. Staying here any
longer wasn't fair on Cam—or herself.

*Tomorrow you're going with Cam to Blenheim to see
your surgeon. You could spend those spare hours after-*

*wards ringing around motels, enquiring about a suit-
able unit.*

She could. It was the perfect solution. So why didn't
she feel ecstatic? Why wasn't she hopping up and down
with glee to know the end of staying here and being a
pain in the butt for Cam was in sight?

She didn't want to leave. She liked it here, enjoyed the
boys, nearly as much as their father. She felt comfortable,
was even relaxing enough to start communicating more
with her mum and dad.

All the more reason to be moving on. Whether she
wanted to or not was irrelevant. Cam Roberts certainly
didn't need the added distraction of her suddenly wide-
eyed, ready-to-roll libido coming between them.

Knock, knock.

She spun round. The crutches slipped, tangled around
her legs and tipped her onto the bed. Pain sliced through
her ankle, ripped up her leg, sent nausea crawling up her
throat. She let out a strangled cry.

'Hey, careful.' Cam pushed open the door and was in-
stantly at her side, reaching down to remove the crutches.
'I'm sorry. I thought you'd hear me coming along the hall.
I wasn't trying to be quiet.'

Deep breaths, in one two, out one two. In, out. Slowly,
slowly the pain ebbed away, leaving her feeling drained.
'Goes to show I'm not improving as fast as I thought,'
she finally gasped out.

Cam knelt down and gently straightened her leg. 'As
fast as you'd like, you mean.'

'I guess.'

'Are you always so impatient?' Straightening up, he
lifted her to stand on the good foot and quickly whipped
back the bed covers before lowering her onto the bed.

'Me? Impatient? Only when I need to get something

done.' Great, now she was in bed, fully dressed and her body craving to relax back into the mattress. But she was damned if she'd undress while Cam was still in the room. Not after that searing moment back in the lounge.

Cam obviously had other ideas. He pulled the over-sized T-shirt she slept in from under the pillow and handed it to her. 'You have something you want to do urgently? Some place you need to be? Or are you in a hurry to leave us?'

'All of the above.' That wasn't a fib.

He crossed to close the curtains, tossing a question over his shoulder. 'What's so important you can't give that fracture a couple of days to start mending?'

'I hate being a nuisance.' Avoid the big questions. Makes life far easier. 'My ankle can heal just as well in a motel as it can hanging out on your deck.'

He turned back to face her. 'Sounds kind of lonely to me.' There was disappointment and something a bit like hurt in that steady gaze locked on her. 'But I guess being stuck with two highly energetic kids and their grumpy father could be worse for someone who obviously prefers her own company.'

Her heart rolled over. 'You're not grumpy.' Well, not often. 'Anyway, I'm not stuck.' Her gaze dropped from that devastatingly attractive face to her encased ankle. 'Not much.' Maybe tomorrow Angus would organise a new, stronger cast for her ankle so she could get around more easily, take in the sights of Havelock the day after tomorrow. Though what would she do for the rest of the day, when she'd finished perusing the few shops?

'You're not used to stopping in one place for any length of time, are you? Especially somewhere as small as Havelock?'

See? She knew he could read her like an open book.

How had he learned to do that? 'That depends what I stop for.'

Again disappointment filtered through his eyes. 'Get some sleep, Jenny. Your eyes are bugging with exhaustion.'

'Bugging now? You need practice on complimenting a woman.'

Heat singed his cheeks but he didn't look away. 'I'll look on line for a book that might give me some pointers.' There was that little smile, albeit a tad reluctant.

That smile warmed her in places she'd been cold all year. That smile came with a danger warning. She really needed to be moving on—fast. Yet knowing and doing seemed poles apart right at this moment.

Not that she'd be falling into a deep sleep easily. Too much going on inside her head for that to happen. Cam had rattled her in more ways than one and she needed to work her way through everything so she'd wake up refreshed and ready to stride ahead and leave him behind—metaphorically if not physically.

But the next thing she was aware of was the sound of the boys calling each other names as they ran down the hall. Glancing around the room, she noted the sunlight at the gap in the curtains where Cam hadn't quite made them meet.

She'd overslept. Hardly unusual. Waking up early was not her thing. Nothing was worth rushing out of bed for. What about a glimpse of Cam's mouth-watering, muscular body to start her day off? What about getting her head on straight? Leaving Cam behind should be the plan. Tomorrow would do for that.

Sitting up straight, Jenny raised her arms over her head to stretch high. She felt good. When she tentatively wriggled her toes even her damaged foot seemed a lot happier this morning. Perhaps some of the swelling had gone down.

Tossing the covers aside, she clambered out of bed and got a shaft of pain for her efforts. Had she spoken too soon? She waited for the throbbing to calm down before limping across to pull open the curtains fully.

There was a light knock on her door. 'Jenny, you awake?' Cam called softly.

'Of course I am.'

The door opened wide and Cam stepped in, taking up all the breathable air at the same time. 'How are you this morning? Those eyes don't appear so bugged.' He stood watching her hop across the room in a T-shirt that barely covered her bottom.

She replied, 'I'm good. Really good.'

Cam gave an affirmative nod in her direction, but his gaze didn't lift to her face. He thought she was good? In what way? The tip of his tongue appeared between his lips, sending her heart rate skittering all over the show.

'Was there something you wanted to ask me?' she croaked. There were a few things she'd like him to ask, but that wasn't going to happen.

He shook his head. 'No, nothing.'

'Then I'll see you at lunchtime?' she asked.

'Yes. You'll have to get your own breakfast. I did poke my head in an hour ago to see what you might like but you were comatose, and now I'm running late.'

'No problem.' Cam had peeked in on her and she hadn't been aware? Running her hand over her mussed hair, she winced. Just as well. No doubt she looked like a train wreck.

Cam's eyes still seemed drawn to the bottom of her T-shirt.

She dropped onto the bed and tugged the covers over her legs. 'If you're late, hadn't you better get moving?'

He blinked as colour reddened his cheeks. 'You're right.' Turning his head, he called, 'Come on, boys. Chop, chop. Pack your bags, put your sandals on.'

'Chop, chop.'

'Chop, chop,' the twins mimicked as they charged along the hall.

Jenny could no longer hold back a smile. 'I remember that. Alison and I repeating everything Mum said. Boy, did we wind her up at times, especially if she was in a hurry or in a bad mood.'

'I'm not in a bad mood,' Cam growled.

'Of course not.' Her smile widened.

His scowl deepened. 'Think I prefer it when you're asleep.' He followed his sons, stomping along the hall.

Laughter bubbled up. 'Temper, temper,' she said, but not so loud that he'd hear. She did need a ride into Blenheim later.

Temper, temper, had been her and Alison's favourite taunt with Mum. They had been naughty at times. But always jointly, each egging the other on. Had Mum looked as tired as Cam did? She had no idea. Though there had been that time that Dad had left them with the neighbour they hadn't liked so he could take Mum out to a fancy restaurant for dinner—to give her a break from them.

Mum and Dad. They'd been the greatest parents any two girls could have wished for. Yeah, and look how she'd treated them these past months—almost ignoring them. Yet they were still so patient with her, waiting for her to work through her grief in her own way, while dealing with their own at the same time.

Where was her tablet?

She found it in the lounge and after making a cup of tea and toasting a slice of multigrain bread she began an email.

Dear Mum and Dad.

It's kind of fun being in this household. Marcus and Andrew remind me so much of the mischief Alison and I got up to. Cam, their father, looks exhausted all the time. I guess we did that to you, too.

I'm going for my check-up with the surgeon today and will have to wait in Blenheim for a ride home with Cam.

She was calling this place home now? What would Cam think of that? Probably pack her bag and put it out on the pavement at the bus stop.

Not sure when I'll be ready to leave here. The car's parked up in the garage here and Cam says I can leave it for as long as I want. Will keep you posted on my next moves.

Loads of love, Jenny.

Tapping the 'send' icon, she shook her head, admitting it felt good to finally have something to say without wondering if mentioning Alison's name would hurt them, or if not mentioning her sister hurt them even more.

Marcus and his skateboard had a lot to answer for. All she had to figure out was whether it was a good or bad thing. Draining the cup of tea she'd all but forgotten, she pushed to her feet. Time for a shower and an end to thinking. Thinking was highly overrated.

In the bathroom Cam had again set up everything for her. Even the rubbish sack was a new one. That man was too thoughtful for his own good. She smiled. But not for hers.

Was Cam like this with everyone? Or just her?

Did he feel attracted to her? Like she did to him?

No point in denying it—she found him physically exciting. And there was more—that thoughtfulness was sexy, as was his tenderness, determination to do the best for his boys, and just about everything about him. This was bad. And exciting.

CHAPTER SEVEN

'WHAT CAN I SMELL?' Cam's nose wrinkled as he sniffed an acrid burnt odour the moment he stepped inside his house. It had been a particularly gruelling day. Lack of sleep over the previous nights while Jenny had tripped through his head had only made it harder to deal with Roy Franks's unwillingness to listen. He'd told the man he'd die if he didn't have the open heart surgery he was booked in for next week, but Roy was still refusing. Sure, the man was scared witless. Who wouldn't be? But the operation had to be better than the alternative.

In the kitchen, standing behind the island, Jenny stared at him, embarrassment written all over her pretty face. Her eyes flicked to him and away again. 'How hard can it be to boil rice? Millions of people cook it every day. They don't burn it to the bottom of the pot, do they?'

Burnt rice? What was she up to now? 'Why do you want rice?' He had new season's potatoes ready to cook with mint picked from Mrs Warner's garden that morning. Lamb patties were on a plate covered with a paper towel in the fridge, all ready for the barbecue. All he had to do was toss together a salad.

Jenny glared at him. 'I'm cooking dinner for you. Thought I could give you a break since you've been so good to me. Guess I got that wrong.' Her glare turned woeful as she glanced at a recipe book on the counter. Asian meals.

She needed a recipe book to cook rice? Guess the disaster facing him answered that in the affirmative. 'Cooking not your strong point?' Despite the mess facing him, he couldn't help grinning at her.

Jenny winced. 'Not really.'

He saw the pot in the sink filled with water, presumably to soak off the layer of blackened rice he could see on the bottom. The pot looked ruined. Turning, he nodded in the direction of a serving dish on top of the stove containing something resembling the cat's biscuits when she regurgitated them on the floor. 'What's that?'

'Chicken chasseur.' Jenny glared at the dish, and continued in a woeful tone, 'At least, that's what it's meant to be but it looks nothing like the picture on the packet.'

'Packet?' Where was her beautiful smile?

'Yes. One of those add-water-and-cook things.' Heat was creeping into her usually pale cheeks.

'Were the instructions in Swahili?'

'So I'm not the world's greatest cook, all right? But I wanted to help out instead of sitting on my behind and being waited on hand and foot.' Jenny locked eyes with his. 'I've managed to empty the dishwasher and bring in the washing without incident.' Then she turned towards the fridge.

Reaching out, he caught her elbow and stopped her. 'Thanks. I do appreciate everything.'

Jenny didn't look at him now so he used his finger under her chin to lift her head and caught his breath at the tears threatening to spill down her face. 'Hey, I meant it. Truly.'

He should step away right this minute but for the life of him he couldn't. Those big beautiful summer eyes were bigger, greener and more beautiful, enhanced by the moisture she was trying to ignore. Big pools that he could easily drown in. Was drowning in.

'Then you won't mind me making the salad.' Jenny pulled back and reached to open the fridge. Lifting the vegetable bin, she once again averted her eyes.

Taking the bin from her hands, he smiled again. This woman had him relaxing even when she'd turned his kitchen into a tip. 'No insult, but I'll make the salad. But, first, why don't we have a glass of wine on the deck?' She did drink wine, didn't she? He hadn't offered before now because she'd been taking painkillers, but that morning she'd announced she'd stopped. Going to tough it out, she'd said, drugs being something she preferred not to take. Her new, lighter cast probably helped too.

'You're offering me a consolation prize?'

'No, you'd be giving me some adult time.' Something he sorely missed whenever he thought about it, which was why he didn't waste time mulling it over. Usually he was so busy just doing what had to be done to keep his head above water that he didn't consider what he might be missing out on, and yet now with Jenny in his house there were many things popping into his mind that hadn't been around for a long, long time. 'Cabernet sauvignon or sauvignon blanc?'

'Sav blanc, thank you. Want some cheese and crackers with that? There's a block of Havarti in the fridge. I only have to open two packets and put them on a plate.' The tears had retreated, and that sweet mouth was starting to curl upwards.

'Can't go too wrong with that.' He found her a serving plate then poured their drinks, white for her, red for him. 'You've chosen one of my favourite cheeses.'

'So the woman in the little café shop told me.'

She'd gone to the trouble of asking? Wow. That showed

her caring side. 'So what do you think of our little town?' She was still here, wasn't she?

'Would quaint be insulting?'

'Depends who you're talking to.' Mrs Warner would agree. Others would hate her for uttering such a word. He led the way outside and pulled out a chair for her. Watching her progress, it was obvious she'd well and truly got the hang of the crutches. 'Delia, my nurse, said she'd seen you out walking when she went to the bakery to buy us all morning tea.'

'I suppose there aren't too many people hobbling around Havelock with one foot in a cast.' She eased herself down onto the chair and slid back before laying the crutches on the floor under the table out of the way.

'You got it.'

'There are some interesting little shops, but how do they survive? It's not exactly downtown Auckland.'

Not even central Blenheim. 'There's a small but steady stream of tourists over the summer months, and in winter some of the shop owners close up and others slog it out.'

'This Mrs Warner? Your neighbour? I haven't seen her yet.'

'She's away visiting family for a fortnight.' Which was why she hadn't done his grocery shopping. Knucklehead that he was, he'd forgotten all about that until he'd been heading to Wairau Hospital to con Jenny into coming home with them.

He watched Jenny sipping the wine, her lips delicate against the glass, her throat moving as she swallowed. His gut tightened, as did muscles lower down. Steady. This fascination was getting out of hand. *So look away. Can't.*

'That turkey been flying over my head again?' she asked.

'No. I'm liking what I see, that's all.' That's all? That's

a lot. Women hadn't featured in his life since Margaret and yet a few days of having Jenny around and he felt as though he was coming alive. Hadn't known he'd been half-dead until this week.

'Your compliments are improving.' She smiled at him, a full-blown, breath-shortening smile that rocked him.

Oh, boy. He was so lost. Standing up, he said, 'I'll turn the barbecue on,' and immediately tripped over his own feet, managing to slosh wine down the front of his trousers. Great, now he had a kitchen and trousers to clean up. Not to mention the stirrings of arousal.

'Go change and bring me those pants. I do know something about removing stains. They won't end up looking like that chasseur, I promise.' Her smile turned to a cheeky grin. 'And watch where you're going this time.'

He spun around, took long, fast steps away from her. If she saw the bulge at the front of his pants she'd call the harassment police. Since when did his lack of a sex life matter so much? Why had his body leapt to life over Jenny?

Because she's beautiful and sexy, and pulls me in with those amazing eyes.

Note to self: stay away from that enticing smile. It's too distracting. Stay away from those eyes. They're dangerous.

And as he headed inside he saw the boys sprawled across the floor in front of the TV.

Second note to self: make those blasted appointments for haircuts.

Jenny worked the stain out and rinsed the trousers. Hard not to envisage the way this fabric had sat over that firm butt just minutes ago. Thankfully Cam had disappeared inside to remove them. Actually getting an eyeful of his rear view, or the front one, for that matter, if he'd shucked the trousers off outside might've given her palpitations.

Hobbling outside, she hung them on the line. The temperature hovered around twenty so with a bit of luck they'd be dry by the morning.

Her gaze cruised the yard. Cam didn't have much of a garden. Guess he didn't have the time. Or maybe he didn't have the inclination.

There was something she'd learned from Mum: how to grow flowers. Nothing more rewarding than seeing beds of brightly coloured freesias, daisies, roses, peonies springing to life over the warm months. To pick a handful of flowers she'd grown and place it in a vase on the table had always made her happy.

Cam's talent seemed to be in mowing the lawn in a circle, starting at the outside and working his way into the centre, by the looks of it. Lines from the last cut were still apparent. She could picture him striding out fast, aiming to get the job done before tackling the next chore. He never seemed to stop, always had more than enough to do. Though tonight he had sat down with a wine. Yeah, look how that had quickly turned to a mess.

At the end of the lawn a swing set looked neglected and unused. She shuffled onto the seat and with her good foot pushed back. When had been the last time she'd been on a swing? With Alison at the park in Surfers Paradise when Mum and Dad had taken them there for a holiday as teenagers. They'd been trying to impress some guys who'd been hanging around and Alison had reckoned they'd look cute on the swings. It had been a big fail.

Another Alison memory and she wasn't shaking with despair. Must be something in the Havelock air for her to be feeling more relaxed about everything that had happened. Would she ever come to terms with her grief? No, that would be expecting too much. Take one small step at a time. 'You lost your mojo in a big way. Don't rush trying to find it again.'

'Where did you lose your mojo?' asked one of the twins from behind her.

'What's a mojo?' asked the other.

'Can we help you find it?'

Stopping the swing, she turned to look at the boys. She hadn't realised she'd been talking out loud until they'd spoken up. 'Mojo is me, who I am, where I came from and where I'm going. The drive that keeps me going.'

Two blank faces stared at her.

'I lost it a year ago and now I want to find it so I can be happy again.' Would they understand that better?

'We can help you.'

They already were. The boys, along with Cam, treated her so normally that she had started coming alive again. 'Thank you.'

'If we help you—'

'Will you help us find something?' Andrew finished the question Marcus had started.

'Sure. What have you lost?' She already knew Andrew was in trouble with Cam for losing a sports shoe this week.

'Our mother. We can't find her anywhere.'

Oh, no. She'd well and truly walked into that one. These poor little guys looked and sounded distraught. Her heart squeezed painfully for them, her stomach sunk in on itself. 'I…' What did she say? Anything that came to mind would only hurt them more. She didn't know the circumstances, and this so wasn't her place. Except they were watching her, each with a plea in his eyes that would be impossible to deny.

'We only want to see her and give her a hug.' Andrew looked ready to burst into tears.

Jenny shoved off the swing and snatched both boys into her arms and held them tight. Not the hug they were wanting but she couldn't not hold them. They trembled against her, clinging to her as if for dear life. 'I know you do. I'd love to hug my sister.'

But that was different. Alison had gone. These boys' mother had to be somewhere. How could the woman leave her sons? Unbelievable. There was nothing that would be a good enough reason.

She sensed Cam's presence a second before his arms went around their little group, like an outer wrapping. His hand on her shoulder was warm and gave her the courage to raise her head and look directly at him.

'Thank you,' he mouthed. His eyes glittered as pain and anger and despair battled for supremacy in his lean face. So he'd heard what the boys had said. How often had he had to deal with this? How did he cope? Then he dropped a kiss on each boy's head and stood up slowly, unravelling himself and then the boys from around her.

What about me? Can I have a kiss too?

What she got was, 'Here, I'll give you a hand getting up.'

She'd forgotten about her ankle, but the moment Cam mentioned it she placed her hand in his and let him pull her gently upright, then leaned against him for a moment before he led her back to the deck to sit down.

'Where's your twin?' one of the boys asked, as he joined them on the deck.

Her shoulders drooped. What should she say? Would the boys think their mother had died too if she told them the truth? But she couldn't lie to them. That wouldn't help anyone. Looking at Cam for guidance, she found sympathy and saw a small nod. After a sip of wine she drew a deep breath and told them as simply as possible.

'My sister had an accident. We were mountain climbing and the track we were on gave out from under us. We fell over the cliff all the way to the bottom. Alison hit her head on a boulder.' The glass twirled back and forth in her fingers. 'She died there. I miss her heaps.'

Andrew clambered onto the bench to sit on her left side. Marcus did the same on her right. Cam looked astonished. Which was nothing to what she was feeling.

'That's sad. I'd miss Andrew if that happened to us.' Marcus snuggled closer. 'He's my best friend as well as my brother.'

Sniff. 'Yes, that's how it is for twins.' Another sip of the wine. 'You know, we're luckier than everyone else because we're twins. No one else has a special person that close to them.'

Marcus pulled back to stare up at her. 'Was Alison as pretty as you?'

'You are a right little charmer, aren't you?' Her smile wavered. 'Alison looked just like me.'

'How did people know who was Alison—'

'And who was you?'

Oh, boy, this wasn't getting any easier. 'Alison was always smiling. She was very funny and made everyone laugh.' Whereas I was the serious one. Except when I was with my sister.

Cam refilled her wine glass, even though she'd barely touched it. 'Here, enjoy that.' He handed it over. 'Marcus, Andrew, let's give Jenny a break now. Dinner will be ready soon so how about you empty your schoolbags and put the lunchboxes on the bench?'

'Thanks.' Jenny watched them scurry to do what

they'd been asked. 'Not sure where in the kitchen they can put anything. I did spread out a bit.'

'A bit?' Cam choked on his wine. She patted his back hard until he held a hand up and drew a deep breath. 'If I didn't know better I'd say a tornado had passed through the kitchen.'

'You do tend to exaggerate.' Reluctantly she withdrew her hand, trailing it across his shoulder blade and upper arm. The warmth Cam radiated hit her deep inside. A rare warmth from touching another human being. That joint hug of Cam's had been the first in a long time.

'Who? Me?' His smile was tight, his breathing a little rapid.

Because of her hand on him? Oh, great. Now what had she done? Did he fancy her? More to the point, did she want him to fancy her? 'Yes, you.' Now which question was she answering? Total confusion reigned in her head and she looked away.

Cam did that finger under her chin thing and tipped her head up and sideways so she couldn't avoid looking into his eyes. 'Thank you for telling the boys your story. I know it's very different from their mother walking away, but they seem to have picked up on something with you, and being twins that's helping them.'

'It must be difficult for you every time they think they've seen their mother. Is that what happened on Saturday? One of them said something about seeing her.'

'You got it in one.' His hands clenched and his body tensed. 'Some days I could strangle her for hurting them. All Marcus and Andrew ever asked for was to be loved. What's so wrong with that?' Spinning on the balls of his feet, he stared across the lawn, seeing who knew what.

'How long has she been gone?' Would he tell her to mind her own business?

'Two years and five weeks.' The desolation in his voice rolled her heart. She wanted to wrap her arms around him in a return hug, to take away that misery, but she couldn't move. What if he rejected her gesture?

Why would he? Why wouldn't he? They hardly knew each other, despite the fact she'd told him very briefly, via the twins, about Alison—something she never told anyone.

Did he still love his wife? Did he look for her in shops, too? Probably, if that far-away gaze was an indicator. Which meant she had no right feeling anything about him other than that he was a nice guy being very kind to her. Time to move on in case she started feeling something stronger for him. She'd talk about that after dinner when the boys were tucked up in bed. Tomorrow she'd head to a motel in Blenheim.

Dinner. The barbecue had waves of heat coming off it. 'Cam, I think you need to turn the barbecue off for a while or we're going to be eating charcoal.' Clomping inside, she retrieved that vegetable bin he'd taken off her earlier. She'd make the salad before cleaning up the mess she'd created.

It took for ever to wipe down all the surfaces, get that pot looking more or less how it used to, and make a salad.

By the time they'd all eaten and the dishes had been rinsed and stacked in the dishwasher Jenny was ready to take the weight off her foot.

Cam sat at his computer. 'Monthly health department requirements,' he muttered over his shoulder in answer to her query about why he was still working.

'You don't have an office person to deal with that?'

Filling the kettle, she flicked it on and found the teabags. 'You want tea?'

'Please. We do have office staff but the partners insist all of us check the figures pertaining to our own work. Pain in the backside at times.' Cam leaned closer to the screen. 'Especially when my receptionist never makes mistakes.'

'You'll have to come and get your tea. I'm done with cleaning up my messes,' she quipped, as she placed a plate of chocolate-chip cookies by his mug, 'I'd have baked a cake but you're out of flour.'

'You got these at the bakery.'

'Hope you like them.'

'They're the best. Don't tell the boys you bought some or they'll be gone.'

Guilt flared for leaving them out of the treat. 'Should I have given them one before they went to bed?'

'No. They'll probably get some on Friday when they buy their lunch.'

'You're not averse to a treat, then?'

Cam smiled, a big, happy smile. 'Who is?'

She could fall for that smile. So rare but when he tried it was beautiful. Which brought her to the next subject. 'I'm thinking I should be moving on soon. Saturday, maybe.' Huh? What had happened to going tomorrow? Saturday had slipped out so easily. She was finding it harder by the day to go. Cam had sucked her in, wrapped her in kindness, and made her start looking at the world differently. That was almost addictive.

Cam leant back in his chair and stared at her. 'Moving on? To where? Not to mention how. You can't drive yet.'

'I don't want to overstay my welcome.' *Lame, Jenny, very lame.*

'I'll let you know when you have.' That smile had well and truly disappeared now, making her sad.

'Now, why doesn't that surprise me?' She tried for a light-hearted tone. Big fail. 'Seriously, Cam, you've done more than enough for me. Think about what you said regarding the twins and them connecting with me. Wouldn't it be better for me to go now, before it becomes a problem?'

Where had that come from? She hadn't consciously thought it through, but now that the idea was out there she knew it to be true. 'No way do I want to upset Andrew and Marcus.'

'Low blow, Jenny Bostock.' He looked taken aback. Why? She was only trying to take his concerns into consideration.

'It wasn't meant to be.' *I don't want to go. Not yet.* But staying would only make her eventual leaving harder for her as much as for the boys. She just knew it. Already Cam featured in her daydreams, and her night-time ones. Even looking at him threw her sex-starved body into a pickle. Considering that sex had never been high on her list of requirements even in the good times, this was hard to understand. Could it be because she'd never met a man as hot as Cam? Just breathing the same air as him turned her on. *Hello? Who am I? I don't recognise myself.*

'What are you doing for Christmas?' Cam stretched his long legs further under the table and crossed his ankles.

'Christmas?' What did that have to do with anything?

'You know. The time when Santa Claus comes down the chimney, bringing sacks of presents for everyone.'

She nodded. 'That Christmas.' Maybe she should go tonight. Christmas used to be filled with fun and love.

She couldn't imagine sitting down to unwrap those presents or to eat roast turkey and hot ham without Alison. Last year the whole issue had been avoided when Mum and Dad had joined her and Colby at a restaurant on Auckland's viaduct.

'It's not far off. Have you got plans?'

Stop right there, Cameron.

'Yes, I have, as it happens.'

I'm going to book into a hotel in some place I've never visited before and spend the day exploring.

Disappointment gleamed out at her from those all-seeing eyes. An uncomfortable silence settled between them, making her fidgety. Finally, when she couldn't bear it any more, she said, 'What are you and the boys doing that day?' Turn it on him, divert his attention.

'Going down the Kenepuru Sound to the family beach house with the whole Roberts clan.'

'You've got brothers and sisters?'

'Three sisters, three brothers-in-law, six nieces and nephews, and my parents. We have a wonderful time.'

She'd got an answer that only caused envy to unfurl deep inside her. Family. Mum and Dad. Back in Dunedin. Christmas would be as lonely for them there as it would be for her in a hotel. She made an instant decision. 'I'm going down south to see my parents.'

'Good idea.' But she noted a hint of disappointment in Cam's eyes before he turned back to the computer and began tapping on the keyboard.

Dismissed. Fair enough. She hadn't exactly been forthcoming about her off-the-cuff plans. Taking the blunt hint, she hobbled towards the hallway. 'Goodnight.'

'Jenny,' Cam called softly. 'Don't make any definite plan about when you're leaving. Stay for the weekend and see how you feel next week. The boys would love to have you here for their school swimming competition on Saturday.'

Yeah. But what about Cam? Would he love to have her standing with him as he encouraged his lads to swim faster?

CHAPTER EIGHT

Cam felt freer than he had for months. His boys were happier than they'd been since arriving in Havelock and that was saying something because they enjoyed living in this tiny place where everyone knew everyone—sometimes far too well. The kids were the only reason he'd hung in here, putting them before the aching need to lose himself in a city filled with people and action and work. Yet today there was a lightness in his chest around his heart that had nothing to with Havelock and a lot to do with the woman walking beside him.

'Hi, Cam,' Braden greeted him, as he placed his 'OPEN' sign outside his tourist info centre. 'You're looking pleased with yourself this morning.'

'Christmas is just around the corner, the sun's shining and my boys are in the swimming team for this weekend's contest against Rai Valley School. Can't get better than that.'

'Sounds like you're taking happy pills,' Jenny muttered.

He laughed. Out loud. A deep belly laugh. What the heck? Maybe he had swallowed something he shouldn't have. Braden probably wore a shocked look on his face after that spewing of words he'd given. He shrugged.

Tough. 'I'd better get that bottle of multivitamins checked out. Who knows what's in them?'

'Maybe you need to see a doctor.' Jenny shook her head at him. 'I know of one who thinks you're decidedly off your rocker. Braden's still scratching his head and staring at you as though he doesn't know you any more.'

'Does that doctor accept responsibility for my deterioration?'

Those gorgeous green eyes widened, and laughter crinkles appeared at their corners. 'You're blaming me for your suddenly apparent motor-mouth?'

'Of course I am.' Not only that. He blamed her for the hours he lay awake at night, wishing she was lying naked in his bed with her legs entwined with his and his hands on those beautiful mounds pushing out the front of her skimpy top.

'Great.'

'Boys, watch where you're going,' he said automatically, before taking Jenny's elbow to lead her across the road after a truck and trailer unit loaded with pine logs rolled past.

Not that she needed his helping hand, despite having left the crutches at home this morning, but he liked doing it, enjoyed touching her. Her skin was smooth and soft under his fingers. The pulse at her elbow rapped a beat on his fingertip and heated his blood fast. Resisting the urge to drop her elbow or the other one to hold on tighter, he just enjoyed the moment, and ignored the sudden intake of breath she made.

The other side of the road came all too quickly, giving him no excuse to continue holding her. But Jenny was ahead of him, tugging free before he had time to loosen his fingers. She stepped sideways, putting a gap between them. Not happy with him? He tried to read her expression, found he couldn't. She didn't appear to be angry. Good, because he really didn't want them getting offside. 'What are you going to do today?'

She flicked him a wry smile. 'I'll have a nana nap, wash my bloomers and scrub my dentures.'

No mention of attempting to cook dinner again. Phew. 'That exciting, huh?' If she was joking with him he had to be in her good books. So taking her elbow hadn't been a bad thing. Did that mean he'd sparked some heat in her as she had done in him? *I hope so. Oh, boy, as I've told myself before, I'm in trouble.* 'Don't nana nap through three o'clock and miss meeting the boys at school.'

'Maybe I'll wait outside the gate all day so I'll be sure to be there on time. Where do they get all that energy?'

The boys had raced ahead, joining other kids on their way to school. 'No idea, but I could do with some of it.' Yet today there was a spring in his step as he tracked the daily route to the medical centre. Until now Havelock had been little more than an anchor around his neck. Today he found himself looking around, smiling at people, watching Jenny as she hobbled along the uneven path, enjoying the twins' enthusiasm for school. Today he actually liked Havelock: liked that he lived here, was making a life for himself and the kids here. Liked walking to work with this woman.

A family. That's what this felt like. Family. How he'd always hoped it would be with Margaret. He shivered, looked up to see if the sun had gone behind a cloud. Nope, not a cloud anywhere to be seen. The ghost had been his dreams and aspirations. Margaret had doused all of those.

Yet here he'd been feeling warm and fuzzy about a family when the woman who'd triggered this was all but a stranger to him. More than crazy, considering his ex hated this ridiculously small place that she believed no one had heard of. No one that counted anyway. Jenny was used to big hospitals and people in her face all the time so it was given that she was unlikely to feel comfortable in Havelock. He needed to remember that next time his hormones woke up.

'See ya, Dad.' Andrew flapped a hand in his direction.

Blink. Oh, right. His corner. 'Wait,' he called to the boys. 'The medical centre's up this street,' he told Jenny. 'I appreciate you doing this. It's one of the things that I worry about: Andrew and Marcus having to go to Amanda's and not being able to come straight home from school. But there's no other way around the problem.'

'The pleasure's all mine.' She sounded so sincere his heart melted a weeny bit more.

Note to self: don't feel bad when Jenny finally leaves. Enjoy the time she's here with us.

Jenny clomped along to the school gate a few minutes before three. It was Thursday and she wasn't at all ready to leave. In fact, she was getting far too comfortable in the Roberts household. It felt like home. Maybe come Monday she'd feel differently. The weekend was bound to be hectic and crazy.

Standing close to but not in the midst of the parents waiting for their children, she glanced around and chuckled. This whole pick-up-the-kids-from-school scene had absolutely nothing to do with her previous life. But when the boys had asked if she would and Cam had agreed if Jenny was happy with the idea, she hadn't been able to come up with any reason why not.

'Hi, I'm Amanda. The twins usually come to me after school. I'm presuming you're Jenny, right?' A woman with bright orange stripes in her black hair stood in front of her.

'Hello, Amanda. Guess the cast's a giveaway, huh?'

Amanda grinned. 'The twins talk nonstop about you. I reckon there's not much about you I don't know.'

Absolutely wonderful. So all the town knew she'd lost her mojo and her sister. 'How boring for you all.'

The grin widened, if that was possible. 'Relax. The twins think you're pretty, and cool for reading to them, and apparently you're hopeless at cooking. Sometimes I wish I couldn't put a meal together then someone else would have to feed my tribe.'

'There is that. But you wouldn't believe the mess I made of dinner and the kitchen the other night. No wonder the boys were talking about me.'

'I heard dinner went in the bin untouched.'

So it was true what people said—there were no secrets in small towns. A piercing ringing sound came from inside the school grounds. Saved by the bell. Now all she had to do was wait for Marcus and Andrew to find her and then they could go home—where she could make some more blunders to amuse everyone.

Amanda said, 'Why don't you come and have a coffee with me tomorrow morning? I do a mean cappuccino, even if I say so myself.'

About to say no, Jenny glanced at this woman who had been kind enough to speak to her. There was nothing but friendship in her eyes. 'I'd like that.'

Yeah, actually, she would. It had been a long time since she'd met a friend for coffee, and while she and Amanda weren't strictly friends it would be nice all the same. Another tick for Havelock. This small place had started doing what nowhere else had managed so far. It had begun chipping away her armour plating that kept the world out and her pain in.

As Amanda gave her the address children swarmed

out the gate to surround the waiting parents, the noise level getting higher by the second.

'Jenny, we're hungry.'

At least that's what she thought Marcus said, but who'd know in the bedlam? He could've told her he'd lost his school bag or his lunch had been stolen, she wouldn't have a clue. 'Just as well I brought my wallet, then, isn't it? We can stop at the bakery on the way home.'

'Can we really?' Andrew bounced up in front of her.

'Better than me making you some biscuits.' She grinned.

Andrew nodded solemnly. 'Would they look like that chicken thing you threw out?'

'Probably.' What happened to the Jenny who hated to fail at anything? The Jenny who didn't do cooking so that no one could laugh at her messes? She'd come to Havelock, that's what.

The boys talked nonstop until they reached the bakery, where they had an endless debate about which treat they'd like. Finally Jenny chose a custard square for herself, saying, 'You've got until the lady gives me my cake to make up your minds, otherwise you're going without.'

Funny how quickly they decided on the brownie. 'Thanks, Jenny.'

'What's for dinner?' Andrew asked, less than a minute later.

'We'll have to wait and see,' she told them. 'You haven't eaten your brownie yet.'

Marcus rolled his eyes at his brother. 'It's Thursday. Sausage night.'

What? 'You have the same thing on the same night? All the time?'

'Of course.'

Probably the only way Cam coped. He was a thoroughly

organised man about the house. Already she'd come to recognise his routines for getting the dinner on, the house tidied, the boys showered and their homework under way.

'Hope you don't mind the meals we have here,' Cam said later that night, as he pulled a packet of mince from the freezer.

'Meat patties tomorrow night, then?'

'You've worked it out already?' Cam's smile was wary. 'I do vary the menu occasionally. It's also different from summer to winter. I make mostly casseroles in the colder months, which are great for being able to slow-cook in the crockpot all day.'

'You're very well organised.' Her routine used to involve going to the supermarket every day after work, where there were all manner and number of solutions for meals and drinks.

'You avoided my original question.'

Handing Cam his mug of tea, she laughed. 'Relax. I'm hardly going to complain, am I? You might tell me to get my own dinner and that would be a disaster.'

'You've *never* cooked?' He did look a little bamboozled by the thought of that.

'You're asking because I'm female and all good women are goddesses in the kitchen?' Her hair swirled around her face as she shook her head. 'Not me. Why bother learning when supermarkets shelves are filled with so many options for heat-and-eat meals? They mightn't be gourmet but compared to what I create they're delicious.'

Heat slipped up his neck and into his cheeks. 'I didn't mean to be all gung-ho over whose role is whose in the house. I enjoy cooking, especially when I'm not rushing around like a lunatic, trying to get everything done so I can get to bed before midnight.' He shrugged. 'There's something special about putting together a meal to share with family or friends. For me it's a way of showing I care.' Another shrug. 'Even if I only barbecue some sausages.'

She hadn't thought of it that way. Sharing with family or friends. She used to share flowers from her garden. That had always made her feel good and hopefully it had done the same for the people she'd given them to. 'I can see how that might be. Except I'd probably lose any friends I might have. Can you imagine sitting down to eat that chicken chasseur I somehow managed to destroy?'

His nose wrinkled and his mouth curved ever so slightly upwards. 'Truthfully? No. It had a distinctly unappealing look to it. Cooking rule number one: remember that people eat with their eyes before they pick up their knife and fork.'

Rule one, eh? 'So it's all about presentation.'

'Yep. You can fool people quite a lot if the plate looks appetising.'

The next morning Jenny swung into Amanda's large kitchen and stopped to gape at the array of cookery books on the shelves. 'You must have hundreds of books.'

'I should really go through them and toss the older ones out but I can't bring myself to do it.' Amanda jammed her hands on her hips as she joined Jenny in staring at the collection. 'So many recipes and no time to read them, let alone use them.'

'Does everyone in Havelock like cooking?' The bakery was beyond excellent; Cam wasn't adverse to putting a meal together; and now this. From a wooden rail above the central island gleaming pots and pans hung off hooks within easy reach of anyone working at the bench. 'Unbelievable.'

'I used to be a chef before I had four kids and took on

teaching swimming.' Behind the orange and black hair was obviously a very smart brain.

'You wouldn't go back into a kitchen here in Havelock?'

As the nostril-twitching aroma of good coffee filled the kitchen, Amanda crossed to a cupboard and found some cups. 'No. It would take most of my time and I far prefer being here for the children. They're growing up so fast already that they'll be gone out into the big, wide world before I know it, and to have wasted these years in a commercial kitchen would be gutting.'

There was a truth in that. Amanda's focus was family, whereas she didn't have to think about anyone else. Yet in the past week she'd started to reach out to Mum and Dad with daily emails that were long, wordy ramblings about her stay with the Roberts family. A family that she was trying to help in any little way she could, even if Cam ran such an organised household that there was little she actually did that made any difference.

'Amanda...' Jenny paused. Was she about to ask something impossible? Not to mention stupid? 'Would you show me how to cook a couple of simple meals that I could prepare for Cam and the boys? I'll pay for everything. If you have the time, of course.'

The woman didn't even hesitate. Not so bright in that orange head after all? 'That would be fun. When do you want to start?'

Oh. Um. Next week? But what if she'd gone by then? 'Today?'

Again, no hesitation. 'Drink your coffee and we'll discuss what we're having for dinner tonight.'

'We will?' Eek. What had she done? Her? Cooking? Yeah, why not? 'I'm absolutely hopeless in a kitchen. Like, really and truly useless.' She'd make a total stuff-up and Amanda would regret agreeing to show her the basics. *Shush, Amanda's talking.*

'I've an idea. I make meals that suit the kids as well as Ross and myself. Why don't we make twice as much and you take home enough for Cam and his lads? That way I can talk you through the process and I'm not having to think up two different meals every time.'

'Sounds perfect.' Every time? Would there be more than one chance at this? Warmth flooded her. Was she really about to embark on a cooking lesson? Unbelievable. 'This coffee's great.'

'Told you it would be.' Amanda grinned. 'Do you like beef stroganoff?'

'I love it. Would Marcus and Andrew like that?'

'My kids can never get enough of it so I'm sure the twins will be the same. They might've had it here some time.'

Uh-oh. 'I'll have to cook rice.'

'Get a rice cooker. I've got one somewhere I'll lend you for starters.'

The rice was white and fluffy. The beef melted in her mouth. And Cam and the boys had seconds. Jenny couldn't stop smiling.

'That was yummy. So you bought a packet with instructions in English.' Cam gave her the biggest smile yet. One that went all the way down to the tips of her toes.

Shaking her head at him, she gave a return smile. 'No packets involved. That was the real article. Made from scratch.'

His eyebrows rose distressingly high. His eyeballs might pop out if he wasn't careful. 'Have you been pulling my leg about your cooking skills?'

'Nope. This morning I had a lesson from an ex chef.'

Wow, she felt good. Not only had she done something other than wipe down benches for this wonderful man but she'd knocked back one of her gremlins. She could cook—with a lot of help from Amanda. *Easy, girl: pride before a fall. One dinner does not make a competent cook.*

'You've been talking to Amanda.' Cam's eyebrows returned to their natural position.

'More like listening as she explained how to slice beef across the grain, and not to over-stir the sauce ingredients. I've had a great day.' A really great day. 'Oh, except Amanda managed to slice three fingers while showing me how fast she was at chopping onions.'

'I take it you weren't required to sew her digits back on?' Cam's eyebrows rose and his mouth curved into a heart-warming smile.

'She refused to even consider stitches so I made some butterfly plasters from her first-aid kit supplies.' It hadn't been a major incident but she'd felt good to have been able to help Amanda medically. The doctor part of her make-up seemed to be waking up here in Havelock too. 'Amanda won't be using her left hand for much over the next few days.'

'Knowing that woman, I wouldn't bet on it. I'm glad you were there for her.'

'Me, too.' Yeah, and leaving Cam just got a whole lot harder. Seeing those smiles as they'd all tucked into dinner had warmed her deep inside in a way she'd never felt, even before Alison's death. This warmth came with a sense of belonging. Finding her mojo?

Maybe I won't leave. Oh, sure, I'm going to settle down in Havelock, lift the population number to five hundred and one, and do what exactly? Sell beef stroganoff at the gate? Like a pricked balloon her happiness shrivelled in on itself. She had to leave soon.

Cam gathered up the plates and stood up. 'That was the tastiest meal we've had in this house. Go, you.' In the kitchen he sluiced the dishes and said quietly, 'The boys love having you bring them home after school, by the way. I prefer it for them. Adds to the stability of their lives, which has been a roller-coaster ride so far.'

Stunned at him even admitting that, she held her breath while thinking about what he'd revealed. She'd wanted to help Cam out, but in this way? The connotations were huge. Doing this involved trust and care and could wreck those little boys' hearts again when she was gone.

'Maybe I shouldn't do it any more. Have you thought how they'll feel when I go away?' *She* was going to feel awful. Leaving the boys would be hard. Leaving Cam—well, she couldn't begin to imagine how that would feel. She suspected gut-wrenching wouldn't begin to describe it.

'I have, but I'm banking on the summer holidays being long enough they won't be at all perturbed.'

Right, he had it all sorted. Except, 'I won't be here until the end of term.'

'You sound very sure.'

'I am.' And because she owed him, she added, 'There's some place I absolutely have to be. No argument.'

'I see.' It was evident in his eyes that he didn't see at all. How could he? He knew nothing about what drove her.

'I'll clean up the kitchen if you've got other things to get done.' She stood up and rubbed the small of her back where it had been aching for a while.

Cam's gaze followed her hands as she rubbed up and

down, working her fingers into the tight muscles. He swallowed hard and pressed his lips tight. The plates in his hands banged onto the bench. She bit down on the reluctant smile about to break across her mouth. It wouldn't do for him to know she'd noticed his reaction. They couldn't follow through. Because of the children. Because she wasn't ready. Because she was leaving and flings, even very short ones, weren't on her agenda. But that didn't mean she couldn't find some sweet pleasure in having him a little bit attracted to her.

He made her feel alive again, reminded her she was a woman, not just someone traipsing the country looking for forgiveness and the incentive to return to medicine.

The only person who has to forgive you is you.

The salt and pepper shakers dropped from her hand onto the table with a bang. What? Where had that dumb idea come from? Not her, that's for certain. Mum and Dad must hold her responsible for Alison's death. Didn't they? They'd never come out and said so but she'd been the only person there when it had happened so, of course, she should've been able to do something to save Alison.

'Jenny? What is it?' Cam was at her side, pushing her gently back onto the chair she'd just risen from. 'What's going on?'

She snapped her mouth shut before she could spill the words that would tell him what a dreadful sister she'd been, not to mention a useless doctor. That would certainly remove any hint of attraction he might feel for her, and she really didn't want to lose that. Not yet. In a few days' time when she went away she'd deal with that. But not tonight. Not now. 'I'm fine. Just moved too fast and cricked my ankle.'

Cam made his usual move and pressed a finger under her chin, raising her face so he could lock eyes with her.

'Try again. I don't believe it.' There was nothing but concern and compassion looking out at her, but she wouldn't fall for it. She had to be strong. Despite telling him about the accident that had taken Alison, she'd not filled him in on all the gruesome details and she wasn't about to start. They were her horrors to deal with, no one else's. Especially not this man's, who'd done nothing but show her kindness.

Pushing his hand aside, she stood again. 'Then we'll have to agree to disagree.' Snatching up the salt and pepper, she slipped past him into the kitchen and started rinsing off dishes. *Please go and find another chore to do, preferably one in another room. Leave me to myself for a bit. I'll come right quicker that way.*

But when she turned around Cam stood right there in front of her, that concerned expression on his face changing, morphing into...? 'What?'

'Jenny.' His hands touched her cheeks, oh, so lightly. 'You're beautiful,' he whispered, as he moved his head closer.

This wasn't what she'd meant when she'd wanted him to find another chore. This was... She leaned closer. This was... The air seemed to vibrate between them. Those brown eyes were locked on hers, watching, waiting, wanting. This was—*is*—right.

Her mouth brushed those lips she'd been dreaming for days of kissing. Brushing her mouth over Cam's wasn't enough. Hunger gripped her. Thankfully Cam began kissing her properly, hard and soft, demanding and giving. Knee-buckling sensations tore through her like wildfire. Heat rose to warm her face. Wrapping her arms around him, she held on for dear life, kissing him back as hard and soft, as demanding and giving as he kissed her. His mouth was hot, hot, hot. His hands on her waist were hot. His chest pressing against her breasts was hard and hot.

And lower down something else seemed to be heating up too, definitely hardening if that bulge pushing into her stomach was anything to go by. How did two mouths touching cause wild reactions south of their waists? Because right in her centre that heat had turned molten, setting her muscles to squeezing and her hormones dancing.

'Yuck, they're kissing.'

'Don't look. That's gross.'

Cam set her back from him so fast it took a moment to regain her equilibrium. Marcus and Andrew. Oh, hell. Now they'd blown it. What were the boys going to think about this? A quick look at Cam told her he already regretted coming near her. The heat suffusing her body rapidly chilled down to cool. Great. She'd definitely be packing her bag now. Hopefully Cam would wait until the morning before kicking her out on the street.

'Marcus, Andrew, where's your homework?' Cam sounded like he was in control of his emotions.

Too in control. Like that kiss hadn't affected him one little bit. But he had been reacting to her as though he wanted her. Or had it been that long for him as it had for her that his body had just woken up all by itself?

'Do we have to do it?'

'There's that swimming competition tomorrow.'

'Go and get it. Now,' Cam snapped.

Jenny snatched up the dishcloth and began wiping down the bench. The sooner the kitchen was cleaned up the sooner she could escape to her room and close the door on this monumental error she and Cam had made. Yes, Cam had a lot to answer for. She hadn't started the kiss, couldn't take all the responsibility for their actions.

But one quick peek at his face and she knew she'd better make herself scarce. For now at least.

Cameron watched Jenny from where he supervised the boys' homework. Her shoulders were tense as she swiped at the bench with the cloth. But just when he thought she was going to spit the dummy out a tiny smile widened that delicious mouth and lifted the corners. So she had enjoyed their stolen kiss. Damn the boys for their interruption. Then again, thank goodness they had burst into the room, otherwise who knew where kissing Jenny might've led? Apart from down the hall to his bedroom, that was. Except those boys were the very reason why it had had to stop when it had. Damn it again.

Note to self: find a time and place where there are no boys so he could repeat that kiss with the hottest woman he'd had the pleasure of knowing.

Note to self: do it soon.

CHAPTER NINE

THE SWIMMING RACES were hilarious to watch. Boys and girls everywhere looked excited and terrified and determined to do well in their events.

Jenny waved. 'Good luck, Marcus. Good luck, Andrew.'

They waved back. Cam gave them the thumbs-up. 'Give it your best shot, guys.' Then, in an aside, he said, 'If only they weren't in the same race. They'll be arguing about the result for days. Marcus swims like a fish while Andrew's more like a concrete block.'

'You haven't tried asking the teacher to separate them?' Hard to believe none of last night's tension had carried over into today. They'd both got up in a great frame of mind, preparing the boys for the swimming and strolling down the main road to the school as though they did it every day.

'On many occasions. Apparently I don't know what I'm talking about.'

Jenny nudged him with an elbow. 'Look at them poised ready to leap in. Like pros they are.' If only she and Cam did do this every day. Not the swimming but taking the boys to school and sharing whatever they were into.

'They watch too much sport on TV, that's what.' Cam's gaze was fixed on his boys.

Say what he liked, Jenny felt sure that was pride swelling his chest. A muscular chest that she'd love nothing more than to run her fingers all over, and tease those nipples till he groaned with need. She definitely had to catch the eleven o'clock bus to Blenheim on Monday. Or should she go back to Nelson and wait out the days till it was time to visit Kahurangi?

'On your marks.' A whistle sounded. The kids were off, some leaping into the water, others belly-flopping, and then there was Marcus. He dived, not neatly but it was a dive.

Jenny grinned. 'Go, Marcus. You're one cool kid.' Hell, *her* chest was swelling with something like pride. 'Where's Andrew?' It was hard to see him amongst the splashes and mini-waves made by the various swimming styles.

'Five metres down his lane. The one with the arms like a windmill having hiccups.'

Andrew might have the most ungainly technique and his legs might be closer to the bottom of the pool than the surface of the water but he was making progress. 'Go, Andrew. Come on, you can do it.' Jenny leapt up and down on her good foot, her hands above her head, waving at him. 'You, too, Marcus. What a champ. You're winning.' Of course, neither of them could see or hear her but she didn't care. This was exciting.

Cam roared his encouragement. 'Come on, Marcus. Ten metres to go. That's it. You're a champ.' Then his gaze cruised down the pool to latch onto Andrew. 'Keep going, my boy. One arm after the other.'

Jenny reached for Cam's hand. 'We should be at the finish line—or whatever you call it in swimming. Those

boys are going to want to see you standing there, smiling at them.'

Cam's fingers instantly interlaced with hers. 'You're
right.'

They got to the end of the pool as Marcus hauled
himself out of the water. 'Did you see that, Dad? I won.'

Cam ruffled Marcus's hair. 'Well done, kiddo. That
was a great race.'

Marcus beamed at him then turned to her. 'Did you
see me, Jenny?'

'I saw you. You're like a seal in the water.' Jenny
dropped a kiss on his forehead, got a whiff of chlorine
and immediately recalled the many hours she and Alison
and their mates had spent at the local pool in the summer holidays.

A warm hand covered her shoulder, warm fingers on
her skin. Cam bent his head so his mouth was close to
her ear. 'You're a marvel with these two. Sure you haven't
got a gang of kids hidden somewhere?'

She heard the words but couldn't answer for the effect
his warm breath was having on her skin. Inside, a gentle wave of warmth quickly became a tsunami of heat,
rolling through her, overwhelming her ability to stand
upright. Just like last night, only this time it hadn't even
taken Cam's kiss to start her off. Placing a hand on Cam's
arm for balance, she struggled to gain control. When her
eyes locked with his she hoped she didn't look as startled
as he did right now. How could one touch, one look make
her feel so—so stunned?

'Dad?'

The twins. She gasped at the same instant Cam swung
his head up. Her heart pounded. What had just gone
down? Here, at the pool. Totally out of place. They were
at the school, surrounded by kids and teachers and par-

ents. And Marcus and Andrew. Far worse than in the kitchen last night.

Cam calmly dropped his hands to his sides. 'I'd better get a move on.' He had to be in Blenheim for the afternoon clinic. 'See you tonight, okay?'

'Is Jenny staying to watch us some more?'

'I'll be here for the rest of the afternoon.'

'Cool. We're going to have a bombing contest after the last race.'

She heard Cam say, 'Be careful,' in a worried tone.

'I'll make sure they behave.' She looked directly at him. 'No broken bones on my watch.'

His smile was strangely relaxed, like he didn't care if half of Havelock had witnessed that near kiss. It seemed for ever before he looked away and focused on the boys. 'How about I get fish and chips on the way home and we can take Jenny down to the marina to eat them?'

The shouts of *yes* were deafening. The warmth returned to her body, this time calm and gentle. This family seemed to like having her around. What's more, she loved being here, with them. Especially with the man who had woken up parts of her body she'd hardly been aware existed before. How could desire for one man be so different from any other she'd experienced in her previous sexual encounters?

'I hear you made a fabulous dinner last night.' Amanda appeared before her moments after Cam disappeared around the corner of the school building, looking too smug for her own good.

Glad of the distraction, Jenny agreed. 'It was delicious, and everyone except me ate two helpings. Thank you so much. You have no idea how much I appreciate it.'

'It seems to have had a strange effect on you and Cam,

if what I overheard the twins telling their mates is true.'
Amanda's eyes glittered with amusement.

'Here I'd been hoping we'd get away with that little
adventure.'

Amanda laughed. 'Not a chance. I doubt there's a living soul in town who doesn't know you two were kissing last night.'

Shrugging, Jenny joined in the laughter. 'Guess there's
nothing I can do about it. I'm not going to wish it hadn't
happened.' Oh, where'd her discretion button gone? It
wasn't as though she usually went around telling others
about her private life. 'How are those fingers?'

'Very sore, but they get me out of washing dishes.'

'Wonder what we can cook next.'

'How about lasagne on Monday?' Amanda asked.

'That's getting more difficult, isn't it?' *Walk before
running, remember?*

'Not at all. You'll be fine with it. Come and meet some
of the other mums. Be warned, they're curious about you,
especially after the stories and that eye-locking moment
you just had with Cam.'

Jenny groaned. 'Great. Think I'd better be making
tracks for home.' *It is not home. And you told the boys
you'd be watching them, remember?* Oh, hell. She'd just
agreed to go to Amanda's on Monday when she intended
leaving that day. She guessed the buses ran the same on
Tuesdays.

'We're keeping an eye on our kids from the other side
of the pool under the shade sail.'

'Are they going to tease me, too?'

'You can bet your dinner on it.' Amanda grinned.
'Might as well face the firing line and get it done with.'

It should've felt exactly like that but the women were

so friendly Jenny relaxed immediately when Amanda
introduced everyone.

'Shelley, Karen, Jocelyn, meet Jenny. She's staying
with Cam and the boys until her foot's come right.'

Fobbing off the comments about hot doctors, Jenny
found a spot on the grass beside Shelley and carefully
lowered herself to the ground.

'How's that ankle coming along?' Shelley asked.

'Not nearly fast enough.' Though if it had healed in
three days, like she'd wanted, then she'd be long gone
and back out on the road heading for the next town. And
not getting to know Cam as much as she had.

Then Shelley asked her, 'Have you got kids? You seem
to know what you're doing with Cam's two.'

'None yet.' Yet? 'Got to find a man first.' Why did
Cam come to mind so instantly? *Don't answer that.* She
couldn't anyway, not having a clue. An image of strong
leg muscles and a tight butt burst across her brain. Okay,
maybe a little clue.

'Looks to me like you already have.' Jocelyn had a
nice smile even when being cheeky.

Amanda had no problem with giving an opinion on
Jenny's single status either. 'Cam doesn't have anyone
in his sights. You could check him out more thoroughly.'

Been there, done that, and so far liked what she'd seen,
tasted, felt. 'I think the man's too busy to find time for
dating. Anyway, I'll be gone within a few days.' How
many times had she said that in the past week? The day
that she packed her bag never seemed to come, always
getting pushed further out. But soon she would have to
make arrangements for that rendezvous with her past.

Shelley looked surprised. 'You're not staying on once
your ankle's better? I'm sure Cam could use your help
at the practice.'

'I think Cam more than handles the centre. Besides, I was an emergency specialist, not a GP.' She shoved to her feet and looked around for the twins. Suddenly she'd had enough of idle chatter that seemed to focus on her too much. Next, these women would be wanting to know why she wasn't doctoring at the moment, and she wasn't ready to share that with them today. Or ever.

Shouts came from the pool. Children were staring into the water. Parents had leapt to their feet and raced closer. Jenny felt her heart thump against her ribs. Where were the boys? Her eyes searched the area as she made her way down to the edge of the pool, found Andrew. Marcus? There, by the changing shed. Phew.

'Lily,' Shelley screamed, and pushed past Jenny to kneel down on the edge of the pool.

A man leapt into the pool, dived deep, aiming for the child on the bottom. The water was turning red down there.

'What happened?' Jenny asked the woman beside her. 'I'm a doctor, I can help.'

'I know. I think Lily was running along the edge and slipped. How many times do we have to tell the kids running is banned around the pool?'

'Can you call the ambulance? I'll do what I can but Lily is going to need oxygen and things that I don't have with me.' If she hasn't drowned down there.

'On it.' The woman was already punching 111 on her cell. 'The ambulance is just next door but the call will go through Christchurch.'

'I suppose it would be asking too much for someone here to have a key?' Jenny asked.

'I've got one. I'm Brett, a volunteer crew member. Simone, tell the dispatcher you've got the ambulance sorted but they still need to record the call.' The man turned to Jenny. 'What do you need?'

'A backboard, oxygen, neck brace, and the defibrillator just in case.'

Brett grabbed a woman by the arm. 'Give us a hand.'

Jenny squatted awkwardly beside Shelley. 'Your daughter?'

'Yes. Is she going to be all right?'

That was the million-dollar question. 'She hasn't been down there more than a few seconds.' But what was causing the bleeding?

Lily was quickly brought to the surface. Thankfully her rescuer had lifted her with his hands under her arms and saved her spine from curving. Now to keep her that way. 'Someone take her for me,' the man called.

'Give her to me.' Shelley reached for her daughter.

'Mummy!' Lily screamed.

'Wait.' Jenny grabbed Shelley's shoulder. Thank goodness Lily was breathing. One less problem. 'Sorry, Shelley, but we have to do this properly in case there's any spinal damage.' Looking around, she said, 'Once we get the backboard I need three people in there to place it against Lily and lift her out.'

Instantly hands were raised, and people were saying, 'I'll help.'

She pointed to the nearest three. 'Get into the water away from Lily so you don't cause her needless movement. Then I want you to stand behind her with…?'

'John.'

'With John. I'll come in and put a neck brace on her before you move her.' She bent down to remove her shoe.

Someone tapped her on her shoulder. 'Here you go. One neck brace. The backboard and everything you asked for. I'll go in with the neck brace. You keep that cast dry.'

Brett gave her no time to reply, already sliding into the pool and pushing towards Lily.

Once Jenny saw Brett knew what he was doing she turned to get the backboard. Passing it down when he nodded, she held her breath as the girl was gently moved upwards and out to the side of the pool.

Shelley grabbed her hand and held on tight. 'She's bleeding from the head. That's serious, isn't it?'

Jenny squeezed back and looked around for Amanda. 'Can you take care of Shelley?' she mouthed.

Amanda joined them immediately, wrapping an arm around Shelley. 'Hang in there, and try not to panic. I'm sure Jenny knows what she's doing.'

'Can someone get a blanket out of the ambulance?' Jenny knelt beside the shivering, crying child. 'Lily, I'm Jenny and I'm a doctor. I want you to lie absolutely still for me. You mustn't move your head at all.' Even with the brace there was room for small movements.

'I want Mummy.' Lily coughed up water. 'Mummy,' she hiccupped.

Brett held her as still as possible but he couldn't prevent some movement. 'Careful, Lily.'

'Mummy's here, love.' Shelley's voice wavered as she crowded closer.

Jenny began gently feeling Lily's skull, looking for a soft patch where she might've hit the side of the pool. 'Tell me if it hurts when I'm touching you. Do you feel any pins and needles in your legs?'

'No. Why?'

'What about in your fingers?'

'No. Am I all right? Is that blood on my face?' Lily's faced puckered up as tears spurted from her eyes. 'I don't like blood.'

'We'll clean it up for you in a minute, sweetheart.' The

blood was pouring from a gash on Lily's forehead but at least the bone didn't appear to be broken. Still, only a scan would be able to totally eliminate that possibility.

'Want me to apply a pressure dressing to that wound?' Brett asked quietly. 'Meg can hold her head.'

She nodded. 'Yes. Are there any slings on board the ambulance?' She'd noticed Lily's elbow was twisted at a slightly odd angle.

'I'll get one.' Brett didn't waste time, just got on with what was needed.

She continued working her hands down the length of the girl's body but found no other injuries. 'Shelley, Lily will have to go to hospital. She needs stitches in her forehead and a cast on her arm. They'll take X-rays of that first and a scan of her head. But I'm tentatively optimistic she's one very lucky little girl.'

A flood of tears streamed down Shelley's face. 'Thank you, Jenny. I'm so glad you were here.'

Brett returned and she helped him tape the pressure bandage on Lily's head, careful not to jar the child's neck. Then they carefully slipped the sling under her left arm and behind her neck. Not that Lily was about to leap up and run around but the sling would prevent unnecessary movement.

'There you go, Lily. Now, we're going to put you on a trolley and place you in the ambulance. Mummy will be with you all the time.' Twisting her head, she found Shelley standing almost on top of her. 'You okay with that?'

'Try and stop me.'

Amanda said, 'I'll take your other kids home with mine. What about Gavin? Want me to get hold of him to let him know what's going on?'

'Please. I think he's on the harvester, doing some

maintenance to the line hauler. Tell him to come through to the hospital as soon as he can.'

Jenny placed her hands on her hips and leaned back, clicking her spine into place. Kneeling all that time hadn't been comfortable. Then she leant forward over Lily. 'I'll see you in a day or two, okay?'

She helped Brett and another guy carefully slide Lily onto the stretcher and watched as he wheeled her over to the ambulance, which was now parked at the entrance to the pool area.

'How do you stay so calm?' Amanda asked from beside her.

'Guess that comes with the training.' Though she had always been calm in emergency situations. If she was going to have a panic it would be after the event, not during it.

'Well, you mightn't be so flash at cooking but you sure know how to fix people.'

Yeah, she did, didn't she? Now that Lily was on her way to hospital and she could relax, she could feel a rush of excitement warming her. She'd helped Lily, made sure she was safe and comfortable. Had been ready if anything more serious occurred. Damn it, she felt good.

The boys ran up. 'Jenny, did you save Lily?'

'No, I just helped her.' She'd completely forgotten about the boys while all that had been going down.

'Relax. I had my eye on them,' Amanda told her.

'Them and half the school, it seems. But thanks. I'm easily distracted.'

'What's to eat?' Marcus asked. 'I'm hungry.'

'When aren't you?' She rubbed his mussed-up hair, which was so long it was in his eyes. 'You need a haircut.'

'Dad forgets to make us an appointment at Kaye's shop.'

'Is Kaye the hairdresser?' She'd noticed the small

house on the main street that had been converted into a salon when she'd walked to the grocery store.

'It's a girls' place but lots of us go there,' Marcus told her.

'Where's Andrew?' Then she spied him chasing a ball around the field with three other boys. 'Shall we get him and head home with a stop at the bakery?'

'Andrew,' Marcus hollered. 'We're going to the bakery now.'

Guess that was a yes, then.

'Hey, who cut your hair?' Cam asked the moment he saw the twins. He'd never got around to making that appointment.

'Kaye. Jenny took us there after swimming.' Andrew screwed up his nose. He hated having his hair cut.

'I hope you behaved.'

'Yes, Dad. We did.'

'Where's Jenny?' The fish and chips needed to be eaten soon or they'd go soggy in their wrapping, and it would take ten minutes to walk down to the marina at her speed.

'I'm here,' her sweet voice called from the deck. 'Andrew, can you put the washing basket away, please?'

'Coming.' Andrew hopped off the couch and raced to do as Jenny asked.

Cam grinned at her. 'You'll have to tell me your secret. A haircut and putting the basket away without an argument. I don't believe it. Thanks a lot for the haircuts. I've been trying to remember to book them in for weeks.'

'Beginner's luck. Kaye had a cancellation.' She grinned back.

'Dad, Lily hit her head in the pool and Jenny saved her,' Marcus called from the kitchen.

Jenny winced. 'Lily slipped and went in, banging her head and elbow on the way.' She quickly filled him in on the details. 'I haven't rung the hospital yet to find out how the scan went.'

'I can do that, if you like. They're more likely to tell me as I'm Lily's GP. But let's have dinner first.'

'Those fish and chips smell divine. I've put a few things together in your chilly bin. Drinks for the boys, wine for me and beer for you, a roll of paper towels for the messy faces, and some tomato sauce. Can you think of anything else?'

'Nothing at all. I'll grab the foldaway chairs and we'll be off.' A picnic. He was going on a picnic of sorts with his kids. And Jenny. His heart felt lighter than it had in yonks. This was fun, pure and simple. The kind of thing any dad should be doing with his boys, and yet he'd never thought to do it. By the time he got to the end of his working day he only wanted to get home and finish all the chores so he could relax for a bit. But with Jenny here he'd suggested it without considering the usual constraints he put on himself.

'Come on, slowcoach,' the woman slowly retraining him as a father called from the front door. 'I'm dribbling with anticipation of those chips.'

'Marcus, grab the box of tissues so we can wipe the slobber off Jenny's chin. We can't take her out in public looking like Socks when she's thrown up her biscuits.'

When Jenny picked up her crutches he frowned. He was being selfish, not considering she mightn't feel up to walking unaided. 'Want to take the car?'

'No way. I'm just being cautious after spending so long on my foot today. I'll toddle along behind you all so that by the time I get there you'll have my chair set up and my wine poured.' Then a furrow formed between her eyes.

'We are allowed to take our drinks onto the marina? I hadn't thought about that.'

'We'll be fine where we're going to sit.' The owner of the bar/café wouldn't mind them using his parking spot for their picnic. As that was attached to the licensed premises, they'd be legal.

'Good. I'll start hopping, then.'

Cam walked beside Jenny, happy to take as long as she needed to get where they were going, steamed fish and chips or not. 'You're going to have a few laughs at the marina. On Friday nights there's always a queue of people wanting to put their boats in the water so they can head out to their beach houses. Tempers get frayed and people try to queue jump. It can be entertaining, especially when someone mucks up backing their boat into the water.'

'Why is it that when you're backing a trailer or boat and people are watching you automatically make a botch-up of the job? I always do that.' Jenny's eyes were wide with anticipation. 'I'll enjoy watching others do the same thing.'

'That's not nice.' He laughed.

'Not at all.' Jenny grinned back at him, speeding up his heart rate. When she smiled or grinned those eyes became greener, warmer and sexier.

Now she asked, 'Do you own a boat?'

'One quarter of one. I've gone shares with my brothers-in-law. None of us uses it a lot, mostly to go to the family property for family holidays. It's a little bigger than what you'll see tonight so we've got a berth at one of the pontoons. We don't have to go through the hassle of lining up with everyone else. Or being laughed at by people like you.'

'Spoil my fun, why don't you?' Her thick hair swung

around her face as she limped along. The long locks shone where the sun caught them, turning the shade almost fire-engine red, and tempting him to run his hand down them to see if his skin burned. Fortunately his brain put the brakes on that idea before he made an idiot of himself. Unfortunately it didn't stop him from wondering what it would be like to make love to her. His fascination had been growing daily to the point he needed to do something about it. Not actually touch her, but go for a hard run up the hill to the lookout. Get a sweat up doing something physical that didn't involve sex.

Who was he kidding? Since last night's kiss there wasn't a doubt in his mind that they should get up close and personal, and soon. It wasn't as though he was alone in his feelings. Jenny had responded to him as quickly as his own body had lit up.

Sex. Sex had been dominating every last one of his thought processes all day. But wanting to get up close and personal didn't make it a wise move. Jenny had never denied she'd be on her way soon. At least she'd been honest, which was what he wanted, right? Right. So should he make a play for Jenny? Or should he ignore his feelings?

Note to self: make up his mind.

CHAPTER TEN

'I CAN'T BELIEVE how long I've been in Havelock.' Aston-ishment made her laugh. Of all the places she'd visited she'd had to pick the tiniest to stop and smell the roses, or was that the salt air? But, of course, stopping hadn't been her doing. She couldn't deny she was enjoying being here, becoming involved in day-to-day routines with the Rob-erts family, and visiting Amanda most days. They were becoming firm friends. 'I might never want to leave.'

'Then don't,' Amanda said.

'It's not that easy.' *Why not? You have to stop some time, somewhere. You can go to Kahurangi and return here afterwards.* On the table her cell vibrated as she tried to squeeze the pasta dough through the rollers of the pasta machine. 'Bad timing.' She had flour from elbows to chin.

'Want me to grab it?' Amanda asked.

'Please.' The phone did ring occasionally these days, usually the twins asking if she was meeting them after school, or had she looked in the laundry cupboard for her mojo yet?

'It's Cam. Something about an accident.'

Her heart dropped. Accident? Who was involved? Cam? The boys? She snatched the phone from Amanda. 'Cam? What's happened? Are you all right?'

Amanda shook her head at her. 'Of course he is. He's phoning you, isn't he?'

'Jenny, I'm fine. But one of the deckhands on Gavin Montrose's mussel harvester got caught in the ropes that haul up the mussel lines and could lose his arm. I'm heading out by boat immediately. I want you to come with me. This is emergency medicine—your kind of medicine—and the guy needs everything stacked on his side we can possible get.' Cam spoke urgently, as though his mind was already on the injuries he'd be seeing.

'I'm a little rusty.'

'Is there a reason you shouldn't do this?'

'No.' Nothing that sounded good enough for her not to help this guy. So stop vacillating. 'Pick me up at Amanda's gate.'

'I'm almost there.'

Closing the phone, she turned the tap on and started vigorously sluicing the flour off her arms. 'You heard?' she asked Amanda.

'Yep, and if you're not back by the time school's out I'll bring the boys here.'

Toot, toot.

'That'll be Cam. See you.'

'I hope you don't get seasick,' Cam said the moment she clambered into his vehicle. 'It's a bit rough out there.'

'Guess we're about to find out.' She snapped her seat belt in place. 'Why are we going by boat? Don't you have a rescue helicopter on call?'

'They'll have been called but we'll reach the harvester long before them. The helicopter has to come from Nelson or Wellington, about half an hour's flying time once they're off the ground.' Cam slammed on the brakes at the wharf. Out of the vehicle, he tossed the keys to a guy coming out of the harbourmaster's hut and grabbed a medical pack off the back seat. 'Park it for me, will you, George?'

They'd barely stepped on the boat and it was pulling away from the jetty. 'This is going to be a very fast ride,' Cam shouted against her ear. 'Want to sit inside?'

'No.' She gripped the rail hard. 'I like to see where I'm going.'

Twenty minutes later they were in the Kenepuru Sound, slowing up to nudge beside a mussel harvester bobbing in the water beside lines held deep by laden mussel ropes. Hands reached down and hauled Jenny aboard with no finesse at all.

'On the other side,' the dishevelled-looking seaman grunted, and turned to pull Cam onto the deck.

Threading her way over and around any number of obstacles, breathing salty and fishy air, Jenny focused on what she was about see and the procedures she'd undertake. It all depended on the depth of damage the rope had done. 'What's the man's name?'

The seaman she was following tossed the name over his shoulder. 'Haydon Tozer.' Then the man stopped and turned back to them. 'The rope's still holding him down. We were afraid if we cut it then he'd bleed to death.'

'You've done the right thing.'

Haydon opened his eyes to a slit when Jenny reached him.

'Haydon, I'm Jenny, a doctor. This is Cameron, another doctor. We're going to get you out of here.' She lifted his good arm so she could take his pulse, all the time assessing the situation. The wire with all its weight had pulverised Haydon's forearm against a steel barrel.

Cam was already opening the medical pack and removing a mask as he asked, 'Can someone tell us what happened?'

Haydon answered. 'I was operating the winch when my sleeve got snagged and the next I knew I was caught like this.'

'Someone must've been quick to stop the wire.'

The man who'd hauled them aboard grunted, 'That'd be me.'

Haydon sat at an awkward angle so as to relieve as much tension on his shoulder and upper arm as possible. Jenny was surprised he was still relatively lucid.

'I'm going to give you some oxygen, mate.' Cam held up the mask.

'The arm's screwed, isn't it?' Haydon croaked through his pain, and his eyes drifted shut. It was as though now help had arrived he was letting go the need to stay on top of everything.

Jenny winced internally. 'Let's check out the situation before I make comment.' But, yes, the sort of weight that rope carried suggested there was no alternative. She glanced at Cam. 'Pulse slow.' There was bound to be blood loss, even with pressure being applied by that rope.

Jenny pulled on gloves. 'I'm going to give you a nerve block so that you won't feel a thing while we get you sorted and out of here.' Which really said she'd already established she'd be amputating.

The guy's eyes opened for a brief moment then he nodded once.

Together she and Cam went through the ritual of checking off the drug dosage. As she plunged the needle into a muscle in Haydon's shoulder, Jenny was aware of the tension emanating off the crew, who stood to one side. She wondered how long they'd stay watching when she and Cam got the scalpels out. Hell, her stomach was rolling with nausea at the thought of removing Haydon's arm, especially in a less than ideal situation.

'You're doing great,' Cam said quietly, as he handed her swabs to clean the skin at the site where she'd amputate.

Thank goodness for that. Cam's calmness steadied the last of her nerves. She briefly locked gazes with him and nodded.

'I'll hold him from behind.' One of the crew stepped forward.

'Great.' Cam tightened a ligature just above Haydon's elbow to slow to a minimum the blood loss that would occur as she operated. Drawing from his calmness, Jenny pressed the scalpel blade deep. As she worked to free their patient, Cam wiped up the blood that escaped the ligature's restraints.

It took for ever. Haydon slipped into semi-consciousness.

She'd never cut Haydon free. He'd die here. She worked harder.

At last. She stepped away so Cam could place a pad over the stump and tape that in place.

A loud thumping from above announced the arrival of the rescue helicopter moments before the downdraught from the rotors lashed them.

'Doesn't the pilot know not to come so close?' she snapped, as she leaned over Haydon to protect him.

'I guess he doesn't have a lot of choice, given he's got to land the paramedic on this harvester,' Cam said a moment later, when the air settled again.

'How's our man doing?' she asked, feeling for a pulse.

'He's one toughie. Let's get him out of here.'

Then the paramedic was standing beside them, taking note of the details of the operation. 'We're taking him to Wellington. There's an orthopaedic surgeon already on standby.

There was a whirl of activity, getting Haydon belted onto a stretcher and raised to the helicopter. Jenny cleaned up the accident site and retrieved everything, placing it all in a bag to go to Wellington with Haydon. Then it seemed only minutes later she was climbing down into the boat and dropping onto a seat in the cabin. She slashed the back of her hand across her forehead. 'Phew. Glad that's over.'

Cam sat down beside her and reached for her hand. 'Me, too.' His thumb rubbed softly back and forth over her palm, like a windscreen wiper. 'Thanks for coming with me. I'd have hated being alone for that one.'

'Some things in medicine never get easy, do they?' She leaned her head against his shoulder. 'It's really only just begun for Haydon, though.'

'He's strong. Somehow I think he'll make the most of the situation and get on with living.'

'You make it sound easy.' Jenny stared at the floor. Was it that easy? Did picking up the pieces and getting on with her life all come down to attitude? 'Thanks for hauling my tail out here. It's been good for me. I felt like a doctor, thought like one, and acted competently.' That surprised her, and now she was very grateful for having had the opportunity. Could she be Dr Bostock again?

'You are a doctor. That was the neatest amputation I've witnessed, and given the circumstances you can be very proud.' Cam squeezed her hand and settled further down on the seat. 'I could do with a strong coffee about now.'

'Me, too.'

'You look pleased with yourself.' And absolutely gorgeous. Cam studied Jenny as he handed her a glass of wine. He looked forward to this half-hour with her at the end of each day when he could relax, talk medicine or boys or fishing. Not that she was into fishing, but she had let him ramble on about it last night until he'd caught her nearly falling asleep.

'Today, helping Haydon, it all came naturally, like I've never stopped practising. Following on from helping Lily the other day and, yeah, I do feel as though I'm getting my mojo back. Havelock's good for me.'

Cam thought so. Jenny looked more relaxed, less drawn than she had that day he'd brought her home with him. 'I enjoyed working with you.' He'd like the opportunity to do it again, though not if it meant someone had to lose an arm. He sipped his wine. 'I wonder how Haydon got on in surgery?'

'Can you find out?'

'I'll try, though not all medical personnel are forthcoming with details when they don't know me. So what did you do with the rest of the afternoon?'

'Had a coffee with Amanda and Shelley.'

'You're making friends with the whole village.' Maybe Jenny could settle here after all. She certainly didn't scoff at the people she met just because they were fishermen or factory hands. 'How was Shelley?'

'In a bit of a state about Haydon. No one seems to understand how it happened. They're so careful on that boat. She and Gavin have had a top rating for health and safety on their harvester and today's incident has gutted them. For Haydon as much as for them.' Her smile dimmed.

'There'll be an investigation by OSH.' Occupational Health and Safety would go over that harvester thoroughly.

'Shelley's flying across to Wellington in the morning to see Haydon and help with whatever he needs. I think they're going to suggest he comes back to stay with them when he's discharged,' Jenny added.

'That doesn't surprise me at all. It's how it is around here.'

She blinked at him. 'I have first-hand experience of that.' Her smile was cute and warming. 'I don't know how lucky I am sometimes.' Jenny twirled her glass between her fingers. 'I've been reminded of that today.'

Interested in getting to know more about what made her tick, Cam asked, 'Is this to do with why you are always restless? Why you're always talking about moving on when you don't need to?'

Her eyes darkened, her fingers whitened on the stem of her glass, and her lips mashed together as she stared out across the lawn.

Reaching for the glass, he removed it before the stem snapped and did some damage. 'Jenny?'

'I'll definitely be gone by the thirteenth.' Her voice was dead.

'Gone?' Within five days? Just when he'd begun to believe she might fit in here full time. What was going on? What had happened to her that was so bad she put up the shutters when he asked about her past? Did it have something to do with her twin? Draping an arm over her shoulders, he tucked her against him. 'Talk to me, Jenny. Tell me what happened. Tell me why you stopped being a doctor, why you're on the move.'

She pulled away, stood up. 'I'll get dinner ready. I'm sure the boys will be starving when they get home from Amanda's.'

'Wait. Talk to me,' he repeated. 'You've been with me for more than two weeks. We're becoming friends. I'd like to get to know you better. Is that such a bad thing?'

She stared down at him as though she'd never seen him before. 'I can't talk about it. Okay?'

Not at all. 'Can't or won't?'

'Does it matter? My sister died, my life stopped. That's all you need to know.'

'No, that answer's for others, not for me.' The hand he took in his was cold and shaky. All his doing, but he wanted to help her, to bring out that humour and fun that she occasionally let slip. Wanted to find the real Jenny Bostock. 'What's special about that particular date?'

She jerked her hand free, stepped further away from him. 'Which bit of leave it alone don't you get, Cam?' Her voice rose on his name. 'I am not prepared to talk about what happened. Ever. To anyone.'

That was so not healthy. But she wasn't about to have a heart-to-heart with him. That was so clear it glittered. Which hurt big time. What was apparent, though, was that this involved her sister. Anniversary of her death maybe? Fighting the urge to follow Jenny into the kitchen and keep trying to get her to talk, he sat staring out across the back yard and sipping his now tasteless wine.

Note to self: try to help Jenny through whatever has turned her life upside down.

He glanced inside, saw the saddest woman he'd ever encountered. The woman he suspected was coming to mean a lot to him. As in love? Did he love Jenny? Enough to get involved with whatever was tearing her apart?

Yes, he thought he did. Scrub that, he knew he did. Somehow, when he'd been trying so hard to keep her arm's length, she'd sneaked under the radar and stolen his heart.

To hell with it. Striding into the kitchen, he gently

removed the stirring spoon from her hand and took her in his arms. 'I'm here for you, okay?' He didn't give her time to answer, just leaned down and captured her mouth with his.

Jenny stood absolutely still, not returning the kiss, but neither did she withdraw.

On her lips he tasted wine and Jenny, a heady mix that zoomed straight down his body, switching on his arousal. Somehow he didn't think this was the time for bedroom activities. His kiss had been about sealing his vow to look out for her, about showing he cared.

Her hands crept up his chest, smoothing over his muscles till she touched his neck, then his cheeks. 'Cam,' she groaned against him, and opened up her mouth, allowing him access to that sweet cavity.

Then her breasts were pressing against his chest, her stomach pushing into his. He saw her eyes widen as she realised his reaction to her, and under his mouth her lips felt as though they were smiling.

Cam placed his hands on the shapely backside that had been taunting him for days. She felt right, so soft yet firm.

The blasted phone rang.

Neither of them moved except to lift their mouths free of each other.

The phone continued ringing. Finally Cam swore and stepped away to snatch the offending instrument from the counter. 'This had better be good. Hello?'

'Cam, Amanda. I'm just leaving with the boys. You've got five minutes.' Click and she'd gone.

'Do you have to go out?' Jenny asked.

Shaking his head, he felt laughter beginning to erupt. 'That was Amanda, warning us the boys are on their way home.'

A twinkle lit up her eyes. 'She's far too cheeky. But I guess we have to be grateful.'

'I think so.' That kiss could've been headed down the hall to his bedroom.

CHAPTER ELEVEN

AT FIVE JENNY gave up all pretence of sleeping and got up to pull on a sweatshirt and shorts. In the kitchen she made a mug of tea and took it outside, where she sat on the deck and watched the sun coming up from behind the hill on the other side of the estuary. As the sky lightened a sense of acceptance flowed over her.

She was going to have to tell Cam what had happened that day Alison had died. Their relationship would stall if she didn't. Last night's kiss told her there was a relationship on offer if she wanted it. She did. If Cam could see past her mistakes. If she could forgive herself.

Too many ifs.

How about another one? What if her feelings for Cam were love? It had to be. It gripped her, squeezed her heart, made her smile, laugh and sometimes cry. If that wasn't love, what was it?

Clink. A cup rattled against another in the kitchen. Cam was also up and about.

Sipping her tea, she waited for him to join her. Had he tossed and turned all night like she had? Even in the half-light his face showed signs of lack of sleep. 'Hey,' she whispered as he sat down in the chair next to her, holding his mug between those same firm hands that had gripped her bottom last night and set her hormones to dancing.

But the sleepless night, this drinking tea out here so early, was only half the problem. 'I have to be in the Kahurangi National Park on the thirteenth.'

She watched him raise the mug to those lips she wanted more of, saw his throat swallow, then heard him say, 'I'll drive you.'

'Just like that?' With no questions asked, he'd drive all that way for her?

'Yes.'

'It's a work day.'

'I'm owed time off.'

Those tears that she'd managed to hold onto all night spilled over and ran down her cheeks. 'Thank you.'

'No problem.'

The last quarter of the sun exploded over the horizon. The new day had arrived. Jenny drained her tea, set the mug on the floor, dug deep for strength, and told him, 'We were hiking along a cliff face. There was a track there, not well maintained but a track.' She swallowed down on the bile rising in her throat. 'I insisted on going first, whereas she usually did. We even joked about me being the bossy twin for a change.'

Cam nodded. 'You blame yourself for that.'

She nodded. 'When I was halfway across the face the track simply fell out from under me. Alison shouted a warning but it came too late.' She swallowed. 'She clambered down the edge of the slip after me, yelling all the time to hold on, she was coming.' Sniffed. 'A boulder broke lose and bounced down the cliff. It clipped Alison's head, crushed her chest.'

Cam's hand enveloped hers. He stayed quiet, waiting as though they had all day if she needed it.

This was hard. Even after all this time. Alison's silence

ricocheted around inside her head. Her own fear blocked her throat, turned her mouth sour.

Cam's thumb stroked the back of her hand.

She hauled in some air. 'I screamed at her to move, to get up. She didn't. No movement at all. When I reached her she was unconscious. I couldn't save her. I had nothing with me to help her. My cellphone was smashed, as was the emergency locator beacon in her pack.' The words spewed out of her mouth now. 'It tore me apart to even think of leaving her while I went out to the road for help. Deep down I think I knew she wouldn't make it.'

'You weren't injured?'

'Hardly, in comparison. Scrapes and bruises, torn muscles. Nothing to hold me back.'

'You stayed anyway?'

'I couldn't leave her, my sister, my twin. She died in my arms an hour later. I'd never have raised help in time to save her so I was glad I hadn't left her alone. How awful would that be? Dying alone?' Her lungs forced the air out in one long huff.

Forget holding her hand, Cam now wrapped her in his arms and sat her on his lap. 'Shh, Jenny, sweetheart.' His lips grazed her forehead and he rocked her.

After what seemed like a long time but probably wasn't she continued, 'With my foot in a cast I can't walk in to that place where it happened, but I have to be as close as I can get for the anniversary.'

'You want to say goodbye?'

'No.' Hardly. 'I want to say sorry, beg Alison's forgiveness.'

The rocking stopped and Cam locked eyes with her. 'Whatever for?'

'Because I couldn't save her.'

The truth dawned in his brown eyes all too quickly.

Except he didn't put her aside in disgust, or even agree she'd failed. Instead he said, 'Tell me if I'm wrong, but you were supposed to save Alison after a boulder smashed her head?' There was nothing but bewilderment and concern in his gaze. No horror at her failure.

Didn't he get it? 'Yes, I was.' She shivered. 'I understand the reality of the situation and how no one would've been able to help her. But the other half of me, the half attached to Alison, doesn't.'

'Oh, sweetheart.' Cam shook his head and wrapped her tight in his arms again. This time he didn't rock back and forth, just settled further in the seat and held her. 'We'll go together to the park.' That's all he said as they sat there for nearly an hour.

Not one word of condemnation, nothing about her responsibilities not being met, just the promise that they would go there together.

Was it possible she might get through this? Have a life on the other side of this? She wouldn't know for a few days yet.

The trip, a few days later, was painfully quiet, and got quieter as the kilometres passed beneath their wheels. Cam kept a watch over Jenny as she drew in on herself, hunching her shoulders forward as the environs of Nelson and Tasman dropped behind and hills and mountains began filling their vision. Should he get her talking to alleviate some of that tension tightening her shoulders?

He couldn't make any of this better for her. He'd give everything he had except his boys to make it go easy for her, though in reality he understood she had to do this and if anything could make her feel more at ease it was getting through today. 'What's the plan? How far in are we going?'

'Since I can't walk the track, I figured the car park is going to be it. I might try walking a little way along the track but it is very uneven and narrow.' She swivelled in her seat to stare at him. Better than watching those mountains getting bigger and bigger? 'The rescue crews used the car park as a base to conduct the search for us. We'd written our trip intentions in the hut books all along the track and when we were a day late Search and Rescue swung into action.'

'How overdue were you?'

'Twenty-four hours. I waited with Alison, holding her to me.'

The hitch in her voice snagged his heart and he lifted one hand from the steering wheel to cover hers. 'You were incredibly brave.' Then and today. He slowed the vehicle. 'This the turn-off?'

'Yes.' Her cheeks had paled more than usual.

As soon as he'd taken the turn he slowed, then stopped and took her hand in his again. A slight tremor shook her, while her skin had turned cold. 'Hey, sunshine, you're doing fine.' But she wasn't really. Why would she? This had to be extremely hard. 'I'm here, okay?'

Jenny stared around. 'How did I think I could do this on my own?' she asked in a whisper. Shoving the passenger door wide, she dropped to the ground and, hands on hips, stared up at the mountain range dominating the skyline.

After parking, Cam strolled across to stand behind her and pulled her slim body in against him. Wrapping his arms around her waist, he dropped his chin on top of her head. 'What do you have in mind now that you're here?' He'd piggyback her along the track if she wanted to go into the bush. Probably cripple him for ever but he'd do it.

As Jenny rubbed her hands up and down her arms

she continued to gaze around. 'The sun was shining the day it happened. A hot, windless day that sapped our strength. But we were impervious to that, loving every step we took through the bush and out in the open, listening to and watching the fantails flitting from bush to branch as they stayed just ahead of us.'

'Did you start out from here?'

Shaking her head, she explained, 'No, we came from the west. We had arranged for friends to walk the track in the opposite direction and we met in the middle, swapped car keys with them. That saved a lot of manoeuvring of vehicles before starting out.'

'I guess it would.'

'Our packs were heavy with gear and wet-weather clothing. I remember complaining about the ache in my shoulders when we reached the first hut where we spent that night. Alison told me to harden up. Sympathy was never her strong point.'

Cam rubbed his chin back and forth across her head. 'You two do a lot of tramping in remote areas?'

'It was our escape from everyday stresses and tensions. Ever since Dad took us on an overnight tramp out of Dunedin when we were ten we were hooked. You couldn't stop us from throwing our packs on our backs and heading out to some hill or mountain. Later, when we were busy with our careers, it became our twin time. We'd go for a week and just be us.'

'Bet you miss that more than anything else.' She had been lucky to have that relationship with her sister. It's what he wanted Andrew and Marcus to always have, a rock in their lives for when the bad times cropped up. His sisters were close to him and he knew how important that had been when Margaret had walked out on him.

Twisting around to look directly at him, Jenny said,

'You're right. It felt as though I'd been sliced down the middle and half of every part of me was missing.'

Her eyes glittered and with his thumb he smudged away an errant tear. 'Your mojo.'

'Yeah.' She drew the word out, then astonishingly her mouth curved ever so slightly upwards. 'I totally bamboozled the boys with that, didn't I?'

'They're still trying to find it for you.'

'Truly?' The smile widened. 'They are great little guys. So caring and thoughtful. They get that from you, I'd say.'

'Of course.' Though to be fair, 'Margaret wasn't always selfish. She used to be the person who turned up on your doorstep with baking if you'd had a bad day, or she'd change an appointment so she could take you to yours when you got a flat tyre.' Funny how now with Jenny he could acknowledge that.

'No one's all bad. I'm glad you told me that. Do you still miss her?' Those green eyes bored into him.

'Not at all. Haven't for a long time. But I still get angry at how she treats the boys.' *I thought today was about you, not me.* 'Want to walk a bit? See how that ankle stands up to the track?'

Her eyes locked with his for so long he began to think she'd gone to sleep with her eyes open, until finally she ducked her chin. 'Yes. You will be there with me, won't you?' Then she sucked a breath. 'Tell me if I'm expecting too much of you.'

'You're not. Trust me.'

After slinging his day pack on his back and locking the car, Cam walked behind Jenny as they stepped along the rutted, root-bound track, holding his breath every time she stumbled, breathing a sigh of relief when she went on. She carried a bunch of pink and white peonies against her chest. Alison's favourite flowers, apparently. After nearly an hour they reached a knoll and sat on the trunk of a large fallen tree. Sweat beaded their brows and dampened their arms and throats.

'It's a hot one.' Cam dumped the pack, then stretched his legs to ease the tightness in his calves. 'I enjoyed that. How's the ankle?'

'It's telling me I'm an idiot and I'm ignoring it. But I guess this is as far as I should go. It's not as if I can make it to the first hut, let alone to where the accident happened.' She bent to remove her boot. 'I know I shouldn't take this off until we get back to the car but I hate standing around in wet boots.'

There'd been a stream where they hadn't been able to avoid wading through knee deep water. 'If we're stopping here for a bit, I'll do the same. We can put them on that log in the sun.'

Jenny looked around. 'I remember stopping here for a nut bar and a juice on the way out with the rescuers.'

Talk about a cue. Unzipping the pack, Cam retrieved two juices and some oat and blueberry muffins from the bakery. 'Will these suffice?' He grinned, feeling like one of his boys when they did something cool.

Her eyes widened and her shoulders relaxed for the first time all morning. 'Thank you. Again. I seem to be saying that a lot this morning.'

'You can quit any time you like. I'm here because I care, because I want to be with you today.' And every other day, but putting that out there had to wait for a more suitable time.

'Thanks.' Leaning closer, she kissed his cheek. Then kissed it again.

Breathing in her scent, citrus overlaid with good, honest sweat, sent a shaft of desire arrowing through him

154   A FAMILY THIS CHRISTMAS

right to his gut and beyond. He loved this woman. And right now was so not the moment to be reacting to her like this. But how not to? Love had brought him to this mountainside with her. He turned, kissed her cheek, then gently grazed her lips with his, before pulling back and deliberately stabbing the end of the straw into the hole on the top of the juice box. 'Drink up. I've got lots of goodies in that bag.'

'Like what? You didn't bring a picnic?'

Had that been the wrong thing to do? Today of all days should he have made sandwiches and left it at that? No. Jenny might be facing her grief but she could celebrate having made it through the first year too. 'Yep. I had to make myself useful.'

'Thanks, again.'

'You're welcome.'

They sat quietly, not speaking, for a while. Then Cam heard a soft sniff and saw a flood of tears streaming down Jenny's pale face. 'Hey, sunshine, come here.' And once again he wrapped her up in his arms.

'I miss her so much.'

His hand rubbed circles on her tense back.

'I still should've been able to save her.'

Huh? He shook her ever so gently and put her away from him enough to be able to gaze into her eyes. 'Being a doctor doesn't automatically make you superwoman. There was nothing you could do.' She must've been in mental agony. His hands tightened on her back, his palms seeking the warmth that told him she was alive and well now. 'At least your parents didn't lose both of you that day.' He brushed his lips across her forehead before tucking her back against his chest.

'I never thought of it like that before. I've been too busy blaming myself. I suggested we climb in Kahurangi

Park. I even chose the track that fell away beneath us and sent us to the bottom. But Alison was with me all the way.'

Silence fell again. Then, 'She's not here. I thought I might sense her presence if I came on the same route but I don't. I remember her laughing and talking nonstop, but it's like any memory—no more, no less.'

She pulled back and stared around. 'But she's with me. Always will be. She's in here.' Her hands crossed on her chest, between her breasts. When Jenny stood Cam remained where he was, ready if she needed him, but giving her the space and time to reflect on what she'd just come to understand. She hadn't lost Alison. She never would.

Picking up the peonies, she crossed the knoll and walked around the edge of the grassed area until something caused her to stop. Slowly she squatted to lay the flowers on a small punga fern log. 'Bye bye, sis. Be safe.'

Tears wet her face, dripped off her chin, but the tension of earlier had eased off. Finally she looked up and locked her gaze with his. 'I'm going to say it again. Thank you. When I landed in a heap outside your house I had no idea how you were going to change my life. You and your boys.'

'Maybe we didn't. Maybe you were ready for it and were already opening up to opportunities.' He added lightly, 'Maybe you wished that skateboard on you.'

'You gave me those opportunities.'

'Okay. I'll take all the credit if it makes you happy.' He felt a lightness settling over him that he hadn't known in a long time. 'If I'd known the changes you'd bring to my life I'd have paid Marcus a long time ago to run you down.'

'Cam, make love to me.' She stood in front of him, her hands reaching for his.

What? Had he heard correctly? Nah, couldn't have. Jenny wanted to make love? With him? Here? All reasoning vanished. Instead, that lightness he'd felt had turned to heat and tension, warming his blood, driving his hormones south. Unfolding himself from the trunk, he said, 'For the record, Alison definitely isn't here? She's not looking down on you? Us?'

Her smile was beautiful. Those deep emerald eyes twinkled out at him. 'No. This is a private party.' Her smile dipped. 'Not a party. But something I want to do with you. You're helping me move on. Making love will help further.' He must've shown disappointment because she quickly added, 'Truth? I've been fantasising about this for days.'

'You've been fantasising about having sex in the bush?'

Her smile wavered. 'Worded wrongly. It definitely wasn't a plan to ask you to make love out here.' He saw the uncertainty taking control of her stance as her shoulders slumped and her back curled forward. She was fragile, very fragile, and he loved her. Besides, he'd been dreaming of holding her naked and close since the first night she'd stayed in his house.

'I like it that you've been fantasising about me, because you've been drowning all coherent thought in my head for days.' He took her face in his hands and leaned closer to kiss her. Her lips trembled under his mouth. His breath hitched as he softened his kiss, not wanting to come on too hard, too fast. Yet his body was screaming for the taste of her, to feel her skin against his, to know her soft curves. He wanted to feel her hands on him, her tongue tracing a line from his nipple to his stomach and beyond. He needed to take this slowly, let Jenny relax into their lovemaking and forget for a while why she'd come to this remote place.

'Jenny, wait. We have to stop. You have to believe me when I say that I want to make love to you more than anything in this world right now, but I wasn't expecting this. I'm not prepared. Hell, I don't even have any protection at home. Haven't needed it for years now. Since long before Margaret…'

Jenny tugged him closer. 'Cam, it's fine. I'm on the Pill. Not that I've needed to be since my last relationship ended, but now I'm so glad I kept filling that prescription.' She smiled cheekily before pressing her mouth against his. She had to taste him. Now. When her tongue slid into his mouth she shivered. Delicious. This was Cam. The man who'd stolen her heart when she hadn't even known if she'd still had one. Now she wanted to know him completely, nothing between them. Today had been hard. So damn hard, yet he'd been there for her, with her, and somehow it had been easier. And now this. This felt right. This was about the future, not the past year.

Cam's body was firm where his thighs pressed hers, where his chest covered her breasts, where his stomach touched hers. And further down the ridge pressing against her told her how much he wanted her. Slipping a hand between them, she reached down, ran her fingertips over the fabric-covered bulge.

Cam gasped, tipped his head back to lock eyes with her. On tiptoe she followed him, her mouth hungry for his, hating the brief break from their kiss. When his hands slid under her shirt and skimmed over her skin she thought she'd died and gone to heaven, except she felt far too alive. Hot need poured through her, swelling up and out from her heart, filling every cell of her body. Drenching her. Yes, she was ready for Cam.

Snatching handfuls of his shirt, she jerked upwards, pulling it free of his bush pants. At least the pants had an elastic waistband and easily slid over those firm hips when she pushed them down. And then he was free, filling her hands; the whole, hot, pulsating length of him. She wanted him, right now, inside her. 'Undress me,' she hissed through clenched jaws.

'You don't want to take your time?' he croaked, even as his hands were scrabbling at her belt buckle.

'I've wasted weeks already.' Her hand slid down the length that was turning her to liquid just with the slick feel of him. 'Cam, can we do this now?' Like right now?

'Help me out here,' he begged. Her belt finally gave way and Cam's hot hands were on her hips, pushing her trousers down. Over her thighs, down to her knees.

Reaching down, she tugged first one then the other leg free of clothing. Then she proceeded to divest him of his trousers.

Cam swung her up in his arms and knelt to lay her on the grass. Quickly grabbing him, she hauled him down to cover her, opening for him. 'Cam, I—' *Love you.* The words were lost on a haze of heat and desire as he pressed into her. Instinctively her hips lifted to receive him. She moved beneath him, making it impossible for him to hold back. And then she succumbed to the oblivion that her release brought.

Cam had made her whole again. By being with her today, by claiming her body so thoroughly. By being Cam, gentle, tough, kind and loving. Jenny held his sweat-slicked body close. When he made to move off her, she tightened her grip. 'I like your weight on me.' Even if he was making breathing difficult. 'I never want to let you go.'

With a wriggle Cam managed to tug his arms free

and rose on his elbows to gaze down at her. His face was flushed and his eyes still held that molten look that had turned her on so thoroughly. 'I'm not going anywhere without you.' His hand brushed her hair off her forehead and cheek. 'Besides, I owe you long and slow.'

A laugh began deep inside her, tripped up her throat and spilled between them. 'Long and slow, eh?'

'Yeah, you know, when I get to touch every part of your delectable body with my tongue? When you're crying out for me to give you what you want? That long and slow.' His grin was wicked and, oh, so sexy.

'I can't wait.'

'I've never taken you for being so impatient. Where's the quiet, controlled Jenny gone?'

'I save her for rainy days. And right now the sun's shining.'

Cam kissed her softly on her now tender lips before slowly sliding off her and sitting up. 'I've got just the thing for sunny days.' When he pulled a wine cooler out of his backpack she gaped.

'You carried a bottle of wine up here?'

'Not any old wine, but this.' With a flourish he tugged the bottle free of the tight cooling bag. 'Champagne.'

'If I hadn't already told you enough times already, I'd say thank you.'

He unwrapped two champagne flutes then popped the cork. 'The best sound in the world.'

'Quickly followed by the fizz and sizzle of bubbles as you pour that into those glasses.' Shuffling on her bottom, she pulled her trousers up to her waist but didn't bother to zip them closed. Who knew what might happen after a glass of champagne?

CHAPTER TWELVE

MARCUS AND ANDREW, followed by two of their friends, raced out the front door of Amanda's house the moment Cam turned into her driveway. 'You're back.'

'Whoopee, we can go home.'

Jenny shoved her door open and stepped down. Wow, she was tired, and that was after sleeping most of the way from Kahurangi. 'I wasn't scintillating company.' She gave Cam a wry smile.

She didn't hear his answer as the boys all but leapt at her. 'Jenny, you came back.'

'We thought you were gone for ever.'

Jenny's heart stuttered, and guilt forced her to glance at Cam, who was watching his boys with a very guarded expression on his face. 'Of course we were coming back. I told you we would.'

'Me, too.' Amanda and some more children joined their group. 'Jenny, you okay?' She knew a little about where they'd been for the day.

Nodding slowly, Jenny sought for an answer, but what the twins had said had rocked her off centre—when she'd only just got back there after all this time. Marcus and Andrew had thought she wouldn't be coming back, which meant they'd believed she was staying on for a while— or longer.

Cam filled the sudden gap in the conversation. 'It's been a long day. Thanks so much for looking after the boys, Amanda.' His brow furrowed as he looked from Jenny to his sons and back again. He wasn't happy.

She didn't blame him. Right from the outset she'd known he didn't want his boys getting hurt.

Marcus nudged one of his friends. 'I told you we're getting a new mother. We've seen Dad kissing her.'

The abrupt silence was only broken when Cam snapped, 'Marcus, Andrew, get in the truck. Now.'

Amanda gave Jenny a swift hug. 'Come and see me tomorrow. We'll have coffee.'

Tomorrow. A whole new day. It should be a blank canvas for her to decide her next moves, but the twins had shown her that was not possible. She had to go before they became even more attached to her. All she could hope for was that she hadn't done any permanent damage, staying as long as she had.

The boys went straight to bed and Jenny headed for the shower to wash away the day—the sweat, the sex, the exhaustion. When she came out wrapped in her sleeping T-shirt and an oversized robe of Cam's, he had mugs of tea waiting.

'Cam, about the boys—'

'It's been a long, emotional day. Let's talk about that tomorrow.'

The problem was tomorrow never seemed to come for her.

Did Cam want time to think about what he would say to her? How he'd explain she had to go for his sons' sakes? *Believe me, Cam, I get it. I am going. This time I mean it.*

For some inexplicable reason she couldn't stop watching his hands as they held his cup and lifted it to his mouth. Those hands had made love to her. She'd wanted to know them on her body once, just once. And now she had. Twice. Only twice wasn't enough. Not by any measure she could think of.

But she'd have to make do with the memories of that afternoon. That's all she'd have. No opportunity to make more beautiful mental pictures for later. She couldn't stay, not even that long. She wasn't the boys' mother, yet right now they'd fitted her into the slot as a replacement.

When she'd first arrived, Andrew and Marcus had been desperate to find Margaret and have her back in their lives. Jenny accepted there was no way the role was hers. She couldn't replace their mum. They wanted, needed, far more than she had to give. Yes, she loved them. More importantly, she loved their father. But she couldn't do what they wanted. Because one day she might fail them and they'd say, 'You're not our mother. You can't tell us what to do, or how to do it. It's not your place.' Cam would be forced to stand up for them, and she'd be broken-hearted again.

Hang on. Wasn't she jumping the gun here? Cam had probably never intended for her to stay on past getting her foot out of plaster—if that long. It wasn't as though he'd come out declaring his love for her. She'd been overlaying everything he'd done and said with her own love, not realising Cam hadn't been at the same game.

So she went for damage control, and told Cam, 'Today I put Alison's death in perspective. I know now it wasn't my fault.' This was way harder than she'd ever have believed. It went to show how much she loved Cam. 'But…' *get on with it* '…just as importantly, staying with you has given me so much. I've started to find myself again.' Her mojo.

'But here's the rub. I'm not sure yet what my future

holds for me. I can't make promises that involve you or your family. I won't guarantee I'll stay around once I finally get myself sorted. I don't even know if I want to return to an ED. Or medicine in any form. And if I don't do that, who am I?' She'd wanted to be a doctor since Donny Browning had stubbed his toe at her third birthday party. Yet knowing she hadn't been able to save her twin hadn't stopped her confidence being undermined enough to terrify her.

'What about that wee girl in the Wairau ED? You saved her life.' Thoughtful brown eyes locked with her gaze.

'Instinct. I didn't stop to think.' She held her hand up. 'And before you say that proves I've still got it medically, it's not the same as making hard decisions about how to treat someone when the situation isn't as urgent.'

'I could mention Amanda, little Lily or Haydon. You were great with them, too.' Cam drained his cup and leaned forward, his elbows on his knees. 'Don't you think it's time to let this go? Be kind to yourself. Forgive yourself.'

He'd missed the point. 'This isn't about guilt now. This is about not knowing who I am any more. I am beginning to think I might return to medicine but I'm nowhere near certain. Until I work that out I can't stay here. It isn't fair on you, and it especially isn't fair on your boys. What if I take off after a few weeks? Or months even? It's going to hurt them and you're already dealing with their mother having let them down.'

She knew Cam didn't get how she could be contemplating giving up medicine for ever. It would be a rare doctor who did. It took so much hard work to qualify, not to mention a ton of dedication, that rarely did anyone ever consider walking away. Tears pricked the backs of her eyelids. Unfortunately, when she opened her mouth there were no more words. She wanted to tell Cam she loved him, and his boys. But she'd still have to say she was leaving so it was probably best she'd become mute.

But the pain. It lanced her, sliced her heart to shreds, twisted her stomach so tight she thought she'd be ill. She should never have stopped here for more than that first night. But it had been too easy to put off leaving. Cam made her feel almost whole again. He'd done more for her in a few short weeks then she'd done all year actively searching for her life.

'The boys still keep looking for your mojo.' Cam's face was sad. 'Though I think you've found some of it already.'

She nodded, slowly drew in air to her lungs and spoke softly. 'I know. But, Cam, they have to stop. I can't complete my side of the bargain.' Not that she'd actually agreed to help find their mother for them. The boys had taken her willingness for granted. 'You have to talk to them about their mother. I can't.'

'You're right.' His smile was rueful and brief, and added to her sadness.

She'd lost Alison suddenly. Losing Cam was going to be slow and difficult. But the pain would be similar. Strange, considering she'd loved Alison since the day they were born, and yet had only known Cam for little more than two weeks.

Cam stood up, stretching his arms above his head. 'We're both tired. Go to bed. We'll talk again tomorrow.'

She should pack her few belongings and hitch a ride out of Havelock right now. But Cam was right about one thing. She was exhausted, emotionally as well as in every muscle in her body. Hopefully she'd manage some sleep tonight.

* * *

Cam watched Jenny trudge down the hall to the room that had become hers. Half of him wanted to follow and crawl into bed beside her, hold her tight, and maybe even make love again. Though that exhaustion pulling at her probably precluded any activity tonight. Just holding her would be fine. He could stroke that soft, satin-like skin, breathe in her scent of lemon and lime.

Rinsing out their mugs, he turned to stare at new photos of Andrew and Marcus pinned to the noticeboard. They stood either side of Jenny, grinning at him as he took the picture out on the lawn, looking so happy. Happier than he'd known them to be for so long he'd begun to wonder if they'd ever know happiness again. Jenny had done that for them.

She could easily break their little hearts by taking off again. Tomorrow might be the day. Or it could be in a month's time. Or a year's. As much as he wanted to believe he could keep her content here with him, an element of doubt picked at his thinking. Jenny was restless. Today's trip hadn't changed that after all. As she'd been direct in pointing out. So, if she was leaving, the sooner the better for his boys.

His heart ached. She'd not only helped the boys, she'd changed his outlook on life. He had a spring in his step, he felt hope for the future again. He could almost taste it: the complete family he'd always wanted, the holidays, showing the boys the way through life's obstacles. Jenny would be perfect for him. He knew that without a doubt.

But bottom line—he couldn't risk the boys being hurt again. Margaret had a lot to answer for. He would not compound their anguish by making a mistake with Jenny. No matter what the cost to him and his heart. He came second in this small family.

Tonight he didn't need to make a mental note about anything, he wouldn't be sleeping anyway. He'd be wide awake, rueing the day that skateboard had smacked into Jenny's ankle and tumbled her into their lives. In a matter of weeks he'd found his soulmate, a woman he loved more than he'd have believed possible. Yet tomorrow he'd talk to her and then, he suspected, he'd watch her walk away. It was the only answer for his boys.

But he had one more thing to ask—make that demand—of her before she walked out the door for the last time.

'You mustn't leave without saying goodbye to Andrew and Marcus.' Cam stepped into the kitchen as Jenny squeezed the teabag and dumped it in the trash can.

Knowing he'd join her out here as soon as the sun began making its appearance, she still gasped with surprise. He'd moved so quietly through the house she hadn't even heard a floorboard creak. Had he been standing there, watching her? Thinking of yesterday or of tomorrow? Forget those days. She had today to get through.

'Jenny.' She'd never heard him sound so harsh, not even when the boys exasperated him. 'It's not space tripping you do, is it? It's avoidance. When my questions get too tough you pretend you didn't hear me.'

Another gasp. 'I've answered more questions this past fortnight than I have in a year. I've told you way more about me and my screwed-up life than I've talked to anyone else about it.' She should've sneaked out in the middle of the night, phoned for a taxi to come out from Blenheim to pick her up. The coward's way out. Easier on her heart. Easier on Cam and his boys. Instead, she'd waited out the long, long hours of darkness so she could see Cam one last time. But there weren't going to be any

happy thank-you-very-much-have-a-great-life farewells
this morning. That was apparent in his strained face, in
those tired brown eyes watching her every breath.

He snapped his fingers in front of her face. 'Hello? Just
this once give me your full, undivided attention. I want
you to explain to the twins that you're heading away and
why. I do not want them thinking they've done something
bad that's made you go.'

He was in full protect-his-sons mode, and for that she
admired him. Nodding her agreement, she said, 'I will
make sure they understand this has nothing to do with
them.' Picking up her mug in less than steady hands, she
gripped it tight and clumped across to the sliding glass
door leading out onto the deck. Might as well sit out the
next couple of hours, watching the sun crawling ever
higher, while trying to come up with something appropri-
ate to say to Marcus and Andrew that they'd understand.

By the time the boys bounced outside to shout good
morning she was none the wiser about how to handle
the situation. Her mind had been focused entirely on the
man she was leaving behind. Cameron had been responsible for her new, improved outlook on life. He'd made
her feel again. And feeling led back to hurting. This time
the pain was self-inflicted.

'Jenny, you haven't forgotten the carols on the marina next week, have you?' Andrew stood directly in
front of her.

Her heart dropped to her stomach.

Marcus added, 'You will wear that Santa's hat I made
specially, won't you?'

Nausea raced up her throat. Slapping a hand over her
mouth, she dug deep to keep her stomach from tossing
her tea at the twins' feet. Twisting her head from side

to side, she waited until she knew her voice box would work in some semblance of normal.

'Why's your bag on the step?' Marcus asked.

Andrew spun around to see what his brother was talking about, spun back. 'Where are you going? Can we come?'

Cam cleared his throat. 'Boys, Jenny has to go home today.'

Gratitude for his intervention was instantly replaced by remorse. He sounded like he was talking through a waterfall, all distorted and deep. She opened her mouth, tentatively tried to speak. 'I'm so sorry, Andrew, Marcus.' Her mouth snapped shut. Try again. That's not enough. Her chest rose as she breathed deep.

'It's time for me to go home.' Now, there was a lie. She didn't have a home. This house had been as close as she'd been to having a home for so long that nowhere else seemed right. As the boys' mouths opened to state the inevitable, she quickly continued. 'I only stayed while my ankle got better. Now I have to find a job and go and see my parents.' Suddenly that left field idea seemed the right thing to do. Go back to Dunedin and mend some bridges with Mum and Dad before deciding where she'd go next.

'But we don't—'

'Want you to go.'

Tears tracked down two small, dismayed faces. Tears that broke her heart all over again. 'I have to.' One day they'd see she'd done the right thing by them. Reaching forward, she dragged the boys into a hug. But they weren't having any of that. They pulled free and ran to stand beside Cam.

'Tell her, Dad.'

'She can't go.'

He placed a hand on each boy's shoulder. 'Sorry, guys,

but Jenny is going.' The eyes that locked with hers chilled her right to the bone.

Standing, she made it to the step and hoisted her bag over her shoulder. Clumping down to the path, she tried to walk away without looking back, but her feet seemed glued to the concrete. Turning, she looked up at Cam, devouring every line of his beautiful face, storing images in her head for those long, lonely nights that would become a part of her life again. 'Goodbye, Cam. Goodbye, Marcus. Goodbye, Andrew.' If her heart hadn't already broken into a million pieces back there on the deck, it would've completely vaporised now.

At the corner of their street Cam hugged his boys to him and cursed Jenny for their tears. Andrew and Marcus had insisted they wave to Jenny as the bus went past, but there hadn't been any answering wave from inside the vehicle as it had sped by. Had she deliberately ignored them? Or had she sat on the far side so she wouldn't know if they'd come to see her off?

'Come on, guys. Let's go home.'

The bus slowed and he held his breath. Had Jenny changed her mind? Would the door open and Jenny hop out, yelling she'd made a mistake and asking if he'd let her stay on? *Yeah, and what would your answer be?* Because if she stayed the possibility of rerunning this scene would always be there. Jenny couldn't commit. *Oh, and you can? Did you once tell her how you feel about her?* Despite the heat in the day already cranking up, Cam shivered. He was looking out for his kids. *Excuses, excuses.*

A dog ran across the road in front of the bus. The bus sped up. Jenny hadn't stopped the driver. A damned dog had.

'Breakfast-time then you can get ready for school and the class picnic.' He nudged the boys towards home.

'I don't want to go.' Andrew stamped his foot.

'It won't be fun without Jenny.' Marcus added his say.

You're not wrong there, my boy. 'We'll make it fun, our fun, like we always have.' Ouch. That was it, really. They'd been full circle and were now back to where they'd been a couple of weeks ago. The three of them. 'It's the last week of the term, remember? That's got to be good.'

Disbelief at his statement blinked out at him from two identical pairs of eyes. 'Yes, Dad.' Their voices were flat, beaten.

His heart crunched. Damn it. Jenny had won him over without even trying. Hard to believe how easily, in fact. 'We won't be beaten.' Neither boy understood what he meant but he did. 'Let's go. We'll have pancakes with syrup.' He'd clean up the resulting mess tonight.

'Yes, Dad.' At least there was some enthusiasm in their voices this time. Some was better than none. Just.

Note to self: keep my boys busy so that they don't get too gloomy over Jenny's leaving.

Second note to self: keep myself busy so that I don't get too gloomy over Jenny's leaving.

Note to self: ignore all notes to myself.

Since watching Jenny's bus roll through Havelock, Cam had been through one of the longest weeks of his life.

Getting Jenny out of his head, out of his system, had proved to be impossible. He missed her so much it was agony.

So call her. Tell her exactly that.

Sure. That would work—until she left again. The boys

weren't coping, moping around the place like someone had stolen their favourite toys. Hell, not even Christmas, only days away, was exciting them.

'Dad…'

'Yes?' Cam clipped the lids on the boys' lunchboxes and glanced at his watch. He'd forgotten to make the lunches last night after getting home from having dinner with Amanda and her family. Forgotten. That never happened.

'Did Jenny find her mojo?' Andrew stared up at him.

He suspected that was the last thing she'd found after all. 'I don't think so, guys.'

'If we keep looking and find it, will she come back?'

'We miss her.'

Me, too. He cleared his throat. 'Me, too.' More than he'd have believed. 'Jenny has lots of things worrying her at the moment.'

'Did you ask her to stay?' Andrew kicked the stool.

'No.' *I was afraid of hurting you both further down the track.* 'Guys, you have to understand you can't make a person stay if they don't want to.'

'How do you know she didn't want to if you didn't ask her?'

Since when had Marcus got so smart? 'I…'

I don't know. Jenny was adamant she had to go and I was adamant I had to protect you two so I never considered asking if there was some way we could get around her problems and make it work for all of us.

'But where will she have Christmas?'

'At school we made her a box to put her mojo in when she finds it. We don't want her to lose it again.'

'Can we wrap it in Christmas paper?'

Cam sat down hard on the stool. They'd made a box for Jenny. So they hadn't given up on her returning.

You have. You gave up before she even left. Same as when Margaret wanted to go find herself. Back then you put the boys first and let her break your heart. Exactly what you've done again. Only this time it feels as though you've lost more than the mother of your children. It feels—feels like half of you has disappeared.

'A box is a cool idea, guys. We'll find a way to get it to her.'

I'll make sure of that, and maybe I could put my heart in it so she knows what she means to me.

After the boys were tucked up for the night Cam sat down with his cell and pressed Jenny's number. His gut tightened as he listened to her voice-mail. Her soft southern lilt tore him apart. When the message ended he pressed redial, listened again, and left a message, asking her to call.

An hour later when his phone hadn't rung and he'd checked a dozen times to make sure the battery wasn't flat, he tapped his computer to life and sent her an email.

Hey, there, wondering how you're doing? The boys are on countdown to Christmas. They...

He tapped backspace four times.

We miss you.
Hugs, Cam, Andrew and Marcus.

At one o'clock he gave up pretending she would answer and dragged himself off to bed. In the morning he'd try again.

Same result.

Lunchtime—same result.

Cam came to a decision. He wanted Jenny back in

his life. He'd risk everything, even rejection, to achieve that, would fight with everything he had to win her back.

Dearest Jenny.

I love you. I think I have from the moment I found you sprawled on the path at my gate. If the way my heart went crazy is an indicator then yes, I did. You looked so beautiful, even when your face was contorted with pain. I wanted to run my hands through that silken hair spilling everywhere. I couldn't take your pain away but believe me, if I could have, I would have. I didn't want to ask you to stay with us but I couldn't stop myself. You were already weaving your way into my soul. I wanted to get to know you, to share some time with you, to laugh and talk together.

And now I have, I miss you so much. It's like someone took a chainsaw and cut me down the middle. I'm not complete.

You're fun, serious, genuine, caring. You even started learning to cook—for us.

Cam hesitated, wiped the sweat off his brow.

There's a place for you here, by my side, in my life and heart, with my sons. There's a niche for you in Havelock, too, if the number of times people stop me to ask after you is a clue. Can you find it in your heart to return? To join us? To join me? For ever?

I understand how difficult life has been for you since the accident that took Alison's life. I'd like to help you continue to get on your feet. I'm prepared to chance it that you might one day wake up and realise you'd made a mistake and leave us.

Another swipe at his brow. This baring his soul wasn't easy. But at least he was trying, and it was a little easier than it would be to say these things out loud to her.

Jenny, I love you. Please come home.

Click. Send.

For a long time he sat staring at the computer, willing his heart rate to slow to normal. He'd done it, told Jenny everything he felt, and now all he could do was wait. She might never answer, but he had given his all and tried.

'Dad, we're bored.'

'Now, there's something new.' Cam unfolded from the chair and stood up. He had the afternoon off. Spending time doing something with the boys would help pass the hours until he could hope to get a reply from Jenny. 'Okay, guys, let's go get our Christmas tree from the pine forest.'

'Yeah.'

'Cool.'

At least he'd made them happy about something.

CHAPTER THIRTEEN

CAM STARED AT the Christmas tree standing in its pot in the corner of the lounge, decorated so heavily only the pine scent and some fallen needles gave a clue to the type of tree it was. The boys had gone overboard in their enthusiasm for hanging baubles and velvet reindeer pulling miniature sleighs. Each had tried to outdo the other with their creativity. When they'd finished they'd placed the one parcel in the house that was ready to go underneath the branches.

A present for Jenny. The box they'd lovingly put together and painted at school.

Cam could feel his heart breaking all over again. Jenny had stolen three hearts in this household.

Well, there was nothing he could do about Jenny right now. If he didn't hear from her soon he might have to resort to tracking her parents down in Dunedin and try coercing her whereabouts out of them. He wouldn't give up in a hurry that was for sure.

He glanced at his watch and groaned. Might as well prepare dinner. In the kitchen Cam stared at the mince defrosting on the bench. His mouth soured. Mince. Patties. Same old, same old. Just the thought of cooking turned his stomach.

'Can we have fish and chips tonight?' Marcus had to be on the same wavelength. 'I'm sick of patties.'

'Why not? I'll phone Diane and put in an order.' Decision made, as easy as that.

'Can we go and get them?'

'On our own?'

'Sure.' The shop was only four hundred metres away and it wasn't as though Havelock was a den of iniquity. Kids were always visiting the shops. 'Let me phone first.'

While the boys were away Cam started to clear away the clutter that had accumulated over the day. One day he might manage to train the boys to put things away as they finished with them. Maybe.

Jenny had seemed to get them to do things so easily. Had she been a novelty? Had they been trying to impress her to stay?

Round and round went the questions that had no answers. *Where are you, Jenny? Dunedin? Or back on the road, this time in a bus, stopping wherever?* She still had to collect her car someday, and hopefully he'd be around when she did. There again, after that email she might wait until he was working at the Blenheim clinic before dropping by here.

'To hell with this.' Tossing two pairs of sports shoes in the shoe basket in the laundry, he headed for the fridge and an ice-cold beer. Out on the deck he sipped from the bottle and stared around his empty yard, and cringed. There was nothing wrong with Havelock, his home or his family. But there had to be more to life. A life with Jenny in it for starters. 'Where is she?'

The front door crashed open. 'Dad, got the fish and chips.' The boys bundled out on to the deck. Then, 'We saw Jenny in the bakery.'

His heart stopped. The bottle of beer fell from a lifeless hand. It was happening all over again. But this time the apparition Marcus and Andrew were seeing was Jenny. Not their mother. Pain and shock slammed through him, kicked at his heart, made it pound against his ribs and send deafening thuds to his ears. Shaking his head, he held his arms out to the twins. 'No. No, you didn't. Jenny's gone. You have to accept that.'

'No, Dad. She hasn't.'

'It's true. We saw her.'

This was bad. How did he make them understand that no matter how hard they tried they couldn't wish anyone they wanted back into their lives? His chest rose as his lungs filled with much-needed oxygen.

'They're not making me up. I am here.'

The air whooshed out of his lungs. His head spun round so fast he felt giddy. 'Jenny? Is that really you?' Who else had red hair that made the day so bright? Who else had such a sweet, heart-melting smile that warmed him to his toes? What other woman could look so beautiful while looking apprehensive? 'Jenny.'

'I got your email.'

Suddenly—who knew how?—he was in front of this woman who'd stolen his heart and reaching for her, covering her mouth with his. Words were beyond him.

When her hands locked at the back of his neck and her breasts pressed against his chest, he prayed that this was true, that he hadn't taken to seeing and feeling apparitions the same way his sons did. Pulling his head back, he stared into those suck-him-in green eyes that had swamped his dreams every night since that day she'd landed in his life. 'You came.' For him? Them all? Then a shocking idea struck. For her car?

But she still had that cast on, was wearing the biggest, brightest smile he'd ever seen, and her eyes were full of—? Love? For him? And, if he needed more convincing, hadn't she kissed him back a moment ago?

'Yes, Cameron, I came back. That email choked me up. You never said a tenth of any of that when I said I was going.'

'I'm not good at verbalising.'

She just grinned at him. 'I know. A real man doesn't say he loves a woman, he shows her. I should've read the manual before I left. But then again I didn't tell you how much I love you either.'

He started to lean closer to that delectable mouth again, but it seemed Jenny hadn't finished.

'You also reiterated what I'd already begun to see for myself. I was running from the best thing that had ever happened to me—you and the boys. A family. A man who loves me regardless of what I've been or who I'll become. A man who had the patience and love to help me through last week and to open my eyes to more than I believed I deserved.'

Then I got it right. The sweat and pain had been worth every drop, and then some. 'Seems you don't have any trouble telling me what's on your mind.' Covering her mouth, he shut up any more words she might have lurking in there. He'd heard what he needed to hear for now. Jenny was back.

'Dad, is Jenny staying?'

'Jenny, will you do some more cooking? I'm sick of patties.'

'And sausages.'

'Can you stay for Christmas?'

This kiss just wasn't going to happen any time soon. Cam shoved a hand through his hair and grinned at Jenny and his boys. 'This is family life. No privacy. Plenty of interruptions. Think you can handle it full time?'

'Try and stop me.'

'Good answer.'

Marcus high-fived his brother. 'She's staying. What night of the week do we want beef stroganoff?'

Jenny laughed. 'What about meat patties night?' Hopefully Amanda would help her get past the lasagne and beef stroganoff and then every meal would be a surprise.

'No, that's fish and chip night now.'

'Dad, the fish and chips are getting cold.'

'Then go and eat them.' He hadn't taken his gaze away from Jenny. 'You hungry?'

Shaking her head, she laughed again. 'Not yet. But a glass of wine would go down a treat. You want to replace that beer you managed to spill everywhere?'

'Yes.' Finally he looked around, then back to Jenny, and felt a well of emotion back up in his throat. 'Thank you for returning. I had decided I'd chase you down if you didn't.'

'I went home, spent two days with Mum and Dad. We talked a lot about Alison and the accident. I guess we had the conversations we should've had twelve months ago.'

'It would've been harder back then. You've had time to come to terms with your loss, as have your parents.'

Her smile softened. 'They were great. I told them all about you and the boys. They can't wait to meet you.'

'Hang on.' Cam looked at her more closely. 'Were you intending to come and see us? I didn't need to email you?'

Her laugh scared the sparrows off the lawn, where the boys were feeding them chips. 'Don't think you could get off that lightly. But, seriously...' Her laughter quietened. 'Putting things into perspective with Mum and Dad made me think about you and me. I flew back yesterday and immediately went to see Angus, who put me in contact with the head of the ED at Wairau.'

Cam held his breath. This was happening too fast. The fact she'd come back to him had only just started sinking in and she was talking about the hospital.

Running the back of her hand down his cheek, she said, 'Starting the first of February I'm working three days a week in the ED. I turned down full-time hours. I want to be a part of your lives, not living on the perimeter—which means there'll be cooking lessons, a house to run and three demanding males to keep in order. I think my life's going to be quite hectic.'

That emotion backing up finally spilled over. Tears rolled down his cheeks, laughter bubbled over his lips. 'Welcome home.'

Home. One tiny word that filled Jenny with warmth and love. She looked around the yard and sighed. One day soon she'd begin digging a garden and planting her favourite flowers so there'd always be colour out here.

Home. Who'd have thought she'd end her travels in Havelock? 'What do you reckon, Alison? Have I done the right thing or what?' Alison would be happy for her. She knew that bone deep. All either of them had wanted was for the other to find love and be happy.

'Here, get your lips around this.' Cam handed her a glass of bubbles. 'We're celebrating.'

She laughed. 'I'm glad this is a celebration.'

'Jenny, have you seen our tree?'

'Dad took us to the forest and cut a big pine.'

'We decorated it today.'

'Come and see it.'

She tapped the rim of her glass against Cam's. 'I know an order when I hear one.'

Cam took her hand and walked inside. 'Boys, quieten down a bit, will you?'

Jenny stopped in front of the tree. 'Wow, look at that. You've both done a fabulous job of decorating it. I've never seen so many decorations in my life.'

'We are allowed to buy three new ones each every year.'

'We haven't got them this year yet.'

She blinked. Where would they put them? 'When are you going shopping?'

'Tomorrow.'

'Can we, Dad?'

'I can't see why not.' Cam looked at her. 'Up for a bout in the shops?'

'Absolutely. I can't wait.'

'You have no idea what you're letting yourself in for.' His grin was wicked.

She nodded. 'Yes, I have. I'm going with my favourite males to load up on presents. What more could a woman want?' It would be like a family outing. Warmth flooded her. How had she thought she could walk away? This past week had been hell, and here she was, back where she now knew she belonged.

'Dad, we're going to be late for the carols.'

Cam's eyes widened and he tapped his forehead. 'Blame Jenny. She sidetracked me.'

'Carols? As in singing and holding candles?' When was the last time she'd done that?

'Yep, down at the marina. Coming with us?' Cam seemed to be holding his breath.

'Be warned, if I sing everyone will leave.'

'We'll take that chance. It would mean we can come home earlier anyway.'

If she'd thought he'd looked wicked before she'd been wrong. Now he looked very wicked. Her stomach flipped at the thought of what they might be doing after they came home. After they'd packed the boys off to bed, of course.

The marina was crowded. Everyone in Havelock and from the outlying bays must have come. The boys bounced around with excitement. Then they found Amanda's kids and dragged Cam and Jenny across to join them all.

Amanda gave her a hug. 'Glad you're home.'

'Was I the only one not to realise this is where I belong?' She hugged her friend back.

'I wouldn't have taken you for a slow learner but that goes to show how little I know.'

'It means you've got a cookery pupil for quite some time.'

Amanda chuckled. 'Guess I'll cope. We'll start with fruit mince tarts this week.'

'Perfect.'

'Here, better be lighting our candles.' Cam handed her and the boys a candle each then lit them. 'Marcus, Andrew, be careful with these. I don't want anybody getting burnt.'

'Yes, Dad.'

'Yes, Dad.'

Jenny laughed. Wasn't she doing a lot of that today? 'Yes, Cam.' She loved it when the boys looked so solemn. It wouldn't last. Any moment now they'd be joining in the singing and would forget every word Cam had said, but that was okay, because she'd be right here keeping an eye on them, along with their dad.

Cam leaned close, his breath warm on her cheek. 'I love Christmas mince tarts.'

'Yeah, but will the boys? Amanda? Can I get a recipe off you? I've got an idea.'

'As long as you promise not to tell everyone you got it from me.' Her friend grinned.

'Make it a very simple recipe, Amanda. Something with no more than two ingredients.' Cam added his two cents' worth.

'I'll surprise the lot of you.' She pulled a face at them both. 'You'll see.'

Cam handed Jenny another present to place under the tree, and told her, 'When I was the boys' age I used to get up early every morning and check out the presents under the tree, counting how many were for me then shaking and squeezing them trying to figure out what they were.'

Yeah, she had those memories, too. 'Whenever Mum was out Alison and I used to search under the window seat for parcels that could be our presents. It never spoilt the fun of opening them on Christmas morning, did it?' She began emptying the carton of neatly wrapped presents she'd bought in Blenheim yesterday. She'd spent hours trawling through shops, trying to decide on gifts for the most important males in her life.

'Hell, no. It was part of the ritual. Drove Mum crazy. I think she expected me to break something.'

'One year Mum wrapped up books, loads of them, and put them under the tree. We really believed that was what we were getting—books.' Mum. She'd have these same memories, too.

Cam must've heard her sigh because his arm wound around her shoulders and tugged her close to his strong body. 'It's not too late to ask your parents to join my family at the farm for Christmas.'

Twisting awkwardly, she stared up into the face she loved. 'Really? Would your mother mind? She already has a house full coming that day.'

He squeezed her gently. 'She'd love it. So would Dad. They can't wait to meet you, by the way.' He'd phoned them earlier in the day and she'd heard him laughing and chatting so easily. Seemed he had a great relationship with his family.

As did she, Jenny acknowledged. When she'd arrived at home last week they'd opened their arms and hugged her like it had been only the day before she'd left Dunedin. 'I'll phone them now.'

'Don't talk all night. I'm looking forward to going to bed.'

The last time this gorgeous man had mentioned going to bed she'd imagined what it might be like. Now, after their lovemaking in Kahurangi and over the last two nights, she had a few clues. 'Maybe I'm worth waiting for.' She grinned.

'Lady, I waited a whole week to make love to you again. That was more than enough.'

Thank goodness Dad answered her call. He disliked talking on the phone so the conversation was brief and successful. 'Dad will email me flight details tomorrow.' Jenny dropped her phone on the table and took Cam's hand. 'Come on. What are you sitting around here for?'

Cam stood up and reached for her. When his lips brushed her mouth she all but melted. 'Bedroom. Fast.'

The next morning she was woken by the twins bringing her a cup of tea. 'Thanks, Andrew, Marcus.' She stretched her toes towards the end of the king-size bed. 'I definitely could get used to this,' she said, repeating what she'd said the first morning she'd woken up in this house. Though that had been in the bedroom down the hall.

'Have you seen all the presents under the tree?' Andrew asked.

'There are lots and lots and lots.' Marcus grinned.

'It's exciting, isn't it?' She grinned back. 'Where's your dad?'

'Getting breakfast.'

'We're having a barbecue.'

'Bacon and eggs.'

'And hash browns and mushrooms.'

Jenny's head was spinning as the boys gabbled at her. 'I'd better get up, then. I don't want to miss out.'

'Finish your tea first.' Cam stood in the doorway, looking at her with love in his eyes. 'We've got all morning.'

She shook her head at him. 'I've got to go to the grocery store later. We're going to make double chocolate chip Santa biscuits this morning.'

The kitchen turned into a familiar mess as Jenny supervised the mixing of the biscuit batter. 'How does flour spread so far?' she mock growled at the boys.

'Something to do with the way you shake the packet as you're filling the measuring cup,' Cam said. 'I've never seen anyone create flour clouds before.'

'Hey!' Jenny caught Marcus's hand before it reached his mouth. 'Don't eat all those chocolate buttons. We need some for the cookies.'

Andrew quickly shovelled a handful into his mouth and began chewing hard. His eyes bulged as he tried not to laugh.

'Not fair,' Marcus grumped.

Jenny let go his hand and reached into the shopping bag. 'Just as well I bought double the quantity needed.'

'You're spoiling them.' Cam helped himself to a few buttons. Then he picked up some more and began feeding her one by one.

Her tongue grazed his fingertips and she saw the jolt

of hot need zipping through his eyes, felt the reciprocal desire heat her body.

In the background she thought she heard 'Yuck' and 'Gross' but she couldn't be sure and she wasn't stopping to ask the boys what they'd said. Then reality slipped into the heat haze that was her mind right now. The boys. They weren't alone. She pulled away.

'Welcome to the real world,' Cam whispered.

Funny how that only made her feel happier. 'Better get these cookies in the oven. Marcus, can you cut the Santa shapes while, Andrew, you can put the liquorice on their chins.'

Cam shook his head. 'Talk about left-field Santas.'

The boys hurried through their tasks and then went over to the tree to rustle amongst the parcels.

'Hey, guys, leave those for Christmas Day.' Cam spoke firmly.

'We're giving Jenny ours now.'

'Are you sure you don't want to wait?' Cam wore a frown.

'She needs it as soon as possible.'

What's going on? Jenny looked from Cam to his sons and back. 'I can wait.'

'No, you can't,' Andrew informed her, as he lifted a square parcel from the back of all the presents.

'We want you to have this.' Marcus took a corner of the present.

Together the boys handed it over to her. 'We made it.'

Jenny took the proffered gift. 'Thank you, Andrew. Thank you, Marcus.' She dropped a kiss on each forehead before glancing up at Cam to see him swallowing hard. *What was this?*

It felt hard and flat-sided, and she very carefully unwrapped the parcel. As the red and green paper fell aside she found a wooden box with a tiny bronze lock and key and it was painted bright green. 'You made this?' she asked around the tears in her throat. 'For me? It's beautiful.'

'It's to put your mojo in.'

'We don't want you to lose it again.'

The floor pushed up at the bottoms of her feet. She grabbed the counter to remain upright, holding on until the dizziness abated. 'Thank you,' she managed to whisper, before the floodgates opened and the tears became a torrent. Running a hand over the box, she twisted the key and lifted the lid. 'Thank you,' she repeated.

Cam's hand was warm on her shoulder. 'You okay?'

'More than okay. You have the world's best two boys.'

'I reckon.'

Marcus said, 'We're glad we found you in the shop.'

'Jenny,' Andrew said. 'Are you going to the farm with us for Christmas?'

'Yes. Your dad asked me last night.' Between kisses. 'Are you staying for ever?'

Jenny raised her gaze to Cam's, gave him a watery smile. 'I hope so.'

One of the boys—she wasn't sure which for all the hammering of her heart echoing in her head—asked, 'Can we have a wedding? Like Toby Sorenson's parents did? That was cool.'

Cam grinned. 'That's meant to be my line, guys.'

Jenny was speechless. Her eyes took in Cam and Marcus and Andrew all staring at her, waiting for something from her. Her mouth dropped open but no words came out. Deep inside the final knot in her stomach unravelled, spreading warmth and love through her. Her chest rose as she drew in a breath. 'Yes, let's have a wedding.'

'Cool.'

'Cool.'

Cam said, 'I love you.'

'And I love the three of you.' Another flood of tears began. Talk about getting all her Christmases in one year.

Impervious to the tears, Cam reached for her and kissed her, long and lovingly. 'I love you,' he whispered again, and went back to kissing her.

And for once the boys refrained from saying a word. Jenny knew that thankfully it was only a respite, not a permanent change. She loved her family just the way they were.

As Cam finally lifted his mouth from those delectable lips he smiled like the cat with the cream.

Note to self: never let a day go by without remembering how much you love this woman.

* * * * *

MILLS & BOON®

Passionate pairing of seduction and glamour!

This hot duo will appeal to all romance readers.
Start your New Year off with some excitement
with six stories from popular Blaze®
and Modern™ authors.

**Visit
www.millsandboon.co.uk/mistress**
to find out more!